BODY TOLL

BRUCE THOMASON

ISBN: 978-1-934666-30-2

Cover Design by Summer Morris

Published and distributed by:
High-Pitched Hum Publishing
321 15th Street North
Jacksonville Beach, Florida 32250

Contact High-Pitched Hum Publishing at www.highpitchedhum.net

High-Pitched Hum
Publishing

DEDICATION

This book is dedicated to the men and women of the Jacksonville
Beach, Florida Police Department, a truly honorable and
professional team.

ACKNOWLEDGEMENTS

To Kyle Meenan: For sharing your expertise as a television reporter to
ensure the dialogue was authentic. Your talent is obvious.

To Doc Tish Galanter, M.D.: For answering my questions about the
proper treatment of injuries.

To Ro Kieran: For your insight into the structure of the story, and for
your friendship. Ride fast. Ride often. Ride safe!

To Jen Zdunkiewicz: For your review of the manuscript. You have a
great eye for detail.

To Jackie, my wife, my best friend, and first in my life: For your
encouragement to write a story based on my experiences in law
enforcement. You were the driving force behind *Body Toll*. Your careful
review of each draft, your suggestions on dialogue and plot development;
and your persistence in presenting your viewpoint, all combined to make
the story so much better.

Proverbs 3:5-6

Prologue

A Nor'easter was howling on this cold and moonless January night as Jimmy Barton headed over the wooden walkover toward the beach, staggering from side to side like a sailboard tacking into a strong wind. He pulled his ragged jacket closer around his throat to keep the bitter wind at bay, the sour-sweet smell of stale beer drifting along behind him like an invisible shadow. Barton stumbled through the soft sand as he made his way beneath the walkover, settling onto a piece of plastic tarp. Pulling an old blanket from his backpack, he curled into a tight ball to conserve body heat, drifting quickly away into a deep sleep.

Barton had no way of knowing his life would end that night, cut short at the hands of a serial killer. An alcoholic living on the streets for almost ten years, Jimmy denied he had a drinking problem. "Hell, I been drinkin' since I was 'bout fifteen or so, but that don't mean I got a drinkin' problem," he would tell his street buddies. "Life sucks, ya know? And havin' a beer or two kinda knocks the edges off." Jimmy couldn't conceive of the possibility that his life sucked *because* of his drinking.

He usually dressed in filthy layers of clothing that hadn't seen the inside of a washing machine since the day he got them. Rather than wash them, Jimmy simply rotated the order of the layers as the mood struck him.

His days revolved around panhandling tourists for beer money, not that they knew what he really meant to do with their gifts. His nights were spent avoiding the cops as he searched for a place to sleep under the stars on the white sands of Jacksonville Beach, Florida. When panhandling slacked off, Barton financed his drinking habit by working at a day labor pool. Daily meals were provided courtesy of the local soup kitchen.

Jimmy Barton's killer was not homeless, nor did he drink to excess. Instead, he took great pains to keep his body in top physical condition. Women considered him attractive, if not handsome. This night, however, those same women would have quickly turned away to avoid making eye contact with him. His head was covered with a ragged old hoodie pulled down to his eyebrows; jeans smeared with so much dirt they appeared brown rather than their original denim blue. His running shoes had turned a grimy shade of grey, long ago abandoning their original, store-bought white. In his disguise, he appeared to be just another homeless man, living a life most people could never understand.

The killer had sat huddled for two hours on a hard concrete bench overlooking the sand dunes and sea oats. He had been feverishly scouring the boardwalk area for the past few days, ever since the local TV stations had identified James "Jimmy" Barton as a witness to the brutal murder the killer had committed on this very beach. Finally, around midnight, he spotted Barton, bobbing and weaving like a punch-drunk fighter as he headed for the beach. He watched his intended victim cross the sand dunes, crushing the tender sea oats under his shoes as he veered under the walkover to seek shelter from the cold and wind.

Before tonight, the killer had focused his lethal attention on prostitutes, a warped tribute to his whore of a mother. Now, he was excited at the prospect of tapping into another target-rich field, homeless people, and especially this homeless man. Most, if not all of them, were alcoholics or drug addicts, in his estimation. People who let addictions control them were pathetic losers, thereby meeting his twisted justification for purging the weak from the human herd.

Even at this late hour, one couple was still strolling along the boardwalk. Pursuing his prey too quickly could draw unwanted attention to himself when Barton's body was later discovered; that would be a fool's choice, he knew. The killer was many things. A fool was not one of them. He patiently waited until the couple left the boardwalk and then moved along in the direction of his intended victim.

Slump-shouldered, weaving his way across the pier parking lot toward the beach walkover, the killer carried a ratty backpack that appeared to contain all his worldly possessions. To anyone still foolish enough to be out in this weather, he would seem to be just another drunken homeless man. Smiling with anticipation, the killer moved under the walkover as he spotted Barton, sunk in the depths of alcohol-induced sleep. Looking both directions, the man saw no one on the beach. He wasn't surprised, considering the time of night and the Nor'easter that had been blowing for the past two days.

He approached the sleeping form and kneeled quietly in the sand beside him as he pulled on leather gloves. From his coat pocket, the killer withdrew a dagger, five inches of black, razor-sharp steel. He leaned forward, heart pounding, his breath coming in short gasps as if he had just run a four-minute mile. The pleasure he derived from taking a human life was like no other, better than sex, better than the most wonderful meal in the finest five-star restaurant.

The killer possessed the ultimate power, to hold a person's very essence in his hands, and then take that essence for his own. This power made him feel immortal. Weak humans the world over recoiled at the very concept of murder. Their petty morality was laughable to him. By adhering to society's rules, they deprived themselves of the most intense emotions and pleasures a human being could ever feel. He had known since that fateful day many years ago that he wasn't one of those weak mortals. Now, he was about to add this bum, Jimmy Barton, to his own private curriculum vitae, thereby ridding the earth of one more waste of oxygen.

Leaning forward, he touched the tip of the knife to the soft, fleshy area below Barton's right eye, pressing just hard enough to pierce the skin. Barton's eyes flew open as he tried to focus on the person looming over him.

"Remember me?" the killer asked.

There was just enough light coming from the boardwalk street lamps to allow Barton to see the man's face, and especially his cold eyes. Along with the voice, Barton instantly recognized the killer. "No, no, please, no!" he exclaimed.

As the blade slashed straight across Barton's neck, his killer jumped back to avoid a gusher of blood spurting straight into the air. The cut was so deep that Barton's windpipe was completely severed, leaving him unable to cry out. As Barton thrashed about, his life pouring onto the sand, the killer watched, no expression on his face. In seconds, it was over.

He kneeled once more beside his victim and used the dead man's sleeve to wipe the blade. Careful to avoid the splashes of blood, he placed a folded sheet of paper on Barton's chest, anchoring it with a small shell he found beside the body. Then he sat back on his heels and contemplated the scene, remembering again the brief message printed on the paper, "One dead child molester, 20 children saved!"

This should push the cops in the wrong direction, he thought, figuring they would check the man's record and find his sex offense conviction in Tampa. *No sense making it easy for them to link this scum to my previous trophy.*

Before leaving, he quickly searched Barton's meager possessions for a souvenir for his collection. The killer picked up a small plastic picture frame with a little girl's picture inside, cradling it in his hands. Written in a childish scrawl across the bottom was the inscription, "To Daddy from Meghan. I love you." He smiled as he slipped the picture into his pocket. *How pathetic is that?* he asked himself. *Carrying around a picture of his daughter from who knows how long ago. As if she still cared about a loser like him.*

The killer turned and headed south on the beach for two blocks before taking another walkover back to the street. As he walked, his heart and breathing slowed almost to normal. He watched carefully for police cars that he knew regularly patrolled the downtown area and the beach. The streets were silent, like an old abandoned cemetery.

Cutting through alleys to the side street where he had parked his car, he climbed in, cranked the engine, and connected his seat belt. He didn't want a cop to have any reason to stop him this night. He turned on the car's satellite radio and found his favorite show featuring an anarchist who spoke of the wretched excuses for leaders who were taking the United States of America ". . . down, down, down!" He believed it to be true. Every worthless human being he killed was one less miserable asshole contributing to the country's downfall. He was proud to do his part.

Driving away, a brief smile crossed his face.

Chapter 1

The alarm went off at 5:00 a.m. Tuned to a local country station, Josh Turner was singing "*Jacksonville.*" Detective Sergeant Clay Randall liked the song and its local connection, just not this early. He rolled over and hit the snooze button, rendering the bedroom almost silent, disturbed only by the faint sounds of waves breaking on the shore outside the condo.

Two minutes later, just as he started to drift off, Dana's alarm buzzed loudly. She slept so soundly that Clay usually had to reach across her to shut it off. By the time he killed her alarm, he was awake. Giving his wife a kiss on the cheek, which she accepted with a soft grunt, he headed off to the bathroom.

He came downstairs five minutes later and turned on the coffee pot. Moving over to the patio doors, Clay scanned the dark beach, seeing nothing but his own reflection in the glass doors. Staring back at him was a thirty-two-year-old man, standing six feet tall and weighing a very athletic one hundred, eighty pounds. He wore his sandy blond hair short in deference to his job, and, even in the glass reflection, smile lines were visible around his dark blue eyes. Clay liked people, except, of course, the criminals he spent his days chasing and locking up.

Clayton Allen Randall was born and raised in Jacksonville Beach. He graduated from Fletcher High School in the top ten percent of his class and was a better-than-average athlete. He entered the University of North Florida in Jacksonville with the intention of getting a degree in marine biology, a field that naturally interested him because of his twin loves of surfing and fishing. Clay discovered early on, to his disappointment, that a career in marine biology required a strong grasp of chemistry, a subject that, with its emphasis on math principles, had largely defeated him in high school. When his college chemistry grades failed to rise above a "D" level, he changed his major to psychology, another field of study that interested him.

Clay had also embraced the social scene at UNF, finding numerous opportunities to get drunk and act foolish, most often occurring in that order. By the time he turned twenty-one, he had changed his major twice more, been on scholastic probation twice, and still didn't know what he wanted to do with his life.

Until one day, while in the local Target store, Clay found his life's calling. He was in the sporting goods section admiring salt water reels when he heard yelling the next aisle over. Curious, he walked around the corner to find a Jacksonville Beach police officer in full uniform on his back with a man almost twice his size straddling him. The huge man had a hunting knife that he was trying to drive into the officer's chest. With both hands on the crazed man's wrists, the officer was gradually losing the contest to the other's superior strength.

Clay glanced around and saw several people standing there, frozen in place. Without thinking, he grabbed a metal bait bucket off the shelf. Swinging it two-handed as he would a baseball bat, Clay connected with the assailant's head. The force of the blow was so strong the man was knocked completely off the officer, rolling onto his back unconscious.

Officer Rafe Santos gasped as he tried to catch his breath, reaching out to knock the knife out of the man's hand. After a few seconds, he had enough wind to call in on his radio for emergency backup and rescue. He then tried to roll the huge man over to handcuff him, but, due to his exhaustion from the fight and the man's three hundred plus pounds of dead weight, he couldn't budge him.

Clay asked, "Officer, can I help?"

With a nod from Santos, Clay grabbed the man's right shoulder, and the two of them succeeded in turning him over. After getting the still-unconscious man cuffed, Santos turned to Clay and said, "Thanks, man. I don't think I could've held off this guy much longer. Damn, he was strong! All I did was ask him for some ID, and he went off on me. Next thing I know, he's got that big blade in his hand, and he's aimin' to do heart surgery on me! You handled yourself good. You jumped in when everybody else was standing around with their thumbs up their asses! You a cop . . . or military?"

"Neither one, sir," Clay answered. "I'm a college student. I was in here just trying to find a new salt water reel."

"Well, thank the Good Lord you picked today to shop, that's all I'm sayin'! What's your name?"

"Clay Randall, sir."

"Hey, man, you don't have to 'sir' me. I'm not that much older than you. My name's Rafe Santos." He stuck out his hand, and Clay shook it, smiling at the officer.

Fellow officers began arriving about that time, and Clay stood back so they could get to the suspect. He had come around by then and was still belligerent, bleeding from a huge gash the bait bucket had opened on the back of his head. The officers helped the paramedics strap the man down and, just in case he became violent again, stayed with the gurney as he was rolled to the rescue unit parked in the fire lane outside the store.

Clay was asked to come to the police department to give a witness statement about what had happened. He was so pumped up from the fight and his rescue of Officer Santos that the detective conducting the interview had to keep telling him to slow down and take deep breaths. By the time he finished his statement, Clay knew he had found his career path. The excitement of the job, the ability to help people in trouble; those things touched Clay deeply like nothing else he had ever done.

Dropping out of college, he entered the regional police academy, graduating at the top of his class. Applying the day after graduation, Clay was sworn in as the newest member of the Jacksonville Beach Police Department four months later. He immersed himself in police work from day one, learning firsthand how and why cops did things a certain way. Just over four years later, Clay was promoted to patrol sergeant. Two years after that, he was assigned as a team leader in the Detective Division. Clay Randall had found his niche and, five years later, still enjoyed the challenge of criminal investigations.

Chapter 2

As the coffee brewed, Clay shut off the security alarm and headed out to the driveway for the morning paper, shivering from the cold, biting wind in the pre-dawn darkness. With the Nor'easter pushing winds over thirty miles per hour, the coast was blanketed with a layer of dark grey clouds so heavy that complaints of winter depression seemed sure to increase.

Clay scanned his neighbors' homes and cars for anything out of the ordinary. There had been a rash of auto burglaries all over Duval County over the past few months. Kids roamed quiet neighborhoods late at night searching for unlocked vehicles in driveways, of which there was never a shortage. They found cash, guns, cameras, mp3 players, phones, computers, you name it. The kids doing this bit of illegal recreation called it "car hopping." Sergeant Randall and his fellow police officers thought it was absolutely crazy that reasonably intelligent people left such expensive items in their unlocked cars at night, assuming their driveways somehow guaranteed a safe haven from criminals.

Clay and Dana lived in Jacksonville Beach, the prime beach community just over the Intracoastal Waterway, or, in the locals' parlance, the "Ditch," from Jacksonville. Their beachfront condo sat a hundred yards from the ocean at low tide. Built in the early 1970s, the house had been completely renovated two years before Clay and Dana bought it. Interior walls of the bottom floor had been demolished to create a large open space so that visitors coming in the front door could see the rolling, white surf as it broke onto the beach, ending its long trip from the distant shores of Morocco.

The condo had an expansive patio on the ground level and a large, overhanging sun deck on the second floor off the master bedroom. Dana spent hours each day on the patio or the deck. She loved experiencing the endless waves as they crashed with a roar or slipped with a soft hiss onto the sandy beach, the morning sun as it eased out of the blue-green waters of the Atlantic Ocean, and the salty smell and taste of the sea breezes. But Dana wasn't there simply to stare at the beautiful view. Working primarily in oils, but talented as well in acrylics, watercolors, and charcoals, she was busy practicing her art, literally.

Dana was an accomplished artist, focusing on land and seascapes. As her reputation continued to grow, prestigious galleries throughout Florida and Georgia had begun exhibiting her works. She had also created a website which offered originals as well as numbered and signed prints for sale.

Dana's annual income was almost double what Clay brought home as a public servant, a fact he sometimes laughed about with his buddies at work. "My goal is to retire and let Dana support me in the style to which I want to become accustomed!" he would say, laughing. Considering how much Clay loved his job as a detective, his buddies knew he wasn't serious, no matter how much money Dana made.

Clay came back in the house with the paper to find his wife sitting at the bar sipping her first cup of coffee, still half asleep. "Man, it's cold out there!" he exclaimed. "Feel my hands," he said, touching the back of her neck.

"A-H-H!" Stop that!" she screamed, jerking away from his touch. "You know I hate when you do that!"

Clay returned his wife's glare with a grin. Slipping behind her, he wrapped his arms around her body, being careful not to let his hands touch bare skin. "Love you, too, babe," he said as he kissed her on the nape of her neck. "You know you can't resist my devilish charms."

She squirmed a little as if to pull away and then relaxed, leaning back into his chest. "I guess I'll let you hang around a little longer . . . but only as long as you promise not to touch me again with those ice packs you call hands!"

Dana Cappella Randall had recently turned thirty-one, a fact not at all obvious from her appearance. With a light olive complexion, short, glossy black hair, and green eyes, she was considered beautiful by anyone's standards. She stood five-four and kept her weight steady at one hundred and fifteen pounds. Unlike Clay, Dana was a Texas native, moving to Jacksonville with her family when she was seven.

Her father, Marty Cappella, was a successful lawyer who transferred his practice to his home state of Florida, settling in the

Jacksonville area and starting a new law firm. He had struck it rich in Texas when the tobacco settlements made multimillionaires out of a few attorneys when big tobacco decided it was better to pay than to fight.

Dana, an only child, entered her teen years with opportunities few children enjoyed. Marty and Roberta, Dana's mom, owned a twelve thousand square foot mansion in Ponte Vedra Beach overlooking the ocean. She attended a private school that catered to wealthy families. Growing up in the rarified atmosphere of money and privilege, Dana wanted for nothing. For her sixteenth birthday, her parents gave her a bright red Corvette convertible, a car that rarely saw speeds below seventy when Dana was behind the wheel.

Her social life was filled with lavish parties attended by all the rich kids from the surrounding gated communities. Dana was pursued by the most popular boys in her private school, usually several at a time, but they bored her with their constant talk of getting drunk, or high, or who had the newest hot car.

What never bored her was her art. Early on, as her exceptional skills at drawing and composition began to emerge, Dana's parents hired private art teachers to hone her innate abilities. On her nineteenth birthday, she had her first showing at a small gallery in St. Augustine, quickly selling the majority of her paintings. That early success revealed a hint of what the future held for her. The price of her paintings increased with each show as more and more art enthusiasts came to appreciate her talents. Her lively and free-spirited personality revealed itself in her paintings, a feeling of warmth and joy that practically leaped off the canvas.

By the time Dana turned twenty-three, she had obtained bachelor's and master's degrees in fine art, and her career was in full swing. She moved out of her parents' big house and bought a small condo in Jacksonville Beach using cash from sales of her artwork for a large down payment. Up to that point, Dana's social life had been limited to the Ponte Vedra Rich Jerk Set, as she called them. She found them all to be more interested in her money and her body than in her as a person. With the move to her new condo, Dana decided it was time to find new friends, also.

Two months after moving in, she was shocked to come home one evening and find her house had been burglarized. None of her paintings were stolen, but the thieves took her TV, DVD player, and various pieces of jewelry.

A couple of days after reporting the crime to the police department, Dana had just returned home from a run on the beach when the doorbell rang. She was still a little spooked from the invasion of her home and debated whether to answer the door. Waiting, the doorbell rang twice more.

They're persistent, whoever they are, she thought. Easing quietly to the door, she peered through the peephole. Standing on the front walk was a rather nice-looking young man wearing a suit and tie and carrying a notebook. She called through the closed door, "I don't need any Jehovah's Witness tracts today. And I go to church, too . . . not yours, though, but thanks anyway!" Dana kept watching through the peephole to see what the man would do.

He paused as if confused by her message before replying, "Ma'am, I'm not a Jehovah's Witness. I'm Sergeant Randall with the Jacksonville Beach Police Department, and I'm here to investigate the burglary you reported."

Dana was still suspicious. "How do I know that's who you are?"

"Well, ma'am. I've got my badge and ID. Will that do?"

"Anyone can buy that stuff over the Internet. How do I know it's real, and you're who you say you are?" Dana asked.

Clay thought a moment and, snapping his fingers, said, "I've got it! Call the police department and ask them if they know Sergeant Clay Randall. I called out here on my radio, so they'll have a log of that. You can even describe me to them since I assume you're staring at me through your peephole. I just need to get some information so I can work on solving your burglary."

Dana said, "You're pretty cocky to assume I'm looking at you."

"No, ma'am, not cocky. I can see the peephole in your door, and I can tell from your voice that you're standing just on the other side. Also, you thought I was a Jehovah's Witness, which means you had to have seen me dressed in a suit and tie like those missionary guys wear. Just simple detective work, ma'am."

Wow, she thought. *He's pretty sharp.*

"Okay, you wait there while I go call," Dana said.

"You got it. I'm just happy to be here. I don't have anything else to do right now, so I'll just be standing here in the hot sun trying not to pass out from sunstroke. If I do conk out before you get back, please be kind enough to toss a bucket of water on me, and I'm pretty sure I'll survive," Clay said with a grin.

Dana giggled to herself, *He's got a sense of humor. And he's got a cute smile for a potentially crazed killer!*

She opened the door. "I guess you can come in."

As Clay stepped into her condo, he saw Dana Cappella for the first time. She was wearing running shorts and a cropped top that showed off her tanned and very fit body. He thought, "This woman is gorgeous! I'm in love, or in lust anyway!"

Over the next hour, they talked about the burglary and the chances of finding her possessions again. While he was not encouraging, he said he would check the pawn shops if she could get him the serial numbers and descriptions of her stuff. Clay found it hard to concentrate on his questions when he gazed at her, so he focused on his notes as much as possible. Dana meanwhile sensed his nervousness and felt sure he was attracted to her. Curiously, she felt something in return. While Sergeant Randall wasn't exactly handsome, he had a very open and appealing manner and a friendly boyishness about him. And the longer Clay talked to her, the more convinced he became this woman was someone special he would like to get to know better.

He never found Dana's property or the burglar, but he asked her out a month later, and she accepted. Two months after that, they were engaged. Dana liked to say, "I was robbed twice. A thief stole my TV, and Clay stole my heart!"

Chez Cappella was a less than cheery place that hot August afternoon when Dana shared the news of her engagement to a cop. Her parents had automatically assumed she would pick a boy from the circle of their rich Ponte Vedra friends. After all, the elder Cappellas thought, their daughter was refined and had enjoyed a privileged upbringing.

Upon hearing the news, Marty hit the liquor cabinet for a few double shots of Jack Black while Roberta took to the bed with one of her classic migraines, a condition that occurred whenever Dana attempted to exercise control over her own life. After two days in bed, she checked into the Mayo Clinic in Jacksonville convinced she had developed a brain tumor caused by her daughter's rebellious ways. One week later, fresh out of her private suite at the Mayo and diagnosed as tumor-free, Roberta called Dana and asked her to come to the house to, "discuss a delicate matter," as she put it.

Dana rushed over, worried that her mother had alarming information about her latest visit to the hospital. She found Roberta in the library, a room with twenty-foot ceilings, mahogany floors, and beautiful floor-to-ceiling bookshelves. Raised in the backwoods of Georgia, Roberta had filled the shelves with well-known authors of all genres. While she had no intention of ever reading them, she believed the books conveyed an exquisite sense of style and exceptional taste.

Roberta Cappella greeted her only child wearing a pale peach dressing gown that, at forty-nine years old, complimented her still voluptuous figure and near-flawless complexion. When she spoke, a faint Georgia drawl came through, try as she might to exorcise any hint of her underprivileged roots.

"Dana, dear," she said as they sat down in the leather wingback chairs facing the expansive natural stone fireplace, "what you've told your father and me is very disturbing. We had every hope and desire that you would settle down with one of those young men like Barry Johnson or Robert Hawkins. You know, someone from a good family."

"Mama, you know I can't stand Barry Johnson. Every time we went out, I felt like I was dating an octopus! He was patting me on the butt with one hand and grabbing my chest with his other five or six hands! And Bobby Hawkins is just a friend. I have absolutely zero romantic feelings for him.

"Besides, why would you want me to be with Bobby anyway? He's a police officer like Clay, and he works in the same department. On top of that, Clay's a sergeant, so he tells Bobby what to do!"

"Well, honey, I know that Robert is a police officer, but he's told me he works right under the police chief. And he doesn't have to deal with those unsavory characters like, like the young man you're interested in apparently has to do.

"Now, you know Robert comes from a truly upstanding family. Maurice Hawkins is one of the most successful builders in Florida, and Martha is a true patron of the arts. It's just a matter of time before his father convinces him to take over the family business and he can leave that silly police job.

"You said you're friends with Robert, honey. I think you'll agree that friendship is the bedrock of a good marriage. So, can't we just slow down and think this through before we make a decision that we'll come to regret?"

Dana frowned, "Mama, what do you mean, 'before *we* make a decision?' I wasn't aware you were marrying Clay."

"Now, sweetheart, you know I didn't mean anything silly like that. I just mean we . . . *you* should think before you go off marrying that . . . that boy. After all, what do we . . . you really know about him? About his family? What sort of education does he have . . . a high school diploma? My goodness, darling, you've got advanced degrees, and you're a successful artist who is only going to be more successful, especially if you associate with the right people. What is he? A boy who wears a uniform and goes around fighting filthy bums. He associates with the most unsavory persons in the community.

"Is the boy even stable? You know you tend to be a little, shall we say, flighty at times, so you need someone who's stable, with his feet on the ground, with a well-paying job, or preferably family money that he can fall back on if things get tight. That's all your father and I want for you. We love you, honey."

"I know you and Daddy love me. And because you love me, you want me to be happy. Right?"

"Yes, but—"

"Well, marrying Clay will make me happy."

"Now, sweetheart, I know you think marrying this boy will make—"

"His name is *Clay,* Mama . . . *Clayton Allen Randall*, not 'that boy' or 'this boy!' I love Clay! He makes me laugh. He's honest. He's a very caring man. And he loves me! He's the man I want to spend the rest of my life with. It's very important to me that you and Daddy accept Clay and grow to love him as I do. But Mama, the bottom line is . . . I intend to marry Clay with or without your blessing!"

Dana stared defiantly at her mother. She had never directly challenged either of her parents, and she waited nervously for her mother's reaction.

"My darling Dana, if you feel that strongly about this boy . . . Clay, then I guess your father and I have no choice but to go along with it," a hint of resignation in her voice. "But you can be sure that we will be watching him closely to make sure he treats you the way our little princess deserves!"

One year to the day from Dana's break-in, Marty and Roberta Cappella hosted a lavish wedding ceremony for Clay and Dana on the large veranda of their oceanfront mansion. Spending lavishly for the affair, Marty mentioned the cost to Clay occasionally when the topic of his meager police salary came up. And Clay's conservative mindset caused any number of tense conversations when the topic strayed into politics.

In spite of the in-law drawbacks, their marriage was a happy one, marred only occasionally by the usual arguments over money, the long hours Clay worked, and his lack of desire to finish college and get a better-paying job. However, their one area of complete compatibility through seven years of marriage was a very active and satisfying sex life.

Chapter 3

"How'd you sleep, sweetie?" Clay asked as he poured himself a cup of coffee. Dana had been in a bad car crash when she was a teenager, and the injuries she suffered caused her lower back to stiffen up occasionally during the night.

"Pretty good. Running every day helps keep the kinks out. I'm doing a quick five miles this morning, and then I've got to finish that watercolor for my show next month. Five, that is, unless this Nor'easter blows any harder. I do have my limits." Dana ran half marathons regularly and at least one local marathon each year. Being a triathlete himself, Clay understood her desire to push the limits, to challenge herself to accomplish things that most people would never dream of even trying.

"Yeah, I'd love to hit the bike myself, but riding into the teeth of this wind isn't high on my list of favorite things. Besides, I have to be in early this morning. Commander Wilson's got me doing a 7:30 briefing on the prostitute that was killed last week."

"Did I hear you tell Cassie on the phone last night that Wilson put you in charge of a task force?"

"Yeah, since ours is the second one killed in the last six months, Commander Wilson thinks we may have a serial killer working the beach. He's assigned me to head up a task force with Cassie Broderick, Jeremy Rivers, and Ty Honchen. We'll be sharing information with Atlantic Beach PD, and they'll do the same for us. Their case has gone nowhere, so the wheels figured a fresh set of eyes, along with evidence from this second murder, might help solve both cases.

"Funny thing about both murders, though. As big as Jacksonville is, and as many prostitutes a city of that size has roaming the streets, they've had none like these two. I'm wondering if the guy lives here at the beach and just feels more comfortable doing his business in an area that he knows. Of course, he could just as easily live in Jacksonville and want to go outside his own backyard to do his dirty work. I've tried to figure out what's in this guy's head that makes him want to kill prostitutes on the beach, but I'm nowhere on it so far."

Dana, who did most of her training runs on the beach, felt a little shiver run up her spine. "I always run north into Neptune Beach and sometimes all the way into Atlantic Beach before turning. Maybe I need to change my route and start going south into Ponte Vedra. Just because this guy has been killing prostitutes doesn't mean he would pass up a woman running alone in the early morning."

"Dana, I worry about you every day out there running alone, 'specially when you go early and there's no one else out there except the transients sleeping on the beach. You need to quit running when I'm not with you," Clay insisted.

"Now, you know that's not going to happen. I have to run regularly or my lower back tightens up, and you're not available to run with me as often as I need. Besides, the soft sand is so much better on my joints than hard concrete streets."

"Then why can't you go to the health club and run on the treadmill? That's soft," he suggested.

"It's not the same. How many times have I heard you gripe about having to ride your exercise bike when it's storming? You want to feel the wind in your face and the sun on your shoulders. That's what I want, too."

"I figured I couldn't change your mind about the beach, but how about carrying your little .380 in a belly pouch? It's not very heavy, but it'll still do a number on a guy if you pop him in the right place."

"Clay, would you please just stop? I'm not carrying that gun! In the time it would take me to get it out of my belly pouch and be ready to use it, I could be half a mile away."

"Okay, then at least be ready to use your D. T. when you're out there."

"My D. T.?" she asked with a quizzical look.

"Come on, Dana. Defensive tactics, remember?"

"Oh, yeah, that. Clay, you tried to teach me so much stuff I hardly remember any of it."

"Okay, fine. Just remember the most important one, the technique you use if someone grabs you around the neck or chest from the back."

Clay could see the wheels turning as Dana tried to recall the simple technique.

"Is that the one where I hit the guy in his, uh, you know?"

"Right. If he's got you from the back, shift your hips to the left and slam your fist into his balls as hard as you can. I guarantee he'll let go in a hurry. Then you run like hell. And one more thing, how about waiting to run until later in the morning when there's more people out there?"

"Yeah, fine. Now will you drop it?" she sighed.

Guessing he couldn't get a greater concession from Dana and wanting to avoid an argument right before his big meeting, Clay conceded with a smile, "Alright . . . and you're right. As fast as you run, a killer would have a helluva time catching you anyway, much less getting his hands around your pretty little neck!"

"Clay, I can't believe you said that. You know I'm freaked out about this!"

"Hey, I'm sorry, sweetie. You know how cops talk. It's our defense mechanism to make jokes about bad stuff. If we couldn't laugh about the crap we deal with every day, there'd be a lot more alcoholics and suicides than there already are. But you're right. I know this has been bothering you, and I shouldn't have joked about it. I love you, and I can't imagine life without my little Italian beauty in it!"

Clay wrapped his arms around Dana and pulled her close. Kissing her neck, he whispered, "It's still early. Since I'm not riding this morning, you wanta slip in a little mattress wrestling? Best two out of three falls?"

"I'm not sure you deserve it," she grumbled, although she didn't really mean it. "But if you can catch me, considering how *fast* I am, you might get lucky!"

Dana jumped off the bar stool and took off running up the stairs. Clay was close behind as they barreled into their bedroom. With a lunge, he grabbed her, and they fell laughing onto their king-size bed.

"Now that you've caught me, what are you going to do with me?" she asked with a giggle.

"This," he said, pulling her close.

"Oh, I like that. I like that a lot," she murmured as their bodies joined as one.

Chapter 4

The killer hated weakness of any kind. His mama had been a weak, pathetic excuse for a human being, in his estimation. Growing up in Miami, Edward Earl Shanklin never knew his father. His mama always claimed he was a soldier she met while he was home on leave. There was seldom enough money to pay the bills, much less any left over for toys and games for the boy. Many meals consisted of store-brand peanut butter and crackers donated from a local church mission.

Over the years, his mama hooked up with the same type over and over again. Names and faces changed, but they all treated her and the boy the same. The constant tension at home caused the child to withdraw into himself. A loner, he seldom interacted with other kids his age. Instead, he found pleasure roaming the woods, hiding among the palmettos as he pretended to be an Indian warrior, ready to attack anyone who ventured into his territory.

As Eddie entered his teen years, he began hunting small animals in the woods, killing armadillos and possums before graduating to the occasional cat or dog that wandered into his range. Eventually, he found greater pleasure not just in killing animals but in torturing them first. As he strung up cats and dogs by their tails and beat them with an old broken bat he had found, he imagined he was beating the numerous men who cycled in and out of their shabby, four-room rent house.

He hated them all. They laid around the house drinking while his mama worked twelve-hour days waitressing at a truck stop. When she didn't bring in enough money, or didn't cook their meals fast enough, or didn't put out when they wanted sex, they beat her, and she took it. When they weren't beating her, they beat him. And he took it, too.

Took it, that is, until the day after his fourteenth birthday. Eddie came home from school early because of a teacher's work period. Slipping quietly through the back door into the kitchen, he hoped to make it to his bedroom without encountering his stepfather, Ray Holmes, a sweat-stained, overweight, forty-six-year-old alcoholic. His mama's fourth or fifth husband, the boy no longer remembered or cared which, had chosen that particular moment to take what he viewed as his right as a husband.

Eddie had just stepped into the hall from the kitchen when he heard his mother crying, begging his stepfather, "Please, Ray, not right now, honey. I'm right in the big middle of my flow, and I'm cramping something awful. You poking at me is just going to make it worse. Can you wait a couple of days? I'll take real good care of you then. Please, Ray," she pleaded.

"I don't give a rat's ass about your period, bitch! I want some pussy, and I want it now!" Ray snarled, slapping her hard across the face.

The boy stood trembling, his fists clenched tightly at his sides. He could tell Holmes was drunk, as usual. The hatred Eddie felt for his stepfather edged closer to a pinnacle as his mind flashed back over the years of physical and sexual abuse heaped upon his mother by Ray and all the rest. He hated his mother, too, for her weakness, for begging when she should have told the bastard to take his clothes and his fat ass and hit the door.

Ray dropped his pants and climbed on top of her. She cried out again, once again begging him to stop. Holmes struck her breast hard with his fist, this time causing her to scream. Before the scream faded, the teenager had bolted down the short hallway to the bedroom. What he saw when he entered the room stopped him in his tracks. In his mind, his stepfather was raping his mother, oblivious to her cries for him to stop. He saw blood staining the bed sheets as his stepfather continued to thrust himself into his mother.

Eddie screamed, "Get off her, you bastard! Leave my mother alone!"

His stepfather paused, looking over his shoulder at the kid, "This ain't none of your business, boy. You better get to steppin' before I give you a whoopin' you won't forget!"

"Eddie, honey, your father don't mean to hurt me. You go on now, and I'll be out in a little while."

"That fat son of a bitch is not my father! Why do you keep putting up with his shit?" he yelled.

"Ray's got needs," she said. "And it's my duty as his wife to satisfy those needs."

The ongoing conversation was making it difficult for Holmes to concentrate on his task, and his erection was rapidly going south.

"You little peckerwood! You got two seconds to be gone out that door, or so help me, I'll beat your ass to a bloody pulp!"

Eddie saw his stepfather's big silver-buckled cowboy belt with metal studs hanging over the closet door. Grabbing the buckle in both hands, he hit his stepfather across the back with the leather end of it, screaming, "I'll kill you!"

Holmes grabbed the belt as Eddie swung again, yanking it out of his hands. He jumped off the bed and struck the boy in the mouth, knocking him over a stool and causing his head to slam against the closet door. Stunned, his ears ringing, Eddie thought his jaw might be broken. Before he could get his wits about him, Ray struck again, this time with the business end of the belt. The buckle crashed against his left shoulder, opening a two-inch gash with the sharp metal studs.

Eddie went crazy. Years later, he still couldn't remember exactly what happened. He sort of blanked out, and, when he came back, he was standing over Ray Holmes with the belt buckle covered in blood. The man's head was a bloody mass of brains, hair and teeth, so distorted that the medical examiner had to rely on his tattoos and fingerprints for a positive identification.

Eddie Shanklin was sent to the county's juvenile detention center where he stayed for sixty days until a public defender got him out on a claim of excusable homicide. Through the years, he laughed every time he heard that term, excusable homicide. It was like a variation on the old Steve Martin routine, "Well, ex-c-u-u-s-e me while I commit homicide on your ass!"

His mother never quite forgave him for killing Ray Holmes. She visited him only once at the detention center. She said she despised him for killing Ray, that he would still be alive if Eddie had done what he was told and left their bedroom. She claimed Ray's actions, and her reaction, were normal for married people.

The boy didn't understand why she blamed him when all he did was try to protect her. Her irrational defense of his stepfather caused Eddie to vow that he would never again do anything for someone else unless it directly benefited him. The incident seared into his mind the realization that he wouldn't get anywhere in this life by being weak and allowing others to have power over him.

In addition to all his mother's other faults, she had also turned tricks in between her many husbands and live-in boyfriends. She was the consummate whore, he thought; a mother who abandoned her duty to her son for money and her own selfish pleasures. He saw that as her ultimate betrayal of him.

His contempt for his mother's weakness warped his emotions permanently. Eddie Shanklin grew to believe his mission in life was to rid the world of weakness wherever he found it. And he found it everywhere he looked, people who had given up on life, people who had surrendered to their baser instincts . . . weakness in all its shabby forms and dimensions. And the experience with his stepfather convinced Eddie he could literally get away with murder.

Chapter 5

"Hey, Mike," Clay greeted his boss, Detective Commander Michael Wilson. Commander Wilson was fifty-five years old and bald, his hairline having gone so far south that he liked to say it was vacationing in South America. He often groused to his detectives that their constant screw-ups caused him to lose his hair.

Although he exhibited a gruff demeanor to everyone except his long-time secretary, Linda Greene, he secretly respected and admired his officers for their dedication to the job.

Commander Wilson had joined the Jacksonville Beach Police Department after serving fifteen years in the United States Navy. In his twenty-one years with the police department, he had served in every division; consequently, there was no stunt or scam his detectives could pull that he hadn't done himself.

"You're late," he growled. "Everyone's here except you, Mr. Lead Detective. Is there some reason why you're dragging your ass in here ten minutes after the meeting was supposed to start?"

Clay suppressed a smile as he thought of his early morning romp with Dana. "Boss, I was doing a last-minute review of my notes so I could sound intelligent in the meeting."

"Oh, so now you decide you want to be intelligent, huh?" Wilson said sarcastically. "It's only taken five years in the Detective Division to come to that conclusion? I'm so impressed, I want your autograph after the meeting! Now, get in there and solve those killings."

"Yes, sir, boss," Clay said with a smile he carefully hid from Wilson. Early on, he had realized Wilson's grouchy persona was just that, a role he played to keep his detectives from getting too comfortable in their jobs. He had the greatest respect for his commander and frequently asked his advice about investigations he was assigned.

Clay walked into the conference room where the detectives and a few patrol officers and supervisors had gathered. "Hi, everybody, sorry I'm late. I've got handouts if someone can help pass them out."

Cassie Broderick, one of Clay's team members on the prostitute cases, grabbed a handful and began distributing them.

"Thanks, Cassie," Clay said. "Guys, take a few minutes to review the material, and then let's go through it. I've included a summary of the killing in Atlantic Beach so we can look for comparables to our case."

After ten minutes, Clay took the floor again. "We have to work together as a team to solve these murders. Atlantic Beach PD has assigned two detectives full time to their homicide, so we'll be sharing information back and forth regularly. For identification purposes, we've designated our task force Operation Street Cleaner."

"That should fire up the media," said Bobby Hawkins, the department's Public Information Officer, or PIO. "Are you sure you want to use a name like that, Sergeant Randall?"

"What's wrong with the name, Bobby?"

"Well, it seems to imply that we're glad a serial killer is ridding the streets of whores."

"It doesn't imply anything like that. Besides, Commander Wilson already approved the name. So let's move on, please," Clay said dismissively.

He had taken an instant dislike to Bobby Hawkins even before he knew of the connection to Dana. And finding out he had dated Dana years before further increased Clay's negative feelings about the man.

Bobby Hawkins had been a cop in Jacksonville Beach for eight years. Bouncing around the department in a succession of jobs, he never stayed long before asking to be transferred to another assignment. Every job had drawbacks that ultimately disillusioned him and caused him to want to try something else. He had been assigned as the PIO for six months, and already his interest was beginning to wane. Hawkins leaned against the wall with his arms crossed, an irritated expression on his face.

Bobby Hawkins' feelings for Clay were similarly intense. He thought Clay had been put in charge of the prostitute task force by kissing up to Mike Wilson. Hawkins figured if they had put him in charge instead he would have already solved the murders.

I worked homicide for a year and got assigned some real whodunit cases. I cleared them on my own and got convictions without any help from Wilson, too. And I'd still be in detectives if he hadn't been such an asshole to work for! Randall thinks he's so hot just because he's solved a couple of murders through sheer luck, and then he gets rewarded with the prostitute homicide cases, he griped to himself, refusing to use Randall's Operation Street Cleaner designation.

Randall's got his nose so far up Wilson's ass, it'll break if he turns the corner too quick. And then he somehow convinced Dana Cappella to marry him!

He had never understood what Dana saw in Clay Randall. He and Dana had been friends in school and had even dated for a while. She had come to him for advice at times when her mother had been particularly difficult. He saw that as true friendship, one he had hoped would grow into a real relationship. That it did not, and led instead to a marriage to Clay Randall, was a constant source of anger and frustration to Bobby Hawkins.

I'm gonna tell the chief about this stupid task force name. I bet he doesn't know anything about it, and he's gonna be pissed at Randall when he finds out, Hawkins thought with satisfaction.

". . . the killing here last week," Clay was saying to the group. "We got a 9-1-1 call last Wednesday morning about 2:00 a.m. from the pay phone in front of Burger King. The guy refused to ID himself, said he had just seen a woman killed under the pier. He described the killer as a white male about six feet, maybe one-eighty, with short brown hair. When the dispatcher asked for additional info, he said he heard the guy say something after he killed her. Let me check my notes so I get it right . . . Yeah, here it is. He said the killer leaned over her and said, 'You have been tried and found guilty of being a weak bitch.'

"The victim was one Marilyn Rene Gibbs, white female, twenty-one, fairly attractive for a, quote-unquote, sex worker, being politically correct here. We popped her once for prostitution, and Atlantic Beach had one case on her, also.

"Cause of death was a stab wound to the heart with a knife blade approximately five inches long. According to Barton, our killer stabbed her in the chest and then stood watching her as she bled out. When she stopped moving, he stabbed her eight more times, three in the pelvic area, two to the right breast, and three to the left."

The assembled detectives and officers quickly realized the MO was very similar to the previous prostitute murder. There was no doubt in anyone's mind they were dealing with one sick SOB, someone who probably had some type of serious sexual disorder.

"By the time an officer got to the pay phone, our witness was gone. As we know now, the caller was a transient named James Anderson "Jimmy" Barton. I had a tape made of his call and played it for our guys. Officer Rafe Santos recognized Barton's voice right off. He's arrested him several times in the past six months for drinking in public and similar stuff and talks to him frequently down on the boardwalk. Rafe found him last Friday and convinced him to talk to us. He said when the killer started stabbing her crotch and breasts, the guy looked insane, growling like a mad dog." A chill ran down the back of just about everyone in the room as they contemplated the monster they were trying to catch.

Paul Shelton, the Jacksonville Beach Patrol Division Commander, had come into the back of the conference room during Randall's briefing. He stood up and said, "Clay, and the rest of you gentlemen and ladies in here, we've obviously got a real problem here. We have to put every available officer and detective on these cases. Just because he's killing prostitutes right now doesn't mean he's going to stay focused on them. While he's apparently got a hang-up on them for now anyway, he might decide all women are whores and start killing them indiscriminately. Our next victim might be a Sunday school teacher that somehow he thinks is a . . . what did Barton say he called her?"

"A weak bitch," Clay read from his notes.

"Right. I want you to hit the streets as hard as you can, push your snitches for any information about a guy with this physical description. Tell them to keep their ears to the ground for somebody bragging about the killings. Between Atlantic Beach and us, we have two prostitutes murdered in less than six months. This guy's sex obsession may be escalating. Toward what end, we don't know . . . but we better find out! So, if you need anything, anything at all, I'll do my best to get it for you. I'll go to Chief Cooper and ask him for more overtime money if that's what we need. Just get this guy! And with that, I'll shut up and sit down."

"Thanks, Commander," Clay said. "We really appreciate your support!"

Absent was any praise for the Chief of Police, Gordon Haynes "Gordy" Cooper. Randall and most of the department despised the chief, a man they viewed as totally devoid of integrity based upon years of questionable actions that always seemed to skirt right up to the edge of unethical behavior but never quite slide over, at least not that any employee had discovered.

Clay was surprised Gordy hadn't stuck his nose in the meeting pretending to care what happened to the investigation. If Cooper really did give a crap, Clay figured it was only because he was afraid the bad publicity might affect him personally.

Clay suddenly realized everyone in the room was staring at him. "Sorry, guys. Just thinking about what Commander Shelton said. Anyway, back to Barton. He told Officer Santos he didn't want to be identified and have the guy come after him. We told him it was extremely unlikely, but we said if he had a place to stay besides the beach he should go there. We offered to get him some help, but he told us he'd head over to the west side of Jacksonville and stay with his sister. Santos transported him over there after we got a statement from him, and he told him to keep his head down until we called, hopefully with a suspect for him to ID.

"As everyone knows, that idea worked really well," he said sarcastically. "Saturday, he talked to a TV reporter, and suddenly his name and face are everywhere. I called Barton and asked him why the hell he contacted the media when he said he was so afraid. He gave me a BS story about talking to his sister about the murder while they were in some store, and the reporter just happened to hear him.

"It's all a crock, but there's nothing we can do now except try to keep him on the west side and away from the beach. Maybe he's trying to get his fifteen minutes of fame, I don't know, but assuming this killer is local, and I believe he is, the odds of him going after Barton have just increased dramatically.

"The MO on Marilyn Gibbs is virtually identical to the Atlantic Beach case. Same size, double-edged blade, same wound distribution, same type of location, on the beach. You'd think our sex entrepreneurs would have gotten smart about taking a customer down on the beach, but apparently Gibbs didn't get the memo.   But that's obviously—"

"This meeting is over, guys," directed Commander Mike Wilson as he walked hurriedly into the room. "We just got a 9-1-1 call of a Signal 7 under the Sixth Avenue, North walkover. Appears to be a white male transient, throat cut, and some kind of weird note on the body. Randall, you and Broderick are lead on this. Ty Honchen, Jeremy Rivers, you're assigned, also. Take an evidence technician with—"

"But Commander," Clay interrupted, "We're up to our necks in follow up now that we have a physical on this guy. Besides, our guy isn't killing male transients!"

"Excuse me," Wilson said with genuine irritation in his voice. "But before I was so rudely interrupted, I was about to mention one additional detail, smart ass. Your Signal 7 is James Barton! Familiar name?"

Sergeant Randall's eyes opened wide. Ignoring his boss's sarcastic tone, he headed for the door at a run, yelling for his team members, "Come on, guys! Grab your radios and get rolling!"

Chapter 6

11:30 p.m. the previous Wednesday night

"Hey, looking for someone?" Marilyn Gibbs asked the neatly dressed man standing on the boardwalk near the Jacksonville Beach pier.

"Yeah, my date said she would meet me here in the parking lot, and we'd go have a drink at that club," he said, pointing at the bar across the street from where they stood. "I've been waiting for a half hour now. I guess she's not coming," the man said with an embarrassed grin.

"Would you like some company?" she asked with a bold smile on her face. She reached out and touched the sleeve of his jacket as she asked the question, at the same time moving in close to the man.

"Well, I, I guess so, sure . . . why not." he replied. "You, uh, want to go have a drink with me?"

"How about we take a walk on the beach instead? I like to walk in the sand," she said.

"Great," he said. Neither said anything as they walked across the parking lot and over the walkover down to the beach. When they reached the sand, Marilyn turned north and headed for the underside of the pier. As they walked underneath, she took the man's hand and pulled him toward the portion of the pier where it originated at the boardwalk. Wooden panels on either side of the pier extended from the walkway down to the sand, creating an effective block against the north wind and screening them from the view of anyone walking by. In that semi-concealed area, the light was much dimmer than it had been on the boardwalk.

Marilyn Gibbs turned to face the man and asked, "What would you like?"

"What do you mean?"

"I mean just what I asked. You gotta tell me what you want. I can't say anything until I know what you want. Then we can talk freer."

"Are you a prostitute?" the man asked with amazement in his voice.

"I didn't say that," she said indignantly. "Are you a cop?"

"Hell, no!"

"Prove it, then. Cops can't expose themselves without breaking the law. So show me your cock, and then we can discuss things."

The man said, "Well, okay, but this is a little bit embarrassing. I gotta turn around. I had no idea when I came to the beach tonight that I would end up being with a, a prostitute."

Gibbs had to check herself to keep from rolling her eyes. The guy was acting like some cornpone hick from South Georgia, trying to pretend he was inexperienced when, instead, she figured him for a player who bought his fair share of street sex.

"Now, honey, you just turn around with your tool in your hand. Then I'll know what this little walk on the beach is all about."

The man turned his back on her, appearing to fumble with his pants. He slipped his hand into his pocket, easing out a double-edged dagger. As he turned back, he grabbed the woman by her left shoulder, pulling her roughly toward him. At the same time, he thrust the knife into her chest directly under the breastbone, angling the razor-sharp blade upward into her heart.

She gasped, an explosion of breath directly into the man's face that carried the smell of the peppermint breath mints she used between customers. He wrinkled his nose in disgust as he pushed her head away, letting her body crumple to the sand, the knife making a sucking sound as it came free from her chest. He stood for several moments without moving, watching her breathing grow shallow.

Marilyn Gibbs had lived her life on the edge since the age of sixteen, trusting no one but herself. She had prided herself on her skills at reading men who wanted more than she was willing to provide, the temporary rental of one or more of her bodily orifices. Until now, she had been able to avoid those men who desired more violent pleasures. As her life ebbed away, Marilyn stared into her killer's eyes, her last conscious thought, *He looks like a devil.*

The man's breathing became labored as he stared at his handiwork. His thoughts were jumbled, part rage, part hate, part contempt for this weak woman who sold her body for money. His bitch mother doing the same thing this dead whore was willing to do flashed through his mind, and he grew more agitated.

The killer turned the dripping knife around in his hand and began viciously stabbing the body directly in the crotch. He then moved to her breasts, driving the knife into each one multiple times. As he wielded the knife, lips peeled back from his teeth, he growled like a dog about to attack someone trying to steal its favorite rawhide bone. Finished, sated at least temporarily, the man stood up. Gazing at the body, he said, "You've been tried and found guilty of being a weak bitch."

The killer raised his head, listening closely for anyone who might have heard anything. Hearing something, a scuffling sound, a sharp intake of breath . . . something, he stared toward where the wooden pier originated at the sand dunes. He could see the dim outline of an opening in the dune that might be an area where someone could hide. The killer considered checking it out but quickly realized that would leave him vulnerable to anyone who walked under the pier. They would see the bitch in the sand, and he wouldn't be able to get away without being seen.

Staring a moment longer, he shrugged. *There's no one there, I'm just a little jumpy. Time to go, as soon as I add a little something to my collection.*

The dead woman was wearing a cheap metal cross on a silver-colored chain around her neck. He grabbed the cross and jerked, breaking the thin chain. Dropping his new souvenir into his pocket, he stood, peering intently at the area under the pier where he thought he had heard something. After staring a few more seconds, he turned and walked away.

After the killer left, Jimmy Barton collapsed to his stomach in the little cave where the killer had thought he heard something. His heart was beating so fast and his breathing so labored he thought he was having a heart attack. Barton was more frightened than he had ever been in his life.

Homeless for years, Barton had often witnessed the terrible things one human being could do to another. But this was beyond anything he had ever imagined. The man he watched kill what was obviously a prostitute was like a demon, evil seeming to radiate from him in waves. He gathered up his meager belongings and crawled out of the cave.

Barton was afraid of being blamed for the murder if anyone found him nearby. He walked quickly past the body of Marilyn Gibbs, not looking for fear he would start screaming and be unable to stop.

He walked north on the beach at a fast pace, constantly looking over his shoulder in fear he was being pursued by the crazed killer. As he fled, he thought about the cruelties of life and how unfair it was for a woman just trying to get by any way she could having to die that way. The more he thought about it, the angrier he got. Barton decided he had to do something, as long as it didn't put him in danger.

Checking in every direction, he headed to a Burger King on Third Street where he knew of one of the few pay phones left at the beach. Barton concealed himself in a stand of fan palms while he checked the area for anyone moving. Seeing no one, he slipped up to the phone and dialed 9-1-1. When the operator answered, he told her what he had seen and then quickly hung up.

Barton walked quickly back to the beach and headed north again. He didn't stop this time until he had covered almost two miles, entering the much smaller community of Neptune Beach. Leaving the beach, he half-walked, half-ran until he came to the rear of Pete's Bar, a local watering hole. The dumpster behind Pete's was filled mostly with broken down cardboard boxes. Barton climbed inside, pulling the cardboard over himself as much to hide as for additional warmth. Drifting off with the help of several swallows of cheap whiskey he kept in his backpack for emergencies, Barton twitched and muttered, his sleep marred by dreams of flashing knives and violent death.

Chapter 7

At 7:30, Dana Randall stepped onto the patio dressed for her morning run. She wore running tights and a jacket to protect her body from the cold wind, a headband for her ears, and light gloves to keep her hands warm. Normally, she carried nothing with her except her driver's license and the house key. Today, as a concession to Clay's concern, she also carried her cell phone. She didn't expect to need it, but she could tell Clay how sensitive she was to his warnings to make him feel better.

As she walked onto the hard-packed sand, Dana debated which direction to run. She knew heading south would make the return trip difficult. She was leaving later like Clay asked, even though the winter daylight made it seem more like night was still blanketing the shoreline.

Go south like I promised him, or run north into the wind while I'm fresh and then coast back home with the wind pushing me? Which one? She mused. Making up her mind, Dana turned north, running with an easy stride as the wind blew hard in her face and the smell of salt air and seaweed pummeled her senses.

She saw no one in the two mile stretch from the house to downtown Jacksonville Beach. Even the transients were sleeping somewhere better protected from the winds than the sand dunes could provide.

The turning point for her regular five mile run was a block past the pier. As she approached the pier, she saw no one anywhere on its thirteen hundred foot length. Usually, there were at least a few diehard fishermen out at the end, hoping to catch a red fish or maybe a shark that the weather pushed in close to shore.

I must be crazy to be out in this weather when even the fish don't bite, she laughed to herself.

Dana ran past the pier and approached the walkover to make her turn for the fast return trip home. Slowing her pace, she spotted what appeared to be a homeless person lying under the walkover close to where the steps led down to the soft sand. Man or woman, she couldn't tell in the still weak daylight.

So I'm not the only one dumb enough to be out in this weather, Dana mused. *Whoever it is must be pretty tough to be sleeping on the beach this morning.*

As she made her turn, Dana suddenly began to feel uneasy. Something about the scene was odd. She could see it was a man lying on his back with his arms and legs splayed out to the sides like a kid paused in the middle of making a snow angel.

Dana felt more and more apprehensive as she stopped and stared closely at the man from about twenty feet away. A blue tarp partially covered with sand lay a few feet from the man's right arm. Although the daylight barely reached under the walkover, Dana was able to see a large amount of blood. It covered the man's neck, chest, and abdomen and had pooled on both sides, creating multiple blood-red clumps of sand.

Dana stared, her mind whirling at the horrible sight. Her heart pounding harder than it had on her run, she tried to make sense of what she was seeing. Then suddenly, the thought exploded in her mind, *This guy's been murdered*! She couldn't take her eyes from the dead man. Her legs felt so weak she wasn't sure she could stand, much less run.

Suddenly, Dana heard a sound behind her. She couldn't identify its origin, but, in her panicked mind, she was instantly convinced the sound was made by the homeless man's killer. In her mind's eye, she saw a tall, dark-clothed man standing directly behind her, a huge hunting knife poised to drive deep into her body. Her bladder felt so weak she thought she couldn't hold back.

She whispered, "Please God. Don't let me die here on this deserted beach." Tensing her shoulders in anticipation of the death blow, she whirled to face her attacker. There was no one there, the beach still empty of human life, except for her. Instead, she saw a seagull trying to stick its head into a Pringle's can to get at a few soggy chips inside.

Dana drew a deep breath, letting it out in a shaky laugh accompanied by a shudder. "C'mon, Dana," she said aloud. "Pull yourself together! Get your cell and call Clay now!"

She grabbed the phone from her pocket, hands shaking badly as she punched in the speed-dial number for her husband. The phone began ringing, and Dana took a deep breath so she could convey a coherent message to him.

"Come *on*, answer the phone!" she said in a loud whisper. After the first ring, she heard Clay's voice mail message come on. Recalling he had told her he would be in a briefing and figuring he must have turned his phone off, she quickly broke the connection and dialed 9-1-1.

"Jax Beach 9-1-1, is this an emergency?" the dispatcher asked in a calm, professional tone.

"This is Dana Randall, Sergeant Randall's wife! There's a man under the walkover at Sixth Avenue, North. He's covered in blood! I, I, it looks like his throat's been cut or he's been stabbed a bunch of times, I'm not sure! I was on my morning run from the house and saw him as I got ready to make my turn. I wasn't sure if it was a man or a woman at—"

"Dana, hold on. This is Donna Lloyd. I know you're upset, but you need to slow down so I can get the right information to the officers responding."

Taking a deep breath, Dana said, "Alright, Donna. Go ahead."

"Now exactly where are you?"

"I'm on the beach right at the Sixth Avenue, North walkover. The man's under the walkover close to where the steps come down to the sand."

"You say you think his throat's cut. Is he dead?"

"Well, I'm standing about twenty feet away, but he looks dead from here. He hasn't moved since I first saw him. Hey, Donna, I see two police cars pulling up in the end zone."

"Good. That should be Officers David Sheasley and Yolanda Jamison. A whole bunch of guys are right behind them, too. I'm going to hang up now and let you talk to them. Are you gonna be okay?"

"Yeah, I guess so. Clay's going to be so mad when he finds out I'm here. We just had an argument this morning about me running alone on the beach. Can someone call him and tell him? He's supposed to be in a meeting this morning on the prostitute killings."

With Donna's promise to notify her husband, Dana broke the connection and waited as the two patrol officers raced over the walkover onto the beach.

With Cassie Broderick riding shotgun, Clay, peeled out of the police parking lot, closely followed by Detectives Ty Honchen and Jeremy Rivers. The unmarked detective cars had sirens and emergency lights in the grill, which were activated as they turned onto Beach Boulevard heading for the oceanfront.

Arriving quickly, they found several marked police cars already crowding the Sixth Avenue, North end zone parking lot. Crime scene tape had been strung for fifty yards in a circle, and officers were stationed in the lot and on the beach to keep the growing crowd of onlookers back from the scene. As they exited their cars, the four detectives pinned their badges to the pockets of their outer jackets to identify themselves.

Yolanda Jamison greeted them as they approached, "Hey, Sarge. I see you got your posse with you. I'm afraid you're gonna need them and probably a bunch more on this one."

Clay didn't smile or crack jokes with her like he usually did. "What you got, 'Landa?" he asked, calling Yolanda by her nickname.

"One deceased white male under the walkover right behind me. On his back, arms and legs spread, throat's been cut, big time. It appears almost like the killer was trying to separate his head from the rest of him."

"Commander Wilson said it's James Barton."

"Yeah, I recognized him. And there's something really strange about this one."

All four detectives stepped closer to Officer Jamison to hear what she had to say. The information could be crucial to the identity of the killer, and they didn't want to risk unauthorized ears overhearing it.

"What is it, 'Landa?" Detective Broderick asked.

"Someone, I'm assuming the killer, left a message on his chest."

Clay stared hard at Officer Jamison. "A message? You mean like another slash mark or something like that?"

"No, no. I mean a typed message, you know, on paper. And it's held in place with a shell."

"What does it say?" Detective Honchen asked.

"Something about Barton being a child molester and a bunch of kids being saved, or something like that."

"Yeah," Clay interrupted, anxious now to get down to the scene. "Anything else unusual?"

"Uh, well, yeah, there is," Yolanda said hesitantly.

Clay waited as she stared at him, not saying anything. Finally, he broke the silence with an exasperated, "C'mon, 'Landa, we're not playing Twenty Questions! What else?"

"It's Dana, Clay. She's the one who found Barton."

Clay was stunned. It was his turn to stare at Yolanda without saying anything as he tried to process what she had just said.

Cassie jumped in. "Landa, You're saying Dana Randall found the body? What was she doing down on the beach this time of the morning so far from . . . oh, she was running, wasn't she?"

"Yes, she was."

"Is she okay?" Cassie asked, almost afraid of the answer.

"She's fine. Barton's cold and stiff, so it's not like she ran up on the murder in progress. She's not hurt or anything, just a little freaked out, as you can imagine. Sheasley left with her heading to HQ just a couple of minutes before y'all got here. You probably passed her coming down here."

Cassie glanced at Clay. She knew he was unhappy with Dana running alone, especially since the two prostitute homicides. Clay was still staring at Yolanda, not saying anything.

"Clay, Dana's not hurt," Cassie said. "She's a tough lady. Now, let's get going. We have another murder to solve."

Clay shook his head as if to clear it. Without another word, he ducked under the police tape and headed over the walkover toward the beach, followed closely by the rest of his team. When they stepped under the wooden bridge, the detectives saw the bloodied remains of their only witness to the Marilyn Gibbs homicide. The note on Barton's chest was flapping in the strong Northeast wind, surprisingly still in place under the seashell.

Jim Childress, the department's primary evidence technician, was taking digital photographs of the body and the area immediately surrounding it. He glanced back at the detectives as they stood quietly behind him. "Sergeant Randall, good morning! And the same to you, Cassie and Ty and Jeremy," he said with a grin.

Jim was one of those rare people who went through life with a permanent smile on his face. He was a cheerful man in a decidedly cheerless job, dealing as he often did with violent, bloody crime scenes.

"I've taken perspective shots from fifty feet in to the body. I shot the note in place, but I haven't moved it yet."

Clay asked, "Jim, can you read us exactly what it says?"

"Sure. Hang on and let me get this last picture of the scuff marks in the sand."

Jim took the shot and then stepped back to where Clay and the other detectives were standing. He scrolled back through the digital photos on the camera drive until he found a close-up of the note. Zooming in so the words appeared sharply, he handed the camera to Clay. As he read, the other detectives leaned over his shoulder trying to see.

"Let's see, it says, 'One dead child molester, 20 children saved' . . . And it ends with an exclamation point. Any idea what it means, guys?"

Jeremy Rivers spoke up. "I think he had a sex offense on his rap sheet. I don't remember the details, but I'll check it as soon as I get back to HQ, Sergeant."

"Thanks, Three, head on back," Clay said, calling Jeremy by his nickname. Rivers had been tagged with the moniker shortly after coming to the department. His rabid support for the Pittsburgh Steelers and his endless stories of trips to Three Rivers Stadium when he was a kid to cheer on his beloved Black and Gold were legendary. A few guys in the department tried calling him "Catsup" when the stadium name was changed to Heinz Field, but Catsup Rivers just didn't have the same punch as Three Rivers.

As Rivers headed back to his car, Clay turned to Cassie and Ty.

"What's the deal with the 'twenty children saved' phrase?" It was obvious from the blank looks on their faces they had no clue.

As Clay handed the camera back to Childress, he said, "I'm drawing a blank on it, too. Maybe it's tied in some way to his sex offense. Three will find it if there's anything there. Meanwhile, what can you tell us about the cause of death, Jim?"

"I would have to say the fact someone tried to remove his head from the rest of his torso with a sharp instrument would probably be a good guess," Jim said with his usual good humor.

"Thanks for that brilliant theory, Jim," Clay said drily. "Anything else you can tell us?"

"Not much, Sarge. In this soft sand, it's impossible to get any shoe prints. But I think I've found what may be a knee impression. See it there?" he pointed.

The detectives started at the spot Childress indicated, but, not surprisingly, none of them could see the impression he was describing. Childress was an expert at identifying shoe, foot, and other body impressions in a variety of surfaces, so it didn't surprise them that he had found something.

"My guess is the killer kneeled on the right side of the body either to commit the act, or to place the paper on his chest, or maybe both. There's not enough consistency in the depression to show the pattern of the killer's pants, but I'm taking a plaster cast anyway. You never know what may show up later," he said, showing his usual attention to detail.

Clay assigned Detective Honchen to walk the beach for several hundred yards in both directions searching for anything that might shed light on the identity of the killer. Honchen recruited some patrol officers to assist him, one going with him while the other two headed in the opposite direction. Before quitting, they would reverse directions and go over the same area their partners had checked in the event something of importance was missed by the first team. Clay assigned additional officers to begin knocking on doors looking for witnesses.

Only after he felt the situation on scene was under control did he allow himself to think about his wife and what she had gone through. Clay stood in the driving wind staring at the ocean as he considered how he should react when he saw her. As the initial shock and fear for her safety faded, his anger began to grow.

I told her not to run north, dammit! he raged to himself. *Why doesn't she ever listen to me?*

His anger was not directed at Dana for defying him but instead was based on his fear of losing her. He thought, *I have to keep my cool. If I go off, she'll get pissed right back, and that'll be a disaster for the investigation and for me when I get home.*

Chapter 8

Dana sat alone in an interview room in the Detective Division, sipping a cup of coffee and reliving over and over the event on the beach. The door opened, and Cassie Broderick walked in. The attractive, thirty-eight-year-old Broderick stood five-ten in her bare feet, with bright red curly hair that her fellow detectives said made her look like the comedian Carrot Top. Considering her size and demonstrated ability to handle unruly suspects, the Carrot Top jokes were usually made when she wasn't around. Cassie was generally even tempered, but she didn't tolerate fools or assholes gladly.

"Hey, Dana, how are you feeling?"

"Still a little shaky. That's the first dead body I've ever seen up close. The blood was everywhere! I don't see how Clay does it, and I especially don't see how *you* do it, Cassie."

"It's not that hard. When you see enough people shot, stabbed, cut, and blown up, you get kind of numb to it. We all put up a wall. That body on the ground is just an object; it's no longer a person. It's evidence, more often than not the most important piece, but still just evidence.

"If any of us, including Clay, ever let our guard down for an instant at these homicide scenes, we'd probably start crying and not be able to stop," she said with quiet feeling.

Dana shuddered, "I wish now I hadn't gone any closer after David Sheasley and Yolanda Jamison got there. I was scared, but I was curious to see his face. Now, all I keep seeing are his eyes. They were only half open, but I swear it felt like he was staring right at me! It was freaky!

"And what's the deal about that piece of paper on his chest? I saw some typed words on it, but I couldn't see what they were. I asked 'Landa, but she wouldn't tell me."

"I'm sorry, Dana, but I can't either. That's part of the crime scene, and I can't talk about it. I hope you understand," Cassie said apologetically.

"Oh, sure, I understand. I didn't mean to put you on the spot. Just more of my curious nature poking its way out. I guess I better get it under control before it gets me in real trouble. I wouldn't be in here right now if I had run south like I promised Clay I'd do."

"Yeah, Clay mentioned out at the scene about his insisting that you run south. He also told me he tried to get you to carry your little gun, but you wouldn't.

"Dana, you have a carry permit, and you really should take advantage of it, especially when you're out running on that beach so early. You know the problems we've had in the past with transients exposing themselves and sometimes chasing women down and assaulting them when they were out walking or running by themselves. It's just not safe for you to be doing that."

"I know, I know, and to top it off, I'm a big coward. I jump at my own shadow, so I guess it was pretty stupid. You know, Clay's always wearing some fruity looking shirt, and when I kid him about it, he says he's secure in his manhood. Well, I'm here to tell you that, after this morning, I'm secure in my chickenhood!"

Cassie Broderick burst out laughing so hard that she almost fell off her chair. "Chickenhood! Omigawd! That is so funny!"

Dana at first just stared at Cassie, not getting her own joke. As she watched, Cassie's curly red hair bouncing up and down in time to her waves of laughter, the Carrot Top comparison suddenly flashed into Dana's mind.

That did it, a smile, followed by a giggle, finally loud laughter of her own. At first, it felt weird considering the terror she had felt earlier, but she quickly realized the laughter served as a release for all her pent-up tension.

"Thanks, Dana! I needed that! This job can really get to you, so any excuse to laugh sure helps keeps thing loose."

As both women still giggled over Dana's inadvertent funny, Clay opened the door to the room.

"Hey, what's so funny about a guy getting his throat cut?" he demanded.

That brought another round of laughter from both of them.

Cassie finally gasped, "Clay, you just had to be here!"

Dana glanced at Clay and then quickly looked away, her laughter fading. She knew he was upset with her over what she had done, and she didn't really want to have an argument about it in front of one of his fellow detectives.

Clay glanced at Cassie, who took the hint and jumped up. "Y'all need to talk. I'll catch you later, Dana. You take care . . . and just stay secure in your you-know-what!" She started laughing again as she left the room, closing the door behind her.

Dana started to laugh but caught herself. "Clay, I know what you're going to say and—"

"Good, but I'm going to say it anyway!" he exclaimed in a loud voice, totally forgetting his promise to himself to remain calm. "I told you how dangerous it was. I told you not to run on the beach so early. I—"

"But—" Dana tried to interject.

"But nothing! Don't even try to justify what you did! You knew I didn't want you running alone on the beach, but you just had to show me you were gonna do whatever you wanted, and my feelings be damned!"

Dana started getting angry. "Just hold on there, bud! That's not fair! You know good and well I didn't do it just to mess with you! I ran north because of the Nor'easter. I didn't want to run back against that wind when I was tired! You know that. You're being an ass!"

"I'm an ass? You're calling *me* an ass?"

"Yes, that's exactly what I'm calling you! I'm fine. No one dragged me under the walkover and raped me! And because of me, you can do your precious detective work sooner than you would have. There was no one on that beach but me. With this weather, there's no telling how long he would have laid out there before somebody found him. You ought to be giving me a medal or something instead of griping at me," Dana said as she stared angrily at Clay.

He glared back, neither of them saying anything for almost a minute. Then Clay's shoulders slumped, and he sat down heavily in the chair next to her.

"Dana," he said hesitantly.

"What?" she asked, still angry at him.

"Look. I knew before I married you that you had a mind of your own. I'm just scared that something bad will happen to you. Don't you know by now how much I love you?" he asked in a pleading voice.

"Nothing and no one in this life matters as much as you. I, I'm sorry I yelled at you."

He grabbed her in an embrace, holding her so tight she could hardly breathe. Dana hugged him fiercely in return, feeling her anger ease, to be replaced rapidly by the emotion of the horrible event. As her body shook with quiet sobs, Clay continued to hold her tight.

"It's okay, my darling. You're safe."

He sat beside Dana with his arms around her as she slowly got her emotions under control. Finally, she pulled back and said with a shaky laugh, "Wow, I must look horrible. I guess it's a good thing I'm not wearing makeup or I'd look like a raccoon."

"If you did, you'd be the best looking 'coon around," Clay laughed in return.

Pulling a couple of paper towels out of his pocket, he said, "Here, sweetie, you don't *really* look like a 'coon, but you'd still probably scare little kids with those puffy eyes."

Dana stared suspiciously at the paper towels.

"Wait a minute. Where did those come from? You never carry paper towels around in your pocket. Were you using them to handle that dead guy?"

"I, I . . . What? No, are you crazy?! I would never do that to you!"

Dana laughed at Clay's expression.

"Got you back for your smartass comments."

Just then, the door opened, and his boss, Commander Mike Wilson, stepped in.

"Hi, Dana, how are you doing?"

"I've definitely been better, Mike, but I'm fine, thanks."

"Have you given your statement yet?"

"Yes. I wrote it and gave it to Cassie Broderick."

"I'm sorry to have to take your husband away from you, but the chief wants to see both of us right away, and he doesn't like to be kept waiting."

"Oh, no problem, Mike. I'll get out of y'all's way. I know Clay is antsy to get back on the investigation and quit babysitting me anyway."

"Hey, I'm not trying to run you off, but, you know, duty calls," Clay said with a smile. "Just hang loose for a few minutes, and I'll get an officer to run you home. Are you sure you're alright?"

"I'm fine, Clay. Don't worry about me." She leaned over and gave him a kiss. "Now get going. You wouldn't want to keep the great man waiting."

Chapter 9

Clay grinned and blew her a parting kiss as he followed Commander Wilson out the door and headed for the chief's office.

"Clay, listen up," Mike said in a low voice as they walked. "I've already had one meeting with Chief Cooper this morning, and I'm here to tell you he's seriously pissed. About what, I don't know. But if I had to guess, it's probably because he's getting political heat over these two homicides. I spent the last half hour getting my ass reamed because we haven't already solved the Marilyn Gibbs homicide. Now, our only witness to her murder gets carved up, too."

Clay rolled his eyes and grunted his disgust. He hated that politics should have anything to do with police work.

A cop is supposed to solve crimes, regardless of how long it takes, Clay thought. *If you cut corners because you're pressured to solve a crime in a hurry, you make mistakes, the kind of mistakes that allow criminals to walk.*

Wilson stopped suddenly and grabbed Clay by the arm.

"Now you pay attention to me, son. I won't say this but once, so you better get it. If you go in that man's office with the attitude I see pouring off you like a heat wave, you'll walk out of there minus your ass, because it will be his! Do you get my drift?"

"Yeah, Mike, I hear you, but—"

"But nothing, no bullshit, do you hear me, Detective Randall? You go in there and show one ounce of attitude, if he don't fire you on the spot, I'll boot your ass out of the division! Do you hear me loud and clear?"

Clay could tell he had stepped over the line with his boss.

"Yes, Mike, I understand. I'll keep my mouth shut and play the game. I wouldn't ever do anything to embarrass you anyway."

"Good," he growled. "Just so we understand each other. And don't call me Mike. Last time I checked, my first name was Commander. You got that, Sergeant?"

Clay hid a grin as he said solemnly, "Yes, sir, Commander Wilson."

"That's what I want to hear. Let's get this over with so you can go back to doing the job I'm paying you all that money to do."

The two men walked into the Cooper's outer office and stopped at Annie Kieran's desk, his secretary.

"Hi, Annie. The chief wants to see me and Randall this time. Is he ready?"

"Hey, Mike. Back so soon, and for more? He's in rare form this morning, so I don't envy you and good lookin' here," she said with a grin at Clay.

Annie Kieran was a short Irish lady who, although living in America for many years, still retained a bit of her Irish brogue and a lot of her bawdy humor. Annie's husband had been offered a lucrative job transfer from their home in Ireland, so the Kieran family packed up, moved to Florida, and began living the American dream.

With a home in Ponte Vedra Beach only minutes from the Jacksonville Beach Police Department, Annie applied for the job when Chief Cooper's secretary retired. After hearing her accent and reviewing her resume, Chief Cooper hired her on the spot, a position she had now occupied for fifteen years.

Clay grinned back at Annie, "Better not let Dana hear you call me good lookin'. She'll be afraid I'll dump her and run off to Ireland with you."

Annie returned the grin. "Oh, now, you go on there. I'm old enough to be your mother, but thanks for the compliment anyway. You're a pet!"

Wilson rolled his eyes. "Pu-leeze spare me the trite dialogue from a 1950's "B" movie, will you?"

Annie's eyes flashed at Wilson. "I'll tell you what, Mike Wilson, if you talked half as nice to the people around here as Clay did, you'd be a lot better off.

"Now, the chief's waiting, and I'm tired of seeing your sour face anyway, so off you go!"

She winked at Clay. "Don't let Chief Cooper take too much hide off."

Chief Gordon Haynes "Gordy" Cooper didn't fit the perceived mold of a typical police officer, much less a police chief. Standing barely five feet, eight inches tall and pushing one hundred and fifty pounds, his physical stature intimidated no one. However, one glance in his eyes was enough to give any big man pause. They were such a pale blue they appeared almost white. And when he stared at someone, they seemed to bore right into a person's brain, allowing Gordy to read every thought. At sixty years old, he still wore his hair combed in a 1950s pompadour, straight up and back, stiffened with enough styling gel to withstand a category four hurricane.

Gordy Cooper knew everyone who was anyone in Jacksonville Beach. And at one time or another, he had done a favor for many of them, from ensuring they got a free ride home when his cops stopped them for drunk driving, to getting the local state attorney to drop drug charges on an influential citizen's son. He used those favors over the years to insulate himself from politicians who came into power with a promise to oust him as the chief. So far, he had outlasted five mayors and countless city council members in his twenty-two years in the power seat.

As Clay and Mike walked into Chief Cooper's office, he was talking on the phone. Gordy Cooper had a voice all out of proportion to his size. It was very deep, echoing throughout any room he entered. He had the usual wad of chewing tobacco stuffed in his cheek, even though smoking and chewing tobacco in public buildings had been banned years before. At the moment, he was berating one of his supporters over his son's latest arrest in Jacksonville on crack cocaine charges.

As he waved them to chairs in front of his desk, Gordy barked, "Dammit, Murray! How many times I gotta tell you your son's a piece of shit? But do you listen to me? Hell, no! I told you to put his ass in rehab six months ago. You didn't hear anything I said! I told you he'd get busted again for that crack shit if you didn't put him somewhere, but you let his mama decide he just needed a little TLC."

In a girlish voice, Gordy mimicked Murray's wife, "Oh, Murray, he's a sweet boy that just needs our love and understanding. He doesn't need to go to some clinic.

"Well, who was right, Murray? . . . You damn right I was! *I* was! You call me crying and wanting me to use my influence to get him off the charges. I tell you what, Murray, that boy needs to do some time in prison. That'll get his ass straightened out!

"Awright, calm down, dammit, quit blubbering. I'll make a call and see what I can do . . . yeah . . . yeah . . . no, don't do anything until you hear from me . . . look, I gotta go! I got more important shit to deal with than your sorry ass kid."

With that parting shot, Cooper slammed the phone down. Spitting a stream of tobacco juice into a spittoon beside his desk, he leaned back with his hands clasped behind his head. Gordy crossed his feet on his desk, scattering papers left and right as he got comfortable. He stared first at Commander Wilson and then at Detective Randall.

"Well? What have you got?"

Clay glanced at Mike nervously and then back at Chief Cooper, unsure if he should speak, until Mike rescued him. "Chief, I brought Detective Randall with me to give you an update on the investigation and let you know what steps we're taking to solve both these homicides."

Cooper didn't say a word. He shifted his cold eyes from Wilson to Randall. Getting no signal from his boss, Clay guessed he was expected to begin his briefing.

Over the next ten minutes, he briefed the chief on both investigations, including the note found on Jimmy Barton's chest. All during his narration, Chief Cooper never said a word or moved a muscle, except occasionally to lean over and make another deposit into his spittoon. Clay wasn't sure, but he didn't think the man even blinked. When he finished, he waited for the chief to say something. The seconds stretched out while Cooper continued to stare at Clay.

Mike Wilson felt Clay's discomfort and stepped in to help. "Chief, we've set up a task force with Atlantic Beach detec—"

"As I recall, you told me Detective Randall would be briefing me. I don't remember asking you for input. I've already heard from you once today, and that's plenty."

Wilson felt his face turning red, and his jaw clenched as he forced himself to keep silent and not explode himself.

"Detective Randall, I've been told by Officer Hawkins that you came up with the brilliant name of Operation Street Cleaner for your little task force. Is that right?"

"Well, yes, sir. It was kind of a collective idea with all of us in the task force. We thought it described what the killer was trying to do . . . you know, clean the streets of prostitutes. It was . . . you know . . ."

Very calmly, Chief Cooper said, "No, Detective Randall, I don't know. Please enlighten me further."

"Well, you see, I guess it was a little bit of black humor . . . you know, cop humor," Clay stammered, thoroughly intimidated by now.

"Cop humor, huh? Cop humor," Gordy murmured to himself. Suddenly, he exploded, "We don't make jokes about killings! Do you have any idea what the press would do with a name like Operation Street Cleaner? They would crucify me! They would say I'm not taking these killings seriously!

"You may not realize it, Detective Randall, but every damn thing that happens in this police department reflects on me. And I haven't been in this chair for twenty-two years by letting bullshit like this go, you understand what I'm sayin'?

"You better clear these homicides, and you better clear them fast. If you gotta have some bullshit name for your little task force, come up with something that won't reflect poorly on me.

"Now, get outa here so I can get some real work done!" Slamming his feet to the floor, Cooper stood up abruptly, a clear message the meeting was over. Mike and Clay moved quickly out of the office, not even pausing to talk to Annie as they fled.

Chapter 10

Neither man said a word until they were behind closed doors in Mike's office.

Clay said, "Wow. That was my first time in all these years to even talk to the man. I've heard stories about his temper, but I've never seen it up close and personal. Why did that bastard Bobby Hawkins have to say anything to him anyway? I'm gonna kick his ass one of these days, I swear!"

"Bobby Hawkins isn't worth the powder it would take to blow him up, so don't worry about him. As far as Chief Cooper, trust me when I tell you that I've been on the receiving end more times than I can count. After a while, your ass gets numb from the bites. I'll do my best to keep him appeased while you work the cases. You just do your best like I know you're capable of doing. Whatever happens, I'll back you.

"I was looking for a job when I found this one, and I can always find another one, or I'll just retire. Either way, I'm not letting Gordy Cooper control my life, and I don't want you to, either. So, get to work, and let's take this guy off the street and into Raiford where he belongs. Now, what's your plan for the next couple of days?"

"I've talked to Barton's sister, a Laura Dahl," Clay said. "She's the relative on the west side we talked him into staying with after he witnessed the Marilyn Gibbs murder. She's handling the arrangements for his body. She said he only had one other relative, a daughter in Beaumont, Texas. Hang on, let me see . . . a Meghan Barton, age twenty-four. Mrs. Dahl said she was driving here and wanted to meet with us about the investigation and also pick up his personal effects. She's supposed to come in sometime this afternoon."

"Has everything been photographed and checked thoroughly for evidence?"

"Yeah. Jim Childress and the other evidence techs went through the entire backpack and found nothing unusual."

"What else?"

"Honchen will attend the autopsy. That'll probably be late this afternoon or first thing tomorrow morning. Childress is processing the note left on his chest and—"

Wilson interrupted, "What do you make of the message?"

"Not sure, boss. I've got Three Rivers checking for any sex offense convictions. If he does, it's public information that the killer could have gotten through the Florida Department of Law Enforcement website. If not, that raises disturbing possibilities."

"For instance?"

"For instance, the killer could be connected in some way with law enforcement. If Barton's not a registered sex offender or predator, he wouldn't be on the FDLE website. So how would the killer know unless he had connections, either by being in the business or by knowing someone who was, and they passed the information along to him? Either possibility raises serious concerns."

"I agree. Keep me posted on that," Wilson advised.

Just then, Linda Greene stuck her head in the door.

"Excuse me, Commander. A Meghan Barton is in the lobby asking to see Clay."

Clay glanced over his shoulder and said, "Thanks, Linda, I'll be right there." Turning back to his boss, he asked, "Anything else before I talk to her?"

"Nothing now. Just keep your feet moving on this. I wanta see nothing but elbows, assholes, and shoe soles until these cases are cleared!"

"You got it, boss," Clay grinned as he left the office and headed to the lobby to meet James Barton's only child.

"I'm Detective Sergeant Clay Randall. Are you Ms. Barton?" Clay asked of the only person sitting in the lobby.

"Yes, I'm Meghan Barton," she said, shaking Clay's hand softly. The young woman was almost five-seven but weighed barely over one hundred pounds. She was wearing a ragged Dallas Cowboys sweatshirt and baggy blue jeans with the cuffs rolled up several times. Her feet were clad in black combat boots.

Meghan had jet black hair, obviously dyed, and styled in spikes all over her head. There were at least a half dozen earrings in each ear, accompanied by a silver ring through her left nostril. Clay could also see a tongue stud glinting as she spoke. As he listened, he wondered how anyone could talk without a major lisp with that crap stuck through their tongue.

"Please come back to the Detective Division," Clay invited as he held the door open for her. As Meghan passed him, he caught a whiff of marijuana on her clothing.

Please don't tell me this woman walked into the police department carrying weed, Clay thought.

Walking toward Clay's office, he signaled for Cassie to accompany them. "Meghan, this is Detective Cassandra Broderick."

Cassie did a split second assessment of Meghan Barton and put her into the "Are you kiddin' me!" category. As with Clay, she gave nothing away as she shook Meghan's hand.

"Hi, I'm sorry we have to meet under these circumstances."

"I guess I've been expecting a phone call for a long time. My dad's been living on the street for so long that I just assumed he would meet a bad end. Anyway, what can you tell me about his death?"

"Let's step into my office so we can talk privately," Clay suggested. "Please have a seat, and Detective Broderick and I will be right back. We have to check on something. Can we get you anything? Coke? Water?"

"No, thanks, I'm fine."

"Alright, we'll be right back," Clay said as he closed the door, gesturing to Cassie to follow him into the conference room. As soon as Cassie came in, Clay shut the door.

"I don't know exactly what I was expecting Barton's daughter to be like, but this wasn't it," he said.

"She's rather unusual, I'll agree. But, you know, with a transient for a father, I guess it's not that hard to see how a kid could be a little strange. Anyway, why did you want to talk to me first?" Cassie asked.

"Did you catch a whiff of her when you shook her hand?"

"No, why?"

"I smelled weed when she walked past me coming in the door. Either she's holding right now, or she's been smoking dope recently."

"I didn't catch that, but you've got one of those bloodhound noses that smells in parts per million, so I'm not surprised. How do you want to handle it?"

"Let's get the business with her father done and then discuss her smoking habits."

"You got it," Cassie said as she opened the door and headed back to Clay's office.

They walked in to find Meghan Barton reading a copy of the incident report of her father's murder. She looked at them with tears in her eyes.

"I'm sorry if I wasn't supposed to read this. I saw the paper with his name on it and couldn't resist. His throat was cut? Who would do such a thing? He was a gentle man. He wouldn't hurt anyone."

"I'm sorry, Meghan," Clay said. "No one deserves to die like that. I want you to know we're working around the clock to find out who did this and get him off the street."

Meghan shook her head. "I just can't believe it. My daddy's gone. I tried so many times to get him to come to Texas and live with me, but he always refused. He said he liked living in Florida, and he didn't want to have to answer to anyone for anything. He said if he lived with me in my house, he would have to follow my rules. I told him he could come and go and do whatever he wanted, but he always said no. Now it's too late."

The detectives waited as she continued to sob. Slowly the tears subsided, and she regained a measure of control. "I'm sorry. I'm blubbering like a fool."

Cassie answered, "Hey, Meghan, it's okay. We understand what you're going through."

"Thanks," she said more calmly. Heaving a big sigh, she said, "I was told I could have his backpack and whatever he had left. Is that supposed to happen today?"

"Yes," Clay responded. "We've got his personal effects here. Let me get them for you."

Clay stepped out of the room, retrieving the backpack from the evidence locker and bringing it into the room.

Meghan stared at the backpack at first, not touching it. She started to cloud up again but made a supreme effort to keep her emotions under control. "Can I open it?"

"Yes, of course," Cassie replied.

Meghan opened the backpack and peered inside. She took out several old shirts, two pairs of dirty jeans, a tattered copy of a novel, *Jetty Man*, by a well-known local author, G. W. Reynolds, and various hygiene articles.

"Is this all there is?" she asked, confused.

"That's all that was in the backpack when we got it," Clay replied. "Why?"

"My picture is missing."

"What do you mean?"

"Years ago for Christmas, I gave daddy a picture of me in a little red plastic frame. I was probably six years old, so that would have been about eighteen years ago. I wrote an inscription on it that said, 'To Daddy from Meghan. I love you.' When he and mama divorced, that's the only thing he said he wanted. He's carried that little picture ever since. Every time I'd see my daddy over the years, he'd always pull out the picture to show me that I was with him wherever he went." As she said this, Meghan started crying again.

"If my picture wasn't in his backpack and not in his pocket, someone took it. That's all there is to it."

The detectives exchanged glances, thinking the same thing. The odds of an alcoholic being able to keep track of a small item like a picture for years were not that great. They both figured he had simply lost it, but neither was willing to say that to the grieving daughter.

Clay responded, "Meghan, we'll add this information to the file in case the picture turns up in possession of the man who mur— . . . took your father's life."

"Thank you. Is it okay if I take my daddy's stuff with me? I need to go to my aunt's house and get some rest before I hit the road for home."

"Sure," Clay said hesitantly. "Listen, before you go. I'm not sure how to ask this delicately, but . . . have you smoked marijuana recently? Because I smelled it on your clothes when you first came in."

She stared defiantly at Clay and Cassie. "Yes, I have. I've got breast cancer, and I'm undergoing chemo, and it makes me so sick I can't function. The only way I can get out of bed and do anything is if I smoke weed."

As she spoke, she grew more upset and agitated. "So . . . what? You wanta put me in jail now? It's not enough that my daddy's had his throat cut from ear to ear. Now, I have to go to jail for using something to keep me from puking my toenails up right here on your nice clean floor? Is that what you want?" she screamed.

Cassie spoke up, "Meghan, calm down."

"Calm down! How can I calm down? Have you ever had to deal with your father being a bum living on the street and then getting slaughtered? And then at twenty-four years old find out you have breast cancer? Have you? Dammit, have you?" she cried, breaking down and sobbing uncontrollably.

Both detectives knew it was useless to say anything. Finally, Cassie said gently, "Meghan, we're truly sorry for what you're going through, and we can sympathize with you even if we haven't suffered as you have. Please go on to your aunt's house. We'll keep you informed of our progress on the investigation. I promise you we'll do everything we can to find your father's killer."

Meghan sniffed, wiping her nose on the sleeve of her sweatshirt. Without another word, she picked up her father's backpack and walked slowly out the door.

When she was gone, Clay said, "I wish now I hadn't said anything about the dope. I'm really not interested in making a minor drug case that'll pile more on her than she's already got. By the way, that also explains why she's so skinny."

"Yeah, chemo is horrible stuff, but, let's face it, the alternative is much worse."

"You're right about that. I'll add this information about the picture to the file, but I seriously doubt it's relevant. Serial killers sometimes take souvenirs from the people they kill, but we're not even sure yet what we're chasing. Odds are the picture was just lost somewhere along the way, in spite of her insisting he would never lose it."

As Clay and Cassie began another review of the reports, Jim Childress was in the evidence processing room examining the note left on James Barton's chest, searching every square inch of the paper for any possible fingerprints. Humming Otis Redding's

"Sittin' on the Dock of the Bay" as he worked, Jim photographed and photocopied the note. Then he dimmed the overhead lights and activated a device that used ultraviolet rays to emphasize any prints. While the UV rays revealed no prints, he did find a watermark on the twenty-four pound bond paper. The watermark depicted the letters **ESE** in the center of the paper.

He stared at the letters, pondering their meaning. *Is this the brand of the paper, or possibly the initials of a company?*

Curious, he swung around to his computer and accessed a search engine on the Internet. He typed in the letters "**ESE**" just as they appeared on the paper, including quotation marks to reduce non-related hits. Pressing the "enter" key, one hundred and thirty million hits popped up in less than one second.

Jim thought, *That wasn't much help. Let's see what I've got here . . . Florida's Exceptional Student Education program, European School of Economics, ESE Espresso machines . . . Aw crap, this is getting me nowhere! I'll note the watermark information in my report in case someone else wants to follow it up.*

He started to turn back to the paper when he had one more thought. *I wonder what font those letters are in.*

Opening a word processing file, he clicked the dropdown menu for fonts. Scrolling slowly through the various fonts, he stopped when he got to "Braggadocio." Jim changed his default font to Braggadocio and typed in the letters "**ESE**" in capital letters.

Comparing the two, he mused, *Well, I've solved one mystery, anyway. This watermark is definitely done in a font called Braggadocio. H-m-m-m. Braggadocio is Italian for braggart. Wonder if that's an inside joke from a serial killer. Or maybe a highly subtle way of taunting the cops. I'll definitely include this information in my report.*

Moving back to the paper, Jim next tried fuming the note with iodine crystals. He poured the crystals into a Ziploc bag and added the note. By shaking up the crystals, any prints would appear quickly in an orange or yellow tint. That produced nothing, so he moved to the last chemical test he would attempt.

He carefully sprayed a 0.6% solution of ninhydrin powder mixed with acetone over the surface of the paper. If prints were present, they would gradually become visible from the chemical reaction.

He set the paper aside and busied himself preparing numerous pieces of evidence from the crime scene that needed to be packaged and forwarded to FDLE for more sophisticated testing. If prints were there, they would begin to appear in an hour or two.

Around eleven o'clock, Jim came back to examine the note and was disappointed to find no prints. He wrote up his report and moved on to other pressing business of the day.

Chapter 11

Making it safely to his car after killing James Barton, the man headed south on Third Street. As he drove, he visualized his victim's eyes again at the precise moment he recognized the man who would take his life. It was as much a thrill, he realized, killing the homeless scum as it was killing prostitutes. Like the taste of an expensive Bordeaux, he savored the intense pleasure and power of taking a life. There was little traffic on the road as he continued driving the speed limit, his thoughts drifting back to another time, another place, another life . . .

———————

Having been cleared of killing his stepfather, Eddie Shanklin was released from juvenile custody to his mother. Due to his age, she couldn't legally refuse to take him in, although she found it hard to be in the same room with him. To survive, they established an uneasy truce in the rent house where Eddie had bludgeoned his stepfather to death.

He went back to school and tried to catch up with his studies. Although well above average in intelligence, Eddie found that studying algebra and English composition no longer held any interest for him. At sixteen, he dropped out, figuring he could learn more about life watching TV than anything his teachers had to offer.

Eddie spent the next few months lounging on the ratty couch in the tiny living room watching TV all day long. Finally, his mother's nagging at him to get off his butt and find a job to help with the bills led him to Clean N' Green Lawn Service. He started out bagging grass and shrubbery clippings before eventually working his way up to the big self-propelled mowers.

In spite of the usually hot and dirty conditions, Eddie discovered he didn't mind hard labor. There was a sense of accomplishment in attacking a lawn and restoring it to its former beauty. Of course, it helped that most of Clean N' Green's clients owned estates that hugged the coastline, the grounds of which were never unkempt.

One of their most lucrative contracts was for an estate owned by Margaret Packer, a wealthy South Beach widow. Her husband had owned a successful real estate firm and had made millions during the Florida housing boom before dropping dead of a heart attack at age fifty, leaving Margaret the sole heir to his company and fortune. She negotiated the sale of the company and walked away with fifteen million in cash and real estate.

At fifty-three, Margaret Packer was an energetic, attractive woman who refused to play the role of the grieving widow. She liked to party, especially with younger men, and she had the money and looks to attract them. When she saw Eddie Shanklin for the first time as he cut her grass in a tank top and shorts, she thought he was the most beautiful boy she had ever seen. The fact that he was only sixteen didn't deter her in the slightest.

He's probably still a virgin, she thought to herself, watching him through her living room bay window as he whirled around the lawn on the company's power mower. *Who better to introduce him to the pleasures of great sex than me?* she asked herself with a smile.

The following week, she took the opportunity to stroll outside and sit on the patio as he worked. Margaret dressed for the occasion in a pair of tight shorts and a low cut top that exposed the vast array of her breasts. As Eddie wheeled by the patio where she sat, he glanced over and promptly ran the mower into the box hedge bordering the patio.

Stopping immediately, Eddie shut down the mower and apologized loudly for damaging the hedge. His boss, Gary Rogers, heard the commotion and ran over. Rogers began chewing him out, threatening to fire Eddie on the spot. Margaret laughed, knowing why he had run into the hedge. She was especially delighted to see that, even while getting his butt reamed, Eddie kept glancing over at her breasts.

She interrupted the tirade, "Don't worry about the hedge, Gary. I've been meaning to have you take it out anyway. I want rose bushes planted along the patio, so your young man just started the project a little early."

"Are you sure, Mrs. Packer?" Rogers asked. "I'll fire this kid right now and replace the hedge at no charge. I don't need a screw-up on a job as important as yours."

"No, no, don't you dare fire him," she insisted. "You go on and finish whatever you were doing, and you, young man, you come back and see me when you finish cutting the lawn."

Eddie wasn't sure if he was out of trouble, but he said, "Okay."

When he finished, he came back to the patio where Margaret was still sitting. "Come sit down . . . Eddie, is that right?" she asked.

"Yes, Eddie Shanklin," he said cautiously as he sat on the edge of the chair, trying to avoid staring at her large breasts that looked ready to leap out of her top at any moment.

"How old are you?"

"I'm almost seventeen . . . well, I *will* be in about eight months," he answered.

Margaret laughed. "Eddie, sixteen's a good age. Don't be in such a hurry to grow up. Enjoy being a teenager. In many ways, they're the best years of your life. By the way, why aren't you in school today?"

"I quit," he said somewhat defiantly. "They can't teach me anything useful. I've learned more about how to survive since I quit than I'll ever learn in school."

"But why would a handsome young man like you need to learn survival skills?"

Eddie hesitated. He had never told anyone about killing his stepfather, and he figured a rich lady like her would freak out if he told her.

"I just do," he said. "I've already learned there are winners and losers in this world, and I don't want to be a loser. In fact, I can't stand losers!" he said vehemently. "I intend to be a winner!"

"I'll tell you what. You seem like a smart young man. I think you have what it takes to be a winner, and I'll help you get there . . . that is, if you want my help."

He stared at her suspiciously. "What do you mean, help me get there?"

"I have more money than I'll ever spend, and no one to spend it on but myself. And I sense you're someone who just needs an opportunity to succeed. So I'm offering you that opportunity, no strings attached," she said.

Margaret wasn't being completely honest with the boy, not yet anyway. She wasn't sure how he would react if she told him she wanted him to rip her clothes off and take her right there on the patio. She would move slowly until he grew comfortable with her. His fascination with her breasts gave her confidence that she would get him into her bed soon.

Eddie quit the lawn service company and began working for Margaret the next week, making twice what Clean N' Green had paid him. He did odd jobs around the estate, anything Margaret found to keep him occupied and near her. The next week after starting, Margaret asked Eddie to clean the Jacuzzi. Gathering tools and chemicals from the utility room, he carried them to the exercise suite on the third floor of the estate.

When he walked into the room, he stared at the Jacuzzi and dropped everything with a clatter onto the floor. Margaret was lounging naked in the swirling waters with a smile on her face.

She crooked her finger at Eddie and said, "Come on in, the water's nice and warm."

Eddie's teenage testosterone was raging, and he didn't hesitate. That afternoon romp in the Jacuzzi led to wild escapades in most rooms of the mansion over the next few months.

Eddie's sex education at the hands and body of Margaret Packer was varied and innovative. For a woman of any age, she was untiring. Over the next year and a half, she taught him all the ways of physical love. Margaret had her boy toy to satisfy her high sex drive, and Eddie had a beautiful, mature woman to fulfill his every sexual fantasy. What was missing from his sex education, however, was the emotional attachment that a mature love provides.

Shortly after Eddie turned eighteen, his mother, driving home drunk from a bar, bonded her twelve-year-old Toyota Corolla to a bridge abutment. The solid concrete structure won the confrontation, and Eddie was left homeless with no known relatives, a situation that bothered him only because he didn't know where he was going to live.

The problem was solved when Margaret offered him a place to live in her home. She told her friends the poor boy was devastated and that the least she could do was to try to fill in for his beloved mother. Meanwhile, she continued to enjoy the boy's growing prowess in the bedroom.

Margaret had her lawyer petition the courts to seal the records of Eddie's killing of his stepfather. Her next step to legitimize Eddie was to adopt him officially as her son, ignoring the "ick" factor of having a long-term sexual relationship with a boy young enough to be her grandson.

Over the next four years, Margaret paid for his education, enabling him to get his GED and then a Bachelor's Degree in Marketing at the University of Miami. As a graduation present, Margaret Packer named her newly-adopted son the sole beneficiary of her estate, estimated by then to be worth more than twenty million dollars.

After six years of service to Margaret, Eddie was getting bored with her. He was a handsome, virile twenty-two-year-old man, bedding a fifty-nine-year-old woman who was beginning to look every day of her years in spite of the many hours spent working out with her personal trainer. Margaret's physical deterioration was helped along by generous quantities of alcohol supplemented with Oxycontin for chronic back pain.

She began to realize she was losing Eddie, and she grew desperate. When he began bringing young girls home to share his bed and the pool and Jacuzzi, Margaret was livid. They argued constantly about it, and each fight ended with her crying and begging him not to leave her. Eddie grew to detest her for her weakness.

One night in June, things finally came to a head. Eddie had made plans to meet friends at a popular South Beach night club. As he was getting dressed for his night out, Margaret stumbled into his room, cigarette in one hand and a Martini glass in the other.

"Going out again, I see," a combination of pills and Beefeater's Gin slurring her words.

"Yeah, what about it?"

"Why can't you stay home with me once in a while? Am I that hard to be with?"

Ignoring her, he headed toward the door.

Margaret grabbed his arm, begging, "Please, Eddie, stay here with me, just for a little while. I'm so lonely when you leave."

Eddie jerked his arm away, causing her to stagger and fall to the floor. The glass hit the carpet, spilling its contents.

Margaret screamed at him, "You bastard! You keep pushing me away, and you'll be sorry! I'll . . . I'll—"

"You'll what, you freakin' old bitch?" Eddie asked with a derisive laugh. "You're a loser just like my mother was! You sit around every day drinking and taking dope until you pass out. You're lucky to get through the day without pissin' your pants! I'm young, and I wanta party. And not with an old woman like you!"

As Eddie headed out the door, he could hear her screaming, not for the first time, that she was going to cut him out of her will, leaving him nothing.

Eddie decided he had to do something before Margaret followed through on her drunken threats. It was time to test his resolve to rid the world of a real loser.

After considering various ways to kill her that involved poisoning her food or alcohol, he finally realized he could take advantage of her twin addictions to painkillers and alcohol, the combination of which caused her to pass out most nights in her bed. Twice in the past month, Eddie had found her unconscious with a lit cigarette dangling from her fingers, mere inches away from the bed sheet.

In the following days, he avoided Margaret as he planned her demise. A week later, he was ready. Eddie approached her in the living room and said he wanted to stay home that night to spend time with her. She was ecstatic at the prospect of being the center of Eddie's attention again.

They ordered in his favorite pizza and ate it on the patio, all the while talking about Eddie's plans to start his own landscaping business using his marketing degree and Margaret's money. She was enjoying herself immensely, unable to take her eyes off her beautiful boy. The unpleasantness of the previous week was completely forgotten.

During the evening, Margaret downed her usual double dosage of Oxycontin chased with the first of several martinis. Eddie kept making her new drinks as soon as one got below half full so that, by ten o'clock, she had passed out on the chaise lounge.

He carried her up to her third floor bedroom suite and flopped her onto the king size bed. Margaret surprised him when she suddenly opened her eyes and, seeing him standing beside her bed, pulled her thin negligee up to her neck, revealing her naked body. She leered drunkenly at Eddie and grabbed his crotch with a coquettish smile.

"Peel those pants off and climb aboard, cowboy. I'm gonna take you for a ride."

The last thing Eddie wanted was to have sex with the old bag, but he couldn't figure out a way to avoid it without angering her.

He delayed, telling her, "I've got to pee. I'll be right back . . . keep your motor running."

Eddie stepped into the bathroom and closed the door. Staring into the mirror, he told himself, *You can do this. Get in there and screw her one last time. She always goes to sleep right after, so you can make sure she never wakes up.*

He stripped off his tee shirt and shorts and walked naked into the bedroom. Margaret was out cold.

Is this my lucky day or what? he smirked.

He stood over Margaret for a moment, looking at the woman who had rescued him from a life of poverty and, more than likely, crime and eventual incarceration. The woman had introduced him to sex, adopted him, bankrolled a college education, and named him sole beneficiary to her sizable fortune. He felt nothing for her. She was a loser, a weakling. He had no use for her, only for what she could give him by dying.

Eddie picked up a pillow and started to place it over her face.

Suddenly, her eyes opened, and, barely coherent, she said, "Eddie, honey, you were fantastic, as usual. You're such a stud. Be a sweetie and get me my cigs off the dresser."

He thought, *She's so stoned she thinks we had sex.*

He pulled out a cigarette and lit it for her. Margaret drew smoke deep into her lungs as she smiled bleary-eyed at Eddie.

"Wasn't I better than that young pussy you've been chasing?" she cooed, arching her hips suggestively at Eddie.

Before he could respond, she leaned back against the pillows and passed out again, the lit cigarette slipping to the bed covers.

Eddie stood watching for a moment to see if she would awaken again. When she began snoring, he took the pillow and pressed it down firmly on her face. She was so deeply unconscious this time that she never stirred.

He watched her chest rise and fall slower and slower, finally stopping. Eddie held the pillow in place for another two minutes just to be sure. When he lifted the pillow, her mouth sagged open. Feeling for a pulse in her neck, he found none.

His breathing was ragged, and his heart was pumping wildly.

Eddie thought, *I did it! What a rush!*

His hands were shaking as he felt a raw surge of power flow through his body. He had killed his stepfather in the heat of passion, an act, if you will, of self defense. Killing Margaret Packer was a calculated act of pure self-interest, without passion. He had planned and executed it without a flaw.

As he marveled at the sheer audacity of his act, Eddie was brought back to reality by the smell of smoking sheets. Easing the cigarette from her limp fingers, he placed it in an ashtray on her bedside table before hurrying down to his room to get dressed.

He ran back upstairs, half expecting to find her sitting up and asking if he wanted another ride. The vision was so real that he stopped outside her door, heart pounding once again.

Finally getting up his courage, he peered around the door frame. Margaret had not moved; she was dead. He suddenly realized he was holding his breath. Exhaling noisily, Eddie went quickly to the ashtray and retrieved the cigarette, positioning it near her hand with the still-burning end touching the sheet.

At the door, he turned to look one last time at the woman who had given him so much. All she had wanted in return was his young body.

He said out loud, "I gave you what you wanted. Now you're giving me what I want . . . your money!"

Eddie watched as the sheets began to burn, creating dense smoke that began drifting toward the ceiling and the smoke detector.

"Oh, shit!" he exclaimed. "The smoke detector can't go off yet!"

He grabbed a chair and quickly set it under the detector, which was mounted in a corner near the ten-foot ceiling. Popping open the device, he yanked the nine-volt battery out, rendering it useless just as the smoke began curling around it.

He knew he couldn't leave the detector empty without some cop or fireman getting suspicious. Then it hit him. He had replaced the backup battery in his clock radio that morning. Closing the bedroom door to contain the smoke from the smoldering bedding, Eddie raced to his room and dug through the bathroom wastebasket until he found the dead battery.

Dashing back upstairs, he barreled into the bedroom. The smoke had gotten so thick that he could barely see, and the smell was getting toxic. Eddie felt his way over to the corner where he had placed the chair. Grasping the back of the chair, he stood up straight and reached toward the ceiling, working entirely by feel.

The dense smoke was starting to make him feel lightheaded, so he quickly stepped down and bent low to the floor. He drew in a deep lungful of relatively clean air before jumping back on the chair. He felt around until he found the smoke detector. Trying to put the spent nine-volt battery into the slot, in his haste, he dropped it.

"Shit!" he raged as he jumped to the floor to search desperately for the battery.

Spying it where it had bounced under the edge of the bed, he snatched it up, took another deep breath, and climbed back on the chair. This time, he was successful in getting the battery in place. Slamming the cover shut, he jumped off the chair and replaced it near the door.

Without a glance back, Eddie ran to the bedroom door, opened it, and stepped out into the clean air of the hallway, closing the door firmly behind him. He knew it was just a matter of minutes before the smoke wafted under the door and made its way to another smoke detector located at the head of the stairs.

He ran downstairs and out the front door, heading for his car. As he opened the door, Eddie caught a whiff of his shirt, realizing immediately that he smelled strongly of smoke.

I won't be able to explain how I smell like smoke when I'm supposed to be at a nightclub when the fire starts, he thought, starting to get rattled.

Eddie stood motionless for several seconds, his brain working furiously. Spinning around, he raced back into the house and up to his room on the second floor. Grabbing a change of clothes, he headed to the pool where there was an outside shower.

Praying the smoke had not reached the working detector, he yanked off his clothes and jumped under the shower. The water was icy, but he hardly noticed as he quickly lathered up his body and hair. Rinsing as fast as he could, Eddie grabbed a towel and dried himself before throwing on the change of clothing.

He bundled up the smoky garments inside the towel, dashed to his car, tossed the incriminating clothing into the trunk, and raced out of the driveway. As he stopped behind a local shopping center to throw his clothes into a dumpster, the smoke detector began wailing.

Eddie returned to the estate two hours later to find somewhat resentfully that police and fire officials were swarming throughout what he now felt was his home. Regardless, he convincingly acted the part of a grief-stricken son come home from a date to find his beloved adoptive mother dead.

When the fire was extinguished, Margaret Packer's body was discovered so severely burned that no forensic evidence was left pointing to the criminal act that took her life. Her blood/alcohol level was four times the legal limit, and the amount of Oxycontin in her body was enough to render her unconscious all by itself. The police investigation concluded with a finding of accidental death, clearing the way for Eddie to inherit Margaret Packer's estate and become a rich man.

The mansion had sustained moderate fire and substantial smoke damage from Margaret's cigarette. While repairs were made, Eddie moved into a suite at a five-star hotel in Palm Beach and lived in the style of luxury he had grown to appreciate and expect.

Two months later, he moved back into his newly-repaired and painted mansion, quickly contracting with a realtor to put it on the market. The estate sold within a week, adding another five million to his already bulging bank account.

The day he closed on the sale and collected his money, Eddie loaded up his newly-purchased Mercedes with two suitcases of clothes and headed north on Interstate 95 toward Daytona Beach, the city he had selected as his new home and base of operations.

As he drove, Eddie Shanklin imagined a limitless future, one filled with money, fine cars, beautiful women, and a nearly inexhaustible supply of losers to purge from the world.

Chapter 12

"Awright, boys and girls, siddown and shut the hell up. I got stuff to pass on, and I want your asses on the street in the next ten minutes," Patrol Sergeant Tim Dawson barked at his squad. The officers mumbled as they sat down in the squad room and got ready to take notes. They knew Sergeant Dawson would be watching closely to ensure they recorded his pearls of wisdom.

Among the six officers assembled for the shift briefing, Officer Roy Connor sat there with pen poised over his notepad. A ten-year veteran and K-9 officer for three, he knew how to play the game, even though he hated it. In fact, he hated most aspects of his job, especially the huge volume of paperwork required for the simplest of crimes.

Connor barely tolerated the citizens he was charged with serving and protecting, figuring most were stupid or they never would have become victims in the first place. However, he did derive real pleasure from rousting criminals and writing people tickets. Most of his fellow cops were reluctant to back him up on certain calls because of his reputation for taking liberties with his baton, his TASER, and his fists.

Officer Connor was thirty-five years old, stood six feet tall and weighed a muscular two hundred pounds, thanks to hours spent each week pumping iron. He kept his head shaved to give himself a more threatening look, and, when he was off duty, wore a large, gold hoop earring in his left ear. He believed it gave him a pirate look, adding to his self-perceived machismo.

Roy Connor liked to use his size and appearance to intimidate people into rapid compliance with his orders, even at times when the subject of his attention was not arguing, fighting, or resisting in any way. He was particularly aggressive with homeless people, tending to punch them sometimes for his own enjoyment.

His K-9 partner was an eighty-pound Belgian Malinois he had named Macho. The dog's high levels of intensity and aggression were traits that Connor worked constantly to enhance. He never hesitated to use the K-9 to intimidate people, especially the homeless.

Connor had been investigated at least a dozen times in his career for excessive use of force and had received a couple of short suspensions. That was it. Chief Cooper liked his style and protected him from the justice he deserved.

Sergeant Dawson said, "Detective Randall has asked us to keep looking for the dude who killed that transient, Jimmy Barton. You've all got the description already, so . . . find him. Also, he asked that you locate and interview every transient you can find. See if they noticed anything unusual about anyone down on the beach or on the boardwalk.

"He figures the prostitute, Marilyn Gibbs, and Barton's killings are related, and he's probably right. So roust all the transients you can find down there and in the woods on the south end under J. Turner Butler Boulevard and see if you can develop a lead or two."

As the sergeant continued the briefing, Patrol Officers Ben "Shank" Wygle and Corri Jennings were talking quietly.

Shank whispered, "Corri, I got five bucks that says Sarge tells us not to do anything that gets him in trouble or do anything that causes him to do any paperwork."

Jennings, new to the squad, whispered back, "You gotta be kidding. He wouldn't say anything that dumb. I'll take that sucker bet."

"But remember, whatever you do . . . hey, Wygle, Jennings, if it's not too much trouble, y'all cut the crap and listen to what I'm sayin'!" Sgt. Dawson yelled.

They quickly turned their attention back to the sergeant, as Wygle flashed a five dollar bill and a grin at Jennings where the sergeant couldn't see.

"As I was trying to say before you two started grab-assin', whatever you do, don't do anything that's gonna get me called in the chief's office. I've been there, done that, got the tee shirt, and I sure as hell don't wanta go back! Oh, and one more thing, don't do anything that's gonna cause me a bunch of paperwork! Now, get outa here, and go do something that'll make me look good."

As the other officers headed for the door, Wygle smiled at Jennings and put his hand out, palm up.

"Hey, Corri, in case you missed it, Sarge just made my bet for me. You'll now notice my palm is empty. It's lonely and needs a friend . . . you know, President Abraham Lincoln?"

Corri smiled ruefully, "I said it was a sucker bet, but I didn't know *I* was the sucker. I should've known better than to gamble with the department's best poker player."

She pulled a five out of her pocket and slapped it into his hand. "Okay, bud, here's your money. Use it to buy me a beer at Pete's Bar tonight. I'm in between training cycles, and a Blue Moon with an orange slice sounds awful good!"

"You're on," Shank said with a surprised and happy grin.

"By the way, I've been wondering how you got tagged with your nickname," Corri said.

"Oh, that," he said, pleased at Corri's apparent interest in him. "I play golf with some of the guys once in a while, and I have this tendency to, uh, you know, hit the ball in ways not associated with making pars. In fact, Ty Honchen wore a bike helmet and a cup the last time we played. He said he needed to protect his brains and his balls from my occasional wild shot. Hence, I have become Shank Wygle, golfer extraordinaire!"

She laughed, "That's a pretty good story, Shank."

Corri Jennings was one of those women whose good looks turned heads whenever she walked into a room. She had short blond hair and striking eyes that alternated between cobalt blue and gunmetal gray depending on the light. Jennings stood five-five and weighed a muscular one hundred and fifty pounds, a result of her passion for power lifting. She had won numerous gold medals in the annual Florida Police & Fire Games and was in training for the international games later in the year.

If Wygle was forced to admit it, he was a little intimidated by Corri. But that didn't stop him from wanting a relationship with her. Corri's invitation to meet at Pete's Bar was, he hoped, a signal of better things to come.

As Shank and Corri headed to the parking lot to get their cars ready for the day's patrol, Roy Connor passed them.

"Fun and games today, huh? Dawson pretty much gave us a pass to hassle the transients, all in the name of poh-lice work. I don't know about y'all, but I'm geared up to root through the woods and find me some dirtbags to mess with."

Jennings couldn't believe what she heard. "Roy, you've been a cop a long time, and I have to give you props for surviving a lot of crap. But your style of policing is not mine. I don't get my kicks out of hassling a bunch of homeless people. Most of them are mentally ill or addicts, and you should maybe have a little of the "C" word for them."

"If you're suggesting that I don't have compassion for the more unfortunate in our society, you're damn right. Nobody gave me a damn thing my whole life. Everything I've gotten has been because I worked my ass off. Those assholes could have done the same thing, but, instead, they chose to turn into alkies and dopers.

"As far as the mentally ill go, as you so politely call them, most of them wouldn't be crazy if they would just take their meds. But they won't. They go into detox, get all regulated, and they're almost normal. Then they get out and stop taking the meds. In no time, they're right back acting crazy again. I have no use for weak assholes like that!"

"You're a great example of everything a cop shouldn't stand for, Connor," Corri said, as Shank stared open-mouthed at the confrontation. "You have absolutely no compassion, no professionalism, and no integrity. As far as I'm concerned, you don't deserve to wear that badge."

Connor moved closer to Corri, towering over her as he snarled, "You listen to me, bitch. You might think you're tough because you pump a little iron, but you're not shit to me. I don't give a damn about your opinion of me or dirtbags or anyone else on this planet. So, you better stay as far away from me as you can get, or I'll make you wish you had never met me. I'm not a man you wanta piss off!"

Shank tried to move between the two officers.

"Hey, guys, cool it. If Sarge comes out here, you're both gonna get your asses in a bind."

Corri glared at him, "Back off, Wygle. I don't need you to protect me from this asshole!"

She turned back to Connor. "Don't think for a second you can intimidate me, Roy Connor. You'll find me more of a handful than those defenseless homeless people you like to bully. You're bigger than me, but if you're stupid enough to try, you'll find that I can hold my own. You won't walk away unmarked, trust me on that!"

They stood toe to toe staring at each other for a few seconds before Connor abruptly turned without another word and stalked off to his car. He jumped in and spun the tires as he raced off the police parking lot, his K-9, Macho, barking loudly as if he wanted to leap out the window and attack Corri Jennings for having the audacity to challenge his master.

"Corri, do you think that was such a great idea to get into a pissin' match with Roy Connor?" Shank asked. "You're obviously not intimidated by him, but you know he and the chief are tight, don't you? The man has protected Connor for years. That's the only reason he hasn't been fired before now."

Jennings glared at Wygle, her eyes flashing. "I don't care who he knows! He's a dirty cop, and I didn't become a police officer to be like him! If you can't see that and don't believe in taking a stand for professionalism, then I guess I misjudged you. Tell you what . . . on second thought, I'm gonna be busy tonight. Forget Pete's . . . just keep my five bucks."

With that parting shot ringing in Wygle's ears, Corri stalked off to her car and quickly drove away. Shank stood rooted in place, his thoughts jumbled. *What did I do? Now, she's pissed at me when all I was trying to do was keep her from getting in trouble. Crap! I'll never understand women!*

Chapter 13

Connor was in a rage over the confrontation with Corri Jennings. *That bitch*, he thought. *Biggest mistake they ever made was letting women into police work. Bunch of sissy liberals! The only thing they can do even halfway right is handle little kids. She'll regret this little conversation. I'll make sure of that*!

Connor cruised to the south end of Jacksonville Beach and parked on the side of Third Street under the J. Turner Butler Boulevard overpass. He was familiar with several transient camps in the woods adjacent to the freeway, so he figured he would start his search there.

He told the dispatcher he'd be in the woods near the freeway checking the camps. She asked if he needed backup, and he told her he did not. Connor didn't want witnesses to anything he might do, depending upon the level of cooperation he got.

Connor took Macho out of his in-car kennel, attached a six foot lead, and headed off down a trail that the homeless had beaten down over the months. As he and Macho moved deeper into the woods, he began smelling smoke, and he smiled. With the cold weather, he figured they would start a fire for warmth.

Connor stepped into a small clearing, observing four tents set up at the points of the compass. All faced a communal fire pit where five men and one woman sat huddled close to each other for warmth. No one spotted him as he moved closer.

When he got within ten feet of the group, he yelled, "Hey, dirtbags! Hit the ground face first, and keep your hands where I can see them!"

As he yelled, Macho began barking and straining at his leash.

The six people jumped at the loud voice and the barking dog, and they quickly turned to see who it was. All but one of them immediately recognized Officer Roy Connor, having been the object of his abuse at various times in the past. Little Billy Bowen, who was afflicted with dwarfism and stood only three feet tall, didn't know him since he had just gotten into town from North Carolina the day before.

While the other five immediately got on the ground, Little Billy continued to sit on a log with his hands extended toward the fire. Connor initially smiled with satisfaction at how quickly the others complied with his commands, but he began frowning at the tiny man who seemed to be ignoring him.

On closer inspection, Connor was startled to see that Bowen had a shaved head and wore a large, gold, hoop earring in his left ear that looked just like the one he wore off duty. It was weird seeing almost a miniature version of himself. But he wasn't about to be sidetracked from his mission, to ensure that the dwarf showed him the proper respect.

"You little prick! Are you deaf? I said get your ass on the ground!"

Little Billy turned his head to look at Officer Connor. In a tiny voice, he said, "I'm not doing anything wrong, and I'm not getting on the ground. It's cold and wet."

This infuriated Connor. He was still smarting from his confrontation with Jennings, and the idea that a little dude with a voice like a mouse would defy him was too much to take. He walked up to Bowen and stood right behind him, commanding Macho to sit and stay.

"I won't tell you again, asshole. Do what I said, and do it as fast as those pigeon legs will let you, or maybe I'll let Macho here have a drumstick for lunch."

Little Billy didn't move, except to raise both short arms and give his tormentor a double-fingered salute. With a roar, Connor grabbed Little Billy under the arms and tossed him over his head. The little man flew through the air and landed hard, banging his head and jamming his shoulder. He lay still several seconds, trying to get his wits about him.

"Any of the rest of you scumbags want a piece of me? I'm in a very bad mood, and I would just love to take it out on every one of you assholes, and that includes you, Caruso. Don't think just because you take a piss sittin' down that I'll go easy on you. I treat all you vermin alike, just like you deserve. You got me?"

"Yes, sir, Officer Connor, sir," said Jerry Bell, a homeless man who had lived on the streets and in the woods in Jacksonville Beach for over fifteen years. "We'll do whatever you want, won't we guys?"

The rest of them all nodded their agreement, letting Bell be their spokesman.

"I'm sorry Little Billy didn't show you respect, Officer Connor. He just got in town yesterday, and he don't know the drill. He'll know what to do in the future."

"Well, for his sake, he better. Bell, you go get him and bring him over here with y'all. The rest of you sit up. Stay where you are, and keep your hands where I can see 'em."

As Bell went over and got Bowen to his feet, the others all rose to a sitting position, being careful to keep their hands in front of them. Nita Caruso was wearing a short skirt in spite of the cold, and it hiked up around her hips when she sat up, revealing her lack of underwear.

"Bitch, I don't wanta have to stare at that bush and imagine who or what's been diggin' around in it, so glue your legs together before I puke!"

As she complied, Bell walked the still-unsteady Bowen over and helped him sit down beside him. They all stared with apprehension at Connor.

"Listen close, assholes. I'm tryin' to find a dude that killed some whore and one of you losers, too."

With the exception of Little Billy, they all knew he was talking about Marilyn Gibbs and Jimmy Barton.

"How can we help you, Officer Connor?" Jerry Bell asked.

"I'm lookin' for a white male around six feet, maybe one-eighty, short brown hair and possibly light colored eyes, unsure of his age, anywhere from early thirties to about forty. He was last seen wearing a knee-length, black leather coat with tan slacks and brown shoes. Any of that sound familiar?"

Little Billy glared at Roy Connor, considering a wiseass comment before deciding he didn't want to try flying again.

Nita Caruso spoke up in a timid voice, "Officer Connor, I've seen a guy like that before."

Connor's nostrils flared, excited at the prospect of finding the man. "Where?"

"I was on First Street around the pier parking lot the other night, and I saw this guy standing there in the lot. The way he was starin' at people as they walked by, 'specially a couple of women that was by themselves, I just got the idea he might be trollin' for someone, like, you know, a hooker, maybe.

"I asked him if he needed somethin'. He stared right at me a minute, which is what made me remember that he had real pale blue eyes. He said that he was lookin' for someone, but not me. Then he walked off and got in a fancy car, a BMW, it was grey, I think."

"What night and what time? Was it the night that prostitute was killed?"

Nita grew more confident since Connor no longer seemed so threatening.

"No, it was a couple of days before, I think. I ain't sure what time it was 'cause I don't have a watch, but I know the bars was still open."

"What were you doing there?"

"I had just finished up with . . . uh . . . a uh . . .," she stuttered and then stopped, staring down at her lap.

"Finished up with what, Nita, a customer? You just finished blowin' a john? Is that what you were gonna say?" he demanded.

Nita glanced at her homeless acquaintances for support, but no one would meet her eyes. Looking down again, she said, "Yes, sir, Officer Connor, but please don't put me in jail. I hate that Duval County Jail."

"I'm not gonna arrest you, at least not for something I didn't witness. Besides, I've seen your arrest dockets. I know you're a hooker. It's good you didn't lie to me, Caruso," he said, leaning in close. "Because if you had been stupid enough to do that, I would have made you pay. You understand that, don't you?"

Reminded once again why she should be afraid of Connor, Nita said meekly, "Yes, sir."

"Alright, let's assume this was the guy that killed Marilyn Gibbs. Why didn't he pick you to cut up like a side of beef?"

Nita started shaking all over as she thought about Connor's question. She hadn't considered the man might have been Marilyn Gibbs' killer. Suddenly, she broke out in a sweat, in spite of a temperature in the low forties. She hugged herself tightly.

"I, I don't know, Officer Connor. I, I guess, I don't know. Maybe he didn't like the way I looked or somethin'," she stammered.

"Well now, I can't say that would surprise me. Let's consider the facts here. A well-dressed man, wearing an obviously expensive leather coat, searching for a little female companionship . . . the kind that he at least pretended to be willing to pay for. And he sees you. What are you, thirty years old? You look like you're at least forty-five, like you been rode hard and put away wet about a thousand times.

"Dressed in filthy clothes you probably don't even take off when your head hits the ground in that tent over there. What's it been, a week since you bathed? So, let's ask these *gentlemen* sitting on either side of you. If you were looking for a piece of ass to buy, and you were dressed in expensive clothes like this guy obviously was, would you flip your pecker out for her?"

At first, no one said anything, and no one dared look at Officer Connor, afraid he would make them answer. Little Billy decided he had to speak up. He was not big in size, but he wasn't a coward, either.

"Yeah, I would. Nita's a nice person, and if she wanted to be with me, I'd take her in a second," he said with defiance in his voice.

Nita glanced at Little Billy with a quick smile of gratitude. She wasn't accustomed to having someone defend her. The fact Little Billy was talking about having sex with her didn't detract at all from the warm feeling his words gave her.

Connor smiled down at Little Billy. He squatted in front of the little man so they were almost eye to eye. Continuing to smile, he stuck his index finger inside the hoop earring in Little Billy's left ear, jerking downward and tearing the earlobe as the earring came free. Little Billy never flinched, in spite of the obvious pain. As the blood began flowing down the side of his neck, he spit directly in Roy Connor's face.

The big cop went berserk. Wrapping his powerful hands around Little Billy's neck, he began to choke him.

As Little Billy's spittle rolled slowly down the side of his nose, Connor screamed, "I'll kill you, you little fucker!"

Thinking his master was in trouble, Macho leaped at Little Billy, trying to devour his tiny legs.

At that moment, Connor's only friend on the department, Officer Syd Padgett, ran into the clearing.

"Roy! Roy! Let him go! You're gonna kill him!"

"This bastard spit in my face!" Roy screamed as he continued to hold Little Billy in the air, choking him while at the same time trying to keep Macho from eating the dwarf.

"Stop, Roy!" Padgett yelled as he tried to pry Connor's hands from around Little Billy's neck. "He's not worth going to prison for! Let him go!"

As Padgett continued to pry at Roy Connor's fingers, his rage began to abate. He finally turned to glare at Padgett, then back at Little Billy, whose face had started turning blue. He opened his hands, letting the man fall to the ground.

Before Macho could attack, Connor grabbed him by his collar and dragged the excited dog away. Padgett took Connor by the arm and walked him away from the group, all of whom had sat frozen as Connor attacked Little Billy, afraid he would do the same to them.

"Roy, listen to me. You can't keep doing this shit. You've got to get control of yourself. Chief Cooper's not gonna keep covering for you. And if you finally kill one of these dirtbags, he for sure can't help you. You'll be in Raiford before you blink your eyes twice, and you know how long you'll last there, considering how many assholes you've sent up. Now get control of yourself, man!"

"*Alright*! I'm calmed down. I just went a little crazy. That little bastard had the audacity to spit in my face!

He started getting angry again as he wiped Little Billy's spit off his face with the back of his hand.

"I know, Roy. I'd feel the same way and want to rip his lungs out through his ass, but you got witnesses here. You can't do that kinda shit when there's others who can back up his story."

"You're right. But, hey, I got some good intel from Nita Caruso that may clear these two murders."

"What does she know?" Padgett asked.

Connor told Padgett what she had said, including the car description.

"That might be solid gold information, Roy. We need to get her in to talk to Randall. Considering what's happened here, do you think she'll cooperate?" Padgett asked.

"Oh, yeah, she'll talk, don't worry about that," Connor said confidently. "She'll talk or I'll give her a taste of what I gave that little gnome over there."

"Roy, you gotta back off. Look, how about you take off and let me handle this. I'll smooth things over here and then bring her to you. Wait for me at Beach Plaza. I'll make sure there's no complaint coming from anyone, and then I'll bring her to you. You can take her in to see Randall and get the credit. That work for you?"

"Yeah, I guess you're right. I'll meet you at Beach Plaza. Call me on my cell when you're close."

Connor spun around and, dragging Macho, walked off down the trail toward his car without a backward glance.

Syd Padgett turned to the homeless group, all of whom had clustered around Little Billy.

"You people listen up. Excitement's over now. "Little man, you got anything you want to complain about?" he asked Little Billy.

Bowen was having trouble swallowing from being choked, much less talk, so he just shook his head.

"Any of the rest of you got anything to bitch about?"

No one said anything or even looked in Padgett's direction, but they all shook their heads in unison.

"Nita, I need you to come with me," Padgett said.

She looked up sharply. "Why?"

"First and foremost, because I said so. Second, and equally important, because I need you to talk to a detective about what you saw. You want to see the man who killed your friends caught, don't you?"

Nita Caruso glanced at the others and then at Officer Padgett. "I guess," she said hesitantly.

"Good. We all want the same thing. So, come with me. We'll get you to the PD for a statement and then bring you back here. And if it takes a while, we'll even see that you get something to eat. Wouldn't want you to go hungry if you missed lunch at the soup kitchen, now would we? That sound good?"

Nita nodded resignedly. She figured he would just arrest her if she didn't agree to go, so she might as well go voluntarily. Nita followed Padgett down the trail and out to his patrol car, climbing into the back seat. He drove her straight to Beach Plaza, where she got into the front seat of Connor's car. Macho lunged at the cage separating him from the front seat, barking furiously at the interloper in his master's car.

"Shut up, you damn idiot dog!" Connor yelled at Macho.

He immediately stopped barking, waiting for the next command from his master. Although even more afraid of Connor since his attack on Little Billy, Nita managed to keep her emotions under control as they rolled toward police headquarters.

Connor pulled into the lot and parked on the patrol line. "Get outa the car."

She climbed out slowly, keeping Roy Connor's hands in sight in case he decided to start choking her like he had done to Little Billy.

"Come on, I don't have all day. Wait by that door over there. Don't go inside. You can't anyway because it takes a code, but don't go in if someone opens the door, you got me?"

"Yes, sir, Officer Connor. I'll do what you say. Just please don't hurt me like you did Little Billy."

Officer Connor stepped close to her, speaking softly, "If you wanta stay healthy for a little while longer, you better never, and I repeat, never, say anything like that again. I didn't hurt that little troll. But I *will* hurt you if you raise a stink. Do we have an understanding, bitch?"

Nita cringed away from Connor, looking down and refusing to stare into his mad eyes.

"I, I'm sorry, Officer Connor. I didn't see nothin', and I didn't hear nothin'."

"That's what I wanta hear. Now, get over there and wait for me like a good little hooker."

Nita walked slowly to the back door of the police building and stood very still. Hanging her head in resignation, Nita's long hair covered her face completely. She continued to stare at the ground as Officer Connor punched in the code. The lock clicked, and he yanked open the door.

"Go on, step into the spider's lair," he said with a sneer.

Connor, in spite of being reasonably intelligent, couldn't alter his basic personality any more than a junk yard dog could stop scratching his fleas. Even though he had attended interview classes that stressed treating witnesses with kid gloves to encourage their cooperation, he believed that was all B.S. In Roy Connor's world, intimidation always reigned supreme as the best technique.

Nita never raised her head; she just shuffled in the door, thinking to herself that she was never getting out of the building alive. After she told the detective what he wanted to know, the monster walking in front of her would take her into some dark room and kill her.

Chapter 14

Roy Connor led the way into the Detective Division, stopping at Linda Greene's desk. A tall woman with short red hair, Linda had been the division secretary for many years, and she was Commander Mike Wilson's right hand. She kept his schedule on track, ensured follow-up investigations were assigned fairly to the detectives, typed all the division memos, made the coffee, kept the little break room clean; in short, did everything but investigate crimes. Truth be told, Mike Wilson thought she would probably make a great investigator had she been a police officer.

Linda was one of those rare people who could find something good in just about anyone. However, Officer Roy Connor presented a difficult challenge.

She looked at him as he walked in the door, thinking, *There's something terribly wrong with this man. I'm not sure he's ever had a kind thought or done something nice for anyone his entire life.*

Instead of voicing those negative thoughts, she smiled and said, "Hi, Officer Connor, how are you doing?"

Connor couldn't figure her out. He figured Linda disliked him like everyone else, but she always treated him with courtesy and respect. Consequently, he tended to be a little more courteous to her.

"I'm good. I brought in this little lady of the night to talk to Randall about the two homicides," he said, indicating Nita Caruso.

"I'll call Sergeant Randall," she said, hiding her irritation at Connor's obvious disrespect for the woman.

"Sergeant Randall, Officer Connor is here with a witness who may have information on Operation Street Cleaner . . . yes . . . oh, sorry, I forgot the task force was renamed . . . right . . . Operation Serial Killer . . . Okay, I'll tell him."

Linda hung up and turned to Officer Connor with a smile, "Sergeant Randall will be right here."

Clay approached the secretary's desk. "What you got, Roy?"

His tone failed to conceal the lack of respect he had for the brutal police officer, knowing Connor's long history of heavy-handed conduct toward the citizens he was sworn to protect.

"This little bi—, uh, *lady* here gave me some information about the murder suspect."

Clay looked at Nita, who was standing with her head down.

"Ma'am, what's your name?"

"Trust me, she's not a ma'am. She's a hooker," Connor interjected.

"Officer Connor, I don't need you to correct my choice of words. And I wasn't talking to you, either. In fact, why don't you get back on the street? There's probably a ticket that needs written, and I know how much you enjoy that."

Connor glared at Clay and opened his mouth to retort. Clay raised his eyebrows, staring back at Roy.

"You have something you'd like to say, Officer Connor?"

Connor knew he was on shaky ground. Randall was a sergeant and could relieve him of duty on the spot if he was insubordinate. He choked back his wiseass comment.

"Nope. I'm good here. Have a nice day . . . Sarge," he said, unable to resist a trace of sarcasm. Spinning on his heels, he stalked out.

Clay looked at the cowering woman. "Ma'am, I'll try again, what's your name?"

Without raising her head, she mumbled, "Nita."

"Nita, what's your full name?"

"Nita Ann Caruso," she said, raising her head to glance at Clay.

"Alright, Ms. Caruso, let's go to my office. Would you like some water or a Coke or something?"

"Water would be good . . . if it's not too much trouble."

Linda stood up, heading for the break room. "I'll get it, Sergeant. You go ahead."

Clay escorted Nita back to his office and got her settled in a chair across the desk from him. Linda came in right after and gave her a bottle of water before withdrawing, leaving the door open since Clay would be interviewing the woman alone.

"I'll hold your calls, Sergeant," she said.

"Thanks, Linda. Now, Ms. Caruso, I understand you might know something about the two homicides we're investigating. Is that right?"

"Yes. Well, maybe. Officer Connor was telling us about a guy . . ."

"Who is 'us' you're referring to?"

"Oh, just some of the guys I was with when he came up on us at our camp."

"I thought you looked familiar. You're one of our regular homeless, aren't you?"

"Yes, sir," she said meekly, figuring his kindness was about to end.

"Listen, Ms. Caruso, you can call me Sergeant Randall, but don't call me sir. We're probably about the same age, so just relax."

Nita smiled for the first time. "Okay."

"I'd like to hear what you told the officer, every detail you can remember."

Nita spent the next fifteen minutes telling and retelling her story to Clay. He let her do a complete run through the first time and then began taking notes as she repeated the story. The woman seemed to have a good memory for details, he thought. She wasn't drunk or stoned, a somewhat unusual condition for most of the hardcore homeless Clay encountered.

When she had given him as much as she could recall of the man's description, including the car he drove, Clay had her write out a witness statement. He read it and was pleased to see that she had documented all the information just as she had told him.

The interview over, he asked, "Do you need a ride anywhere?"

"If it's not too much trouble, could you have someone take me back to the camp down at the south end?"

"Sure," Clay said with a smile. "I'll call dispatch and have an officer come right in."

"Uh, Sergeant, is . . . is there any chance you could get someone besides Officer Connor or Officer Padgett to take me back?"

"I understand about Connor, but Padgett is a problem for you, too? What did he do to you?"

"Nothing," she said quickly. "And neither did Officer Connor. I, I would just like someone else to take me. If you can't, that's no problem. I can walk."

"It's no trouble. Listen, did something happen out there with Connor or Padgett? Did they do anything to you?"

"No! They didn't do anything to me, but . . ."

"But what, Ms. Caruso? If something happened, you can trust me to take care of it. Not every officer in this department is like Connor or Padgett."

Nita struggled with her desire to tell Randall what happened to Little Billy Bowen. He seemed to be an honest cop, something she had seldom encountered. But she was too afraid of Connor to speak up.

"Nothing, Sergeant Randall. You've been very nice to me, and I thank you for that. But I'd like to go now."

Clay realized she was afraid to tell him about something Connor or Padgett had done. He had no choice but to let it go, at least for now.

"Sure," he said. "Hang loose for a few minutes, and I'll get Officer Jennings to take you back to your camp. She's a good cop, you can trust me on that. In the meantime, here's my card. Call me if you think of anything else, and especially if you ever see this guy again."

Chapter 15

"Clay, do we really have to go to this party tonight?"

"Dana, you only turn thirty once. Remember how you walked around like somebody died for a week before you hit thirty? Well, all week 'Landa Jamison's been acting the same way, so we decided to surprise her with a party at the FOP Lodge. Her sister, Fontana Jones, set the whole thing up."

"Is Fontana still in vice and narcotics?"

"Yeah, 'Tana does a great job, too. She can pose as a drug dealer one minute and a high class hooker the next. She's such a great actress she sometimes even plays a drug-dealing hooker! The woman's only twenty-five and looks like a model, but she can dress and act like a fifty-year-old grandma when the occasion calls for it."

"Well, anyway, I've still got two paintings that need work before my show at the Reid Lansing Gallery in mid-May, and it's already April. I could really use the time tonight to—"

"Sweetie," Clay interrupted. "We haven't been to a party for months. I really need a break. This homicide investigation has got me going in so many directions that I think I may have run into myself the other day."

Dana giggled as she visualized two Clays coming from opposite directions and banging into each other as they rounded the corner. In her mind's eye, she saw both of them carrying a box of packing peanuts they planned to use to secure evidence going to the crime lab.

As they collided, the boxes went straight up in the air, a cloud of peanuts flying out and then drifting down around their ears like monster-sized snowflakes. She had a vivid imagination that enabled her to visualize landscapes in a way that was not only appealing but also very profitable.

Clay failed to notice that Dana had temporarily gone away.

". . . And you know how good you are and how fast you work. If you only have two to finish, that's like nothing to you. You know what I mean?"

"Um, yeah, I guess," Dana said as she tried to regain the thread of his monologue.

"So, we need a break. It's Friday night. Rafe Santos and Ty Honchen are grilling hamburgers and chicken, and there's enough alcohol to get the party started and running all night. What more can you ask for?"

"I guess you're right."

At eight-thirty, Clay pulled into the parking lot in Dana's midnight blue Lexus LS. He never drove his detective car off duty when he knew he would be drinking. Clay was pretty conscientious about following the rules of the department. He believed the rank of sergeant required him to maintain a higher standard of conduct since officers lower in rank tended to pattern their own behavior after supervisors.

There were already a dozen cars and trucks in front of the lodge. Yolanda's Jeep was missing, but Fontana's Chevy pickup was backed in next to the front door. He could see 'Tana and several others unloading cases of beer from the bed.

"Hey, that's outstanding! No one's gonna be thirsty tonight," Clay said. "Especially me. I can't wait to knock back a few cold ones."

"Clay, we've talked about this before. You know how you get when you've had too much to drink."

"Come on, Dana," Clay said, irritation evident in his voice. "Last time I checked, I was way over twenty-one. I think I can handle a few beers without the need for Mother Dana to watch over me."

"You're over twenty-one, alright, but when you get to drinking with your cop buddies, you lose all sense of perspective and proportion. You start thinking you're ten feet tall and bulletproof, like that Travis Tritt song you like. Look, Clay, I didn't want to come anyway. Please don't make me regret my decision."

"Okay, I give. I'll be a good boy, anything to keep my little lady happy" he said.

They got out of the Lexus and started toward the door. Dana slipped her hand in Clay's as they walked.

"I hope they brought something besides beer. I wouldn't mind a glass of Pinot Noir myself."

Clay rolled his eyes. "Dana, cops don't drink wines with French names," still somewhat annoyed over her comments about his drinking. "They drink beer, mostly. Well, some of us drink Jack and

Diet, or maybe Dos Equis or Corona when we cook fajitas, but Pin-not Nore? Come on!"

"Clay, it's pronounced Pee'-No Nu-wah', not Pin-not Nore. I swear, sometimes I wonder what kind of an education you got at Fletcher High."

Clay glared at her. "Better a half-assed education at Fletcher than that snotty-ass private school for rich snobs you went to."

Dana stopped in her tracks. "What did you say?"

Before Clay could think of a response, she was off and running. "I was just kidding with you, and you know it. But you just had to take a shot at my education, didn't you?"

"What? I was just popping back at you for you taking a shot at *my* education. It's a two-way street, last time I checked."

"We've had this conversation before about you making fun of my school. I'll remind you that I graduated at the top of my class. What were you . . . third from the bottom or something like that?"

"Oh, that's low. Look, why do you have to make such a big deal outa this? I was just kidding about your precious wine pronunciation. I know how the stupid wine is pronounced. I guess you forgot that I took four freakin' years of French in that low class school I went to. Remember? I can probably speak more French than you, even. Wanta hear?"

"No. Not only do I not want to hear you speak French, I don't want to hear you speak at all, at least not right now. I'll see you at home."

Dana turned and stalked to her car. Sliding behind the wheel, she locked the doors and started the engine. Before she could back out, Clay ran up and tried to open the door. Finding it locked, he banged on the window.

"Dana, wait! What are you doing? Roll down the window! I wanta talk to you!"

Dana stared angrily at Clay, both hands remaining on the steering wheel.

"What?" she mouthed through the closed window.

"Dammit, roll it down so I don't have to shout!"

"Don't you dare shout at me!" she mouthed back at him as she put the car into gear.

Realizing she was going to leave if he didn't back off, Clay said in a softer voice, "Dana, wait, don't go. Please, roll down the window."

She looked at Clay a moment and then lowered the window.

"Why are you doing this to me? I'm up to my ass in this investigation. Cooper chewed me out over the name I gave our task force, and he's demanding that I clear both murders, like yesterday! I just wanted to get out for a few hours and relax a little bit with my wife. I don't think that's asking too much. If I offended you, I'm sorry. But you offended me, too. You started in on me about drinking as soon as we got here, and then you badmouthed my school and my education. I know I don't have a master's degree like you, but that doesn't mean I'm a dumb ass either. Look, can we just forget all this and start the evening over?"

Dana thought he was being insensitive to her. He had already forgotten about the trauma she had suffered when she found the homeless man's dead body. But she admitted to herself that she hadn't realized the amount of pressure Clay was under at work.

She thought, *As always, I'll be the bigger person and cut him some slack, even though my stress is probably off the charts in comparison to his.*

She turned off the engine and got out of the car. Smiling at her husband, she said, "Okay, truce. We'll start over."

"Thanks, babe. You know I love you."

"I know you do, and I love you, too."

As they headed back toward the lodge, Clay looked slyly at her.

"I still don't think anybody brought any Pin-not Nore."

Dana punched him on the arm, laughing, "You jerk!"

Chapter 16

Unknown to both of them, their arrival and argument had been witnessed by Bobby Hawkins. Standing in the shadows on the east side of the lodge, Bobby swayed as he took another big gulp from a bottle of Coors Light. It was his fourth in less than an hour. As he watched the two of them approach the front door, his expression shifted back and forth between rabid dislike for Clay and sheer lust for Dana.

"Sorry bastard," he muttered too low for them to hear. "Thinks he's so great just because he's got the hottest and richest woman on the beach. One of these days, I'll make him pay for stealing Dana away from me."

With that mumbled threat, he turned and walked around to the back side of the lodge where the burgers and chicken were being grilled.

"Hey, 'Tana," Clay greeted Fontana Jones. "I was interviewing that transient you popped for dope yesterday trying to get some intel on the homicides. Turns out he didn't know anything, but you should have heard him talking about you and your dope-dealin' hooker act. He said you were so good lookin' he couldn't wait to get outa jail so he could come buy from you again."

"Well, bless his heart," Fontana said. "I'll be happy to sell to him again . . . dope, that is," she clarified quickly.

"I was wondering there for a second," Clay grinned.

"Now, you just get your mind out of the gutter, Clay Randall. I swear, Dana," she said laughing, "I don't know why you put up with this wiseass white boy! You know you could do a whole lot better!"

"Aw, you know, 'Tana, he's good for yard work and hauling groceries and carrying paintings to my shows. And sometimes when I got an itch that needs scratching. So I guess I'll keep him around a while longer . . . at least another week anyway."

They both laughed as Clay tried to ignore the shots he was taking.

"You need any of that beer hauled inside, 'Tana? Might as well do something I'm good at," he said, a mock hangdog look on his face.

"No, thanks, sugar. Y'all go on inside. I got a couple of mindless drones to take care of it. Oh, hey, here's David and Shank. Thanks for helping me, guys," she said enthusiastically to Patrol Officers David Sheasley and Shank Wygle as she winked at Dana.

Clay opened the screen door and pushed open the inner door, standing aside so Dana could go in.

They had no sooner stepped inside when they heard, "Hey, Clay, glad to see you brought the good-lookin' half of the Randall household! Damn, you're lookin' fine tonight, Dana!"

Clay and Dana turned to their left at the same time and looked at one of Clay's task force members, Detective Ty Honchen.

Ty was a short man by typical cop standards, only about five foot, six, but he was built like a tank. The muscles in his arms and chest strained to escape the sweater he was wearing. At forty-two, he had given up the longer hairstyles of his early years in favor of keeping his blond hair cut very short in a "high and tight" military style. Honchen seldom found the need to use his brute strength on the job. One look at his muscular physique was usually enough to calm a situation quickly.

Tonight, Ty had clearly started on the liquid cheer early. He raised his Jack and Coke in a toast, "To a person I have the greatest respect for, welcome . . . oh, and you, too, Clay!"

The twenty or so other cops and their significant others all hooted at Honchen for his good natured shot at Clay.

"Thanks, Ty," Clay retorted. "Can somebody run this guy on a breathalyzer? He's either drunk or crazy to be hustling my wife!"

Just then, Ty's wife, Ann, walked up and popped him on the back of the head. Ann was only about five foot, three, but there was no question who was in charge in the Honchen family, at least that night.

"Clay," she said. "Just ignore the little man. You know how he gets if he has more than one drink. It breaks the connection between his pea brain and his big mouth."

Turning to look at her husband, Ann said in mock anger, "Tiberius Honchen, can you control yourself, or am I gonna have to take you home?"

Before Ty could say a word, the lodge exploded with laughter. "Tiberius! Your name is Tiberius?" Clay asked incredulously.

Ty looked sheepishly at his friends as they continued to whoop and holler. When the laughter died down, Clay asked what everyone in the room was dying to hear, "Now, Tiberius, all of us are your friends. You know that, right?"

Ty took another swallow of his drink, "Yeah, right, my *good* friends."

"Alright, now that we've established that, all these inquiring minds here would sure like to know just how the hell you ended up with a front-end name like Tiberius! Oh, and before you share that story, please tell us your middle name. It starts with an "A," doesn't it?"

"Yeah, it does." After a brief hesitation, he said in a low voice, "Aurelius."

The screams of laughter started all over again. "Tiberius Aurelius Honchen!" Clay hollered. "I had no idea you had a Greek god's name!"

As the laughter continued, Ty muttered, "Ancient Roman, not Greek."

"What, what did you say, oh great one?" Clay sputtered.

"It's an Ancient Roman name. Now do you wanta hear or not?"

Dana stepped next to Ty and put her arm around his shoulder. "Go ahead, Ty," she encouraged. "Don't let these cretins get to you. I'm sure your parents had a very good reason for your name."

"Thanks, Dana. It's nice to get a little support from the only member of the Randall family with class. Okay, friends and jerks, gather 'round, and Uncle Ty will educate you on the finer points of given names."

The group moved a little closer so they could hear Ty's soft voice.

"My dad was stationed in Italy when he was in the Army. That's where he met and married my mother, Alessia, God rest her pure blood Italian soul. Anyway, Dad fell in love with the country, the language, the food, you name it . . . he was a true Italian aficionado. And for you hicks from the sticks, that means devotee or admirer.

"So, a couple of years after Dad and Mom came back to the states, I was born. I was a little short when I was born, only about seventeen inches at birth."

"Yeah, well, you're not much taller than that now, are you?" 'Tana Jones asked from the back of the crowd, again to much laughter.

"Hey, I expect to catch crap from the guys and my wife, but 'Tana . . . you? I'm crushed! Anyway, in closing, and I am getting to the close of this story, believe it or not.

"By the way, just as a side note, Ann always says I take too long to tell a story and include way too much extraneous B.S., that means irrelevant or superfluous to you dumb asses in the back row, not that I believe I'm longwinded," he rambled as his friends rolled their eyes.

"Don't anybody say another word or we'll never get to the end of this story!" 'Tana yelled to the crowd, all of whom were hollering at Ty to finish.

"Thank you very much, you pack of addle-brained doofi . . . that's the plural of doofus, 'cause I know y'all haven't been schooled enough to know that. And now, uh, where was I? Oh, yeah, I was short, so my Dad wanted to name me Napoleon Bonaparte Honchen after, well, you know. But my Mom wouldn't hear of it. I was solid as a rock even at that age, so she wanted me to have a strong name to go with this fabulous body you see before you tonight," he said as he quickly stood and did a little flex for the crowd.

"Whoo-Hoo! Flex them pecs, Tyberius!" Cassie Broderick shouted.

"Thanks, Cassie. I love you, too. Oops, Ann, honey, and Mickey, I mean that in a totally platonic way," he said with a side grin at his wife and Cassie's husband.

She gave him a love tap on the arm. "Would you puh-LEEZE finish this story? I swear, it's taking you longer to tell how you got your name than it took for you to incubate in your mama's oven!"

"Awright, awright! Anyway, she picked Tiberius for my first name because he was the second emperor of Ancient Rome and was a strong and powerful man. And since I had a full head of gorgeous blond hair at birth, she gave me the middle name of Aurelius, which means golden.

"With an Italian mother and a father who loved all things Italian, you gotta know that I didn't have a prayer of getting a good old American name like Clay, wait . . . Clay isn't exactly common, now is it? Let's see, what does Clay mean . . . dirt? Soil? Earth? I'll stick with Tiberius Aurelius myself, thank you!"

As the crowd laughed and clapped, Ty stood. "Story tellin's thirsty business," he said, moving toward the table where the alcohol and mixers were located, trailed by his wife, who was steadily voicing her concern about drinking too much.

As Ty told his story, two others sat back in a corner knocking back one beer after another. Bobby Hawkins was on his eighth beer while Roy Connor had just finished his second six-pack. Both men were very drunk, and both shared a common antagonism toward Clay Randall and Ty Honchen.

"Asshole," Roy Connor muttered, his voice slurring.

"Which asshole you referring to, Roy?" Bobby asked. "I see quite a few in front of me, starting with Detective Sergeant Clayton Randall."

"I was talking about Honchen, you idiot. But Randall fits in that category, too, so I guess you're not a total idiot."

"Thanks," Bobby slurred, not realizing through his alcohol fog that he had just been dissed. "How can such a beautiful, intelligent, rich piece of ass like Dana be married to that scumbag?"

"Hawkins, you're a pathetic human being, you know that?" Connor growled.

Bobby was normally intimidated by the hyper-aggressive Roy Connor, and he wouldn't have even been talking to him if he hadn't been so drunk.

He replied in a hurt voice, "Whata you mean, Roy?"

"Look, lemme give you a piece of advice. If you want something in this life, you gotta take it. No one's gonna give you a damn thing. Take it, you hear me? Take it! If you want her so bad, take her away from Randall. Be a man about it instead of whining and crying like a baby. One way or the other, I don't care!

"Only thing I'm interested in now is you gettin' your ass up and away from me before I decide you need chokin' out like those . . . well, like some people need."

The glare he turned on him as he said this made Bobby jump to his feet and scurry across to the other side of the lodge, putting as much distance between himself and the crazy cop as he could.

At nine, the birthday girl, Yolanda Jamison, arrived. She walked in the door of the lodge to shouts of, "Happy Birthday, 'Landa!" "You're only thirty, you're not dead yet!" "Somebody from AARP just called wantin' to sell you some life insurance!"

The catcalls continued as someone handed her a beer. The crowd cheered as she turned the bottle up and set it down empty.

"I have to tell y'all I suspected something was going on. There's been too many closed door meetings when I'm in the station, and I knew it couldn't all be about Clay's murder task force!" she said.

Everyone crowded around 'Landa and continued to wish her a happy birthday as several volunteers began carrying in the hamburgers, chicken, and sausage that had been grilled for the occasion.

The party moved into fast forward with the guest of honor there, and alcohol continued to flow freely as people stuffed themselves with barbecue and enjoyed the mix of music playing loudly on the lodge's CD stereo system. No one worried about making too much noise since the FOP lodge was located in the woods at the south end of the city, well away from homes and businesses.

The rules of the lodge were that no one was supposed to drive away drunk. Someone would be the designated driver, and, if no one volunteered, cots were available to sleep it off right there. Most of the partiers had taken advantage of the lodge's sleeping quarters at one time or another.

Chapter 17

By one o'clock, there were only four couples still on the dance floor, swaying to a Brian McKnight love song. Clay and Dana were dancing along with Ty and Ann Honchen, Cassie Broderick and her husband, Mickey, a fireman, and Fontana Jones and her husband, Michael, a deputy with the Jacksonville Sheriff's Office. The guest of honor, 'Landa Jamison, was sitting at a table with her boyfriend, Rafe Santos, Three Rivers, Shank Wygle, and Corri Jennings.

As the song ended, the back door to the lodge opened, and Roy Connor staggered inside, holding a beer. He took a long pull as he surveyed the room, taking note of the people he disliked or outright hated, which was just about everyone there.

Shank Wygle leaned over to Corri Jennings and whispered, "Great. That's all we need. He's a world class jerk when he's sober. Drunk as he is, I got a bad feeling things are heading south in a hurry."

Corri stared at Connor briefly and turned back to the table, ignoring him. Connor saw her looking at him, and his blood began to heat up. On the one hand, he hated her for standing up to him in the parking lot earlier that week, especially in front of another officer. He also hated her because she was good looking and sexy, and he knew she would never let him taste her charms. Her every look and action made it clear she thought he was dirt.

Taking another long swallow, he let out a loud belch that caused every head in the room to turn toward him.

"What's your problem?" he snarled at the group.

Shank Wygle, wanting to score points with Corri, decided he had to say something to make up for his inaction during the parking lot confrontation with Connor.

"Roy, you oughta step away from that beer. You've had way too much to drink tonight."

Roy had been looking at Corri all the time Shank was talking. He slowly turned his head and stared at Wygle.

"I oughta what? Step away from my beer? Aw, that's rich. 'Step away from my beer.' You tryin' to come up with some snappy little sayin' that everyone will start repeatin' so you can bring some meaning into your pissant little life? That what you tryin' for, Wygle?"

Connor staggered over to the table where the officers were sitting, stopping directly behind Wygle's chair.

Yolanda Jamison said, "Roy, I do appreciate you coming to my birthday party, I really do. I've had a great time tonight, so please don't turn it into something ugly right here at the end. Let me give you a ride home, how about it?"

Looking at the birthday girl, Connor sneered, "Landa, you always so fuckin' nice to ever'body, even me. I'm here to tell you that nice don't get you shit. It's all about power. And I got lots of power," he said, flexing his big biceps the way Ty Honchen had done earlier. "So don't try to get in the way of the conversation I'm havin' with this pissant sittin' in front of me."

Wygle had finally had a bellyful of Connor's insults. "That's it, asshole! No more!" he yelled as he started to rise from his chair.

Connor bellowed in rage, grabbing Wygle around the neck and dragging him backward out of the chair. Connor was trying to execute the control technique known as the Lateral Vascular Neck Restraint in which an officer places his forearm and bicep on either side of a person's neck, cutting off blood flow to the brain and quickly rendering the person unconscious.

In his drunken condition, Connor had positioned his forearm across Wygle's throat, a move that, given enough pressure, could crush his esophagus and kill him. Shank struggled unsuccessfully to break the bigger man's grip on his throat. Everyone was yelling at Connor to let him go, but he was a wild man, intent only on choking out Wygle.

Clay and Ty grabbed Connor's arms, yelling at him to let go, while Corri Jennings delivered knee strikes to Connor's upper thigh. In spite of their efforts, he continued to choke Wygle, whose face was turning an ugly shade of purple.

Clay raced out the door to his car, grabbing his TASER and handcuffs that he carried with him at all times. Running in the door, he saw that Wygle was rapidly losing consciousness.

He yelled at the officers fighting Connor, "Get back!"

They saw the TASER in his hand and jumped away like they had been shot themselves. As Clay pulled the trigger, two barbs exploded out the end, flying through the air and striking Roy Connor in the middle of his broad back.

Fifty thousand volts surging through the wires to the barbs embedded in his back did what all the officers' physical strength had been unable to do. His arms flew up into the air as he fell forward to the floor. Shank, suddenly free of Connor's massive forearm, slumped to the floor beside him.

Three Rivers and Rafe Santos dragged Wygle away as Connor's five second ride on the electric highway ended. While the current flowed into Connor's body, he was unable to do anything. His muscles were frozen, his jaw clenched tightly. As soon as the current stopped, however, he struggled to his knees, shaking his big head like a fighter trying to unscramble his brains after a crushing uppercut.

"Stay down, asshole!" Clay yelled. "If you try to get up, I'll take you for another ride!"

"I'm gonna kick the everlovin' shit outa you, Randall. Your stripes don't mean shit to me down here," he roared, starting to rise.

Clay pulled the trigger, sending another fifty thousand volts into Connor's body. When the second cycle ended, Connor stayed on the floor, staring at Clay with intense hatred in his eyes.

Clay handed his handcuffs to Ty Honchen. "Cuff him, Ty. I'm arresting this asshole for aggravated battery on a law enforcement officer!"

The words sunk into Connor's alcohol-soaked brain. "What? You're arrestin' me? You can't arrest me. I'm a cop!"

As he said this, Ty Honchen forced his hands together and snapped the cuffs. Connor started to struggle again at the feel of his arms handcuffed behind his back.

"The barbs are still in your back, Roy. I'll tase you again if you don't stay still, you hear me?" Clay asked.

Ty whispered to Clay, "Are you really gonna arrest him?"

"Damn right I am! Everyone here is a witness to his unprovoked attack on Shank. The guy's been getting away with this crap for too long. Cooper can't protect him this time."

Chapter 18

"Cooper can't protect who?"

Every eye in the room turned toward the door as Police Chief Gordy Cooper strolled in. Officer Bobby Hawkins slipped in right behind him, a smirk on his face. Everyone was so stunned to see the chief that no one spoke. Chief Cooper walked over to the table where the group was standing. His pale blue eyes bored in on each of the people present, resting finally on Clay Randall.

"Sergeant Randall, I asked a question, and I believe it was in response to a statement you made. Do I need to repeat it?"

Clay glanced nervously at his fellow detectives, Ty and Cassie, and then flicked his eyes at Dana, looking desperately for support, before looking back at the chief. "Chief, I just meant that, uh," he stammered.

"Yes, Sergeant, you meant what?"

"It just seems like Roy Connor has a history of doing things that would get someone else fired, and, well, I would hate to see him get off for his unprovoked attack on Officer Wygle."

Chief Cooper stared at Clay for a moment before responding. "A lesser man might think you're accusing him of showing favoritism toward an officer, almost like I'm covering up improper conduct for some underhanded reason . . . some unprofessional motive.

"Should I assume instead that your alcohol consumption at this little gathering tonight caused you to have a breakdown between your good common sense and your tongue? That this caused you to misspeak, and that it did not and does not reflect your true feelings? Is that an accurate assessment of your motives, son?"

Clay knew his answer could very well make or break his career. He knew Cooper had fired other officers for daring to challenge him. He was aware also that, if he said nothing, his integrity was shot, not only with himself but also with other officers who admired him for his honesty.

"Chief," he said carefully, "Officer Roy Connor attacked a fellow officer here tonight, and it was totally unprovoked. You can see that Wygle is still having trouble breathing over there. Connor tried to choke him out using the LVNR, which he had no business doing.

And to make matters worse, he applied it wrong. He had his forearm across Wygle's throat. He could have crushed his larynx and killed him. Wygle probably should go to Beaches Baptist ER to get checked out."

The chief glanced over at Officer Wygle, who was being administered to by Dana Randall. He was sitting on the floor, his head between his legs. Dana had her arm around his shoulders and was trying to get him to take a sip of water. Without saying anything, Cooper looked back at Clay, indicating he wanted him to continue.

"This isn't the first time or even the tenth time that Connor has attacked someone without provocation. I mean, you can ask just about any officer in the department. They don't want to go as a Signal 35 on his calls because he has a tendency to get in citizens' faces and be verbally and physically abusive. He's been pulled off more prisoners than I can count, and he's still here. We . . . *I* think he dishonors the badge of the Jacksonville Beach Police Department!"

Cooper looked around the room at the officers and wives and asked, "Does anyone else here agree with Sergeant Randall's characterization of Officer Connor?"

Ty Honchen spoke up immediately, "Yes, Chief, I do. He's a loose cannon."

"I agree with Clay and Ty, too," Cassie Broderick added.

Each of the officers present added murmurs of assent to what had been said, all but the PIO, Bobby Hawkins. He had stood behind the chief the whole time, smirking at Clay and the others as they spoke.

He leaned over and spoke softly to Chief Cooper so that the rest of the group couldn't hear, "Chief, these guys just don't like aggressive cops. They think you have to kiss people's asses to get them to do things. Roy is a cop's cop. I would rather have one Roy Connor backing me in a tight spot than ten Clay Randalls."

Without responding to Bobby Hawkins, the chief looked at Roy Connor. He was still face down on the floor, his arms bound behind his back. The probes were still in place, wires running to the TASER Clay held in his right hand.

"Sergeant Randall, do you believe you need to keep that TASER attached to Officer Connor?"

Clay looked down at Connor along with everyone else in the room. He was asleep, snoring heavily. In the excitement and tension of the last few minutes, no one had noticed that the dozen beers had worked their magic, sending Roy Connor into a sodden slumber.

"No, sir, I guess not."

He reached down and yanked the probes out of Connor's back. The man grunted but otherwise gave no indication he felt anything.

"I don't think Officer Connor is an immediate danger to any of you here. Would someone be kind enough to remove those cuffs?" Chief Cooper asked.

"I'll take care of it, Chief," Ty volunteered.

He kneeled down and unlocked both cuffs, removing them from Connor's wrists as the big cop continued to enjoy his sleep on the floor.

"Officer Hawkins, would you please assist Officer Connor out of here and get him home? He doesn't appear to be in any condition to drive," the chief said sarcastically.

Bobby Hawkins immediately stepped forward and grabbed Connor by the left arm, rolling him over and pulling him to a sitting position. Connor's head rolled forward as he continued to snore.

"Roy, hey Roy!" Bobby yelled as he pulled up Connor's head. "Roy, wake up! Time to go home!"

Connor opened his eyes slowly, looking around the room. Spotting Clay, his eyes narrowed. "You bastard! You shot me! I'll—"

"Officer Connor," Chief Cooper said in a quiet voice as he squatted in front of Connor. "Do you recognize me?"

Connor stared bleary-eyed at the chief for a moment, trying to focus his eyes. They widened as recognition flooded in.

"Uh, yeah, I recognize you, Chief."

"That's good. Officer Connor, it will be to your distinct advantage if you don't say another word when I finish talking. I want you to get your drunk ass off this floor and walk out the door without looking left or right. I want you to get in Officer Hawkins' truck and allow him to drive you home. When you get there, I want you to go inside and go straight to bed. You with me so far? Nod your head if you are."

Roy Connor nodded his head slightly, turned to his right and let out a loud belch before looking again at the chief.

"You're doing fine. Stay with me a minute longer. I'm suspending you from duty, effective right now. That means I don't want you carrying your gun or your police identification with you anywhere. Come to my office Monday at 0800 hours. We will discuss your behavior here tonight at that time. Do you understand what I've told you?"

"Yes," he said.

"That's fine. Officer Hawkins, get Officer Connor out of here."

Hawkins helped Connor to his feet and walked him out of the building. The chief watched until they drove away before turning back and approaching Officer Wygle.

"How you feelin', son?"

"My throat's sore, Chief, but I'm alright. I don't need to go to the hospital," he said in a raspy voice.

"That's good news. Let me know Monday how you're doing. I'll deal with Officer Connor over this little incident. I guarantee it will never happen again."

Chief Cooper looked around the lodge at the remaining members of the birthday party.

"It appears it was a good thing that Officer Hawkins called me when he did. A few minutes later and something bad could have happened. This shows me these parties here are getting out of hand. I may have to shut them down for a while to save y'all from yourselves. It's obvious some of you can't hold your alcohol and act responsibly. I mean, the idea of using a TASER on one of your cop brothers," he said, shaking his head.

Clay couldn't let that pass, even if it pissed off Cooper. "Chief, if I hadn't tased him, he might've killed Shank, uh, Officer Wygle. Even with me and Ty and several others pulling on Connor's arms, we couldn't break his hold. I was the ranking officer here, so it was my decision to use the TASER."

"I'm sure you thought you did the right thing, but I'll have to think about whether I agree with you or not."

Glancing at his watch, he said, "It's late, and I want this building vacated immediately. Go home, all of you."

With that parting command, Chief Cooper strode out the front door, fully expecting his orders would be obeyed.

"What a sanctimonious asshole," Ty said. "He's not gonna do anything more than slap Connor on the wrist as usual. And that little weasel, Bobby Hawkins! I'd love to get his skinny neck in an LVNR and watch him do the funky chicken!"

"Well, I don't know about y'all," Yolanda said, "but this was the best thirtieth birthday I could possibly have had. Great food, plenty to drink, a fight, Roy Connor riding a TASER, Chief Cooper showing up at the party; it don't hardly get any better than that!"

Nobody wanted to test the chief's direct order to break up the party. They did a quick cleanup, gave 'Landa a last birthday hug, and headed out the door for home.

As Clay and Dana drove home, she asked, "How do you put up with a guy like that?"

"Who, Cooper or Connor?"

"Well, now that you mention it, both! They're two of a kind. Connor intimidates with his size and his willingness to use his fists. Obviously, Cooper's not physically threatening, but he does a good job with his voice and words. With both of them, it's all about exercising power over others. I just don't understand people like that. And I truly don't understand why you stay in a police department with people like them, especially with a man like Cooper in charge."

"Honey, I seldom have to talk to the man, and I don't see Connor very often either. But you know a lot of people in the department, and most of them are honorable. There are very few like Connor, fortunately.

"Anyway, it's just a matter of time before he goes over the line far enough that Cooper won't be able to cover for him anymore. Or Cooper's finally gonna get into a big enough political switch that some mayor will finally get the balls to fire him. I'm just hanging on waiting for one or both of those things to happen."

"Well, sweetie," Dana said as she slid over to cuddle beside him, "for your sake, I hope it happens soon."

Chapter 19

On Monday morning, Clay met with his team, Cassie Broderick, Jeremy "Three" Rivers, and Ty Honchen. "Guys, before we talk about the murders, does anyone have anything they want to say about last Friday night?" Clay asked, referring to the birthday debacle at the FOP lodge.

"Yeah, I do," Cassie spoke up immediately. "That weasel Bobby Hawkins oughta have his butt kicked for calling the chief to come to the lodge. I've never liked the guy ever since he hit on me a couple of years ago even though he knew I was married. My opinion of him is even lower now that I know he's a spy for Cooper!"

"Oh, you have no idea how devious he is. He's made snide comments to me over the years about me not being good enough for Dana. You know he went to high school with her, and I'm sure he's still pissed because she never gave him a second look. He's also the reason the task force name was changed from Operation Street Cleaner to Operation Serial Killer."

"We wondered why you changed the name," Ty said. "What did Bobby do?"

"Weasel, not Bobby. That's his new nickname," Cassie exclaimed.

Ty grinned, "I'm good with that. What did Weasel have to do with the name of the task force getting changed?"

"Y'all remember how he objected to the name in the briefing?" Clay asked.

All three detectives nodded.

"He whined to the man about it, so Cooper called Mike and me in right after we got back from Barton's scene and chewed me out over the name. Said he heard it from Bobb-, 'scuse me, Weasel. Trust me, I have absolutely no use for the man on a whole bunch of levels."

Ty Honchen spoke up, "In the pecking order of dirtbags in this department, he takes a back seat to Roy Connor in my book. If that SOB even so much as looks in my direction again, I swear I'll beat him 'til his dog's eyes bleed!"

The team members howled as Ty sat there looking quizzically at them.

"What? What's so funny about it? I meant it! And his damn dog is just like him. He's Roy Connor in a cheap fur suit!"

That only made it worse. Three laughed so hard he fell out of his chair, tears streaming from his eyes. The commotion attracted Linda Greene, the only other person around at the time.

She stuck her head into the conference room and, seeing Three rolling on the floor, asked, "Jeremy, are you okay? Should I call Rescue?"

That set them all off on a fresh round of laughter that didn't subside until their stomachs hurt and they were gasping for breath.

Clay decided it was time to get down to business. "I'm sorry I raised the issue, guys. Let's get back on the murders. I'm still on the chief's radar for not clearing the cases, and I'm sure tasing Connor didn't help me."

As they started grinning, he held up his hand. "Let's stick with the homicides. Three, any prior sex offenses in Barton's background?"

Rivers, having recovered from his roll on the floor, cleared his throat and said, "There's at least a small amount of truth to the killer calling Barton a child molester. His rap sheet shows one conviction in Tampa for exposing himself to a sixteen-year-old female. He was homeless at the time, and he was taking a leak behind a building against a dumpster. Apparently, he was also drunk. He told the arresting officer that he thought it was okay since he was behind the building in an alley, and he really had to go. He claimed he had an enlarged prostate, and, when you gotta go, you gotta go.

"The female was an employee of Dunkin Donuts carrying trash out to their dumpster when she encountered our now-deceased friend. Barton heard a noise and turned around in mid-stream, giving the young lady a clear shot at his pecker. Problem was he just kept standing there staring at her as he pissed.

"A witness said Barton shook his pecker at her. She screamed, ran back inside, and called the cops. The witness grabbed Barton and held him until officers arrived. Barton's explanation for waving his wand at her was that he was, get this, 'just shakin' the dew off the lily.' He was convicted for exposure of sexual organs and served six months. Right after he got out, he left the area. Unfortunately for him, he picked Jax Beach as his new home, and the rest is history."

As the discussion continued among the detectives, Roy Connor was sitting in the chief's outer office watching Annie Kieran type memos. He had reported promptly at eight o'clock as he had been ordered, but after waiting an hour, his mood began to sour.

"It's nine o'clock. The chief said he wanted me here at eight. Do you know when he's gonna call me in?"

Annie continued to type a moment longer, paused, and then peered at Connor over the top of her glasses.

"Officer Connor, you can see the chief's door is closed. I've told you already that he's in there. He will call you in when he's ready to talk to you. Now, be a good lad and allow me to finish this memo."

Connor slumped in his chair, irritated at the little Irish woman for talking down to him. *Sorry broad*, he thought to himself. *They shouldn't allow foreigners to take jobs away from hard-working Americans. She still talks with that Irish accent after being here all these years. Called me a 'good lad.' I'd love to put her in a chicken hold and see if her accent still hangs in there.*

Annie was spared further vicious musings as Chief Cooper opened his door and crooked his finger at Connor. Without waiting, Cooper walked back to his desk. He settled into his high-back chair, leaned over and sent a stream of Redman into his spittoon, and kicked back, propping his pearl-grey, lizard-skin cowboy boots on the corner of his desk. Connor stood in front of Chief Cooper's desk.

"Close the door, Officer Connor," Gordy said in his deep voice.

Connor walked back and closed the door before returning to stand again in front of the chief's desk.

"Sit down," Gordy commanded.

As Roy settled into the straight-backed chair, he glanced at the man, trying to read his mood. Chief Cooper was the one person who could intimidate the big cop. He didn't feel physically threatened because he knew he could easily break the little man in two. It was the man's aura of power and intensity that was very disconcerting to Roy.

"Officer Connor, I see you have your uniform on this morning. I don't recall authorizing you to wear it. In fact, I specifically recall suspending you and directing you not to carry your weapon or identification, which obviously would mean that you couldn't wear your uniform.

"I realize I'm getting older, and sometimes my memory isn't as clear as it used to be. So, is that what has occurred in this instance, Officer Connor? Has my memory failed me, or have you disobeyed my direct order?"

"Uh, no . . . I, I mean, yes . . . I mean, I guess I forgot what you told me, Chief."

"I can buy that, Officer Connor. After all, you were not exactly sober at the time we discussed this, now were you?"

"Well, I uh, I had a few beers at the party, so . . ."

"So . . . what? Do you agree or disagree that you were not sober?"

"I agree. I was drunk, Chief. What can I say? It was a party, you know? Free beer."

"Oh, now I understand. Party plus free beer equals freedom to get wasted and act like a complete fool. Is that what you're saying, Officer Connor?"

"No, not exactly. I guess I just didn't pay close attention to how many beers I was drinking. I'm sorry to cause a problem, Chief. I won't let it happen again."

"Let's set aside the drinking issue a moment and move on to the incident with Officer Ben Wygle. Do you recall that, or did the alcohol cause you to forget that little incident the way you forgot about being suspended?"

"No, I remember it," he said, glancing at Cooper and then dropping his eyes.

"Would you like to share your recollection of the events that led up to your attempt to choke out a fellow officer?"

"I uh, got upset at something Wygle said."

"And what would that be, Officer Connor?"

"He dissed me, Chief."

"And how did Officer Wygle . . . diss you, as you call it?" the chief asked, continuing to speak in a calm voice.

"He told me I oughta put my beer down and that I had drank too much."

By the end of his explanation, Connor was almost mumbling as he realized how foolish he sounded.

"So, let me see if I understand this correctly, Officer Connor. You had too much to drink, by your own admission, and Officer Wygle was kind enough to point that out to you. Is that correct?"

"Uh, yeah, I guess that's right."

"Alright. Then your thoughtful response to Officer Wygle's sincere efforts to take care of a fellow officer was to try to choke him out by means of the LVNR, which you used incorrectly."

Connor couldn't look at the chief. "That's about it."

"And that action is what led to Detective Sergeant Randall deploying his TASER and then handcuffing you like a criminal."

"Yeah," Connor said loudly, eyes flashing and temper rising. "Randall didn't have any right to do what he did! What I did to Wygle didn't deserve getting tased and then cuffed!"

Cooper abruptly stood up, leaning across his desk as his eyes narrowed to slits and his voice got even softer, "Officer Connor, don't ever, and I mean *ever*, raise your voice to me again. I'll rip that badge off your shirt and send your ass to the unemployment line so fast you won't have time to think about your stupidity. Do I make myself clear to you?"

"Yes, Chief. I'm sorry. It won't ever happen again."

Gordy sat back down, continuing to stare at Connor. "What am I going to do with you, Officer Connor? I have had to address your overly-aggressive actions several times in your career here. You hustle on the street and arrest plenty of criminals, which makes me look good to our citizens. But then you turn around and punch out someone who didn't need it, or you do something like this little stunt at that party. Then I have to smooth things over, and I don't like doing that.

"When you do your job right, you make deposits with me in your goodwill account. And when you screw up, you make withdrawals from that same account. I'm afraid your account is just about empty, Officer Connor. And you don't have overdraft insurance, you understand what I'm saying? It means you're about overdrawn, and, when that happens, I'll take your badge from you.

"So, considering your actions at the party, this is my decision. Effective today, you're no longer a K-9 officer."

"But Chief," Connor started to protest.

"Shut up!" he bellowed at Connor. "Don't interrupt me! Turn in your dog and your gear to the K-9 sergeant and report out on the midnight shift tonight! And if you say one more word or do anything other than walk out that door and follow my directions to the letter, I'll fire your ass! And I'll make sure you never get another job as a cop!"

Connor stood without a word and walked out the door. Although livid that he was losing his dog, he was still relieved the chief hadn't fired him or given him a stiff suspension without pay.

As Connor left the building, he raged, *This is all Randall's fault. I'll get that bastard. I'll shove that TASER so far up his ass he'll take a ride every time he farts*!

Chapter 20

By late April, Operation Serial Killer was floundering. Clay and his team of detectives had examined every scrap of evidence from the murders of Marilyn Gibbs and James Barton. The backgrounds of both were exhaustively reviewed, but nothing they found provided sufficient information to allow the detectives to focus in a specific direction. Clay had been on the local Crime Stoppers program discussing the cases and asking for anyone with any information to contact the police department, all to no avail.

The team had discussed the watermark on the note left on Barton's chest, and they had spent many hours scouring the Internet looking for something, anything, that would reveal the meaning of the **ESE** letters. No luck.

Chief Cooper demanded weekly updates from Clay on the progress of the investigation. The meetings with Gordy were agony for him since he didn't have anything positive to report. Clay expected at each meeting to be told he was being replaced as the lead investigator, but, at least so far, he had been spared that particular humiliation.

Clay and his team were in the conference room going over the case files yet again when Mike Wilson stuck his head in the door.

"I've got something. Panama City Beach detectives are working a homicide involving a hooker. A witness was running on the beach around midnight two nights ago when he heard a woman scream. He saw a man standing over a woman, who turned out to be the prostitute. The killer had apparently just opened her up like a can of soup.

"Turns out the witness is a Navy SEAL. He yelled at the guy and started running toward him. When the killer saw him, he took off. He had about a twenty yard lead, and the SEAL had to run through loose sand. As soon as he saw all the blood, he figured she was dead, so he kept going after the killer."

The detectives focused intently on the information Wilson was giving them, all taking notes as Mike talked.

"The witness hit the street just in time to see a light colored BMW take off with its lights off. He saw one person in the car when it passed under a streetlight, but he couldn't read the tag. The man said he didn't see any other cars moving or anyone walking, so Panama City is pretty confident the killer was in that car."

"Could we be dealing with a traveling serial killer?" Ty Honchen interjected.

"Maybe," Clay said. "Contact the lead detective, and get a copy of their paperwork. Check with them also to see if they had the witness look at various BMW models to try to narrow down the specific car. Then we need to get the information out to the troops."

12:30 a.m. the previous Monday night

Everything had gone according to plan at first. The killer had been in Panama City Beach two days, cruising the beach area looking for his latest victim. The first night yielded no hookers, so tonight, he had changed tactics. Parking his car a block away from the Catamaran Beach Club, he strolled into the bar and ordered a beer. The music blaring from huge speakers was Jimmy Buffet at his finest, just what you would expect from a beach bar, he thought.

As he surveyed the crowd, the killer sensed someone moving close to him. He looked down into the face of a pretty young woman who couldn't have been more than nineteen or twenty. She stood only five feet tall and may have weighed a hundred pounds with all her clothes on, a weight she didn't come close to this night.

She was dressed in a string bikini top that showcased pert breasts and very short shorts that covered less of her butt than was left exposed. As the man admired the cute beach bunny, his eyes were drawn to a tattoo on her right breast of a red and black ladybug sitting on a yellow sunflower. In her ears, the young woman wore tiny red and black ladybug studs.

"Hi," she said, almost yelling to be heard over the music. "Big crowd tonight, isn't it?"

"It sure is," he responded with a smile, also speaking up. "I'm in town on business and thought I'd check out the night life. It's loud and lively, I'll say that."

She smiled back at the man. Leaning close, she spoke directly into his ear, "Are you meeting someone tonight?"

"You," he grinned.

"Well, here I am. I'm Stacy," she said, extending her hand.

He took her hand in both of his. "I'm happy to meet you, Stacy. I'm Bob. Uh, if I'm not being too personal, not that I'm trying to stare at your breasts or anything," he said with a disarming smile. "But, what's the story on your ladybug tattoo and the ones in your ears?"

Stacy glanced down at her breast and then back at the man, smiling. "I've always liked ladybugs. They're tiny but cute, you know? Like me," she said with a mischievous grin.

The man grinned back at her. "I can see that."

"You wanta go somewhere quieter so we can get to know each other better?" Stacy asked with a coquettish smile.

"Sounds good to me," he said as he drained his beer and followed her out the door.

After strolling along the street for a couple of blocks, she stopped. "Let's walk on the beach. I love to feel the sand between my toes," she said, pulling off her sandals and stepping onto the soft sand.

They continued their leisurely walk until they came to a wooden bridge leading to the beach from one of the numerous hotels facing the Gulf of Mexico. Without hesitation, Stacy grabbed the man's hand and pulled him under the walkover.

"Alright, Bob. It's just you and me here all alone. I had a feeling you were looking for something when I saw you at the bar. Was I right?"

"Wow, you must be a mind reader."

"So, let's get down to business. I've got other appointments. What do you want?"

"Man, you don't waste any time, do you?" the man asked in an "aw shucks" tone of voice.

"As the saying goes, 'time is money,' and I'm in the business of making as much as I can," Stacy retorted, not at all fooled by the man's innocent demeanor.

"Okay, since you obviously know what I'm looking for, what do you charge for a blow job?"

"For you, because I like you, twenty bucks," she said crisply.

"It's a deal," the killer said.

"Then, Bob, if you'll show me President Andrew Jackson, I'll get to work!"

The killer pulled out a twenty and held it in his left hand as he unzipped his pants with his right. Stacy took the bill and slipped it into her bathing suit top. Without pausing, she went immediately to her knees and got to work.

The killer looked quickly in both directions, seeing nothing but deserted beach. He carefully slid his hand into his coat pocket, trying not to give his newest target any warning of what was to come. As he began to withdraw his hand with the knife, she sensed the movement and looked, spying the instrument of her coming death.

Stacy immediately leaned away from the killer, rocking back on her heels as she started to get to her feet.

"Hey, what's the deal? What's with the knife?"

In one fluid motion, the killer slashed the young woman's face, opening her left cheek from ear to chin. Stacy took two stumbling steps backward, screaming in a strangled voice as blood from the massive wound flowed down her throat, threatening to drown her. The killer lunged at his victim, swinging the knife in a deadly arc that opened a gaping wound in her abdomen.

He watched as she fell forward onto the sand, her life's blood turning the white sand a muddy red color. At that moment, he was interrupted by shouts. Looking over his left shoulder, he saw a man running toward him. The killer quickly reached down and ripped one of the ladybug studs out of the dead woman's ear before sprinting away, dashing across the sidewalk and down the street to his car.

As the man headed northeast on State Highway 231 in the direction of Interstate 10, he looked down and saw the whore's blood on his pants. Cursing steadily at his close call, he maintained the presence of mind to keep his speed under the limit. He knew he couldn't explain the blood on his pants if a cop stopped him.

The killer reached into his shirt pocket and pulled out the tiny ladybug stud he had ripped out of Stacy's ear. He regretted he had not had time to acquire both of them and even fantasized a moment on how stimulating it would have been to have removed her ladybug tattoo with his knife and taken it, also.

The man had not expected the interruption as he harvested his latest victim. But, being the very intelligent, highly adaptable, and evolved human he knew himself to be, the man was not surprised that he was able to escape unscathed.

As the killer drove on through the night toward Jacksonville, he tuned in the car's satellite radio to his favorite late-night program and listened intently, smiling and nodding frequently with the ideas espoused by the program's ranting political extremist.

Chapter 21

Clay and Dana sat in the bar in Harry's Seafood Bar & Grille. They both loved the New Orleans-style food Harry's served as well as the relaxed and friendly atmosphere. Clay ordered a beer while Dana stayed with water and lemon.

"You don't want your usual glass of wine?"

"No, I'm a little tired, and one glass would put me under the table," Dana said with a smile. "So, tell me how your murder investigation is going."

"It's not," he said in a discouraged tone. "We've found no solid connection between Marilyn Gibbs and James Barton other than they were both killed with a double-edged knife similar to a dagger. But I have no doubt our man killed Barton because he witnessed him killing Gibbs. And then there's the note left on his chest. I'm not sure what to think of it unless it was put there to try to throw us off."

"I tried to get 'Landa and Cassie to tell me what the note said that morning, but they said they couldn't. What did it say, anyway?" Dana asked, still very curious since everyone involved seemed to be treating the note so mysteriously.

Clay leaned toward Dana, lowering his voice. "I'll tell you, but you have to keep this very confidential. If word leaked out that I told you, my ass would be in a sling."

"Clay, don't you know by now that I never repeat anything you tell me in confidence?"

At that moment, the server stopped at their table. "Are y'all ready to order, or would you like a few more minutes?" she asked.

"We're ready," Clay said, ordering Jambalaya for both of them, a spicy Cajun dish with shrimp, chicken, and smoked sausage. As the server jotted down the order and headed off, Clay leaned forward again. "The note said, 'One dead child molester, twenty children saved.' Only problem with that is Barton wasn't really what would be classified as a true child molester. He got arrested down south for taking a leak behind a donut place and then shaking his pecker at a sixteen-year-old employee who came out there to dump trash. I don't know for sure, but, taking everything into consideration, the message just doesn't feel right. I really think it was done in hopes of sending us in the wrong direction. That's what I told Mike Wilson and the guys, and they agree with me."

"Since you don't think the message means anything, what's the big deal about revealing it then?" Dana asked in confusion.

"Because it's part of the active investigation, and it could still end up being a key to solving both murders. So we don't want it plastered on the front page of the newspaper or hear Kyle Meenan talking about it on the news."

"Why not? It seems to me the more people who know what the note says, the better chance you have for someone to call and say, 'Hey, that sounds like something so-and-so would say,' don't you think?"

"That might be a remote possibility, but I seriously doubt it. There's just too great a risk of our publicizing it and then having it screw up the case. So, anyway, what's happening with your show at the Lansing Gallery?" Clay asked, trying to steer the conversation away from the murders.

Not to be deterred, Dana persevered. "Well, if you won't talk about the message, what's with the picture in a frame I heard you talking to Cassie Broderick about on the phone last night?"

"You know, I sometimes forget how relentless you can be when you want something."

"Yeah, so? You should know by now that persistence is one of my best qualities."

"I could argue that point, sweetie," he said with a bemused grin. "About the picture. Barton's adult daughter, Meghan Barton, is the child in the picture. It was taken when she was about six. She wrote an inscription on it, 'To Daddy from Meghan. I love you.' The picture was mounted in a small, red plastic frame. Meghan claimed her father always kept the picture with him wherever he went, but it wasn't in his personal effects. She thinks the killer took it, but I'm kinda doubtful. I mean, c'mon. The guy's been a transient for years, traveling around the state, living outdoors the whole time. I'm pretty sure he just lost it somewhere along the way, but we logged the information just in case. Cassie thinks there's something to it, so she still brings it up occasionally.

"Now, enough about the homicides. I'm spending every day all day living with it, and I'm pretty sick of talking about it. It's your turn to tell me what's happening with you. Are you ready for your show?"

"Yeah, I'm good. I've got eight watercolors and six oils wrapped and ready to go to the gallery. I'm so pumped about it! It's actually a dual show with my work and Peter Pettegrew! Can you believe it?"

"Who's Peter Pettegrew? Wasn't he that guy who could turn into a rat in one of the Harry Potter movies?" Clay asked Dana innocently.

"Oh, boy. No, my love, he's not that character. I forget you're absolutely clueless about the art world. *This* Peter Pettegrew is one of the top landscape artists in Florida, if not the country, and I'm getting equal billing with him!"

"That's great, Dana! I mean it. I know my art education is somewhat limited, but I'm smart enough to recognize true talent, and I've never doubted that you're a fantastic artist. So I'm not surprised that you're getting a show with what's-his-name, Peter . . . "

"Peter Pettegrew, sweetie. And thanks," Dana said with a grin.

The food arrived, and their conversation turned to other topics. Halfway through the meal, Robert Trevino, Harry's Proprietor, stopped by their table.

"Hi, Dana, how's it going? Still keeping Sergeant Randall around, I see," he said with a grin.

"Oh, yeah, Robert. He makes a good bodyguard and chauffeur," she said, returning the grin.

"Everything okay with your meals?"

"Outstanding as always, Robert," Clay said, mumbling through a mouthful of Jambalaya.

"Okay, guys. Let me know if you need anything," he said, moving on to greet his other customers.

When they finished, Clay ordered their favorite after-dinner drink, coffee with a snifter of Amaretto liqueur on the side, but Dana stopped the server before she could leave.

"Make mine decaf, please, and no Amaretto."

"You got it," the server responded, as Clay looked at Dana with raised eyebrows.

"No Amaretto? What's going on? You always have coffee and Amaretto after dinner. And what's with decaf?"

"I, uh, I'm just not in the mood for alcohol tonight. Remember? One drink and I'll be under the table," she reminded him.

Dana avoided looking at Clay, instead staring intently at the cocktail napkin under her water glass as her fingernails turned it into confetti.

Clay watched her hands flutter nervously. "What is it, Dana? Are you sick?"

"No, no, I'm fine. It's just . . ."

"Just what, Dana? What is it?" Clay asked as he leaned across the table and took her hands in his. "Talk to me, babe."

"This isn't the way I wanted to tell you," Dana said with regret in her voice as she looked up at her husband.

Clay was becoming more confused and more tense as the moments passed. He didn't understand what was wrong, but it was obvious his wife was struggling to tell him something.

"Just say it. Whatever it is. We'll deal with it. Wait. I remember now. You went to the doctor today. Do you . . . is there something wrong?" he asked, anguish clear in his voice.

"Oh, Clay, my darling, nothing is physically wrong with me. I'm very healthy. It's just . . . I wanted to be someplace romantic, like walking on the beach, but here goes. I'm pregnant," she said with a huge grin on her face.

Clay stared at his beautiful wife trying to process what she had just said. He had already convinced himself that the woman of his dreams, the love of his life, the best part of himself, had cancer or some other deadly disease.

"Wha, What did you say?"

"I'm pregnant. I'm with child. I have a bun in the oven. I'm knocked up. I'm going to have a baby . . . our baby! Is that descriptive enough, my love?"

"Oh, my God! You're pregnant!" Clay gasped.

"Wow! Your vast experience as a detective enabled you to decipher my coded phrases and draw the correct conclusion! I am *so* impressed," she laughed, squeezing his hands.

Clay grinned back at his wife as he came to a full realization of Dana's pronouncement. He was going to be a father. He raised both of her hands and kissed each one tenderly. Then he stepped to her side of the table and took her in his arms, planting kisses all over her face and neck.

He said in a voice loud enough for everyone in the bar to hear, "Hey, everybody! My beautiful wife is going to have a baby! I'm going to be a mother! And she's going to be a father!"

As the twenty or so people all laughed and cheered at the announcement and Clay's botched description, Dana corrected him, "Clay, I think I'll be the mother, if you don't mind, and you can be the father, okay?"

He was confused for a moment before he realized his mistake.

Blushing, he said, "Hey, mother, father, I don't care. I'm just so happy I can hardly stand it!"

After a round of champagne on the house for everyone and a glass of sparking water for Dana, they finally escaped to their car and headed home. As Clay drove, he held Dana's hand.

"I'm still having trouble believing it. We've been trying for what, six months? I was beginning to think it wasn't going to happen."

Dana looked at Clay and felt tears of joy welling up.

"I've been doing a lot of praying about this. I felt strongly when I went in to see the doctor that he was going to tell me I was pregnant, and I was right. My prayers were answered. We're going to have a baby, Clay," Dana said as the tears rolled down her cheeks.

"I would love for you to scoot over here, but you have to stay in your seatbelt to protect our baby," Clay grinned.

He pulled into the garage at home, shut off the engine, and leaned over, tenderly kissing her tears away. "You're going to be an awesome mother. And our son is gonna be so handsome, and he's gonna be a world class athlete, and—"

Dana laughed as she pulled away, "Son? We're having a daughter, sport. She'll be beautiful, with long legs, dark hair, gorgeous blue eyes like her daddy, *and* be a world class athlete!"

"That's okay with me, too," Clay said as they entered their home, both contemplating the dramatic changes that would affect their lives in the coming months and years.

The gathering storm clouds were still below the horizon, hidden in the future; events unseen, unanticipated, personal trials for which they were totally unprepared.

Chapter 22

"Clay, tell me again why we're riding up and down First Street on a Friday night when you could be home with Dana, and I could be watching reruns of Sex and the City," Cassie said.

"Sex and the City reruns? What about Mickey, that 'gorgeous hunk of a fireman,' as you refer to your husband? Did you forget him?"

"No, of course not. But he's on duty tonight, hence TV and a glass of Merlot for me. Anyway, you're avoiding the basic question."

Clay grimaced as he drove their unmarked detective car through the pier parking lot, dodging the dozens of revelers who crowded into downtown Jacksonville Beach every weekend to enjoy the beach during the day and the bars and restaurants at night. Jax Beach, as most locals called the town, was considered the playground of the county. Of the three beach communities, it was the only one with substantial parking, all of it free.

"Aw, it's probably a waste of time, but we've run out of leads to chase. The only thing new to come up recently is the murder in Panama City Beach. I'm still not sure it's related to our cases, but the physical description is similar, and the Navy guy who witnessed it gave a so-so description of the man's car. Consequently, I figured we might as well look for a light-colored Beemer occupied by a white male about six feet, one-eighty, with short brown hair."

"So, get with the program, Detective Broderick. Let's find this guy so I can stay at home and satisfy my pregnant little wife's every whim, feeding her ice cream and pickles or whatever weird food fetishes women in her condition have. And you can get back to reruns and wine, whataya say?" he asked with a smile.

By 1:45 a.m., the bars began disgorging their customers onto the sidewalks, and most had made it to their cars to leave after another night of hard partying. Clay and Cassie had parked in a dark corner of the pier parking lot to watch for the target car as well as any hookers trolling the streets or parking lots. Cassie, who had been slumped down in the passenger side of the front seat, sat up straight and stared wide-eyed at a light blue BMW cruising slowly southbound on First Street.

"Clay!" she hissed loudly. "Quit staring at that woman. She's not a hooker, even if her boobs are about to fall out of her top! See the BMW? There's a guy driving it," she exclaimed, pointing toward the car as it continued to travel slowly along First Street.

"Got it," Clay said as he cranked up the engine and headed for the exit. They entered First Street about one hundred yards behind the Beemer.

"And I wasn't staring at the woman *or* her boobs," Clay protested. "I was reading the words on her shirt. It said, 'If you lie **TO** me, you can't lie **WITH** me.' I thought that was pretty cool. I bet there's plenty of guys and girls who have trouble living up to that."

"Yeah, you're probably right," Cassie agreed. "Look, the car's slowing down by that girl walking by Chicago Pizza."

It was obvious from the young woman's reaction that the person driving the car was saying something to her. Clay pulled into a parking lot about fifty yards away where they both had a clear view. As they watched, the woman shook her head and walked off in the direction she had come. Looking over her shoulder, she said something neither detective could hear, but it was obvious from the look on her face that she was angry.

They were still not close enough to tell anything about the driver other than the fact it was a man. When the car started to move on, Clay gunned the engine and pulled out onto First Street again, staying about a half a block back. As the BMW passed Sneaker's, a local sports bar, the driver ran the stop sign, turning west onto Beach Boulevard.

"Aw, what a shame," Clay said. "The guy runs a stop sign right in front of the poh-lice, thereby requiring us to do our traffic duty and stop him."

Clay flipped on the unmarked car's grill lights and bumped his siren to get the man's attention while Cassie called in their location along with the car description and license tag. The Beemer eased through the stop sign at the next intersection and pulled into the Walgreen's parking lot.

"Let's do this by the book. We don't have enough PC to do a felony stop, but let's be extra cautious anyway. If it's our guy, just remember he carries a very sharp and very big knife."

"I won't have any trouble remembering it. You be sure you don't either, Clay Randall. First and last rule is always, 'Go home safe at the end of the night.' Everything else takes a back seat to that," Cassie said as they exited the car and started toward the BMW.

Clay walked slowly toward the driver's side while Cassie moved up toward the passenger's side. As he eased past the trunk of the car, he placed his hand on it to ensure it was closed. They had all been educated about criminals hiding in the trunk of a car and then jumping out to ambush an officer after he passed.

Small trunk, Clay thought. *Probably too small to hide anyone but a midget, but no sense taking any chances.*

He stopped just short of the driver's door, taking a position that would put the driver at a sight disadvantage. That allowed him to see over the man's shoulder and into the interior of the car.

He scanned quickly for weapons and, seeing nothing to raise an alarm, said, "Good evening, sir. I'm Sergeant Clay Randall with the Jacksonville Beach Police Department. I stopped you for running the stop sign back there on First Street as you turned onto Beach Boulevard. May I see your driver's license, insurance, and vehicle registration?"

The man looked over his left shoulder with an irritated expression on his face.

"Officer, I don't know what you're talking about. I didn't run any stop sign."

"Sir, please provide your license, insurance, and registration," Clay repeated evenly.

The man's voice started to rise. "You have *got* to be kidding me! This is bullshit! I'm minding my own business, and you decide to hassle me! Why don't you just trot on back to your car and go do something constructive? Like arrest a real criminal maybe. This city's full of them."

Clay continued to speak in a calm voice. "Sir, since you've failed after two requests to provide me with your driver's license, insurance information, and vehicle registration, I'm forced to assume that, one, you don't have a driver's license; two, you have no insurance on this obviously expensive car; or three, the car must be stolen, which means I *have* found a real criminal."

The man sputtered, "That's not true! None of it!"

"If it's not, please give me the information I've asked for, right now, without another word, or I'm going to take you out of this car and put you in handcuffs. And while you're at it, go ahead and step out of the car."

The man retrieved the three documents and handed them to Clay, all the while glaring as if he wanted to kill him. Clay noted immediately that the man was about six-one and weighed around two hundred pounds. He had short brown hair that, in the right light, looked almost blond. With a physical description similar to the serial killer, Clay's antenna rose higher. He signaled to Cassie to move closer.

Looking at the man's driver's license, he asked, "What is your name, sir?"

"You've got my license. Can't you read it?" the man responded sarcastically.

Clay looked up from the license. "I'll ask the question one more time, and, if you force me to ask any further questions more than once from this point onward, I'm going to arrest you for opposing a police officer. Do you understand?"

The look he gave Clay was filled with contempt, but he answered, "Yes."

"Fine. What is your name?"

"Emory Elliot Stovall."

"Thank you, Mr. Stovall. Where do you live?"

Stovall started to respond scornfully that his address was on the license, but he stopped himself.

"I live at 887 Ponte Vedra Boulevard, Ponte Vedra Beach, Florida, United States of America, Earth," obviously incapable of hiding his disdain entirely.

Clay suppressed a smile as he continued, "Thank you, Mr. Stovall. What model is this vehicle?"

"It's a BMW 750i, and it cost $90,000 as you're looking at it. Probably twice what you make in a year."

Clay ignored the jibe. "Mr. Stovall, what were you talking about with that young woman on First Street?"

Stovall looked warily at Clay. "What woman on First Street?"

"The woman you stopped your car and talked to in front of Chicago Pizza. Young, maybe late teens, about five-three, long blond hair in a ponytail, wearing a white long-sleeved top, faded blue jeans, and white sandals. You know, *that* woman."

"I don't know what you're talking about."

"Mr. Stovall, my partner and I sat and watched you pull up beside her and talk to her about something. She obviously wasn't buying whatever you were selling, because she was angry as she walked away. Now, I sense that you may be heading down that uncooperative road again, a road that will inevitably lead to metal bracelets and trips in the back seats of cars with a permanent odor of puke, urine, and other vile smells. Please tell me you're not going there."

Stovall stared at Clay before speaking. "Okay, I did stop to talk to a young lady. So what? I was asking her for directions."

"Really? Directions to where, Mr. Stovall?"

"To, uh, to the police department."

"The police department?" Clay asked in disbelief. "Why would you need directions to the police department?"

"I heard about your citizen police academy, and I wanted to sign up," he said without hesitation.

"With all due respect, that sounds highly unlikely to me. And assuming for a moment that you *were* asking the young lady for directions to the police department, why would that make her angry?"

"I'm not aware she was angry," Stovall said coolly. "I just asked her for directions, and she told me she didn't live here and couldn't help me. So, if that's all, why not give me my papers back and let me get on my way. And I believe I'll just wait on signing up for your little academy. Quite frankly, if you're typical of the officers in your department, I think *you* should attend it instead so you can learn how to treat innocent citizens like me."

"You'll be on your way shortly, Mr. Stovall. Just as soon as I issue you a traffic citation for running that stop sign. By the way, what is your occupation, sir?"

"Why do you need to know? Oh, never mind. I don't care. I'm wealthy and therefore am not required to drag myself to some boring job where I have to punch a clock every day and do menial tasks for small change. Certainly a man like you would understand that," he said scornfully.

Continuing to ignore Stovall's sarcastic digs, Clay observed, "You said you're wealthy, but you didn't say how you came into your money."

"I didn't, you're correct. Let's just say a wealthy relative died and left me a fortune, and I have parlayed that small fortune into a much larger one through my own innate skills."

"What exactly do you mean by *innate skills,* Mr. Stovall?"

"I invest in things that end up appreciating in value, and that's all that you need to know. Write me your pathetic little ticket so I can be off. I have a nice little bottle of Dom Perignon waiting for me at home."

Clay went back to his car to write the citation while Cassie stayed near Stovall to ensure he didn't get in his car and get a weapon or try to leave.

As she stood at the trunk of Stovall's car eyeing him, he said, "My, you're a tall, good looking woman. Don't tell me you're a cop, too."

Cassie just looked at Stovall, saying nothing.

"You're attractive in a masculine kind of way. That's a compliment and not a putdown, I assure you. I could use a woman who looks like you in one of my businesses." Stovall said with a slight smile.

"What kind of business would that be, slick? Streetwalking?" Cassie asked as she turned fully toward Stovall, glaring at him.

Stovall laughed out loud. "Oh, no, nothing so gauche as that. Much more refined, shall we say. And the pay is highly competitive. Let's say it would probably pay you twice what you're making now."

"I think your mouth just lost its connection to your brain, hotshot. If you're propositioning me to be a hooker, I'll figure out some charge to put on your ass and hook you up right now. If that's not what you're talking about, I'm not interested. I have a problem working for people I want to punch out. So, back off before I decide you're resisting a police officer."

As she said this, she put her hand on her TASER. Stovall looked at her a moment, smiled, and then turned away, staring toward the ocean.

Clay finished the ticket and came back to explain what Stovall had to do. After signing the citation and being given his copy, Stovall got into his car.

Clay said, "Mr. Stovall, we're going back to try to find that girl. And if we do, we'll see what she has to say about your conversation with her. Because I don't believe you asked her for directions. You also don't strike me as someone interested in learning about police work through our citizen police academy. I have a feeling we'll see each other again. Until then, you drive carefully."

Clay went back to the car and climbed behind the wheel. Cassie got into the passenger seat still steaming over Stovall's comments and wishing he had given her a reason to, as she liked to say, cuff him and stuff him.

Emory Elliot Stovall stood watching until the police car turned onto First Street and disappeared from sight. With a scowl, he got into his BMW, and took off, squealing tires as he hit A1A headed for his mansion in Ponte Vedra. As he drove, he tore the ticket into several pieces, letting them flutter out the window.

Chapter 23

"Think he's our guy?" Cassie asked.

"He's very cool. Maybe too cool. Most people are nervous when they get stopped by the cops, but he never showed any fear or hesitation. I don't know. What I *do* know is his story about asking her for directions is pure, unpasteurized B.S. Even if we don't find the girl, he's definitely someone to watch."

Clay drove along First Street from one end of downtown to the other, but she was nowhere to be found. He parked once again in the pier parking lot.

"Let's stroll around for a few minutes. Odds are slim she's still here, but we have to make sure."

"No argument from me. After that jerk tried to recruit me to be a hooker, I've got a personal stake in this."

"Cassie, you don't know that's what he meant. He may have wanted to hire you to be a model. You've got the height and the looks. Besides, you're telling me you're not at least a little flattered that he would think you're good-looking enough to be a high class call girl?" he asked with a grin.

"I got your high class call girl right here, buddy!" Cassie exclaimed, giving him the finger.

Clay laughed as they got out of the car. "That's one of the many things I like about you, Broderick. You're not intimidated by anyone or anything."

"I realized early on that I wouldn't get anywhere being a sissy. Only the strong survive in this world, and especially in police work."

As Cassie spoke, she and Clay were walking by a pickup truck in the parking lot. The window was down on the passenger side, and Cassie heard a girl crying. She stopped so suddenly that Clay almost ran into her.

"Hey, anything wrong?" she asked the young woman sitting in the passenger seat.

As she turned to look at them, they both realized she was the one they were trying to find.

"No, nothing's wrong. Go away," she said as tears rolled down her face.

They showed the young woman their badges and asked her to get out of the truck. She stepped out and leaned against the door, arms folded defensively across her chest.

"What do you want? I haven't done anything wrong. I'm just sitting here minding my own business."

"Miss, are you sure you're okay? The fact you're crying tells us that something is wrong. We'd like to help if we could," Clay said sincerely.

The young woman continued to sniffle, but she smiled slightly.

"No, thanks. Gary, he's my boyfriend, we had a fight earlier, and he walked off on the beach. He said he wanted to cool off. So I took a walk myself. I didn't want to be the first one back to the truck. I wanted him to be waiting and worrying about me. Pretty stupid, huh?"

"Listen, honey, from a woman's point of view, it makes perfect sense. I'm Detective Cassie Broderick, and this is my partner, Sergeant Clay Randall. What's your name?"

"Rene Carter."

"Could you show us some identification?" Cassie asked.

Rene reached into the truck and retrieved her purse, handing Cassie her driver's license. She noted Rene Carter was eighteen years old.

"Do you still live on Stilwell in Jacksonville?"

"Yes, ma'am."

"Rene, when you were walking along First Street, what did the man in the light blue BMW say to you?"

The young woman immediately looked down, obviously uncomfortable. "I guess you saw us, huh?"

"Yes, we did. You looked upset. Were you?"

"Yes, I was. I still am! I can't believe what he asked me!"

Clay and Cassie looked at each other. "What did he ask you, Miss Carter?" Clay prompted.

Rene glanced up at Clay and then immediately down again. They could see her face start to turn red even in the dim lighting on the parking lot.

"I, I'm embarrassed to say," Rene stammered.

Realizing the young woman was reluctant to reveal what happened in front of him, Clay glanced at Cassie.

"Detective Broderick, I've got to make a quick call. Would you talk to Miss Carter while I take care of it?"

"Got you covered, Sergeant," Cassie said, winking at Clay as he walked away.

As soon as Clay moved out of earshot, Rene looked up at Cassie and smiled weakly.

"I'm sorry I'm acting so silly. I was embarrassed to repeat what he said to me in front of your partner because, well . . ."

"Because he's a man?" Cassie finished.

"Yes, ma'am. I'm a pastor's daughter, and I've been pretty sheltered all my life, home schooled and all that. I'm just not used to people talking to me the way that man did."

"I understand, Rene. So tell me what he said, as near as you can remember, word for word."

"Well, as I said, I was walking just so I wouldn't be there when Gary got back. I heard this car driving really slow coming up behind me. I didn't think anything about it I guess because I was still thinking about the argument. Then I heard the guy in the car saying something. I looked over, and he was waving at me to come over to his car.

"He asked me if I needed a ride, and I told him I didn't and just kept walking. So he pulled up beside me again. I was starting to get freaked out, and I looked over at him to tell him to leave me alone. That's when he said it. I, I still can't believe he was so crude!"

"Go ahead, it's okay." Cassie said gently.

Rene took a deep breath, letting it out as the tension eased a little. She found Cassie easy to talk to.

She spoke softly, "He told me, 'I've got fifty bucks if you'll climb in and blow me,' and he had the most evil smile when he said it."

"What did you do?"

"I turned around right away and started walking away. And then I looked back and told him he was a disgusting pig and I was going to call the cops on him. Oh, I'm sorry, call the police on him."

"It's alright. We don't mind being called cops, Rene. Anyway, you did exactly the right thing except, I assume, you didn't call to report him."

"No," she said sheepishly. "I don't have my cell phone with me. I just went back to the truck and was sitting there still waiting for Gary when y'all came up."

"We were in the area and saw what happened, but we couldn't hear what was being said. We pulled him over for running a stop sign, so we know his name and where he lives. But what he did is not a crime, so we can't arrest him."

"It's not a crime?" Rene asked incredulously. "I can't believe it. It was just so offensive to me!"

"I understand your feelings, believe me, I do. There's nothing I'd like better than to put him in handcuffs and haul him off to jail, but he hasn't committed a crime. If you had been younger, a child, that's a different story, but . . . I'm sorry. There's nothing we can do, at least with this incident. I imagine he'll keep doing this sort of stuff, though, and, he may step over the line next time. And I hope I'm there when he does!"

"Thank you for being so understanding. I hope I never experience anything like that again. And if Gary would just get back, I could go home."

At that moment, she spotted him walking over the dunes from the beach.

"There he is, finally! Thank you again," she called over her shoulder as she ran to her boyfriend and grabbed him in a fierce hug.

Cassie walked back to the car and got in, briefing Clay on the conversation.

"I agree we don't have a case on this one, and that's a shame," he said. "I don't think we can classify Stovall as a suspect, but we can't eliminate him either. The physical description is in the range of what we got from Jimmy Barton on Marilyn Gibbs' murder, and the car and physical are similar to the killer's information from Panama City Beach. He's definitely somebody we need to put on our list of possibles. And how about the way he identified himself? Emory Elliot Stovall. What a pompous ass!"

"I thought the same thing. And when he implied that he wanted to hire me as a call girl, that *really* got to me. I came this close to choking him out right there in the Walgreen's parking lot," Cassie said, gesturing with her thumb and index finger about half an inch apart.

"If Roy Connor can choke out people who don't deserve it, I should be able to do it to a prick that does," she said with a grin.

"You know, now that you mention it, there *is* a resemblance to Connor. Not necessarily in looks, but definitely in personality. I bet if you looked up 'arrogant' in the dictionary, you'd probably find Roy Connor and Emory Elliot Stovall pictured side by side."

"You're right. Connor and Stovall are truly a pair of flaming assholes," Cassie said laughing.

"I think we've done as much as we can do tonight. Let's pack it in and get a fresh start on Monday. I believe I hear my pregnant wife calling me," Clay said with a grin as he headed for police headquarters to end their shift.

Chapter 24

The following Monday, Division Commander Mike Wilson met with the Operation Serial Killer task force for an update meeting.

"I asked Commander Wilson to sit in so he could get up to speed on the investigation and especially about our encounter with a guy last Friday night," Clay said.

Over the next twenty minutes, Clay and Cassie took turns sharing the events surrounding their encounter with Emory Elliot Stovall. When Clay told them about Stovall's thinly-disguised offer to hire Cassie as a hooker, Ty and Three looked at each other and burst out laughing.

"What's your problem?" Cassie asked indignantly, glaring at the two detectives.

"Cassie, we know you. I bet Clay had to grab you to keep you from knockin' his dick in the dirt!" Ty said with a laugh.

Even normally serious Mike Wilson had to smile at the mental picture of Cassie popping the haughty Stovall.

"Let's just say that Emory Elliot Stovall wouldn't want to see me seriously pissed."

"Trust me, we wouldn't either, Cassie," Clay agreed.

"Enough of the macho posturing," Mike Wilson said. "What do y'all have planned for this week?"

Clay said, "First, I've got Ty digging into Stovall's background. He'll do a workup on all previous residences, cars registered in his name, any jobs he's held, even though he claims he's independently wealthy. The usual. Second, we want to put out a prostitute detail using one of our female officers posing as a hooker to see if we can entice our killer to show himself."

"No. Out of the question. Way too dangerous. Next suggestion," Wilson objected.

"Hold on, Mike. Hear me out on this, please. We've been talking about this since we got the information from Panama City Beach. There are enough similarities between that one and Marilyn Gibbs, along with Donna Martin, the Atlantic Beach prostitute, that we think they may all be connected to the same guy.

"We also sent out a statewide message asking for information on similar killings. We got hits from Daytona Beach on two prostitutes killed with knives within the past year. Also, Tampa had one, and Key West had two. That makes seven hookers killed with knives in the past four years, plus Jimmy Barton. And we feel sure Barton was popped because he witnessed the Gibbs murder.

"One of the hookers killed in Key West lived long enough to describe her attacker. She said he was about six feet tall, one-seventy-five, short brown hair, medium build. That fits Barton's description of Gibbs' attacker as well as the Navy SEAL's description of the killer in Panama City Beach."

"You're telling me there's a guy bagging hookers all over the state, and now he's doing it here in *our* beach?" Mike asked.

"It sure looks that way, Commander," Cassie said. "That's why we think we should be more aggressive. They're prostitutes, yes, but they're still human beings, and we shouldn't be showing any less interest in finding the guy who killed them," she said vehemently.

Three Rivers spoke up, "Commander, the detail can be put together so our decoy is completely protected. We'll have a bunch of us in the immediate area, and the decoy will be wired, so we'll know everything that's being said at all times. If anything starts to get hinky, we'll move in and take the guy down. It'll be safety first."

"I'm not saying I'm approving this crazy idea, but, just for discussion purposes, who would you use as the decoy hooker?" Wilson asked.

Clay spoke up immediately, "Corri Jennings."

Mike Wilson thought about it for a moment. "She's tough, that's for sure. What is she, a black belt in karate or something like that?"

"No," Three said. "Corri is a power lifter. She could probably bench press all of us at one time. Anybody who screws with her will wish they had taken on a bear instead."

"Guys, I'm not feeling good about this, in spite of all your precautions. We all know the killing range for someone with a knife is twenty-one feet. Any cop who lets a guy get within that zone is just asking to get sliced and diced. And now you're talking about putting one of our cops within a foot of a possible serial killer. A guy who, if you're right, has already killed eight people in Florida alone. At least eight that we know of. Have any of you brilliant detectives even thought about asking Jennings if she wants to do this?"

The task force members glanced at each other. They knew they had the Detective Commander leaning their way, but Clay had to close the deal.

"We talked to her, and she's ready to go right now, today, if you give the approval, Mike. The body toll is eight so far, and we have no reason to think this guy's going to stop until we either put cuffs on him or a bullet in his head."

Commander Wilson looked at Clay and then each team member in turn. They stared back with anticipation on their faces.

"I probably should be committed for approving this. If it goes bad, I can just imagine what Chief Cooper will have to say. But that's my problem. As y'all have heard me say a time or two, 'The cloak of responsibility hangs heavy on the shoulders of a supervisor.' I got a feeling this cloak is going to end up breaking my back before it's over. Go put your operational plan together. I want to see it and be able to make adjustments as I see fit before you go forward. Understood?"

The task force members grinned at each other. "We already roughed out a draft, just in case you approved it, boss," Clay said.

"Anticipating my decisions is gonna get your ass in a sling one of these days, Randall!" Mike snapped at Clay. "Now get the hell to work so I can justify signing your pitiful paychecks."

As Commander Wilson left the conference room, the four detectives stayed, elated that they had convinced their boss to go along with the prostitute decoy idea. At the same time, they were mindful of the extreme danger Corri Jennings would be in if she encountered the knife-wielding killer.

"Where's Corri right now?" Cassie asked Clay.

"She's waiting in the break room for the verdict," Clay responded. "Would you go get her?"

Cassie left the conference room, returning within moments with Corri Jennings. She took a seat at the head of the conference table.

"Cassie told me it's a go," Corri said to the group.

"Yeah. Commander Wilson resisted at first, but we convinced him we could protect you, so he gave in," Clay said. "Let's talk about how we can ensure your protection. We all know that a vest is designed to stop bullets and not sharp instruments. And we also know from the autopsies on Gibbs and Barton that the guy uses a very sharp knife. So, any ideas how we can protect Corri in the event she gets up close and personal with our killer, and he decides he wants another notch on his knife handle?"

Three spoke up, "What's wrong with her wearing her vest? It won't totally stop a knife . . . wait, guys, don't look at me like that! I'm just speculating here. God forbid that it would ever get that far, but, in the unlikely event he was able to get his knife out and stab Corri, the vest would stop most of the force, and she would most likely . . . uh . . . you know . . . survive," he finished lamely.

"Three, your sensitivity for Jennings's feelings knows no bounds!" Clay said sarcastically. "I'm sure you just made her feel one hundred percent better!"

Turning to Jennings, Clay said, "Corri, just so you know, we don't plan to put you in a situation where the best you can hope for is to survive."

"Listen, guys. I'm a big girl. I pinned on the badge with my eyes wide open. I know there are risks in this job, and I'm willing to take them when it's necessary. In this case, I believe y'all can give me good enough coverage. And I'm confident in my own ability to take care of myself," Corri said with determination.

She turned to Rivers, "Three, not to put you down, but have y'all thought about the fact that I'm supposed to look like a hooker? A ballistic vest under a tee shirt is going to be a little obvious, don't you think? I mean, anything I wear short of a turtleneck will show the top of the vest, and I think you'll agree it's not exactly turtleneck weather in April."

All four detectives sat there a moment pondering the reality of what Corri had said.

"I can't let you do this without some type of body armor. It's just too dangerous," Clay said.

"Hey. I just thought of something that might help," Cassie interjected. "You know our vest covers have a pocket in the front for a ballistic plate, right?"

"Right," they said in chorus.

"And the vest plate covers basically the heart area, right?"

"Right again," Clay said.

"So, how about we contact the company that makes our vests and see if they could make a ceramic plate that would fit Corri's upper body . . . you know, at least the front side?"

"I don't know, Cassie," Ty said. "I imagine they fabricate those plates from one standard pattern. To make one specifically for Corri would probably be so expensive that the department would never pay for it. What do you think, Clay?"

Clay contemplated the problem for a few moments. "I tend to agree with Ty. While it would protect Corri much better than that small plate, I might have trouble convincing Mike Wilson to spend the money, depending on what it costs.

"Tell you what, Cassie, you and Corri contact the vendor and tell them what we're looking for and ask them what it would cost. I'll go to the Commander if it's not some crazy amount and try to get him to cut loose some money. In the meantime, Ty, you and Three start putting together an operational plan as if we're going to go forward with the decoy operation."

The team members nodded their assent and left to get started on their assignments.

Chapter 25

"I'm so nervous about this show," Dana said to Officer Bobby Hawkins as they stood in the entry hall of the Reid Lansing Gallery, located on First Street in Jacksonville Beach overlooking the ocean. "I've done small showings in St. Augustine and Gainesville, and they were great. But this is the big time. The Lansing Gallery is well-known in the art world. Outstanding artists like Deborah Southfield and Jamison Alexander have exhibited here. And I'm doing this show side-by-side with Peter Pettegrew."

Dana paused, frowning at the look that suddenly appeared on Hawkins' face. "Uh-uh. Don't go there, Bobby."

"Go where?" Hawkins asked with a grin.

"You know exactly what I'm talking about. *This* Peter Pettegrew is a very accomplished landscape artist, not a character in a novel. I swear, your jokes are as lame as Clay's!"

Bobby's grin vanished instantly at the mention of Dana's husband. "Dana, why do you put up with a jerk like him?"

"Bobby Hawkins, don't you dare talk about Clay that way!" Dana exclaimed with a scowl. "You and I have been friends for a lot of years, and I like you. But I won't stand here for one second and have you run down my husband. I love him with all my heart, and, if you ever want to have a civil conversation with me again, you better never, and I mean *never*, say another bad word about Clay where I can hear it!" she said heatedly, shaking a finger in his face.

Stalking out of the room, she left Hawkins standing there with his mouth open, unable to think of anything to say.

Damn, he thought. *I just don't understand what she sees in that guy. But I gotta be a little more cool if I'm ever gonna have a chance to get her away from him.*

Bobby turned and took up his position near the door. He had been hired by the gallery in his capacity as a police officer to provide security for the show, a gig known as an extra duty job. The pay was pretty good, and the nicely air conditioned gallery was just an extra perk. In addition, he got a chance to see the moneyed people who lived in the area, many of whom he knew through his parents from growing up in the wealthy Ponte Vedra Beach community.

Patrons of the arts had been arriving over the past half hour or so, and there were probably close to a hundred in attendance already. As Bobby surveyed the crowd, he caught the eye of a man about twenty feet away who was staring intently at him. When their eyes met, the man walked over, carrying a glass of champagne in his right hand.

"Good evening, Officer . . .?" the man said with a question in his voice.

"Oh, hi, Mr. Stovall. I'm Bobby Hawkins. Don't you remember me?"

Emory Elliot Stovall looked closely at the officer. "I'm sorry. Could you refresh my memory?"

"My parents are Maurice and Martha Hawkins. I was at your house years ago with my parents for a big party you threw for Al Gore when he was thinking about running for president. I was still in high school then, I think. I'm the one who did CPR on that woman who had a heart attack."

Emory Elliot stared at Hawkins as he tried to recall the incident from years ago. Suddenly, recognition dawned in his eyes.

"Okay, I remember you now, and I know your parents well. I must say I wasn't aware you were a police officer. I guess it's been a while since I've spoken to Maurice and Martha, what with my investments taking me around the world. How are they doing?"

"They're fine, Mr. Stovall. I'll tell them you asked about them. So, are you here to see Peter Pettegrew's or Dana Cappella's paintings?"

"I expect I'll peruse both artists before I leave tonight. I'm aware of Pettegrew's work. In fact, I commissioned Peter several years ago to do a rather large piece for my home. But, I must admit I'm not familiar with the work of this young lady, Dana Cappella."

"You probably know her parents, Martin and Roberta Cappella. They live in Ponte Vedra not too far from you."

"Of course, I know Marty and Roberta. Do you mean to tell me this Dana Cappella is their daughter?"

"Yes, sir, she sure is."

"I had no idea. Well, I'll have to cast a closer eye on her work, then."

Stovall hesitated a moment as a large group of patrons walked by, the men in tuxedos, as was Stovall, and the women dressed in varying styles of evening wear, jewels and cleavage abounding.

As they moved on, he stepped closer to Bobby, speaking softly, "I was wondering, Officer Hawkins, Bobby, are you familiar with a member of your force named Clay Randall?"

"Oh, I know him," Hawkins said, unable to keep the disdain out of his voice. "He's a sergeant with the department. And not very well liked, I might add."

"Well, well. I must admit I'm not surprised by your opinion of this man. I had the unfortunate occasion recently to encounter him, and I was most unhappy with the disrespectful manner in which I was treated."

Bobby perked up. Anything bad said about Clay Randall was like music to his ears.

"Mr. Stovall, I don't normally talk bad about a fellow officer, but Sergeant Randall has a reputation for treating our citizens with disrespect. I'm surprised Chief Cooper hasn't fired him before now. I think the only reason he keeps his job is because of the police union backing him no matter what he does," Hawkins lied with a straight face. "What did Randall do to you, if you don't mind my asking?"

"He and a large red-headed woman, her name was Border or something like that, claimed I ran a stop sign, and he wrote me a ticket for it. I have never been so insulted in my life by the way that man treated me. And the woman who was with him wasn't any better.

"If Gordy Cooper can't do any better in his hiring practices than those two, then I guess I need to discuss with some of my friends on your City Council about whether it's time that Gordy retired," Stovall said with rising indignation in his voice.

"Mr. Stovall, I'm sure Chief Cooper was not aware of the way Sergeant Randall and Detective Broderick treated you, but I assure you he'll know first thing tomorrow. I report directly to him, and I know he would want to know if a man of your standing in the community received poor treatment from one of his officers."

"Well, thank you, Bobby," Stovall smiled. "I appreciate your attention and your courtesy. This town needs more officers like you. One more question, if you don't mind."

"No, sir, not at all."

"Wasn't Randall on the news recently talking about those murders here in your fine community?"

"Yes, he was. He's been put in charge of a task force to solve the murder of a prostitute and a homeless man."

Hawkins glanced in both directions and then leaned in close to Stovall in a conspiratorial manner, "And I'll tell you, just between you and me, the chief is not happy with him because he can't solve either one of them. He's talked about replacing Randall with somebody with real investigative experience. Chief Cooper has even hinted he might want me to take charge of the task force," Hawkins said, a note of self-satisfaction in his voice. "If he gives it to me, I'll find the killer in no time at all."

"Really?" asked Emory Elliot. "Do you have a specific person in mind?"

Not expecting to be asked for specifics, Bobby hesitated as he tried to think of something intelligent to say. "Well, I, uh, I really can't say. You know, confidentiality of the investigation and all that."

"Of course, I completely understand. It's just that I've always been fascinated with police work. In fact, I briefly considered a career in law enforcement until I realized the standard of living was much lower than I wished to tolerate.

"About your investigation again, and I wouldn't want to put you in a bad position by asking you to reveal a confidence, so if you can't say anything, I certainly understand. But I heard a rumor that the man who killed these people here in Jacksonville Beach and Atlantic Beach also killed a number of other prostitutes throughout Florida."

Bobby looked at Emory Elliot in surprise, wondering how he could have found that out since, to his knowledge, the information had not yet been made public. He looked both directions again as if afraid the killer lurked behind one of the gallery columns, waiting to overhear the police department's secret plans to capture him.

"Mr. Stovall, I'm shocked that you know that. We just found that out yesterday, and it hasn't been publicized anywhere that I know of. If you don't mind my asking, where did you hear about that?"

"Oh, I just keep my ears open and pick up things here and there," he said vaguely.

Bobby looked so distressed that Stovall felt sorry for him. "Okay, I guess I can share this with you since you shared some inside information with me. I happen to be good friends with one of your fellow officers, Roy Connor. I rode with him in his police car last night when he was on duty. He was patrolling here in downtown Jax Beach, and he told me all about it. And by the way, he has the same opinion of Sergeant Randall."

Bobby Hawkins was amazed that a man of such sophistication and breeding as Mr. Stovall could be friends with a low class prick like Roy Connor. He kept those thoughts to himself, figuring if a wealthy man like Emory Elliot Stovall could have a friendship with Connor, then he should have no trouble developing a similar relationship. After all, it never hurt to have rich and influential people who claimed you as a friend.

"Well, since Roy told you, it's obvious he trusts you, but please, Mr. Stovall, don't repeat that information. Chief Cooper said he didn't want this information out until *he* was ready to release it. I'm really surprised that Roy told you, anyway. He's not high on Chief Cooper's list of favorite officers right now."

"I assure you, Officer Hawkins, that his, and your, secrets are safe with me," Emory Elliot said with a smile as he patted Bobby on the shoulder. "Now, if you'll excuse me, I should go mingle with the crowd and take a quick look at Ms. Cappella's work."

As he started to walk away, Bobby said, "Mr. Stovall, there's something else you should know. Dana Cappella paints under her maiden name, but her married name is Randall."

He waited to see if Stovall would make the connection. He didn't have to wait long.

"Bobby, you're telling me that Dana Cappella is married to Sergeant Randall?" he asked incredulously.

"Yes, she is," Bobby said with a smirk.

Stovall stood there looking at Hawkins, but it was obvious his mind was elsewhere as he processed this very interesting piece of information.

Walking away, he said over his shoulder, "Thank you again for your help, Bobby. You've just made my day."

Bobby Hawkins smiled as he watched Emory Elliot Stovall walk into the gallery where Dana's work was exhibited.

Always nice to have the opportunity to wreak a little havoc in Randall's life, he thought. *And to score a few points for myself. I just hope he won't try to hurt Dana's career just to get back at Randall, but, if she's so dead set on thinking he's a great guy, maybe it's time she found out that a lot of other people besides me think he's an asshole.*

Chapter 26

Stovall moved purposefully through the gallery looking for Dana Cappella, finally spotting her talking to a tall, well-dressed man as they stood in front of one of her larger pieces. The man was sipping from a flute of champagne as they talked.

Emory Elliot was curious to learn more about her, not only because he knew her parents, but also because she was married to Clay Randall, a man he intended to punish for having the audacity to treat him with disrespect. He casually positioned himself in front of another of Dana's pieces so he could hear their conversation.

"Ms. Cappella," the man said, "I've been to galleries all over the country, and I have seen literally hundreds of artists' works. I'm not sure exactly how to express this, but there's something about your work that just makes me feel good. Do you know what I mean?"

"I've been told that before. I don't think I can explain it, but I'll try. It's . . . well, it's like, when I start a piece, I have a definite idea of what it will look like when it's complete. But, as soon as my brush touches the canvas, something, or someone, takes over, and I'm no longer in control. It's like I become a spectator, standing back and watching someone else paint.

"I've heard writers say that they start with an outline that includes the way they plan to end their book. But then the characters take over, and they dictate to the writer what happens. And the ending is quite often very different from what the author initially envisioned. That's the way I feel when I paint.

"I don't know. Maybe part of it is that I'm a positive, happy person, and my paintings are a reflection of my subconscious. Whatever it is, I don't try to analyze it too deeply for fear I'll lose it. Does that make any sense?"

"It makes perfect sense to me," the man said. "By the way, my name is Ethan Hunter," he said as he extended his hand.

Dana shook his hand. "I'm glad to meet you, Mr. Hunter."

"My father is named Mr. Hunter. Please call me Ethan," he said with a dazzling smile.

"Okay, Ethan, and I'm Dana," she said, smiling in return.

Emery Elliot Stovall could wait no longer. He stepped directly in front of Dana, startling her and causing her to step back involuntarily.

"Ms. Cappella, Is it true you're married to a police officer named Clay Randall?"

Dana was startled by the man's abrupt question. Before she could speak, Hunter placed a hand on Stovall's shoulder.

"Excuse me, sir, but Ms. Cappella and I were having a private conversation."

Stovall shrugged off Hunter's hand, ignoring him as he continued to stare at Dana. "I asked you a question."

Hunter moved around Stovall and got in front of him. Staring into Stovall's eyes, he said, "I don't know who you are, and I don't care. But if you don't step away from Ms. Cappella right now, you may find that you have the ability to fly. Would you like to try?" Hunter asked, his eyes narrowed to slits.

Stovall looked at Ethan Hunter for the first time, recognizing a man who was not intimidated by him and who, from his size, appeared capable of doing exactly what he suggested. He glanced around and saw people shifting their attention from the many beautiful pieces of art to the confrontation taking place in the normally refined gallery. He thought of calling Bobby Hawkins over but decided he couldn't afford to create a bigger scene than he had already done.

Stepping around Hunter, he said, "I apologize if I came across a little strong, Ms. Cappella. My name is Emery Elliot Stovall, and I've known your parents for years. I'm very unhappy with the rude way your husband, Sergeant Randall, treated me when I was simply minding my own business. I intend to file a formal complaint against him with Police Chief Gordon Cooper," he said as his voice rose. "I planned to buy several of your pieces tonight, but there is no way I'll part with any of my money now, knowing your husband will get to enjoy it!"

Dana was stunned and didn't know what to say. She couldn't understand why the man was verbally attacking her over a disagreement he had apparently had with Clay, and right in the middle of her first, and maybe only, show at the Lansing Gallery.

Hunter once more came to her aid. "Mr. Stovall, You've said enough. It's obvious that you've greatly upset Ms. Cappella at a time when she should be experiencing great happiness. I think you should leave . . . right now," Hunter said as he put his hand on Stovall's arm and started walking him toward the front door.

Stovall tried to jerk away, but Hunter's grip was like steel. Before he could create any further disturbance, Ethan leaned close and spoke softly so that only Stovall could hear.

"If you continue to act like an asshole, I'll be more than happy to kick the shit out of you right here in front of your rich friends. If that's what you want, keep it up."

Emory Elliot felt the strength in the man's grip and heard the quiet intensity of his voice. He decided it would be in his best interests to leave without further resistance.

When they got to the front door, Ethan released his arm. Stovall turned to say something sarcastic to Hunter, but the look in the man's eyes stopped him. He walked away from the gallery without another word. Hunter stood watching Stovall until he rounded the corner out of sight.

As he turned to go back inside, he stepped on Dana's foot. "Oops! I'm sorry, Dana, I didn't know you were standing right behind me. Are you okay?"

"No, uh, yes, yes, I'm fine," Dana said with a smile. "As I tell my somewhat clumsy husband when we're dancing, 'You walk on the tops and I'll walk on the bottoms!' "

"I haven't heard that expression in years," Ethan laughed. "My mother used to say the same thing to my father when they went dancing, too. Seriously, are you okay? That guy was really harassing you."

"I was a little flustered, I'll admit. I don't know what happened between my husband and him, but it must have been pretty intense for him to be so agitated."

"Some people are just quick to anger. It's like they live their lives at two degrees below the boiling point, and it takes very little for their lid to pop off. Anyway, getting back to our discussion before we were so rudely interrupted," Ethan said, "I was about to ask if you take on commissioned work. I am so impressed with your talent that I would love to have you come to my home and paint a beach scene from my terrace. Is that something you do?"

Dana hesitated, not sure how to respond. She had just met this guy and knew nothing about him.

"I assure you my intentions are completely honorable and above board. I have a home on Duval Drive here in Jacksonville Beach, and my view of the ocean through the palm trees and other vegetation is spectacular. It's something I would love for a person of your talent to capture. By the way, do you know Gerard Harrison?" he asked.

Dana nodded, "I believe I've seen his work. Isn't he a well-known nature photographer here in Florida?"

"Yes, he is. His work is absolutely beautiful. Well, anyway, I hired him to shoot the view from my terrace, and I selected one to have enlarged and framed. In fact, it's hanging in my living room right now. But even though it's a gorgeous work of art, there's still something missing. Your work captures an indefinable essence that I'm convinced makes real-life photography pale in comparison. What do you say? Have I persuaded you yet?"

"Well, I don't know . . ."

"Tell you what," Hunter interrupted as he pulled a checkbook out of his jacket pocket. "Let me give you a down payment on the work. You take this check with you, and if you decide you don't want to do it, just tear it up, and there will be no hard feelings on my part. If you decide to accept the commission, though, this down payment will be one-third of the total price," Hunter said as he finished writing the check and handed it to her.

Dana glanced at the amount he had written. Her eyes widened as she saw ten thousand dollars written with a flourish. It didn't take a mathematician to figure that this man was offering her thirty thousand dollars for one painting, and they hadn't even discussed the size he wanted. That would be the largest commission Dana had received in her career thus far.

He must want me to paint his entire ceiling like the Sistine Chapel for that kind of money, she thought.

"I know. You're probably thinking I'm a head case to pay that much money for one painting. But I see what you're capable of doing, and I would consider it money well spent. An investment that no doubt will appreciate over time."

Dana glanced down at the check again and then up at the man. "Mr. Hunter . . . Ethan," she said as she extended her hand with a big grin, "You've just commissioned yourself a work of art."

Hunter grinned back as they shook hands to consummate the deal.

"Great! Here's my card with my cell number and address. Give me a call the first of the week to arrange a time to meet me at my home. And if he's available, please bring your husband with you. I've always been fascinated by the field of law enforcement, so this would be a perfect opportunity for me to get to talk to a professional about what police really do instead of what is shown on TV. Actually, if I'm not mistaken, I believe I've seen your husband on the local Crime Stopper's show. Isn't he in charge of the investigation into those terrible murders here at the beach?"

"Yes, he is. Clay is a very dedicated police officer and a great detective. And he's not rude to people either!" she said vehemently.

"I'm sure he's nothing like what that Stovall man claimed," Ethan said to reassure her. "After all, any man smart enough to marry a beautiful and talented lady like yourself couldn't be all bad. By the way, would you satisfy my curiosity about something? I heard Stovall refer to your husband as Clay Randall, and your name is Cappella. Is there some reason for the different last name?"

"No, it's not unusual. I had already started my career under my maiden name of Cappella. I kept it so people seeing my work wouldn't think Dana Randall and Dana Cappella were two different artists."

"That makes perfect sense," he said with a smile. "And now, if you'll excuse me, I think I should quit monopolizing your time as I see many other patrons wanting to discuss your work. I believe I'll go find a glass of champagne to celebrate what I know will be a magnificent addition to my home!"

As he moved off into the crowd, Dana folded the check and slipped it into the pocket of her dress. True to Hunter's observation, she was immediately inundated with art patrons. She spent the rest of the evening basking in the warm glow of positive feedback of her work and delicious anticipation of the moment she would tell Clay about her lucrative commission.

Chapter 27

The killer was angry, not the out of control rage he felt when he killed his stepfather, but certainly more so than he had been in a long time. Things were not going well at the moment. A speculative investment had gone belly up, shrinking his net worth by about five million dollars. It wasn't fatal. He had weathered market fluctuations before. But this wasn't a fluctuation in the market. His financial advisor had pushed him hard to invest in an Internet start-up firm hawking software that supposedly would make the iPhone as out-of-date as the rotary dial phone.

The man imagined using the "tool of release" on his financial advisor for being such a loser as to push him into this financial loss. Missing from his reverie was any conscious thought that he was ultimately responsible for decisions made about his own money. He simply was not wired to think negative thoughts about himself.

He was also angry because of a recent event in which he had not been accorded the respect he knew he deserved.

He thought, *I look forward to the opportunity to show him why he should have been respectful of me. Only a loser would fail to recognize my strength and power. He will live only long enough to regret his actions. When he looks into my eyes as I take his last breath, he will know why.*

Imagining murder and mayhem was nowhere nearly as satisfying as the real thing, the killer knew. That lust for blood was the reason he was once again dressed in his homeless disguise and prowling the Jacksonville Beach boardwalk near midnight. In the past week, he had twice donned his disguise searching for a suitable target.

Tonight, he was in luck. An hour earlier, he had spotted a woman sitting on a bench near the lifeguard station at the foot of Beach Boulevard. From the looks of her ratty clothing and a large handbag that appeared to be stuffed with the accoutrements of her pathetic life, she was obviously one of Jacksonville Beach's homeless.

The killer recognized her. He had an excellent memory for faces and places, as he liked to say. He remembered she asked if he needed anything one night in the pier parking lot when he was looking for a new victim. He had briefly considered taking her but ultimately decided there were too many people around who might remember seeing a well-dressed man walking onto the beach with a raggedy homeless woman.

He had no idea what her name was. Names weren't important to him anyway, only losers. He wouldn't have cared that her name was Nita Caruso. Since the horrible incident with Officer Roy Connor and Little Billy Bowen, Nita had stayed with friends across the ditch in Jacksonville, afraid to return, afraid she might encounter the brutal cop again. She had only come back to Jax Beach because she missed the funny, brave little dwarf who had stood up to Roy Connor. She hoped that, if she hung around the boardwalk, she would eventually run across him.

The killer stationed himself on another bench half a block away, pretending to read a dog-eared paperback as he watched Nita out of the corner of his eye. Two police officers had passed by while he watched, asking him for identification and what he was doing. He showed them a Florida identification card in the name of one of his mother's old boyfriends, a man dead for fifteen years. Having discovered that a man with sufficient cash could easily purchase false identification, the killer had half a dozen IDs in different names and addresses to use on his hunting expeditions if he were stopped.

The officers found nothing unusual to pique their interest. As they headed north on the boardwalk, the killer visualized lunging at them from behind, slashing the first one across the throat and stabbing the second in the back of the neck. In his mind's eye, he saw them fall, blood spurting from their wounds. He imagined the thoughts that would have raced through their minds as their lives faded away, *We should have checked this guy out closer. He looked a little too healthy and too alert to be a transient.*

The vision was so vivid that he almost missed his target getting to her feet and greeting a dwarf. She bent over and gave the little man an enthusiastic hug. He watched as Little Billy Bowen sat on the bench close to the woman. The bald-headed little man reminded him of the dwarf actor who starred in the Austin Powers movies.

Wouldn't it be ironic if that's who he was? he mused. *I haven't added a dwarf or an actor to my collection. What a hoot if I could kill two birds with one stone, or knife as it were*, he laughed to himself, amused at his own dry wit.

After talking a few minutes, the dwarf reached over and squeezed the woman's breast, saying something in her ear. She smiled in return and put her hand on his crotch. The killer felt revulsion at this open display of sexual attraction between two losers.

I was looking for one loser tonight, but I'll take a two-fer when it's right in front of me, he smiled to himself.

Nita and Little Billy stood and started walking toward the killer, the little man only coming as far up as the woman's hip. As they walked, he kept goosing her in the butt, Nita jumping with a laugh each time. Just before reaching the bench where their worst nightmare sat, they turned and started over the ramp, heading for the beach.

Oh, this is sweet! he crowed silently. *They're making it too easy for a man of my talents. Well, I takes 'em any way I gets 'em*, he quipped.

He waited until they were past the arch of the walkover before easing off his bench and strolling casually in the direction they had gone. He watched his targets step onto the sand and move under the walkover. Had they only looked up, they would have seen the cold-eyed man staring intently at them from the peak of the walkover.

His targets were in full-on heat and thinking only of satisfying their urges. He waited until he heard the distinct sounds of two people in the throes of sexual passion. Looking north and south of his position, he saw no one within range. He was ready.

The killer's heart rate started to increase as he quietly covered the short distance remaining until his shoes touched the beach. He slipped his knife out of his pocket and held it open in his right hand, razor-sharp blade pointing at the sand. The man took one more quick look in both directions. He didn't want a repeat of Panama City Beach.

The man was repulsed by the action taking place in the sand. The woman was on her back, naked from the waist down, her legs spread wide, toes pointing at the underside of the walkover. And the tiny man was on top of her, his pants around his ankles. His feet only reached the woman's knees, and his head barely reached her chin. The killer's disgust at the two homeless people going at each other was heightened by Nita's moans of pleasure as the dwarf attacked her body with great enthusiasm.

The man hesitated as he started to move toward Nita and Little Billy.

Wait, he thought. *I've got two for the taking, but, whichever one I take first, the other isn't going to lie there quietly waiting their turn. I need to silence them both quickly. How can I do that?* he asked himself.

And then it came to him. The killer smiled as he started forward again, Nita and Little Billy so engrossed in each other that they heard nothing except their own sounds of sexual delight. He slipped up and stood directly beside the two. Nita sensed another presence and opened her eyes, seeing a dark figure standing over Little Billy and her, holding something in his hand.

She gasped, "Billy, stop! Wait a second!" But Little Billy was nearing his climax and heard nothing.

"Billy!" Nita said sharply, "Stop!" as the man stood poised with what she could now see was a knife held only inches from Little Billy's neck.

The agitation in Nita's voice had finally filtered through the blood rushing in his ears, and he raised his head to look at her. Seeing the terror in her eyes, he peered up just in time to see the knife as the killer drove it down with such force that the blade cut straight through his neck and into Nita's chest. Little Billy's spinal cord was completely severed, leaving him instantly paralyzed, unable to move, speak or even breathe. His position on top of Nita ensured the blade would continue on its path directly into her heart.

Little Billy never got a chance to see the face of the man who sent him to his death. But Nita did. As she began to lose consciousness, Nita recognized the pale blue eyes of the man she had propositioned weeks before in the pier parking lot. She took the vision of those dead eyes with her as she followed Little Billy into eternity.

The killer left the knife in place and stepped back to admire his handiwork. Nita and Little Billy were literally bound together in death as they were in their last moments in life. After a few seconds, he realized it was time to leave.

The man grasped the handle of his knife and pulled, but it wouldn't budge. It was held in place by the stiff cartilage of Nita's breastbone and Little Billy's neck. He rocked the knife back and forth several times, but it still wouldn't move. The killer stood and placed his foot in the middle of Little Billy's back. Gripping the knife handle with both hands, he gave a violent yank. The blade came free of both corpses with a sickening, wet sound.

Kneeling once again, the killer examined Little Billy first to find his memento. He saw a gold-colored hoop earring in the little man's right ear and paused.

I thought only gay men wore an earring in just the right ear. What's he doing with a woman?

Then he noticed Little Billy's left ear lobe was torn open. *Okay, he can't wear one in the left ear*, he surmised, unaware that Little Billy's left ear lobe had been reshaped in his violent encounter with Officer Roy Connor.

Jerking the hoop from Little Billy's ear, the killer turned to Nita. This memento was easy. She had a pink rubber bracelet on her left wrist, the kind people wore to support women with breast cancer. *If you had breast cancer*, he thought, *I just saved you a lot of pain and suffering. That's because I'm such a nice guy.*

As he turned to go, pocketing the knife along with his newest trophies, he looked back, thinking, *Rot in hell with the rest of the pathetic losers this world has spawned.*

Chapter 28

Less than thirty minutes after butchering Nita Caruso and Little Billy Bowen, the killer pulled into the driveway of his expansive estate. Parking his BMW in the attached garage, he hit the button to lower the door. The killer got out of the car and turned to admire its sleek lines for a moment before heading into the house, shutting off the security alarm as he entered through the kitchen.

Opening the door to his Sub-Zero refrigerator, the killer removed a bottle of Dom Perignon Champagne, circa 1993, which had been chilled to the perfect serving temperature of 45 degrees. Carefully removing the cork, he filled a Baccarat flute two-thirds full with the delicious nectar before taking a small sip, just enough to savor the unbelievably rich taste.

The man was still dressed in his filthy disguise. Looking down at his tattered clothes, he laughed out loud at the absurdity of the situation. He thought, *I'm standing in my five million dollar home, drinking very expensive champagne to celebrate ridding the world of two more pieces of trash, while I'm looking and smelling exactly like the fucking losers I just killed! That's rich!*

Draining the champagne, the man climbed the Italian marble staircase to the second floor, stripping off his disguise as he entered the master bathroom. Reaching into the coat pocket, he pulled out the cheap rubber bracelet and the hoop earring. Flipping the bracelet around his index finger, the killer savored the memory of Nita's terror-filled eyes when she recognized the man who would collect her life as a hunter collects a trophy deer.

The killer felt an erection growing as he stared at the two mementoes. In addition to the sense of power that killing gave him, the act was tremendously erotic. Since murdering his adoptive mother years before, he had masturbated to relieve the sexual tension generated from each killing, now ten in all. As he did, he re-lived the feel of the knife cutting through skin, muscle, cartilage, and bone. He savored the fear that flooded his victims as their lives seeped away. Their pain became his pleasure, momentarily quieting the twin demons of rage and lust.

The man carried the items to a beautiful red oak bookcase covering most of one wall in the master bedroom suite. There, he placed them beside the small picture of Meghan Barton and the cheap metal cross he had taken from James Barton and Marilyn Gibbs after collecting their lives.

He stood a moment letting his eyes roam over the rest of the mementoes from his previous kills. There was the nose ring he had taken from Donna Martin, the hooker he killed in Atlantic Beach six months before. Next to it was the set of silver earrings he had torn from the ears of Marta Bailey after collecting her life in Daytona Beach the year before.

Picking up the earrings, he thought about Marta. She had been clean for a whore. He had met her through an escort service and had actually allowed her to give him a blow job before killing her, stopping short of ejaculating so he wouldn't leave any DNA for the stupid cops to discover.

Replacing the earrings, he brushed his fingers over the sunglasses he had taken off Mary Stein's face, noting again the spots of dried blood that had splashed upward when he had cut her throat in a cheap motel room in Daytona two months before he killed Marta.

Only glancing at the rest of his little keepsakes, the stud earring in the shape and color of a ladybug that he had ripped from the ear of the young woman in Panama City Beach, a lighter, a pack of breath mints, a house key, his trip down memory lane was over for now.

He stuffed the clothing into a large plastic bag, tying it off securely to prevent the smell from leaking out. He would dispose of the clothing tomorrow in a dumpster far from his home and the beach. The killer put the knife he used on all his victims into a locked drawer in the vanity before stepping into the shower. After a vigorous fifteen minutes of scrubbing and lathering his body, he exited the shower feeling refreshed.

Ten minutes later, he was back downstairs for another flute of champagne and a few chocolate truffles to compliment the fabulous wine. He strolled into the main living area, a large room with floor to ceiling windows that gave him a panoramic view of the beachfront and the Atlantic Ocean.

The interior of his tastefully-appointed home had dark oak and limestone flooring, with intricately-carved, mahogany dentil molding in every room. No expense had been spared on the furnishings, for, after all, the killer wanted to project an image of taste and refinement to the rich elite of the Jacksonville area with whom he associated.

He settled onto a massive Le Corbusier cowhide chaise and propped his bare feet on a cocktail table with exquisite Cocobolo wood inlays that set him back more than ten thousand dollars on a recent trip to Honduras. As he sipped his Dom Perignon, the man's thoughts once again drifted back over the intimate details of each of his conquests, drawing great satisfaction from the continued success of his life's work.

Chapter 29

Officer Roy Connor was working the midnight shift patrolling the downtown beat, an area that also included the beach. He had struggled at first to adapt to the new hours after working for several years on the day shift. He also missed his K-9 partner, Macho.

Whenever Connor thought of what he had lost, his anger toward Sergeant Randall was rekindled. The resentment fed the desire to take out his frustration on the citizens he was paid to serve. Since his meeting with Chief Cooper, however, Connor was more careful than he had been in the past. He avoided punching out and otherwise abusing homeless people. It was hard, but he knew Cooper was serious when he told him he wouldn't get any more chances.

Connor's inability to relieve his hostility on other people was taking a toll on him. His only recourse was to become even more aggressive in his enforcement of the law. Consequently, Roy Connor became a ticket-writing machine. Anything that moved was stopped, and he would, in most cases, find some violation, no matter how minor or obscure, that would allow him to cite the violator. In his first month on the midnight shift, Connor wrote two hundred and thirty-four tickets, a number that exceeded the combined efforts of all three shifts.

Connor's new patrol supervisor, Sergeant Randy Tanaka, had initially objected to the transfer. But Patrol Commander Paul Shelton had told him the chief had made the decision to send Connor to his shift, and it was his job to make it work.

Sergeant Tanaka had met with Connor on his first night and made it clear what he expected. Surprisingly, Connor's attitude was positive and upbeat. The sergeant didn't know the extent of the threats Connor had received from the chief, but he was happy with the man's attitude regardless.

After his initial ticket blitz, Roy asked Sergeant Tanaka if he could be assigned to the downtown beat on a regular basis. The sergeant was so pleased with Connor's work that he approved the request, much to the irritation of a couple of his fellow officers who had been sharing the beat for the past year and didn't want to be reassigned. Connor didn't care whether they were pissed or not. He wanted the beat because he knew it would give him greater opportunities to work out his frustrations on more people, especially the homeless who hung around the Seawalk Pavilion and slept on the beach.

The city had passed a law a few years earlier making it illegal for anyone to camp on public property or sleep on the beach overnight. Because many of the homeless ignored the law, his sergeant told him to check the beach a couple of times during each shift. Connor didn't mind the assignment since it gave him another excuse to roust homeless people, a hobby he continued to enjoy even if he had to do it in a kinder and gentler way.

Tonight, Connor had been disappointed when Emory Elliot Stovall cancelled his plans to ride with him during the shift. Stovall had called Connor on his cell phone to let him know he was tired and didn't feel like coming out after midnight.

It was a topic of frequent speculation among the officers on his squad as to the reason a rich man like Stovall would want to spend hours riding around in a police car with the likes of Roy Connor. Strangest of all was Connor's reaction. His normal demeanor was sour and uncooperative to just about everyone. But Stovall was an exception. He was polite and deferential to the man whenever he showed up to ride and always jumped at the chance to volunteer for the assignment whenever Sergeant Tanaka asked.

"The son of a bitch is probably sucking up to Stovall hoping he'll give him some of his money," groused one of his fellow officers, Dan Engels. "When the guy finally comes to his senses and tells Connor to take a hike, I'm bettin' Connor chokes out that rich SOB like he did Wygle at the party."

Engels had no takers on his bet. They had all seen Connor in action at one time or another and figured it was just a matter of time before he blew.

By five-thirty in the morning, Roy had issued nineteen tickets, arrested three drivers on warrants, bagged a DUI, and checked the beach on foot. He figured he could take a ride along the beach this time since the low tide had just turned. He drove his marked Chevrolet SUV onto the sand at the lifeguard station, turning south. Connor used the patrol car's spotlight to illuminate the area under each of the walkovers.

Reaching the end of his beat without finding anyone, Connor made a wide sweeping turn. As he neared the water's edge, he stopped the patrol car, staring through the windshield at the waves breaking onto the sand a few yards away. It was peaceful this time of the morning, and he enjoyed the solitude. Hiding out on the midnight shift, away from the suits that ran the department, especially the head suit, Connor began to feel a small sense of satisfaction with his new assignment.

He completed his turn and headed back north to continue his patrol. As he passed the lifeguard station again, Connor lit up the first walkover, spotting a form underneath.

"Just when I'm feelin' all chilled, I gotta deal with some pissant transient!" he said out loud.

He turned his car toward the walkover, switching on the high beams as he did to provide more light. Seeing no movement, Connor advised dispatch he would be out on a 13T, the call type for a suspicious homeless person. The communications officer acknowledged and dispatched Dan Engels as backup.

Connor had no intention of waiting until Engels arrived. He was confident in his size and ability to handle some weenie homeless guy. Besides, he carried a TASER and an expandable baton in addition to his Glock .45, so he had no qualms about approaching the guy alone.

As he exited his patrol car, Connor saw that what had looked like someone dressed in light-colored clothing was actually a person lying naked on the sand. Leaving his patrol car on firm sand, the headlights and spotlight still pointed at the person, Connor moved forward.

He was still thirty feet away when he stopped, staring at the scene in front of him. He saw a large amount of blood on the head, neck, and back of a dwarf. The man's pants were around his ankles, and the woman he was on top of was naked from the waist down, her legs splayed out to the side.

From the size of the man and his shaved head, Connor thought, *That's gotta be the little dude from the transient camp, and he's on top of some woman gettin' his rocks off. Or he was, anyway.*

Continuing to see no movement from either one, Connor eased closer, not wanting to disturb any evidence if this was a crime scene as it appeared to be. From the side, he shined his flashlight at the woman, recognizing Nita Caruso.

"Well, I'll be damned!" he exclaimed. "She's the bitch who had information on the serial killer that I brought to the station to talk to Randall! Looks like he's added two more!"

Connor grabbed his radio mike and advised the dispatcher he had an apparent double homicide. Within seconds, Dan Engels arrived. Connor directed him to start putting up crime scene tape in a large arc around the scene. He told the dispatcher to call the on-call detective and evidence technicians and then stood by to wait for the homicide investigation chaos to begin once again.

Chapter 30

"Sergeant Randall! Hey, Clay!" Kyle Meenan called from the other side of the crime scene tape.

Clay looked up from his examination of the two bodies to see the assertive field reporter for one of the Jacksonville TV stations. He waved and held up his index finger to let Kyle know he saw him and would be over to talk to him shortly.

Clay watched Jim Childress intently as the evidence technician knelt beside the two bodies, taking close-up shots of the knife wound in the back of Little Billy Bowen's neck. He had not run across Bowen in the short time the man had been in town, so Officer Engels filled him in on what little the department had on the man. However, Clay had immediately recognized Nita Caruso, as had Cassie Broderick.

"Jim, is that a single stab wound that passed through this guy and into Nita Caruso?" he asked.

"That's what it looks like, Sarge. Course, we won't know for sure until the ME cuts them up."

"Does it appear the blade went into her chest deep enough to penetrate the heart?"

"Yeah. Again, I'll know more after the autopsy, but it sure looks like it. The craziest part of this is that it looks like they were in the midst of . . . shall we say, friendly relations, when the guy stabbed them."

"That's a helluva way to go, dying in the saddle, so to speak," Clay said.

Cassie Broderick walked up at that time, her red hair sticking out in all directions.

"What have we got?" she asked, staring at the two bodies locked in their lethal embrace. "Whoa! When dispatch called me, they didn't tell me we had a case of the ultimate coitus interruptus!"

Three Rivers, closely followed by Ty Honchen, arrived on the scene at that moment. Hearing Cassie's attempt at dark humor, Three couldn't resist.

"Actually, Detective Broderick, you're not entirely accurate. Coitus interruptus is the act of withdrawing prior to ejaculation," he said with a sly look. "That doesn't appear to be the case here. I'd call this more of a coitus deadus."

"Three, you're so full of crap your ankles gotta be hurtin'!" Cassie exclaimed.

Three laughed as Ty asked Clay, "This little dude was actually having sex with the woman at the time they were killed?"

"That's what Childress is saying."

Rivers couldn't resist another opening. "Man, I wanta be a hundred years old and drop dead of a heart attack right after I've finished puttin' some heavy lovin' on Corri Jennings. That's what I'm talkin' about!"

"Jeremy Rivers, you are one disgusting human being, you know that?" Cassie said, rolling her eyes.

"Just tryin' to keep things light in the face of tragedy, darlin'."

"Okay, that's enough clowning around. Put on your game face," Clay insisted. "Y'all know who the woman is, don't you?"

"No, who?" Honchen and Rivers asked in unison.

"Nita Caruso."

Ty frowned, "The name's familiar, but we've interviewed dozens of people, so . . ."

Three snapped his fingers. "She's the prostitute Roy Connor found down at a transient campsite around JTB, isn't she? She claimed she saw our killer and tried to hook up with him, but he blew her off. Too dirty, I guess," he said, wrinkling his nose.

Clay looked around. "Y'all come over here. I don't want anyone else hearing this," he said, walking out toward the water to get away from the half-dozen media types as well as the curious early-morning walkers, runners, and bikers crowded on the other side of the police tape. When they had moved out of hearing range of the crowd, Clay said with a frown, "This is bad, real bad."

"Yeah, one homicide is bad enough, but two? The press will eat us alive!" Cassie exclaimed as she glanced over at the media horde, which seemed to be expanding by the minute.

"Well, there's that, of course. But I was specifically talking about the fact that we now have two people who provided information about a possible serial killer and then ended up dead. Both apparently at the hands of the serial killer. You understand what I'm saying?"

Cassie's eyes widened as she realized what Clay was implying. "You're not suggesting that someone, like a cop, tipped off the killer, are you?"

Clay stared at Cassie, saying nothing.

"Oh, come *on,* Clay!" she said in a loud whisper. "You're thinking a *cop* is the serial killer?"

"Maybe."

"No, no, no," she retorted, shaking her head vigorously, her curly hair flying back and forth. "I don't believe we've got a rogue cop on the force. Nope, don't buy it."

"I dunno, Clay. That's pretty wild," Three said.

He looked from Cassie to Ty to Three. "You don't believe Jax Beach PD has a rogue cop? None? C'mon, y'all are not that naïve!"

Suddenly, the light bulb came on for Cassie.

"You're talking about Roy Connor, aren't you?" she asked, glancing around as she tried to spot Connor among the large number of officers milling about. "You think *he's* our serial killer? What are you basing that on?"

Clay ticked off the points on his fingers. "Number one, Roy Connor hates everybody, especially hookers and transients. Number two, he recently had a run-in with Nita Caruso and Billy Bowen at their camp under the JTB overpass. Three, who allegedly found the bodies? Connor, that's who."

"What do you mean, 'allegedly', Clay?" Three asked. "He's the one who called it in."

"Yeah, so? Use your detective skills, Jeremy. Of course, he called it in. That doesn't mean he was patrolling the beach and just happened to find the bodies, though. He might have actually done it and then pretended to find them."

Seeing the skepticism in their eyes, Clay continued to argue his case.

"Think about it. Two people impaled with one knife thrust. That takes someone with real strength. Connor's a powerful guy, no question about it. And it fits right in with his abusive personality."

The team members glanced at each other, hoping someone else would be the first to speak.

Finally, Cassie said, "Clay, I want to say this in a respectful way, so . . . you're full of crap! Look, the physical we keep getting on this guy doesn't fit Connor.   He's about the right height, I'll concede, but he probably weighs twenty or so pounds more than the descriptions we've gotten on the killer.   Then, think hair, as in, the killer has short hair.   Connor is follically challenged.   And the guy can barely make it from payday to payday.   I can't see him having the money to buy an expensive Beemer and then hide it in a barn somewhere, bringing it out only on nights he wants to party with his blade. Next—"

"Wait a sec—"

"No, Clay, you wait a second. I think you're letting your dislike for Connor cloud your reasoning. It's true, none of us can stand being in the same room with him, but it's a huge leap from asshole to serial killer!"

"Hold on, Cassie!" Clay said, the irritation evident in his voice. "Just because Connor weighs more and shaves his head is no reason to reject him. You know how unreliable eyewitnesses can be. All of you do," he said, looking at Ty and Three.

"We've had eyewitnesses three feet away from a suspect and then describe him afterwards anywhere from five-six to six-two and weigh between one-fifty and two hundred. So you can't say with certainty that our killer is exactly six feet tall and weighs one-eighty and has short hair.

"For all we know, the killer could have worn a cap of some kind, and the witnesses just didn't notice it. And Connor could also be wearing a short wig or something. The guy is bad to the bone. I know that, and y'all know that. So, don't reject him so quickly just because you think no cop could be a killer!"

By the time he finished, Clay was almost loud enough for the crowd to hear from thirty feet away. His hands had balled into fists as he ranted about the rogue cop. Clay felt tremendous anger that such a brutal, dishonest man had been allowed to continue wearing the badge that meant so much to him.

"Why can't you see this?" he asked, looking at each in turn. "Connor has the perfect opportunity to commit these crimes. When he's working, he has a legitimate reason to be on the street and on the beach. And he can be down here on his days off in plainclothes and blend in. If an officer ran across him, they wouldn't think anything about it."

Cassie broke in, trying to calm him down. "Clay, I'll agree that maybe Connor shouldn't be completely eliminated, but don't we have more pressing avenues to explore right now, like Emory Elliot Stovall?"

"I'm glad you brought him up. I forgot to mention this. I was up talking to Annie Kieran yesterday, and Bobby the Weasel was in the chief's office. I overheard him telling Cooper that Connor was riding the other night on duty with none other than our three-name friend."

"What?" Cassie exclaimed. "Why would a rich guy like Stovall be out riding around in a police car, and especially with a flaming asshole like Connor, unless . . ."

Clay smiled at Cassie as he saw her processing the information.

"Right. Unless there's a connection that goes beyond Connor simply trying to do a little community relations by allowing interested citizens to ride with a cop. And that connection might be what?" he asked his team members collectively.

Ty spoke up. "From what y'all told us about your encounter with Stovall, he sounds a lot like Connor, personality-wise. But I agree that neither of them is doing the ride-along thing just for the hell of it. They must be up to something together."

"That's what I concluded after overhearing that little tidbit from Hawkins," Clay said. "Of course, he didn't bother to share it with me. I mean, after all, I'm just in charge of the task force, so why should I know about it?" he asked sarcastically.

"I'm smart enough to see some holes in my theory about Connor being the killer. So, let's look at it from another perspective. Stovall is cruising First Street in an expensive car similar to our killer's. It's late at night, and he's trying to pick up a woman. Maybe he thought she was a hooker. Maybe he didn't care and just wanted to kill any woman he could entice into his car and take somewhere quiet.

"Or maybe, since there's apparently a friendship or some type of association between him and Connor, he's either taking victims to Connor so he can kill them, or Stovall's loaning Connor his car so he can commit the killings using Stovall's car instead of his own. Let's face it. There's no way Connor could slip around in that bright yellow Hummer he's leasing for who knows how much a month."

Ty said, "Speaking for me alone, I'm just not there on Connor. Clay, you're an outstanding detective, better than I'll ever be, but I'm seeing very few signs pointing directly at Roy Connor. Trust me. I wouldn't piss on him to put him out if he was on fire, but I don't think he's our man. Three, what do you think?" Ty asked, looking at Three Rivers.

"No sermon from me, Clay, but I agree with the guys. I don't think Connor's a serial killer . . . serial asshole, maybe, but that won't get you the needle in this state. It'll just get you promoted to chief!"

They all laughed at Three's joke; it was just what they needed to lighten the tension of the moment. .

Clay conceded, "All I'm saying is we can't eliminate Connor or Stovall. This might be a two-man job, you know? So we need to dig into Connor's background along with Stovall and see what we find.

"So, start filtering through the crowd and see what you can pick up. I'll go talk to the media since Bobby Hawkins apparently couldn't drag his sorry ass out of bed this early."

As the team headed back to the crime scene, Clay stopped them.

"I'm keeping the information about Nita Caruso being a possible witness off the table for now. We've got enough negative publicity without that coming out. With four killings here and one in Atlantic Beach, we'll be lucky if we're not on CNN and Fox News tonight.

"But if they get wind we think this guy's killed ten people, and two of our four victims might have been killed because they were potential witnesses, we'll get our asses handed to us. The FBI will probably claim jurisdiction, and then we'll be lucky to see the case file again except when some Fed is carting it around. Let's get to work and keep that from happening."

Chapter 31

As Clay and his team arrived back at the scene, they were dismayed to see the size of the crowd. There were at least two hundred people standing behind the police line now. Four TV crews were there with tall antennas pointed at the early morning sky, obviously prepared to do live remotes from the scene.

As he scanned the crowd for Kyle Meenan, he was bombarded with questions from reporters.

"Sergeant, over here! We need to ask you a couple of questions!"

"We're going live in five minutes. Can you tell our listeners what's happening here?"

He kept moving until he spotted Meenan. He was taping a teaser to attract the interest of viewers and hopefully keep them tuned in over the commercial break.

As Clay walked up, trailed by the news crews who had continued to pepper him with questions, Kyle finished and turned to Clay with a grin.

"Hey, man! You've got a real circus out here this morning. The only thing missing are the elephants."

Clay laughed. He liked Kyle Meenan, which was not something he could say about many in the media. Kyle was a straight up guy. If Clay said something was off the record, he never had to worry about seeing it on Kyle's station, at least not based on anything Clay had said.

At the same time, he knew Meenan had a job to do that was considered important by the citizens of the community. They got along well in an atmosphere of mutual respect and professionalism. That was why Clay had sought him out. He knew the other media types would film his statements, so he didn't feel bad about talking to Meenan first.

"Okay, Kyle, I assume you want a statement."

"Thanks, Sergeant Randall. I know things are hectic right now, but can you release anything for our viewers? And maybe do it live with me in a couple of minutes?"

"Sure, no problem."

As Kyle and Clay spoke, other TV crews and newspaper reporters were either positioning their cameras to get a tight head shot of Clay or extending their cordless microphones and tape recorders up close to his face, determined to catch every word, breath, sneeze, or cough to come out of his mouth.

"Ready?" Kyle asked.

"I'm ready," Clay said.

At that very moment, Officer Bobby Hawkins stepped up, moving between Clay and Kyle Meenan.

"Thanks for holding it together until I got here, Sergeant Randall. I'll take over now," Hawkins said with a smirk meant only for Clay.

He turned his back on Clay and addressed Meenan.

"Morning, Kyle. The official Jacksonville Beach PIO is here and ready to share what information is available for publication. What are your questions?"

As Bobby spoke, he nodded at the other news crews to reassure them that he knew their questions were equally as important as Kyle Meenan's.

Meenan respected Sergeant Randall; he believed Clay was an honest cop. Conversely, he saw Bobby Hawkins as a pretentious, self-serving twit. Regardless, he had a job to do.

"Okay, Bobby, we're going live," Kyle said, looking into the camera.

"We're live in Jacksonville Beach where a double homicide has just been reported. Two individuals, one male and one female, possibly homeless, have been found under one of the beach walkovers. Here with us is Jacksonville Beach Police Public Information Officer Bobby Hawkins."

Turning to Bobby, he asked, "Officer Hawkins, can you tell us what happened here?"

Bobby looked directly into the camera, assuming a serious yet friendly demeanor.

"Certainly. One of our best officers was patrolling the beach about two hours ago, checking to ensure no crimes were being perpetrated against our citizens. As he checked under the First Avenue, North walkover, he found two persons who were deceased. He advised our Communications Center, and detectives and various support personnel were dispatched. They are presently examining the scene and gathering information for a report." Hawkins stopped and smiled for the cameras.

Kyle stared at Hawkins, thinking, *What a pompous ass! 'Crimes perpetrated against our citizens.' What a load of crap!* His professional face revealed none of these thoughts, however.

"Officer Hawkins, is it true the victims were homeless and that they were stabbed to death? Also, assuming that is the case, have you found any connection to the previous murders in Jacksonville Beach and Atlantic Beach committed by the serial killer?"

"Well, Kyle, that's a lot of questions in one breath. Let me see if I remember all of them," Hawkins said with a grin, trying to come across as witty.

"The two victims are indeed members of our homeless community. As for the cause of death, that's still under investigation, so I can't release any details on that. And what was your third question, Kyle?"

"Is there any connection to the previous killings in Jacksonville Beach and Atlantic Beach?"

"Oh, right. I really can't comment on that at this time. Now, any questions from our other friends in the media?"

But Kyle would not be pushed aside so easily. "Officer Hawkins, one more question for our viewers. I understand the female victim recently came to your department and gave you a statement describing a man believed to be involved in the previous murders."

Clay had been listening to the exchange and became immediately alarmed. He stepped up to Hawkins and whispered, "Don't go there, Bobby. That's not to be released!"

Hawkins gave no indication he heard the warning. He wasn't about to let Clay Randall tell him how to do his job. He knew how to handle the media, something Randall obviously had no clue about. Answering this question wouldn't jeopardize the investigation, he was sure.

"Kyle, that's a good question. And the answer is yes. She came forward a few weeks ago and provided information about a man she saw in the pier parking lot who appeared similar to the previous description we received from Mr. James Barton, the homeless man who was murdered several months ago."

That triggered a rush of shouted questions at Hawkins about witnesses being stalked and murdered and what was the department doing about it and didn't he think the state police or the FBI should be called in and weren't the resources of little Jacksonville Beach simply not up to the challenge of finding this serial killer. Hawkins realized belatedly that, hard as it was to admit, Randall was right. He shouldn't have gone there.

He finally stammered, "Sor, sorry, guys. We have to cut this short and get back to conducting the investigation. Thank you for coming out. I'll send out a press release shortly. Thanks again."

Hawkins spun around and almost ran to his car, driving quickly away. The questions were then fired at Clay, but he said no comment to all of them and ducked under the police tape heading back to the scene. All the way back, he silently cursed Bobby Hawkins for being the world's most arrogant asshole in addition to being a first class weasel.

Chapter 32

"Commander Wilson, please tell me why we keep having these homicides in our city, and yet you can't seem to catch the perpetrator," Chief Cooper said quietly with an angry glint in his eye.

Wilson had been abruptly summoned to the Chief's office to discuss the latest double homicide victims, Nita Caruso and Little Billy Bowen. Clay sat beside his boss, wishing he were somewhere else; directing traffic at a busy intersection, digging through a garbage dump for evidence; attending an autopsy . . . anywhere but here watching Chief Cooper get ready to blow like Mount St. Helens.

"Chief, we've been working non-stop on these homicides for several months now. We're satisfied that both prostitutes, Marilyn Gibbs here and Donna Martin in Atlantic Beach, were killed by the same person. The Gibbs witness, James Barton, we're sure was killed *because* he witnessed her murder and then identified himself by going on TV.

"We've also found similarities between our killings and murders in Panama City Beach, Daytona, Tampa, and Key West. This guy is popping prostitutes all over the state, and he's hitting hookers and homeless people here. Chief, I've got Sergeant Randall and his core team of detectives on it full time. Their cases have been reassigned so they can spend all their time working to find this guy."

The chief had remained motionless during Wilson's summation, never blinking, hardly appearing to breathe. When Mike finished, Gordy leaned over and spat a stream of Redman into the spittoon beside his desk. He settled back in his chair, letting his head recline against the high back as he stared at the ceiling, his hands steepled together. Wilson and Randall watched silently, waiting to see if the chief's reaction would be measured or a full bore verbal assault. They didn't have long to wait.

Gordy leaned forward, continuing to speak in a quiet tone. "Commander Wilson, I am rapidly coming to the conclusion that I have appointed an incompetent supervisor to the position of Detective Division Commander. I—"

"Chief, I can accept constructive criticism, but I don't appreciate being called incompetent. And especially in front of one of my officers."

Clay held his breath, knowing something bad was about to happen.

"You don't appreciate . . . *you* don't appreciate," Gordy repeated in a voice even softer than before. "Well, *I* don't appreciate being made a fool of in the media because *you* can't solve a couple of simple homicides. I've been catching more heat from the newspaper and TV stations this past week than in all my previous years as chief combined.

"They're talking about a violent crime wave in Jacksonville Beach on CNN. They're implying we're all a bunch of redneck idiots out here at the beach. And now they're writing editorials pushing the city to disband the police department and let the Jacksonville Sheriff's Office take over. Now, I happen to like the sheriff, but I wouldn't care to work for him.

"And the worst part of all this is that those pissants on the City Council are starting to criticize my leadership. *My leadership*! As if they could do what I do."

Looking at Clay, he asked, "Sergeant, have you got anything constructive to add to this conversation?"

Clay swallowed hard, discovering his mouth was so dry he was afraid he would croak like a frog.

Clearing his throat, he said, "Chief, we've got a good suspect we're looking at. We're digging into his background to see if he's been around when the other murders around the state were committed. I hate to say this, Chief, because you put Officer Hawkins in the position of PIO, but he screwed up bad out there at the scene."

"How so?" Gordy asked.

"One of the reporters asked if it was true that the female victim, Nita Caruso, told us she had seen a guy in the pier parking lot who might be our killer. I don't know how he found that out, but it's not something we wanted publicized.

"I whispered to Bobby, Officer Hawkins, that he shouldn't answer the question. But he went ahead and told all the media it was true. Then, all the reporters started attacking the angle that two witnesses were killed in retaliation for speaking up and speculating about leaks inside the department, and, well, I'm sure you've seen the news . . ."

"I can assure you I've seen the coverage from every media outlet, Sergeant," Chief Cooper said smoothly. "I haven't survived in this position all these years by being tone deaf when it comes to the media. But as far as Officer Hawkins' statement to the press, you're wrong. He did exactly what a good PIO should do. He put out a tiny bit of information that might cause someone in our community to come forward with facts that will crack open this case. No, I'm afraid the problem we have here is a singular lack of quality investigative work."

Continuing in the same soft voice, he said, "So, I need to do something that shows I'm taking these murders seriously, even if they're just a bunch of damn hookers and transients."

Looking at Mike Wilson, he said, "What I've decided to do is remove you as the Detective Division Commander. Effectively immediately, I'm demoting you to sergeant and assigning you to the midnight shift."

Turning to Clay, he continued, "As for you, Sergeant Randall, I'm not going to demote you, but I *am* removing you as head of your task force. You will be replaced by the man I should have put in charge in the first place."

Clay and Mike both stared at Cooper, unable to believe what they were hearing.

"I'm putting Officer Bobby Hawkins in charge of this investigation. I feel sure he will be able to solve these crimes in a timely manner. Sergeant Randall, you and the other members of your task force will report to Officer Hawkins on the task force. Any questions?"

Mike Wilson said nothing. He stood up, reaching to his belt where he carried his badge and pulling it off. Staring at it a moment, his fingers closed around the gold badge, squeezing it hard as if he didn't want to forget what it felt like. Then he placed it on the edge of the chief's desk. He pulled his police identification card out of his pocket and dropped it beside the badge.

Looking up, he said, "Gordy, I've put up with your crap my whole career."

Chief Cooper bristled at the words and the use of his first name by an underling.

As he started to retort, Mike said, "I'm not through, Gordy! I've watched you pull stunts that skirt right to the edge of ethical behavior more times than I can count. But this latest decision will prove to be your crowning underachievement. You're dumber than a box of rocks if you think an idiot like Hawkins can solve these crimes. He couldn't detect his way out of a room with arrows pointing to the door," Wilson said.

Unable to stop the flood of feelings he had bottled up for years, Mike continued, "I've endured your browbeating and intimidation tactics all these years because I was afraid of losing my job. Well, I'm not afraid any more. I just can't take your bullshit another second. I've got my time in, so I'm officially retiring, effective immediately. Find another flunky to banish to the midnight shift."

With that parting shot, Mike Wilson turned and started for the door. Clay was so stunned he couldn't speak. He sat rooted to the spot as his eyes swiveled between his boss, his mentor, his friend, and then at Chief Cooper.

Before Mike made it to the door, Cooper growled, "Wilson! You forgot something!"

Mike turned and said, "What? To thank you for hiring me? To thank you for my promotions? I don't think so, Gordy."

"You're carrying a department weapon on your hip. If you walk out that door, I'll have you arrested for theft of city property!" Cooper yelled.

Wilson glanced down at the pistol on his hip and then back at Cooper.

"You're right, Gordy. I wouldn't think of stealing city property. And you know, when I wake up tomorrow morning and walk into the bathroom, the man I see staring back in the mirror will be someone I'm proud of. Can you say the same . . . *Chief?*"

Taking the gun and holster from his hip, he dropped them on the table by Gordy's door and walked out.

Chief Cooper was so red in the face Clay thought he was about to have a stroke or heart attack.

He glared at Clay, screaming, "GET OUT! GET OUT OF MY SIGHT!"

Clay needed no second invitation. He almost ran out of the room. Before he got past Annie Kieran's desk, Gordy had slammed his office door so hard that three framed pictures fell to the floor, shattering the glass. The last thing Clay saw as he headed down the stairs was Annie staring at the chief's door with her mouth hanging open.

Chapter 33

Clay headed back to the Detective Division to find Commander Wilson. As he went by Linda Greene's desk, she said, "Clay, what's going on? Mike just stormed past me with a look on his face that would freeze molten lava!"

"Can't talk now, Linda," Clay muttered as he kept moving. He got to Wilson's office and found the door closed. Knocking, he called, "Mike! You in there?"

After a moment, Wilson opened the door and growled, "Come in. Shut it behind you." He turned and went back to his desk where he had started piling items in a box.

Clay shut the door quietly and stood watching his boss as he continued to rummage through drawers, throwing items haphazardly into the box. After watching Wilson silently putting years worth of his professional life into the battered cardboard box, Clay felt he had to say something.

"Mike, I'm sorry I've caused this. If I had just worked a little harder—"

"Cut it out, Randall. This isn't about anything you've done or not done. I know you and your team have busted your asses trying to find this guy. Anybody with a lick of sense in this business knows how hard it is to catch a serial killer until he makes a mistake, which, by the way, this guy hasn't done yet.

"Look how long Ted Bundy was running around the country killing women. And what about Danny Rolling in Gainesville? Sure, it took smart cops to catch them, but they both eventually made mistakes that caused those cops to focus directly on them. Whoever this guy is, he just hasn't screwed up yet.

"What makes this crap so hard to stomach is that Gordy Cooper knows all this. He'd never admit it, though. He's so weighed down with his massive ego and his public image that he can't handle the slightest criticism. He tries to project this image of the great Gordy Cooper, all-knowing and all-powerful, always in charge. But it's all B.S. The man's afraid of his own shadow. If he was as tough as he wanted everyone to think, he'd be out front telling the media to piss off and give his guys room to work.

"The chief of police should be a leader to his employees, but Gordon Haynes Cooper doesn't know the meaning of the word," Mike grumbled. "I'll tell you, Clay, I'm disgusted with the man and all he represents. I can't stay another minute in a department run by an egomaniac with no integrity. That badge I put on his desk means too much to me."

As he said this, he piled the last certificate in the box, which was close to overflowing. On the very top, he balanced his nameplate. Hoisting the box in both arms, Mike Wilson walked past Clay without another word.

"Commander, what are you doing?" his secretary asked with alarm in her voice. "Where are you going?"

"I'm going on permanent vacation, Linda. Thanks for all your help through the years. I'll be seeing you," he said, never breaking stride.

Clay had followed Mike down the hall from his office, still too stunned and emotional to speak. He looked at Linda, whose eyes were clouding with tears as she watched Mike Wilson walk out the door.

She turned to Clay, openly crying. "Clay, what happened? Why did Mike leave?"

"He finally got a bellyful of Cooper. He retired rather than take a demotion."

"A demotion? But why?" she wailed.

"Because we haven't cleared the murders, and he said he was getting pressure from the media. Oh, and he's putting Bobby Hawkins in charge of the task force, so I'll be reporting to him."

"What's all the yelling about?" Cassie Broderick asked, coming up to Clay and Linda.

"Commander Wilson has retired, and Bobby Hawkins has been put in charge of your task force over Clay!" Linda exclaimed.

"What? What did you say?" Ty Honchen asked as he and Three Rivers came out of the conference room.

"Mike and I were in Cooper's office to give him a briefing on the murders when the man went off on him. He said he was demoting him to sergeant and sending him to the midnight shift. Then Mike told him where he could stick his job and retired on the spot. Left his badge and ID card on the man's desk and walked out. And I've been replaced as lead of the task force by *Bobby Hawkins*," Clay spat, unable to keep from snarling the name of a man he detested only slightly less than Roy Connor, and now Gordy Cooper.

"Oh, man, we're screwed," Three Rivers moaned. "Hawkins is a dumb shit . . . oh, I'm sorry, Linda. Pardon my language, but I just can't stand the guy. And Mike is gone?"

Clay nodded. "I watched him pack all his stuff in a box and head out the door. I couldn't say anything to get him to change his mind. Actually, I don't think there *was* anything I could have said to change it. He was done, you know what I'm saying? Done!"

"Will he come back, you think?" Cassie asked.

"I doubt it seriously. Even if he changed his mind, there's no way in hell Cooper would let him come back. Mike really got in his face big time. Cooper would have fired him if he thought he could get away with it. But he knows how well respected Mike Wilson is in this community. There's no way he'd fire Mike and take the chance that he would talk to the media. Especially with all the negative coverage he's already getting over the homicides."

"What happens now?" Ty asked.

"You keep plugging away until you hear different. I expect our new leader will show up soon to gloat."

"That little pimp doesn't know shit about police work," Ty snarled. "He's spent so much time up Cooper's ass that his nose is permanently brown. Hell, when his nose isn't there, he's got his whole head up his own ass so far he needs a Plexiglas bellybutton to see where he's goin'! If he thinks I'm taking orders from him, well, let's just say that won't happen!"

"Cool it, Ty," Three cautioned. "Gordy won't hesitate to fire you if he thinks you're screwing with his lapdog."

"Three's right, Ty," Clay said. "We're not going down that road. We're gonna do our best to solve these murders in spite of Hawkins. All of you are outstanding detectives; that's why I wanted you on the task force.

"We can come up with sufficient dead-end leads for Hawkins to chase that will keep him out of our hair while we do the real work. Whataya say?" Clay asked as he extended his hand, palm down into the circle of team members.

They looked at each other and then at their leader. "I'm in," Cassie said, putting her hand on Clay's. "How about it, guys? You in, too?"

"Damn right, I'm in," Three growled as he slapped his palm on top of Cassie's, closely followed by Ty's strong hand.

"You *know* I'm in!"

Linda Greene, who had finally gotten her emotions under control, tentatively extended her hand to join the group.

"Can I be a part of your pact, too? Mike Wilson is the finest man I've ever known besides my husband. So, if it will help solve the murders, and maybe, just maybe, convince Mike to come back, well, if you need my help giving Bobby a little misdirection, then I'm your girl."

"Welcome to the team!" Clay said with a grin, bringing her into their scheme to isolate Hawkins while they solved the serial killer homicides.

Chapter 34

"Alright, gentlemen and lady . . . oh, and you, too, Clay," Bobby Hawkins said, failing to keep the sarcasm out of his voice. "Let's get this meeting started. I've got a lot to cover and not much time to cover it.

"As you may have heard, Chief Cooper put me in charge of the task force because he was unhappy with the lack of progress you four have shown. He gave me specific instructions about how I'm to run this investigation. Unfortunately, I'm not at liberty to share those instructions with you at this particular time," he smirked.

Ty Honchen stood up and leaned across the table toward Hawkins, the muscles in his massive arms and shoulders bunching up as they strained to burst through his shirt.

"You listen to me, you little weasel," Ty said in a menacing tone as Bobby leaned back against the wall, trying to put as much space between himself and Ty as he could. "You don't know shit about these cases. In fact, you don't know a damn thing about how to conduct a criminal investigation, much less one involving a serial killer!"

"Ty!" Clay said in a sharp tone as he stood, putting his hand on Ty's arm. "Don't do this. He's got Cooper's ear. You're not helping yourself."

Ty glanced at Clay, "If I don't say what's on my mind, I'm gonna explode."

Turning back to Hawkins, he continued, "You can go around telling everyone you're in charge of this task force, but don't think for a second that you're *really* in charge. The four of us have been busting our asses for months while you've been lying on your back in the chief's chair so your lips come in direct contact with his skinny ass every time he sits down. So, and I'm speaking only for myself here, keep outa my way unless you have a burning desire to have me rip your head off and piss down your neck! Got it?"

Clay pulled Ty back from the table, "Detective Honchen! That's enough! The man put him in charge, and you're jeopardizing your job acting like this! Cut it out!"

Ty's nostrils flared as he glared at his Sergeant. For a tense moment, he looked ready to take a swing at Clay.

With a visible effort, he swallowed hard and nodded. "I'm done. I've said my piece. I'm not gonna kick his ass, not right this second, even though he deserves it. Anyway, this little pussy would rather have me talkin' all up under his clothes than stand up to me. Whataya say, *Bobby*, am I right?" he demanded, glaring at Hawkins again.

Bobby stared at Ty's massive upper body. He looked into the man's eyes, seeing both utter contempt and hopeful anticipation that he would challenge him.

He sputtered, "You, you can't talk to me that way! I'm in charge of the task force. I'll tell the chief you threatened me!"

Ty started across the table after Bobby, who cringed back into the corner, throwing his hands in front of his face. Clay, Three Rivers, and Cassie all grabbed Ty and held him in a bear hug.

"Okay! Okay! I'm calmed down," Ty yelled after a brief struggle. "Let me go. I'm not gonna do anything."

Clay looked at Bobby Hawkins, who was still cowering in the corner of the conference room. He was muttering to himself, "When I get out of here, I'm telling Chief Cooper what these assholes did."

Clay said, "What are you talking about, Bobby? Nobody did anything to you. We've all been sitting here discussing the homicides. Haven't we guys?"

"Yeah, that's right," Three said.

I've been going over the Marilyn Gibbs case this whole time with Ty. Are you okay, Bobby? You got a fever or something causing you to hallucinate?"

"Oh, is that how it is?" Bobby asked, getting a little of his bravado back when he realized Ty wasn't going to pound him into the carpet. "Well, who's the chief going to believe? Me or a bunch of assholes like y'all? Trust me, he'll believe me!" he said triumphantly.

"Hold that thought," Clay said, stepping to the door and opening it. "Linda, could you come in here?"

Linda Greene stepped to the door of the conference room. "Hey, Clay, what do you need?" she asked with an innocent look on her face.

"Linda, how long have you been outside the conference room?"

"Since right after you closed the door to start the meeting. I've been making copies of reports. See?" she said, holding up a sheaf of offense reports.

"Did you hear what we were saying in here?"

"Of course I did," she said with a smile. "You know how thin these walls are. I can hear someone breathing in here, for goodness sakes!"

"Alright, and would you summarize for us what you heard," Clay asked, glancing at Hawkins' smirking face.

"Sure. I heard Officer Hawkins talking about being put in charge of the task force, and I heard the four of you telling him how you would support him . . . that all you wanted was to get these homicides solved."

"Now, wait just a damn minute here!" Hawkins yelled. "That's not what happened, and you know it! Honchen threatened to kick my ass! You must have heard him!"

"Why, Officer Hawkins, I don't know what you're talking about," Linda replied sweetly. "I heard nothing of the kind. These four detectives are just about the finest, most dedicated and honest officers in this department. You should be proud to serve with them instead of attacking their integrity!"

Clay grinned at Hawkins. "Uh, Bobby, in case you forgot, Linda is Chief Cooper's sister-in-law, and he holds her in very high esteem. So who's he going to believe? A lying little weasel like you? Or a fine upstanding lady who also happens to be family? Man, that's a tough one. I can't decide. What do you think, guys?" he asked his team.

They all grinned back at Clay and then looked in unison at Hawkins.

"Gee, Sarge," Three said. "I'll bet my next paycheck the chief takes option two."

"Well, then, it's settled," Clay said. "Thanks for your leadership on the task force, Bobby. We've all got our assignments, so we'll just leave and get started. Oh, wait," he said, glancing at his watch. "It's lunch time, and I'm buying. I'll meet y'all at Sneaker's Sports Grille in ten. Linda, you can ride with me if you like."

"Of course, we're disappointed that you can't join us, Bobby, but we know you'll want to get familiar with the investigation. There's only about a thousand pages of documents in those six notebooks there on the table. You'll probably need to commit them to memory in case the chief asks for a briefing. See you later, Bobby . . . oh, sorry, task force leader!"

They all headed for their cars, leaving Bobby Hawkins alone in the conference room and wondering how he had lost control so quickly.

Chapter 35

The specially-designed ceramic plate for Corri Jennings was delivered to the department in late June. The factory rep had found the request intriguing and convinced his boss to absorb the cost, which was considerable. Team members were examining the plate as they waited for Jennings to finish a call and come in for a fitting.

Bobby Hawkins was feeling the contours of the ballistic plate. He eyed Clay. "Whose idea was it to do a special order like this? This has to have cost a fortune. The chief's not going to be happy paying for something like this when we're facing budget cuts."

"The plate was provided to the department gratis," said Clay. "And who said we're facing budget cuts, anyway?"

"Oh, well, see, Chief Cooper told me the other day things are kinda tight right now. He didn't tell you?" he asked with a sneer.

Three Rivers spoke up before Clay could get fired up. "Dude, if the chief told *you*, the information's not important."

As Hawkins started to respond, Clay spoke up, "Zip it, Three. Stop the arguing, and that goes for you, too, Bobby. Our job is to find the killer, and nothing else. As soon as Corri gets here, we need to have her try this thing on to see if it fits. Then we need to finalize our plan."

As Clay spoke, Corri stepped into the room. "Hey, guys, dispatch said you needed me. What's up?"

"The ceramic plate just arrived. Go into my office with Cassie and try it on. If it fits, we'll get the detail scheduled," Clay said.

"Hold on just a damn minute!" Bobby Hawkins exclaimed. "Have you forgotten that I'm in charge of this task force? Appointed by Chief Cooper, remember? I don't recall approving this detail."

"It was approved before you got here, and we've got the team and the plan almost complete," Clay said.

"Yeah, but I'm the one who calls the shots, not you, Clay. And who approved it?"

Clay stared at Hawkins, his jaw clenching. "Commander Wilson approved it and also got approval from Chief Cooper. You want to go ask the chief?"

Bobby looked around at the detectives and Corri Jennings. The hostility emanating from them was palpable.

"No, I don't need to ask him. It's just that I keep getting cut out of everything, and then the man asks me what's going on, and I sound like a dumbass when I have to tell him I don't know."

Three said, "Bobby, you *sound* like a dumbass because you *are* a dumbass."

Hawkins glared at Three Rivers, about to retort, when Clay jumped in.

"Bobby, will it make you feel better if you tell Officer Jennings to go try on the plate?"

"No, that's alright," he said, still feeling a little uncomfortable.

Corri picked up the ceramic plate and, followed by Cassie Broderick, headed for Clay's office. Within minutes, they were back.

"It's fine," Corri said. "I expected it to bind a little in the obvious places, but it felt okay."

Her comment triggered for Three Rivers the erotic vision of her firm, full breasts. He and Jennings had been dating for about three months, much to the disappointment of Shank Wygle, who had finally given up on getting a date with her.

Rivers had been pressing her to move in with him for the past month, but she wasn't convinced he was ready to make a commitment to her alone.

She had told him, "I'm not shacking up, Jeremy. I've never done it before, and I don't intend to start now. You say you only want to be with me, but your track record says something else."

Three wasn't sure himself if he was ready to settle down. If he did, though, he knew he could never do better than Corri Jennings.

"Then the detail is a go for Friday night," Clay said. "You agree, Bobby?" he asked to head off further complaints from Hawkins.

"Yeah, that's good. I'll brief Chief Cooper on what we're doing. How many officers do you have scheduled, and what's the plan?"

"Ty put together a good plan with everybody's input, so I'll let him give the basics. Ty?"

"We've got ten cops to cover Corri. There's the four of, uh, five of us," he corrected with a curt nod to Hawkins, "and five from patrol. The detail will start at 2300 hours and run until something happens or the streets are empty. Corri will primarily be cruising the pier parking lot, depending on traffic, and she'll be wired up so we can monitor her conversations.

"If our guy shows and is stupid enough to make a play there on the lot, we'll take him down right there. But it's more likely he'll play it cautious and try to get her down on the beach. If that happens, we've got it covered, also.

"Two officers will be hanging out under the pier posing as transients. If Corri starts moving that direction, they'll duck into the little sand cave under the pier but be ready to pop out if a takedown presents itself. Okay so far?" Ty asked, glancing around the room.

Seeing no questions or comments, he continued. "If nothing happens in the first couple of hours, then we'll have her start trolling First Street."

"What happens if the guy tries to get her into a car?" Bobby asked.

Clay interjected, "We've discussed that at length. Corri won't get into a car because we can't cover her. And since we can hear what's being said, we can stop the car after it leaves and do a felony stop on the driver."

Bobby continued to question the plan. "What if the killer approaches Jennings and pulls a knife. What's she supposed to do?"

"I'll answer that," Corri said. "I'll kick his ass up between his shoulder blades and use his own knife to cut off his balls!"

"You can't do that!" Hawkins gasped.

Everyone stared at Bobby as if he had sprouted an extra set of ears.

Corri burst out laughing, immediately joined by the rest of the team. "Bobby, I'm kidding, okay? I'm not like your buddy, Roy Connor!"

He looked around the room, his face turning red. "I knew you were kidding, and anyway, Connor's not my buddy," he said indignantly.

"Yeah, *right*," Three said. "The fact is, we'll be close enough that Corri won't have to engage in prolonged hand-to-hand combat. Besides, if he comes out with a knife, she knows what to do, right Corri?"

"Two shots, center mass, followed by one to the head. Then we call the medical examiner's office to send a meat wagon. Cause of death . . . acute exposure to lead."

"That's the drill if he pulls his knife, Corri," Clay said. "But if he doesn't, do an arm bar takedown and get him on the ground fast. Then we'll be all over him."

"Sounds like a plan," Corri said. "Do you have anything to add, Bobby?"

"No, I guess it's okay," he said, disappointed that he couldn't think of anything to criticize.

"Okay, people, let's be prepared for anything to happen. And remember that our first and last priority is to protect Corri," Clay concluded, bringing the meeting to a close.

Bobby Hawkins offered no objection to Clay ending the meeting. Recognizing the fierce loyalty the police officers in this room felt for Clay Randall, he knew they would never accept him as their leader in spite of any title he was given.

Chapter 36

"How you feeling, babe?" Clay asked as Dana grunted and groaned through her morning stretches on the floor beside their bed.

"I've had morning sickness every day this week. Thanks to my mother's genes, I guess I'll be sick the whole nine months like she was with me. I'm bloated up like a swollen toad. My face is all broken out. Let's see . . . yep, that about does it. Other than those minor issues, I'm fine. Thanks so much for asking."

"Wow, you've always been a little grouchy in the morning, but you've taken it to a whole new level of crabbiness!" Clay said with a grin.

"You try carrying this baby for a few days and see how cheerful you are, bud."

Clay flopped down on the floor beside Dana and began stroking her stomach gently. At four months, she was starting to show slightly. Dana had continued her daily regimen of running and stretching, which had kept her weight gain to less than five pounds. She had a glow about her, a fact she attributed to the child growing inside her.

"Have you felt him move yet?"

"No, I haven't felt *her* move," she corrected with a smile.

"Whatever. We'll see who's right in a few months. You still don't want to know the sex?"

"No. I want the anticipation to build until the big day. I've always been into deferred gratification, you know that," Dana said, sighing with contentment at Clay's continued stroking of her stomach.

"What's on your agenda for today?"

"I'll be at Ethan Hunter's house continuing the landscape. Clay, you wouldn't believe the guy's home. You've got to come see it and meet him. He asks me every time I'm there when you're coming. He says he wants to meet the famous detective who's investigating the serial killer murders."

"I'm not famous. I haven't solved any of them yet. Besides, I'm not too interested in meeting some pompous rich guy, even if he did throw thirty thousand bucks at my wife for one painting."

"Clay, he's not what you think. He's nothing like the guy that got in my face complaining about you at the Lansing Gallery during my show. What was his name? Emory something . . ."

"Emory Elliot Stovall."

"Yeah, him. Ethan's not that way at all. He's very professional, but he's personable, too. I was a little nervous the first time I went to his house, but, like I told you then, he was a perfect gentleman. Now, it's more relaxed. He helps me get my easel and case from the car and sets it up for me on the terrace whenever he's there. And when he's not there, his maid lets me in. I'm very comfortable working there now, if I can just stay out of the bathroom puking up my toenails at least once a day."

"But you said he keeps asking you about the cases and what I'm doing and when we're going to find the murderer. Doesn't that seem a little strange to you?"

"No, it doesn't. He's curious and a little nervous like every other resident of the beaches."

"I can understand being curious, but what's he got to be nervous about? Our guy's killing hookers and transients, two categories of people that Hunter has probably never encountered in his whole life except to drive past and look the other way. Well, we don't really know him, so it's possible he's not driving past the *hookers*."

"Clay, that's silly. Ethan is a caring person who donates a lot of money to various charities focused on helping the homeless. And he's a good looking guy, so I can't imagine he would have to buy a woman, much less a streetwalker like the ones being killed."

"Wait a minute. How do you know he donates money to homeless causes? Did he tell you?"

"Yes, he did. While we were talking about the killings, he mentioned feeling sorry for people who got down on their luck. He said he thought it was the least he could do considering how much money he had."

"Dana, just because he said he supports the homeless doesn't mean it's true. This guy sounds like he's playing you. For what reason, I'm not sure. But the fact he keeps wanting to talk about the murders and what I'm doing bothers me a little bit. And the fact he's so friendly to a gorgeous, talented artist who happens to be my wife bothers me, too."

"Oh, Clay, you're just being a typical cop," Dana said as she turned to her side to ease the pain in her lower back. "You're suspicious of everybody, but not everyone you meet is a criminal. And he's not the least bit interested in me except in a professional way."

"You're probably right," Clay said as he shifted and began kneading the muscles in her lower back. "But just about everyone has an angle or an agenda. Few people are what they seem to be. Everyone puts on different faces when they interact with others. Think of yourself. You have one face when you're with me. You're kind, loving, sexy . . . did I mention that you're still hot even though you're pregnant?" he asked as he shifted one hand to caress her swelling breasts and the other to rub softly between her legs.

"Um-m-m," she smiled. "I can't concentrate on what you're saying when you do that."

"Okay, I'll pause while I finish my thought and then pick up where I left off," Clay said as he began massaging her lower back again. "Where was I? Oh, yeah, faces. You have a face you present to me, a different face to your parents, a different one to this Hunter character, and so on."

"But I'm still the same person," Dana protested.

"Of course you are. But you act differently depending on the person or group you're with. You show me the true Dana Randall, in all your warts and glory. You would never act that same way around other people, even with your parents . . . *especially* with your parents," he said with a grin.

"My point is this Ethan Hunter has a public face he's presenting to you. He wants you to see him as this rich yet humble humanitarian. I'd be willing to bet there are plenty of other people who see a very different person entirely and would be shocked at your opinion of him. That's all I'm saying.

"Just be cautious what you tell him about my job and this investigation. That's all on a need-to-know basis, and he simply doesn't need to know!" Clay concluded as he immediately moved his hands back to her sweet spots.

This time, Dana didn't protest, instead turning onto her back so Clay's hands and body could more easily grant her the sexual pleasure she craved even more as her pregnancy progressed.

Later, their physical urges temporarily satisfied, Clay and Dana sat on their patio sipping coffee while they watched the never-ending procession of people walking, jogging, biking, and sunning themselves on the beach.

"When are you going to do your prostitute detail with Corri Jennings?" Dana asked.

"It's on for this Friday."

"Is Corri really okay with this? It sounds dangerous."

"She's fine. Corri's a cop, and we have to take risks sometimes. We got her a ceramic chest plate molded to protect her upper body in the event she encounters our guy, and he tries to use his knife. The plate will stop any knife he could possibly have."

"Well, what if he cuts her face like the girl in Panama City Beach you told me about?"

Clay hesitated before answering, obviously feeling a little uncomfortable with the question.

"We've talked about that, and Corri is aware that he's gone for the throat before. She's very strong and athletic, and she feels confident she can keep him off her until she can grab her Glock and send him straight to hell."

"I could never do something like that. I'd be so scared I wouldn't be able to breathe. I still have nightmares thinking about walking up on that dead guy. When I heard the stupid seagull behind me, I just knew it was the killer," she said, shivering as she reached over and grasped Clay's hand.

"It's okay, babe," Clay said, giving her hand a reassuring squeeze. "You were very brave to stay there and call 9-1-1. No one would have criticized you if you had hauled it back to the house before you called."

A thought occurred to her, "Are *you* in any danger?"

"No, not at all," Clay said, mentally crossing his fingers behind his back. Throughout their marriage, Clay had seldom told Dana more than the briefest details about the dangerous parts of his job. He knew she worried about his safety, and he figured she would only get worse with a child on the way.

"Are you sure? I mean, dealing with a guy who's killed so many people, he could cut you before you could even get your gun out."

"Trust me, darlin'. I'm not letting this guy within cutting distance of me unless he's unarmed, disarmed, or dead. Now, you sit here and concentrate on growing our son while I go make us some lunch," he laughed, jumping up to avoid her swat at him with the morning paper.

Clay was relieved to escape the increasingly uncomfortable conversation with Dana. He knew there were risks involved, particularly for Corri Jennings, and he knew the rest of the team, including himself, faced dangers, also. If they were successful in finding the killer, odds were pretty high the confrontation with such a man would prove deadly.

His imagination took off as he went to the refrigerator to gather ingredients for a salad. Slicing ripe tomatoes with a sharp paring knife, he envisioned a vicious altercation with the killer that had both their lives hanging in the balance. After a few moments, he shook his head in a conscious effort to clear the violent images from his mind.

I doubt seriously this guy will even show. We'll burn up some overtime and get Cooper pissed at us for that, and have nothing to show for it, he thought.

Clay had no way of knowing how wrong his assumption would prove to be.

Chapter 37

Friday night was unusually hot for the beach community, the temperature at eleven o'clock still hovering around eighty-five degrees. With no ocean breeze, the officers working the prostitute detail were sweating heavily. Cassie Broderick used powerful binoculars to watch cars and people from her vantage point on top of a parking garage a block south of the pier. Her focus was on Corri Jennings as she strolled along appearing to search for someone. She was dressed in tight shorts and a sleeveless blouse that did a barely passable job of hiding the ceramic chest plate, at least as long as no one actually tried to touch her. Inside a small shoulder bag, Corri had wedged her badge and gun.

Clay and Ty Honchen were sitting half a block away from the parking lot in the back of an old Dodge van the department had seized from a drug dealer. The windows were darkened to allow them to see without being seen.

Three Rivers had drawn the unenviable task of pairing up with Bobby Hawkins, a partnership Hawkins disliked as well. They were lying on their stomachs, hidden in the sea oats planted on the sand dunes just east of the boardwalk. Their job was to be Corri Jennings's first line of defense if she came onto the beach with a possible suspect.

The rest of the officers on the detail had been assigned positions of concealment in spots north and west of the parking lot so that all possible avenues of escape were covered. Each team member wore an ear piece so they could hear Corri's voice on the body wire she wore under the ceramic plate, the microphone disguised as the top button on her blouse.

She kept up a running monologue about the heat, her sore feet, and anything else that came to mind, partly to relieve the boredom, and partly out of nervousness. They had begun the detail at ten o'clock, and she had yet to have anyone approach her fitting the general description of the killer. Two men had tried to pick her up, but she quickly blew them off. One appeared to be about seventeen years old, his face blotchy red with acne.

"Hey, baby, you lookin' for some action tonight? I got it hangin' just for you!" he said in a squeaky voice that hadn't decided if it would eventually become a tenor or a baritone.

Corri looked at the young man with unconcealed contempt. "Little boy, I think your mama's looking for you. Now run along."

The kid's face blushed red, and he turned without another word and walked away.

"He needs to work on his snappy patter. I don't think a real hooker would go for that BS line unless he was waving a hundred dollar bill around," she said for the amusement of her listening audience.

A few minutes later, a man who looked to be at least eighty years old walked by her. As he passed, he grabbed her left buttock, giving it a healthy squeeze. Corri spun around, ready to grab the man and take him to the ground. His toothless grin and loud cackle caused her to pause.

"Old man," she snapped, "don't be touching my butt unless you want me to slap that nose of yours to the back of your head!"

He hooted louder this time. "Thanksh for the memory, sugar," he slurred, obviously very drunk. "I ain't had me a piece of ass since I cain't recollect when. 'Course, I ain't been able to git ole Charley up higher 'en 'bout seven o'clock for just 'bout as long."

With a big grin plastered on his face, the old man staggered off down the boardwalk, still chuckling as he held up his right hand, admiring the appendage that had touched the butt of a goddess.

The hilarious encounter with the old drunk was the high point for the team that night. They called it at 1:00 a.m. after Corri had left the parking lot and begun trolling First Street without anyone hitting on her. Over the next two weeks, they tried three more times without success. Everyone was getting discouraged as they discussed what to do next.

"Chief Cooper is really starting to get on my ass because we haven't cleared the murders," Bobby complained. "Even the national media have been here trying to get him on camera. And since he's refused to be interviewed, they're hammering him. He's starting to get worried that the Mayor is going to get the rest of the City Council together and vote to fire him. He's so pissed he's even talking about taking me off the task force!"

Cassie, Ty, Three, and Corri, newly assigned to the task force, all looked at Clay, waiting for him to respond to Bobby. He didn't hesitate.

"What did you expect, Bobby? Did you really think you'd come in here and solve these murders through the shear force of your personality?"

Three snickered at the comment, causing Bobby to scowl at him. "Well, if I had gotten a little cooperation, maybe I would have."

"Bullshit," Ty said. "You have no talent for investigations. In fact, your only noticeable talent is your ability to stick your nose up Cooper's ass and still be able to breathe through it."

"Back off, Ty," Clay warned. "Stop deliberately trying to provoke him. It serves no useful purpose. What we need is a new plan. Does anybody happen to have one handy?" he asked, looking at each of his teammates.

They all dropped their eyes or suddenly got busy shuffling through the hundreds of pages of the case files. Everyone, that is, except Corri.

"I realize I'm on temporary assignment here, and I don't have the experience you guys have, but I've got an idea." She hesitated, "You know, if you're interested."

"Everyone can contribute to the cause, Corri," Clay said encouragingly. "Let's hear your idea."

She looked around, cleared her throat, and stood up. "I think better on my feet," she explained. As she talked, she paced back and forth.

"I've walked the pier parking lot and First Street so many hours that I've memorized every crack in the pavement. And the results were getting propositioned by a pimply-faced teenager and my butt squeezed by Grandpa Moses.

"I think I should be hitting the clubs as well as walking the street. The killer hooked up with the Panama City Beach victim in a club and then got her on the beach to attack her. Maybe we'd have better luck trying that angle," she concluded. "And one other thing . . . I think I should dump the plate."

"Whoa, hold up. What are you talking about?" Clay protested. "You know Mike Wilson refused to approve the detail until we told him about the ceramic chest plate. You can't get rid of that. It's your only protection against a knife."

"First," Corri said, "Commander Wilson's. Second, the plate is so bulky that I look like a guy, and I don't think our killer is targeting guy hookers. It was a good idea, and the plate would work well in cold weather under a bulky sweater or jacket. But it just doesn't work when everybody at the beach wears as little as possible to stay cool. I can't dress appropriately for the assignment, you know, a low cut blouse to show off my, uh . . ." she hesitated, gesturing at her chest as her face turned red.

Three Rivers jumped in immediately. "I don't like it, Clay. This guy's proven he's a meat cutter. If he gets his knife out, Corri's gonna be carved into little pieces before she or any of us can stop him. This is *not* a good idea," he said, objecting to Corri's idea more out of personal worries for her than officer safety considerations.

"Jeremy, it's not your decision," she retorted.

Turning to Clay, she pleaded her case. "I know it's ultimately not mine, either, but I want you to agree. It's the only way I can create the right look. And besides, we're getting nowhere with me wearing the vest, so why not give my idea a try?"

Clay thought about the potential consequences, primarily that Corri could be seriously injured or even killed.

He looked at Three Rivers. "I've heard your feelings on the subject, although I question your objectivity, for obvious reasons."

"Hold on," he said, holding up his hand to stop Rivers before he could object. "Cassie, what do you think?"

Cassie glanced at Corri and then back at Clay. "It's definitely a risk. We all know what could happen if he gets his knife out before Corri can react. But . . . I guess if Corri is comfortable with it, you should let her do it."

Clay looked at Ty Honchen, raising his left eyebrow in a 'What do you think?' expression. "I thought from the start the ceramic plate would be a problem this time of year. I say go for it as long as Corri is okay with it."

"Okay, Corri, I'll stick my neck out as long as you're sure you want to try it without the plate. It's clear what we've been doing so far isn't working. Like that old saying, the mark of insanity is to keep doing the same thing over and over expecting different results. That's us.

"So, if our team leader has no objection . . . ," he paused, looking at Bobby Hawkins. "Seeing none, it's a go. Let's get our ops plan together for this Thursday night."

Chapter 38

Music blasting from the surround-sound speakers inside the Surf n' Sand Club made it hard to think, much less carry on a conversation. It also had the disturbing side effect of making Corri's conversations difficult for team members to pick up on the wire she wore. Because of this, Clay had sent Three Rivers into the club as an eyes-on backup for her.

It was 1:00 a.m., and the place was crowded with twenty and thirty somethings looking for a buzz, a high, or a one-night stand. Corri was dressed in shorts so brief and so tight that a large portion of the cheeks of her well-toned butt were on display for all the guys to admire. She wore a low-cut blouse that showcased her full breasts. As before, she carried her pistol inside her little shoulder bag.

Corri's outfit and good looks had earned her appreciative stares from guys in every bar she went. She had politely rejected the come-ons of half a dozen men who obviously didn't fit the physical profile of their target. Finishing the non-alcoholic O'Doul's beer, her on-duty drink of choice for the night, she stood up from her seat at the bar, preparing to leave. Corri thought she would try the pier parking lot for a few minutes before hitting one of the other clubs.

"Hi, don't I know you from somewhere?" a voice from behind her asked.

Corri turned and saw a man staring at her who closely fit the description of the killer they so desperately wanted to find. Her heart began racing as she looked at him, her face and eyes revealing none of the inner tension she was feeling.

"That's the most lame and unoriginal line I've heard in years," she said with a smile. "You tell me, where would that somewhere be?"

He smiled ruefully at Corri, "Well, nowhere, really. I saw you sitting here alone and realized I was looking at the most gorgeous woman in the place. Hell, the most gorgeous woman *any* place. I just had to introduce myself and hope you would allow me to buy you a drink. And it *was* pretty lame, wasn't it?"

"Yeah, it was, but your follow-up compliment, although not true, makes up for it. And as for a drink, I've had enough for one night. I was going to take a walk and clear my head before I drove home."

"I realize I'm being a little forward, but if I let you walk out that door without at least knowing your name and trying to get your number, I'll spend the rest of my life cursing my stupidity," he said, adopting the look of a scared teenager trying to work up his courage to ask the prettiest girl in school to the prom.

Corri laughed at the man's humorous come-on, momentarily forgetting she was possibly talking to a serial killer. Snapping back to reality, she extended her hand, "Hi. I'm Robin. And you are . . .?"

"Hi, Robin. A beautiful name for a beautiful lady. I'm Emory, and I'm very happy to meet you."

As he introduced himself, the man executed a little bow, somehow pulling off a move that was clearly out of place in a beach night club.

"May I accompany you on your walk, Robin?"

She hesitated a moment and then, thinking of the back-ups who would shadow their walk, said, "Sure, why not."

As they walked out the door and began strolling along First Street, Clay called the rest of his team on the radio, "Did anyone hear the guy's name? I couldn't pick it up over the noise in the bar."

Shank Wygle was dressed in ragged old clothes and riding a beach cruiser on the boardwalk. He responded on a tiny handheld microphone, "He said Emory, I think."

"Say again! Did you say Emory?" Clay asked, agitation evident in his voice.

"Yeah, that's what it sounded like. Why?" Shank asked.

The next few seconds of radio traffic were garbled as multiple team members talked over each other. Finally, Clay broke through.

"Everybody stand by! I need the air clear. We may have our killer! Cassie, do you have eyes on Corri and this guy?"

"They're headed north on First Street on the east side. They're approaching the pier parking lot now."

"Can you see the guy's face, Cassie? Please tell me you got a clear eyeball on him. Tell me it's Emory Elliot Stovall!"

Cassie kept adjusting her binoculars as they continued walking, trying to get a clear view of the man's face.

"I can't see his face, Clay. I don't know if it's him or not."

Keying the radio, he asked, "Anybody on the radio besides Broderick and me who knows Stovall on sight? If so, respond now."

Hearing no response, Clay grew more agitated. "That damn Bobby Hawkins has to call in sick the one time he could be of use since he knows Stovall," he raged to his empty car.

Ty spoke up, "Cool it, guys. Corri's voice is coming in fine now. Listen up!"

Team members shifted their attention from their talk-around channel back to the body mike channel in time to pick up the man talking to Corri, ". . . like to walk barefoot on the beach."

"I do, too. I've been surfing since I was about ten, so I guess I'm a true beach bunny."

"Would you like to take a stroll on the beach?"

Corri hesitated, calculating the risk involved and the ability of her team to cover her if this guy was really the serial killer. "Well, I don't know . . ."

"If you're worried about being on the beach in the dark, don't be. I've got a black belt in Tae Kwan Do, so I can handle anybody who tries to mess with us," he said, a hint of boastfulness in his voice.

"Okay, I'm not scared, anyway," she said with false enthusiasm in her voice.

That's just great! she thought. *This guy's probably carrying a pigsticker a foot long, and now he tells me he knows karate! What have I got myself into*? she asked herself as they weaved their way between the parked cars heading for the beach.

Clay and the rest of the team were frantically shifting their coverage.

"I want Honchen and Wygle under the pier right now! Get in the sand cave so the guy can't see you when they pass by. Three, get David Sheasley, 'Tana Jones, and Rafe Santos and split into two teams north and south of the pier to give us coverage both directions. Whichever way they go, I want the other team closing up to be ready for a takedown. Everybody go!"

Team members scrambled to their positions as Corri and the man calling himself Emory approached the entrance ramp to the pier.

"What do you do for a living, Emory?"

"Oh, I dabble in stocks. Well, I guess to be fair, I should say the stock market is my avocation. My vocation is the real estate business. I buy distressed properties at bargain basement prices, spend a little money fixing them up, and sell them for a profit."

"Is that a profitable business, I mean, right now with the housing market in flux like it is?"

"I do okay," he said, trying and failing to project an image of modesty.

As they reached the sand, he said, "Hang on while I get my shoes off."

Hopping on one foot, he stripped off one shoe and sock, then turned to Corri.

"Give me a hand while I get the other shoe off so I don't end up face down in the sand," he laughed, reaching out to Corri with his left hand.

She reached out with her right hand to steady him while he took off his other shoe. As he started pulling off his sock, he staggered off balance, pulling Corri toward him.

"Whoa," he said as he grabbed her with both hands, pulling her to the sand and landing on top of her. Suddenly, he was all hands, squeezing her breasts with one hand while he pulled down her shorts with the other.

"Wait! Stop!" Corri said loudly, grabbing his hands as the man feverishly continued his assault.

Panting with the effort, he snarled, "Quit fighting me, bitch!" as he struck Corri in the side of the head with his fist.

Stunned by the vicious punch, she stopped struggling, giving him time to get her shorts and panties pulled down with one hand while he unzipped his pants and pulled out his penis with the other.

As he tried to force himself inside her, Corri regained her senses. Screaming, she slapped her hands together on his ears as hard as she could, trying to break his eardrums.

"OW!" he screeched. "You bitch! I'll kill you!" he yelled as he wrapped his hands around her throat and began to choke her.

Ty Honchen and Shank Wygle got there first. Ty grabbed the man by his belt and the collar of his shirt and literally yanked him over his head as if he were completing an Olympic lift. With a loud roar, he threw the man through the air, where he landed on his face in the sand. Amazingly, he was on his feet in an instant, assuming a karate stance.

Emory snarled, "You just fucked with the wrong man!"

He moved slowly toward Ty, his hands and body in a classic karate fighting position. Behind Ty, Corri scrambled to her feet, pulling up her shorts as she tried to get her bag open to get to her gun and badge.

Emory suddenly screamed in pain as the barbs from Shank Wygle's TASER hit him squarely in the back, sending fifty thousand volts through his body and driving him face down onto the sand for the second time in less than a minute.

As the five-second ride continued, Ty yelled, "POLICE, ASSHOLE! Don't move!"

As soon as the current stopped flowing, Emory started to get up, so Shank shocked him again. The man writhed side to side, getting sand into his nose and mouth. The rest of the team had come running up by this time, panting from their all-out sprint to reach the scene before the action was over.

When the flood of electricity stopped for the second time, Emory stayed down but raised his head to look around. What he saw unnerved him. He was surrounded by eight men and women, all pointing guns at his head and waving badges so he couldn't possibly miss them.

"Shit," he muttered. "Bunch of cocksuckin' cops."

Clay dropped down beside him, staring at his face a moment before recognition flooded in.

"Well, I'll be damned. Emory Elliot Stovall, as I live and breathe! You just made my day. Hell, you've made my year!"

Stovall stared at Clay, not speaking.

"Listen up, *Mr. Stovall*," Clay said, unable to keep the sarcastic delight out of his voice. "I'm gonna put cuffs on you. If you fail to follow my instructions to the letter, Officer Wygle here will give you another shot of the juice. Do we understand each other?"

Stovall continued to stare, saying nothing.

"I'll ask you just once more. Do we have an understanding?"

When Stovall remained mute, Clay looked at Shank Wygle, "I think he wants to ride that horse again."

"Wait! Wait! Don't do it again! I couldn't hear you because of that bitch!" Stovall spat, looking with hatred at Corri Jennings. "I think my eardrums are broken. I'm suing every one of you bastards! I didn't do anything she didn't ask for. I never would've left the bar with her if she hadn't begged to suck my cock. I'm innocent!"

Corri started toward Stovall, fire in her eyes. "Back off, Jennings. He's trying to provoke you," Clay ordered, grabbing her arm to keep her from attacking Stovall. "I'll handle this."

Kneeling beside Stovall again, he asked, "Are you going to cooperate? Tell me you are, or he's going to tase you 'til your eyebrows turn white."

"Yeah, I'll cooperate," he growled.

"That's what I wanted to hear," Clay said, grabbing and cuffing his left arm first and then his right. With Ty on the other side, they hoisted him to his feet.

"How did you know my name?" he asked Clay.

"Don't you remember? My partner and I stopped you after you tried to pick up that young girl on First Street several weeks ago."

Stovall had looked away from Clay as he talked. His head spun around at Clay's words, his eyes narrowing to slits.

"I remember you now. You're the cocksucker that wrote me a bullshit ticket! Where's the big, red-headed hooker you had with you that night?" he sneered.

"I'm right here, slick," Cassie said, stepping into the circle of flashlights.

She was sweating from her dash down the stairs from the top of the parking garage, and her unruly red hair was flying in every direction. She was furious that someone had attacked a cop, yet ecstatic that it was Stovall.

"I had a feeling we'd see you again. You're in deep shit this time, pal. A jury will be only too happy to lock your ass up for a bunch of years for trying to rape a cop. But I have a feeling that charge will get lost in the shuffle when we put the heavy stuff on you."

"What are you talking about? What heavy stuff?" Stovall demanded.

Clay looked at Cassie, shaking his head. He didn't want to give Stovall advance warning so he could invent alibis for the murders. In the department's interrogation room, he hoped the shock of hearing they suspected him of committing ten murders would cause him to break and give them a full confession.

"Never mind, Stovall," Clay said.

Turning to Fontana Jones, he directed, "'Tana, you and Ty transport Stovall to the station."

As she took Stovall's left arm, Ty warned, "He claims he knows karate, 'Tana. Watch him close."

"Don't worry," Shank spoke up. "I'm leaving the darts attached just in case he decides to get stupid."

As they escorted Stovall to the patrol car, Clay checked on Corri Jennings. "Are you hurt? Do you need to go to the ER?"

Shaking her head, Corri was bent over with her hands on her knees, taking deep breaths in an effort to stave off the urge to puke as the adrenaline dumped from her body. Three Rivers stood beside her gently rubbing her back. His hands were shaking as he realized how close his girlfriend and fellow officer had come to getting seriously hurt.

"You okay, Corri?" he asked anxiously.

"Yeah," she responded in a raspy voice "Throat's a little sore from him trying to choke me. My pride's hurt more than anything. I can't believe the rotten son-of-a-bitch tried to rape me. If I could have gotten my gun out of my bag, I would have put two . . . hell, I would have put *ten* in his K-5 ring. Next thing he knew, that bastard would have been knocking at Satan's door asking for his pitchfork and horns!"

Rubbing her temple, she said, "His punch packs a ton. I was out of it for a few seconds. I hope I broke the bastard's eardrums!"

Pausing to take a deep breath, she looked up hopefully at Clay, "You think he's our killer?"

"Right now, based on what he did to you, I'll say it's a very high probability. We've been watching him ever since he tried to pick up that girl on First Street a while back. I thought then from the way he acted that there was something really wrong about him. And tonight just proves it."

Turning to Cassie, he asked, "Did he have a knife on him?"

"Unfortunately, no. Just some cash, cigarettes, and his wallet."

"Any identification?"

"Yeah. His Florida DL issued to Emory Elliot Stovall, same address in Ponte Vedra as when we stopped him. The only record he's got is a failure to appear charge on the stop sign ticket you gave him. Dispatch ran a criminal history on him, too. No hits anywhere."

"When we get to the station, let's put him in Interview Room One. It has the new recording equipment with a color camera and voice activated recording. I want to start interviewing him before he hollers for a lawyer. We may just have our serial killer in the back of that car!" Clay said in an excited tone.

He clapped Shank Wygle on the back. "Great job with the TASER. If this guy really knows karate like he claims, you may have saved us from having to shoot him. And I'm sorry to have to do this to you, Shank, but I need you to stay until we get an evidence tech out here to process the scene."

"Uh, process what scene, Sarge? There's nothing here but sand," Wygle said, confused.

"He didn't have a knife on him, so I want to be absolutely sure he didn't dump one in the sand during the fight. Plus, I want Jim to take pictures of the sand and the surroundings to show exactly where the attack took place."

"Oh, right, right. That makes sense. Okay, I'm your man. If a knife's here, I'll find it."

Chapter 39

The caravan of police cars rolled into the parking lot. Transporting Stovall, 'Tana Jones and Ty Honchen pulled into the sallyport with Clay and Cassie right behind. They got out of their cars and waited until the overhead door closed, ensuring their prisoner couldn't escape. With the exception of Shank Wygle, the rest of the team came in through the side door, creating a show of force in case Stovall wanted to fight again.

Opening the car door, Clay unbuckled Stovall's safety belt and told him to step out. With his hands cuffed behind his back, Stovall had to shift his body sideways and swing his legs out.

"Don't forget his feet, Sarge," 'Tana warned.

"Are you going to give us a problem?" Clay asked, watching Stovall closely for his reaction.

"No. No problem," he answered dejectedly.

Clay reflected on the man's abrupt change in demeanor. It was surprising, even unusual. He wondered again if he was looking at a serial killer, the notorious murderer who had haunted his dreams and most of his waking moments for the past six months.

Man, if he's the one, this will be a media spectacle around here, he mused. *And poor, pitiful Bobby Hawkins is too sick to preen in front of the cameras. I guess I'll have to do it. It'll be nice to get a little credit instead of my weekly ass chewing from the chief. We all deserve a pat on the back for getting this guy off the street.*

Clay took Stovall's left arm and pulled him to a standing position. Cassie took his other side, and the two of them escorted him through the booking area into the interview room, closely followed by Ty Honchen. The interrogation room they entered was sparsely decorated with three plastic chairs and a small table. The walls were painted off-white with nothing to break the neutral monotony.

The camera and microphone were hidden inside the air conditioning register in the ceiling, feeding signals to the recording equipment in the adjacent room. A one-way mirror allowed other officers to watch the proceedings without being physically in the room. As soon as Clay and Cassie escorted Stovall into the room, Ty shut the door and stepped into the viewing room.

"Have a seat," Clay said to Stovall, indicating a chair directly across from the one-way mirror.

"Do I have to keep wearing these things?" Stovall asked, swinging his hands around to reveal the stainless steel handcuffs firmly locked around his wrists.

Clay stared at him for a moment as he tried to decide if the guy was faking his subdued demeanor.

"What do you think?" he asked Cassie.

She addressed Stovall in a firm voice, "Sergeant Randall is thinking about taking the cuffs off. It would be a serious mistake for you to flip out. Why should we trust you?"

Stovall looked at Cassie and then dropped his eyes to the floor.

"I'll cooperate," despair clear in his voice.

Clay watched Stovall closely, looking for signs his aggression was returning. Seeing none, he made the decision.

"Turn around, and I'll get those cuffs off."

Stovall raised his head and looked at Clay through teary eyes, turning around so he could get to the cuffs.

"You sure you're calmed down?" Cassie asked, still a little nervous about letting the man have full use of his hands.

Stovall turned his head slightly to look at Cassie. Nodding, he dropped his head again. Clay exchanged looks with Cassie. Neither knew how to take the new Emory Elliot Stovall.

They weren't sure if it was an act to get them to let their guard down. The other possibility, occurring to the veteran detectives almost simultaneously, was that he was the serial killer and was depressed at having finally been caught. Offering no resistance, he sat as soon as the cuffs were removed and laid his head on the table.

Clay and Cassie sat across from Stovall, saying nothing. After three minutes of almost total silence, the only sound an occasional sniff from Stovall, he raised his head.

"What do you want to know?" he asked softly.

"First, I need to advise you of your rights," Clay said.

He proceeded to read Stovall his Miranda rights from a card he pulled from his wallet. When he finished, Clay asked, "Do you understand these rights I've read to you?"

Stovall nodded.

"I need a verbal response," Clay clarified.

"Yes, I understand."

"Understanding those rights, do you wish to speak to us?"

Stovall glanced at Clay and then at Cassie. He then shifted his gaze to the one-way mirror.

"Is someone on the other side of that mirror watching us?"

Figuring Stovall knew the answer, Clay saw no advantage to be gained by lying.

"Yes, there are several detectives in the room. The ones from out there on the beach."

"Is the guy who shocked me in there, too?" Stovall asked, a hint of anger returning.

"No, he's not. Now, do you want to talk to us?"

He shrugged, "Sure, why not? I've got nothing more to lose anyway."

"What do you mean?" Cassie asked.

He shrugged again, a slight smile playing across his lips, disappearing almost as fast as it appeared.

"You're the big shot investigators. You figure it out," his innate arrogance starting to reappear.

"Okay. For the record, let's pretend we don't know you. Please state your full name and address," Cassie prompted.

"Emory Elliot Stovall. I live at 887 Ponte Vedra Boulevard."

"Where do you work?"

"I don't."

"How do you support yourself? You know, pay your bills, buy food, gas for your car, etc." she asked.

"I get by," he said, smiling again.

"Could you be more specific, Mr. Stovall?" Clay interjected.

"I could, but I won't. Let's just say, for the second time, I believe, because I told you when you harassed me before . . . that I'm independently wealthy."

At that moment, Clay's BlackBerry vibrated. Glancing at it, he saw a message from Shank Wygle, in capital letters, "FOUND THE KNIFE IN THE SAND! HE'S THE KILLER!!!!!"

Stunned, Clay stared at the words as he tried to assimilate the message. He looked up at Stovall, who was staring at him curiously, as was Cassie. He began to smile.

"Emory, do you own a knife?" Clay asked.

Stovall suddenly grew fidgety, shifting back and forth in his seat. "What do you mean?"

"A knife. You know. A sharp instrument, made of steel, you use it to cut something . . . or somebody. Do you own one?"

Glancing left and right, licking his suddenly dry lips, Stovall said, "Yeah, I own a *bunch* of knives. They're in a drawer in my kitchen. I use them for cutting vegetables and steak and stuff. So what?"

"Did you have a knife with you when you attacked Officer Jennings tonight?"

"I didn't attack her. She propositioned me in the bar. She could tell how well-hung I am, and she said she would pay to give me a blow job. I didn't need a knife, except maybe to protect myself against her. She's a female predator. And she's a cop? What a joke!"

"Now, Emory," Clay said in a tone a parent would use on a child caught lying about breaking the living room window. "You didn't answer my question. Did you have a knife with you tonight?"

Stovall clenched his fists, his shoulders hunching together. Clay and Cassie tensed, ready to react if he suddenly became violent.

Suddenly, he sat up straight, letting out a loud sigh. "I'm through talking to you. If you're going to put some bullshit assault charge on me, do it so I can get my lawyer to post bond for me. I've got better things to do with my time. You know, you're a pitiful excuse for a cop, Randall. I don't understand what a fine piece of ass like Dana sees in a loser like you," he smirked at Clay as he leaned back, crossing his arms over his chest.

Clay exploded to his feet, the chair flying backward, slamming into the wall and rattling the one-way mirror.

"You sorry piece of shit! Don't ever speak my wife's name again, or I swear I'll . . ."

Stovall's crude reference to Clay's wife was a trigger, causing all the emotional pressures of the past six months to erupt. Working fourteen hour days; replaced as head of the task force by the weasel Bobby Hawkins; anger at the chief for forcing his friend and boss,

Mike Wilson, into retirement. Stovall's snide comment was too much.

Clay's whole body shook as he tried to control the intense desire to lunge across the table and bash Stovall's head into a bloody pulp. His logical side fought for dominance over his raging emotions. Attacking Stovall was exactly what the man wanted, he realized. After a few seconds, his professional switch came back on, and he was once again in control.

Staring at Stovall intensely, he said, "This interrogation is being halted at your request so you can consult with an attorney. You'll be transported to the Duval County Jail and booked for attempted sexual battery and related charges for your attack on Officer Jennings."

Spinning around, Clay started to leave. As he reached the door, he stopped, turning back to Stovall, who had started to rise from his chair.

"Oh, and by the way, we'll be talking to the state attorney about adding more charges, also."

"What charges?" Stovall asked, a wary look in his eyes.

"Murder."

"What? Murder? What the hell are you talking about?" Stovall yelled.

"We found your knife on the beach where you dropped it during your attack on Officer Jennings," Clay said, calmly, once more the professional cop. "We believe you're a serial killer, Mr. Stovall. You've killed at least five people here in Jax Beach and probably another six or seven across the state. But rest easy. We'll only charge you with our cases. That should be enough to get you the needle in this state."

With that parting shot, Clay left the room as Ty Honchen and Three Rivers came in to take Stovall to the county jail.

As he walked away, Stovall yelled at his retreating back, "I didn't kill anybody! You're fucking up bad now! I'll get you for this!"

Ty grabbed Stovall's arm and jerked him around. His eyes narrowed to slits as he got within six inches of Stovall's face.

"Clay Randall is a good cop, and we don't take kindly to threats against our own. If you even dream of doing anything to him, every cop in this place will join me in making your life a living hell!"

Without giving Stovall a chance to respond, Ty spun him around, cuffed him, and marched him out to the sallyport to a waiting transport car. Opening the door, he shoved Stovall inside roughly, then held him back against the seat with a powerful forearm while he connected the shoulder harness.

Stepping away, Ty slammed the door, at the same time telling the patrol officer, "Get this son-of-a-bitch downtown and book him."

As the officer drove out of the sallyport, Stovall looked back at Honchen, thinking, *You just bought a one-way ticket to hell*!

Chapter 40

At 2:00 a.m., Clay and his team met in the Detective Division. Realizing they would need something strong to stave off the inevitable fatigue that would hit as the night wore on, Three Rivers brewed a pot of the special coffee blend he liked. Everyone avoided looking at Clay, feeling sympathy for him at Stovall's crude comment about his wife yet surprised over his angry explosion at the man. Rarely had any of them seen Sergeant Clay Randall lose his cool, so, naturally, they had all assumed he wasn't capable of most normal human emotions where the job was concerned.

As they sat around the conference table sipping the strong and bitter-tasting coffee, Clay spoke. "Guys, I apologize for losing it in there. I guess—"

Cassie Broderick interrupted him. "It's okay. The son-of-a-bitch deserved it."

"Yeah, I gotta hand it to you, man. You got more control than me. I'm not sure I could've held back if he'd said that about Ann," Ty said.

Corri Jennings, still berating herself for letting Stovall get the best of her, added, "Clay, I was so pissed at him that, if you hadn't stopped me, I think I would have shot him. Then I'd have probably been in trouble myself. You just acted like a human being for a few seconds. But you never stepped over the line, so don't beat yourself up over it."

"Thanks, guys. I appreciate your support."

Shrugging his shoulders to loosen the kinks, he said, "Guys, this is the calm before the storm. As soon as word gets out that a Jacksonville Beach police officer was the victim of an attempted sexual assault by a rich guy from Ponte Vedra, we're going to be swamped by the media. We can handle that.

"But if they find out we're looking at Stovall as the serial killer, too, the national media are going to descend on us with more cameras, satellite trucks and reporters than this town has ever seen. There'll be so many talking heads here the entire supply of hair spray and makeup will be sold out within a twenty mile radius," he said with a grin.

"So, before the horde arrives and starts reporting everything we *do* say and making up things we didn't say, tell me if I'm overreacting to think that Stovall is our man. Can we charge him with Marilyn Gibbs, James Barton, Nita Caruso, and Billy Bowen here, and Donna Martin in Atlantic Beach?" he asked, ticking off the names on his fingers.

Cassie said, "I don't think we have enough evidence to convince the state attorney, at least not right now. We all know they would prefer cases sewed up so tight the defendant has no choice but to plead out. Since there were so many witnesses to the attack on Corri, that probably meets their requirements, but the murders? I don't have the same level of confidence about them. We just don't have anything that ties him directly to any of the victims. Sorry, Clay."

"No, that's okay, Cassie. I'm looking for straight talk here, no emotion, no B.S. Tell me what you really think, not what you think I want to hear. Anybody else? Ty?"

"Yeah, Clay," he said, sighing heavily. "I would love to nail this asshole for the murders, but I agree with Cassie that it's a stretch."

He explained, "One, he attacked a police officer, but his previous victims have been exclusively hookers and transients. Two, Wygle found a knife in the area where the struggle took place, but we can't put it in his possession, at least I don't think we can. I'll come back to point two in a second. Three, the knife blade appears similar in size to the knife wounds on the homicide victims, but that in and of itself proves nothing. And four, he drives a light blue BMW, which is similar to the suspect vehicle in Panama City Beach. But there are probably dozens if not hundreds of light blue Beemers sold. Since that appears to be all we have to tie him to the murders, I doubt seriously if that's enough.

"Back to my second point. We may have a little problem with the specific charges we can stack on Stovall for his attack on Corri. Can we say conclusively that the knife is his? Corri, did you ever see the knife?"

"No, I didn't," she conceded. "Of course, after he punched me, I was seeing stars for a few seconds, so he could have pulled it out then," she said, visualizing the attack and getting angry all over again.

Ty continued, "To put the knife on Stovall in the absence of a witness, we have to connect him through fingerprints. The knife needs to be checked for any usable prints and, if there are, see if they match up with Stovall. It also needs to be processed for blood traces to see if there's a match with any of our murder victims. By the way, who has the knife?"

Shank Wygle said, "Jim Childress took it."

Clay jumped in, "If there's blood on the knife, DNA testing will take weeks or even months to complete. Jim can at least test for the presence of blood, and he can type it to see if it matches with any of our victims, but that's as much as we can get right away."

Turning to Wygle, Clay said, "Shank, go find Childress and tell him I want that knife processed *yesterday*. If we can put it in Stovall's possession, it will bump up the charges considerably. Then a judge will be more inclined to hang a high bond on him and increase the chances that he'll stay in jail while we try to tie him to the murders."

As Wygle left the room, Clay looked around at the remaining officers. "I've got to call Cooper on this. Does anyone think we should tell him we've caught our serial killer?"

Hearing a chorus of no's, he adjourned the meeting, directing everyone to start the huge volume of paperwork required to charge Stovall with the assault on Officer Jennings. Clay went to his office and called Chief Cooper, who arrived at the station at 3:00 a.m.

Before Clay could brief him on the events surrounding the arrest of Emory Elliot Stovall, Cooper demanded, "Where is Officer Hawkins? Why isn't he here to brief me?"

"Chief, I talked to him about five yesterday afternoon, and he gave no indication anything was wrong. Then about fifteen minutes before the detail kicked off, he called and said he was sick. We already had a bunch of officers in on OT, so I figured it would be best to go ahead with the detail," Clay said, maintaining a blank look that masked the pleasure he was feeling as he envisioned Bobby Hawkins trying to explain his way out of this one.

"Alright, I'll deal with him. Tell me what you've got," he commanded in his deep voice.

Clay spent the next twenty minutes taking Chief Cooper through the incident, starting with Corri Jennings' initial encounter with

Stovall, the attack, finding the knife they were processing for prints and blood evidence, and ending with Stovall's statements in the interview room. Cooper didn't interrupt, instead writing notes to himself.

When Clay finished, the chief asked, "Didn't you write this man a traffic ticket some time back?"

"Yes, I did," Clay said, figuring Stovall must have complained on him.

Briefly wondering if Cooper had dismissed the ticket as a political favor to a rich Ponte Vedran, he continued, "I wrote him for running a stop sign after he tried to entice a teenager into his car, a light blue BMW. Detective Broderick and I were out that night cruising the downtown area looking for a light blue or grey Beemer like the one the killer used in the Panama City Beach prostitute murder. With the car being similar and him trying to pick up the girl, and then lying to us about what he said to her and what he was doing at that time of night, all of that combined naturally aroused our suspicions about him."

Clay purposely avoided telling Cooper of his earlier discussion about Stovall's possible connection to the serial killings. In spite of that, the chief, under increasing pressure from the media and the mayor to solve the murders, latched onto the similarities.

"From what you're telling me, it sounds like you've caught the serial killer," Gordy said, excitement creeping into his voice.

Clay hesitated, "We talked about the similarities, but we're not satisfied he's the one. The biggest drawback in proving it is the lack of DNA evidence at any of the crime scenes that we can try to match with Stovall."

"I'm getting more and more pressure every day from . . . well, let's just say I'm getting pressure to get these cases cleared. I've got fine, upstanding citizens calling me demanding that I put more officers on their streets, even though all these killings have happened on the beach and not in a neighborhood. It's a load of crap, the hassle I'm getting."

Gordy suddenly stopped, realizing he was not talking to Bobby Hawkins or one of his other cronies.

"Anyway, I feel really good about this guy Stovall being the one. From the points you cited, there are too many similarities for them to be a coincidence. I'm going to call a press conference and announce that we've caught the serial killer," he concluded.

Clay fervently wished Commander Mike Wilson was still there to intercede on his behalf with the massive ego and strong will of Chief Cooper. After the discussion with his team, he had come to agree that the evidence to charge Stovall right now was weak. He was concerned that bringing homicide charges now would start the speedy trial clock and result in losing the cases entirely if the state attorney wasn't ready to proceed within the arbitrary time limits set by state law.

"Uh, Chief, is that a good idea? I mean, we don't have a smoking gun, so to speak, that ties Stovall directly to any of the murders."

Gordy Cooper stood to his full height of five feet, eight inches, staring down at Clay, who wisely remained seated.

"I don't recall asking for your opinion about my decision, Detective Randall. In the event I ever have such a weak moment, you can feel free to offer your thoughts. Until then, don't make that mistake again.

"I'm going to my office to prepare for a press conference. You're in charge of it since Officer Hawkins has seen fit to be ill at a most inopportune time. Set it up for 10:00 a.m. in my conference room. Be sure all the television, radio, and print media are contacted. Any questions?" he asked in a tone that clearly implied he wanted none.

Not trusting himself to speak as anger flooded through him again, Clay simply shook his head.

Without another word, Gordy Cooper turned on his heel and walked out.

Chapter 41

The press conference was an unmitigated disaster. Gordy Cooper almost pranced onto the raised platform he had ordered placed at the front of his conference room, the better for everyone to see him. His specially-constructed podium, fully four inches shorter than a standard pedestal, was placed on the platform, allowing him to look down at his audience and at the same time giving him the appearance of being taller than he was.

The story was big. Gordy had hinted in the press release that a major announcement about the status of the serial killer investigation would be made at the press conference. This was like throwing chunks of bloody meat into a pool full of ravenous sharks. The media read between the lines and surmised Chief Cooper was about to tell them the killer had been arrested.

Every local television and radio station was represented along with the major national cable news outlets. They were joined by reporters representing the print media in the Jacksonville area as well as newspapers from as far away as Miami. Clay wondered how reporters had traveled over three hundred and fifty miles from south Florida on such short notice until he overheard them talking about commandeering their publisher's private jet with his blessing.

Gordy opened the press conference with a prepared statement detailing the circumstances of the attack on Officer Jennings. Then he summarized the four murders in Jacksonville Beach and the single homicide in Atlantic Beach.

When he finished, Clay silently pleaded with the man to stop, but he didn't. Gordy was in his element. There were at least a dozen television cameras rolling, all trained directly on him. He went on to summarize the other homicides in Panama City Beach, Daytona, Tampa, and Key West.

Print and electronic media types were hurriedly scribbling notes, each in their own brand of shorthand, not wanting to miss any tidbit dropped by this cocky little man. His message was clear even though he had not yet stated it. He had a man in custody. This man had attempted to rape a female police officer, and this man was the serial killer wanted all over the state.

Gordy ended his prepared statement by reading the name of the suspect, Emory Elliot Stovall, and listing his address in Ponte Vedra. He said Stovall was an independently wealthy man who dabbled in a number of things, none of which he named, primarily because he had forgotten to ask Clay for the information before the press conference.

When the chief concluded his prepared statement, pandemonium ensued as every reporter in the large conference room tried to outshout the others in asking a question. Cooper did fairly well on most of them, declining to answer obvious ones such as, "What specific evidence do you have that points to Mr. Stovall as the killer?"

Unfortunately for Gordy, Kyle Meenan zeroed in on the holes in the case against Stovall. His probing questions quickly sent the chief's blood pressure into orbit.

"Chief Cooper, since you've declined to identify specifics, can you state here today that your department has evidence that directly links Emory Elliot Stovall to ten murders across the state?"

"I believe I've said already that I wouldn't answer questions about specific evidence," Gordy said smoothly.

"You did," Kyle persisted, "but I'm asking if, without identifying *what* the evidence is, you can confirm that you *do have* evidence that directly incriminates Mr. Stovall."

"Well, yes. We do," Gordy said.

Kyle continued quickly, irritating the hotshots from several of the large networks because they couldn't get their questions asked.

"So, you're saying that your officers will be filing multiple murder charges against him here in Jacksonville and then providing that direct evidence to the police agencies in Daytona Beach, Tampa, Key West, and Panama City Beach. Is that correct, Chief Cooper?"

Realizing he had overextended himself, Cooper tried to back up. "Now, Kyle," he said in his most condescending tone, "that's not entirely accurate. I have to present the information to our fine state attorney here in this judicial circuit and get his blessings to file the appropriate charges. Then—"

"Are you saying you're not sure whether you have sufficient evidence to file these murder charges, Chief Cooper?" Kyle hammered.

"YOU STUPID SON OF A BITCH! GET THE SHIT OUT OF YOUR EARS, BOY! IF I SAY SOMETHING, YOU JUST REPORT IT AND QUIT CHALLENGING EVERY DAMN WORD I SAY," he bellowed.

Gordy stopped, his mouth hanging open as he realized he had just cursed on live television. In every direction he looked, television cameras were pointed directly at him, their red lights shining as they recorded his humiliation.

But Gordon Haynes "Gordy" Cooper was nothing if not confident, to the point of supreme arrogance. He swiftly calculated the potential damage to his career, coming to the conclusion his outburst would be excused by his supporters. They would see it as a strong law and order response by their chief, fed up at the harassment by an incompetent, egotistical reporter. He gave no thought to the potential damage he might have done to the homicide investigations themselves.

Smirking at the huge throng of media, he said, "This press conference is over."

Cooper marched off the platform and into his office directly behind, slamming the door on the shouted questions directed at the puffed-up little man who had shown such overwhelming impudence.

Chapter 42

The fallout from Gordy Cooper's tantrum was swift. By the next day, after seeing and hearing his bleeped response to Kyle Meenan replayed dozens of times on both local and national media, Mayor Carolyn Hudson summoned the chief to her office.

Prior to her election to office, Hudson had grown disgusted with the sleazy methods Gordy Cooper used to crush anyone who disagreed with him. She ran for mayor determined to get rid of the tyrant if she could. Gordy's meltdown in a nationwide forum gave her the ammunition she needed. Thirty minutes after entering the mayor's office, Gordon Haynes Cooper left, officially the former Chief of Police of Jacksonville Beach.

The day after that, Mike Wilson was convinced by the mayor to come out of forced retirement. She administered the oath of office, and Mike officially took the reins of the police department as the new chief. He returned to the department he loved amid the cheers and applause of officers and civilian employees alike. Chief Wilson's first official act was to convene a meeting of Clay's serial killer task force in his conference room, scene of the recent Gordy Cooper fiasco.

Clay came in first, shaking the new chief's hand and clapping him on the back. He was followed by Cassie Broderick, Ty Honchen, Three Rivers, Shank Wygle, Corri Jennings, and Fontana Jones.

As the group settled in with coffee and donuts, Mike stood up to speak, "I can't begin to describe my feelings at being back here, so I won't try. Just know that I'm proud to serve with you again, and that's as much emotion as you're going to get from me," he said, ending with his typical growl.

Everyone in the room grinned at their new chief, happy for the first time in their careers to have a man of integrity leading them.

"Now what I'd like—"

"Hey, sorry, I'm late, Chief," Bobby Hawkins interrupted, barging into the room. "Someone apparently forgot to tell me about the meeting. Fortunately, I heard about it and rushed right down.

Just let me get a quick cup of coffee, and I'll bring you up to speed on the investigation."

As Bobby talked, he moved to the coffee pot and poured a cup. Grabbing a donut, he started toward the head of the table to sit next to the chief. No one, including Wilson, had said a word since Bobby charged in the door. He walked up to the chair he wanted, which happened to be occupied by Three Rivers.

Standing behind him, Hawkins bumped the chair slightly, leaned over, and said, "Rivers, you're in my seat. As the task force leader, I sit at the head of the table next to the chief."

Mike Wilson had deliberately stayed silent, watching Bobby Hawkins to see what he would do. He had seen enough.

"Officer Hawkins, tell me why you're here in this meeting."

Bobby looked at the new chief in confusion. Then he caught on, and he smiled.

"Oh, right. Well, see, Chief, I'm in charge of the serial killer task force."

"Really?" he asked, his eyebrows raised. "I thought Sergeant Randall was in charge."

"No. Well, he was, but, he was replaced. By me, so . . ."

"And who put you in charge, Officer Hawkins?"

Bobby hesitated, realizing the conversation was not going in the direction he expected. "I, uh . . . I was put in charge by Chief Cooper, uh, former Chief Cooper."

Pretending to be unaware of the move Cooper had made the day he was forced to retire, Mike said, "Let me see if I understand this. You're telling me that the former chief put you in charge of the task force, thereby forcing a supervisor, that would be Sergeant Randall, to report to a non-supervisor, that would be you. Is that what you're telling me, Officer Hawkins?"

Everyone in the room was riveted at the scene taking place before them, trying their best not to laugh at Hawkins' growing nervousness and discomfort. Bobby stood rooted to the spot, nervously licking his lips, his hands shaking so badly he spilled some of his coffee on the carpet. Quickly setting the cup on the table, he grabbed a napkin and began blotting the liquid. Mike waited patiently until Bobby stood up again, holding onto the wet napkin.

"Well? I'm waiting for your response, Officer Hawkins."

"I, I don't know what to say, Comman—, uh, Chief. I just did what I was told," he responded lamely.

"That's probably the truest statement you've made in a long time. Now listen up. The reason you didn't get the word on this meeting is that you are no longer part of this task force. From what I can tell, you added nothing of value to the investigation. In fact, I'm not clear on exactly what your value has been to this department in your entire career.

"So, effective immediately, you will report out on Sergeant Tanaka's squad on midnights where I expect you to do your job, Officer Hawkins. Serve our citizens first, this department second, your fellow employees third, and yourself last. Always last, Officer Hawkins. If you do that, you will get unqualified support from me. Fail, and I will allow you to maximize your opportunities outside this organization. Do we have an understanding?"

Bobby was in shock. He was losing his prestigious position, and he wasn't even being sent back to the cushy former job of public information officer. Instead, the chief was bumping him back to patrol officer status. Working the midnight shift that he hated. Working for Sergeant Tanaka, who expected his officers to give ten hours of work for ten hours pay. Working with Roy Connor, a man he feared. Numb, he could only nod as he moved to the door and out of the conference room, banished to a fate he couldn't have imagined only three days ago.

Dismissing Bobby Hawkins from his mind, Chief Wilson turned to Clay, "Now, tell me how strong a case we have on this Stovall character."

"Mike, I mean Chief, sorry," Clay apologized, realizing it would no longer be appropriate to use his former division commander's given name. "We booked Stovall on attempted sexual battery and kidnapping. The kidnapping charge is fairly weak, but it meets statutory requirements because he kept her from leaving.

"The judge set a five hundred thousand dollar bond on each charge, so he's eating and sleeping on the county's dime for the moment. But considering the size of his mansion on prime beachfront property in Ponte Vedra and the high-priced attorney he hired out of Miami, I expect him to hit the bricks any time."

"Have you discussed the homicide cases with the head of the felony trial division?" Mike asked.

"We've given them everything we have, which isn't all that much. Jim Childress processed the knife and got zip, no prints and no blood, so DNA is out on the homicides. Chief, we've just about beat this topic to death since we popped Stovall, and, bottom line, we're not sure he's the killer."

"So, what's your plan?" Mike asked, feeling the frustration of every officer in the room.

Clay looked at Cassie, nodding for her to pick up the briefing.

"Chief," she said, "I'm the official monitor for the various investigative tracks, so I'll summarize. Jeremy Rivers is en route to the Miami area to dig up background on Stovall. He grew up there and left in his early twenties, as best we can tell. After that, he's going to Key West to meet with the detectives who handled their prostitute homicide. Ty is heading to Daytona tomorrow to meet with their detectives and then on to Tampa to check on their case. Finally, Ben Wygle is in Panama City Beach checking on their case information."

Clay jumped back in, "They're taking picture lineups with Stovall's mug shot included to show to witnesses. We know there are at least two. One of the Daytona cases and the Navy guy in Panama City Beach, so we're hoping for a positive ID on one of them at least."

Mike asked, "I don't suppose we've got enough to get a search warrant for Stovall's house, do we? I would really like to get inside and see if he's got anything that could tie him to our murders. Also, can I assume you've considered the possibility that the serial killer took a souvenir from each of his victims?"

"We have," Clay responded. "At least two of our victims may have had something taken. We interviewed James Barton's daughter early on, and she insisted he always carried a little framed picture of her with him, but it wasn't in his backpack or his clothing.

"Then there's Billy Bowen, the dwarf. His right ear lobe was freshly torn like the killer ripped out an earring. His left one was also torn, but it was scarred over. A couple of transients told us Little Billy, as they called him, wore big hoop earrings. They said the one in his left ear was torn out by someone during a fight sometime in the recent past. According to one of his buddies, he was wearing the one in his right ear the day before he was killed. So, yes, we'll look for those if we get a chance to search Stovall's house."

"Okay, guys, I'll let you get back to work," Mike said, smiling for the first time since the meeting started. "I've got a police department to run."

Chapter 43

By the end of the week, Emory Elliot Stovall was a free man. Attorney Gerald Strahan appeared on his client's behalf at the bond hearing before Judge Lenny Baker, a mediocre judge who had been on the bench so long that defense attorneys and prosecutors alike joked that his butt had put down roots into the fabric of his high-backed chair.

The assistant state attorney presented her case for keeping Stovall's bond at five hundred thousand per charge, for a total of one million dollars. Her arguments were well-reasoned, avoiding histrionics, a trial tactic more commonly used by defense attorneys. When she concluded, it was the defense attorney's turn.

"Thank you, your Honor," Gerald Strahan said in his folksy manner as he gestured to Stovall, sitting beside him in a two thousand dollar Italian suit.

"My client, Mr. Emory Elliot Stovall, is a fine, upstanding gentleman, a prominent supporter of many philanthropic causes, both locally as well as nationally. He has deeply embedded ties to his community that absolutely guarantee he is going nowhere. He will be here today. He will be here tomorrow. I say, your Honor, Mr. Emory Elliot Stovall plans to be here until the Good Lord calls him home!"

Putting his hand on Stovall's shoulder to show support for his client, Strahan continued his oratory, "He will be here because he wants to answer the scurrilous charges that have besmirched his outstanding character. Mr. Stovall has truly been the victim of a vicious witch hunt by an inexperienced and incompetent police force. The Jacksonville Beach Police Department is so backward that the chief got himself fired, *fired* for the use of such vile language that my beautiful granddaughter ran crying from the room when she heard him utter it on national television!

"Your Honor, my client has been falsely accused of attacking a police officer in a way that is simply outside the realm of possibility for him to even imagine doing. Our position is that Mr. Stovall was instead attacked by the police officer herself and —"

"Hold on, Mr. Strahan," Judge Baker interrupted. "This is neither the time nor place to litigate the charges against your client. This is a bond hearing, nothing more."

"Your Honor, please accept my humble apologies. I just feel so strongly about the innocence of my client that . . . well, there I go again! I do apologize and will conclude my remarks by asking that you allow Mr. Stovall to be set free from the horrendous conditions he is currently enduring in that hellhole . . . oh, forgive me, your Honor, I apologize profusely for my inadvertent use of slang before this honorable Court.

"In conclusion, I beg the Court to release Mr. Stovall from the Duval County Jail on his own recognizance, with the understanding that he relinquish his passport and stay within the confines of Duval County or St. Johns County where he currently resides, except with the Court's permission."

The assistant state attorney leaped to her feet to argue vociferously against Strahan's request, citing the particularly vicious nature of his attack on a female police officer, an attack that was witnessed by at least half a dozen police officers.

After several more minutes of arguing by both sides, Judge Baker ruled the bond would be reduced to twenty-five thousand dollars per charge. As he banged his gavel to close the hearing, Stovall smiled at his attorney. He could easily have posted the full million dollar bond if required, but he enjoyed the game of trying to get it reduced.

By the time he was released from the jail an hour later, Emory Elliot Stovall's overriding obsession, nurtured over the week he had spent in the filthy conditions of the jail, revolved around his detailed plan for revenge against Clay Randall and Ty Honchen.

Chapter 44

Over the next two weeks, as summer advanced, tropical waves began forming in the Atlantic Ocean and the Caribbean. Every year, Floridians braced for the storm season, packing their hurricane kits with bottled water, clothing, and boxed and canned foodstuffs. Important records and valuables were loaded into small containers that could easily fit into the trunks of cars.

Clay had already put together his hurricane kit and arranged for Dana, as in previous seasons, to evacuate with her parents to their vacation home in Stone Mountain, a picturesque little town northeast of Atlanta. Depending on the direction of the storm, their other evacuation destination was a townhome on Sanibel Island on the southwest coast of Florida.

Clay's job required that he stay and work. It was an arrangement neither of them liked but understood to be necessary, given the responsibility of police officers to protect the city from looters in the event of an evacuation.

At 5:30 a.m. Saturday morning, Clay sat at the bar with his high-test cup of coffee and bowl of oatmeal, his normal pre-ride breakfast. Dana sat beside him eating eggs with toast and jelly and drinking decaf coffee. Her belly was showing a little more each week, although she was still fairly trim due to her continuing regimen of running and Pilates exercises several times a week.

"How long is your ride today?" she asked, looking sideways at Clay as she buttered her second piece of toast.

"Fifty today," he said. "I've got a triathlon next weekend, so I need to get in one more hard training ride before I start tapering off."

"Is anyone riding with you?" she asked, concerned about Clay riding in the pre-dawn darkness on the busy highway from Jacksonville Beach to St. Augustine.

"Not today. Sam left a message saying he had to babysit his daughter, Lily, so I'm riding solo."

Seeing her look of concern, he tried to reassure her. "It's okay, babe. Those LED lights on my bike are so bright a driver would have to be blind to miss them flashing. And if he's blind, I'll be the least of his worries!" he said, laughing as he got up to rinse off his dishes.

"Okay, but call me when you get to your first rest stop so I'll know you're not lying in the palmetto bushes somewhere with a car's side mirror welded to your butt."

"Wow, don't we have a vivid imagination!" he exclaimed. "Okay," he said, raising his hands in mock surrender at the thunderous look she was giving him. "You'd think I was a novice rider the way you're freaking out."

"Not at all. I just keep thinking about that Stovall guy threatening to get you and Ty. He's out of jail, and you have no idea where he is. He could be following you without you knowing he's there and run you down in his car. I'm worried about you."

"You're starting to sound like me when I was on your case about running on the beach."

"Yeah, and look how that turned out. I'm just scared, Clay. I can't forget how angry he was that night at my show at the Lansing Gallery. If Ethan Hunter hadn't been there, he might have attacked me just to get back at you. He really hates you! The man is frightening," she said, shuddering.

Clay walked back around the bar, sitting beside Dana as he wrapped his arms around her. "I'll be fine, darlin'. I can hear cars coming up behind me, and I always look back as they get close to let them know I'm aware of them. Worst case scenario? I'll get off the road until they pass.

"And besides, I always carry my little .380 in the bike pouch, so, if someone deliberately tries to run me off the road, I'll fire a shot across their bow, then *they'll* be the one heading for the bushes! And they'll need toilet paper when they get there!" Clay said, grinning at Dana as he copped a feel of her swelling breasts.

"Hey, those babies are getting huge," he said, taking advantage of her thin cotton tee shirt and lack of a bra.

"Alright, Mr. Magic Hands. That's enough. If you keep on, all your blood will head south on you, and I don't imagine an erection is the best thing to have on that tiny bike seat of yours."

Clay leaned over and kissed her neck softly, caressing her breasts a moment longer before stepping back.

"Keep your motor running, babe, and I'll take you for a ride on the pole express when I get back. Get it? pole express . . . Pol-*ar* Express?"

"Oh yeah, I got it, stud," Dana said, rolling her eyes as she laughed at Clay's corny play on words. "Now head on out of here, big boy. I'll be working on a new piece. I've got some more to do on Ethan's piece, but that's next week. Just be careful and come back to me soon."

"Always, my love," Clay said, kissing her and heading for the garage to get his bike ready for the ride.

Clay's route took him south to the county line where he connected with Ponte Vedra Boulevard. He had ridden past Stovall's mansion several times since the man had bonded out of jail, a fact he was glad now he had not shared with Dana. No lights or activity had been visible on his previous rides, and this morning was no exception. The house sat slightly elevated with a circular drive sloping down to the roadway. As Clay rode past, he spotted Stovall's BMW parked near the front door.

Man's got enough money to have a four car garage, but he parks his eighty thousand dollar car outside in the salt air. Go figure, he thought, dropping down into his tri-bars to make himself more aerodynamic and increasing his speed to thirty miles per hour.

His rear light was set to strobe, casting a brilliant red flash at least a mile to the rear, hopefully to alert drivers and thus avoid making him a hood ornament. A couple of miles past Stovall's house, Clay's heart rate and breathing were slightly elevated, his pedal rhythm a steady ninety strokes per minute.

Instead of listening to his mp3 player, Clay used the time on his rides to sift through the facts of the murders, looking for some area of the investigation he may have missed. As he contemplated the facts of the Billy Bowen and Nita Caruso murders, he heard what sounded like a truck approaching from the rear. Clay glanced over his left shoulder and saw headlights about half a mile back.

Dawn was breaking, but the section of road he was riding was still in deep shadows from large overhanging trees. *Whoever it is can't help but see me with the strobe*, he thought, resuming his mental review of the murders.

As Clay rode on, the sound of the approaching vehicle broke into his reverie. Looking back, he saw what appeared to be a large pickup truck, moving fast. Being cautious, he shifted from his tri-bars back to a more upright position just in case he had to make an evasive maneuver. As the sound of the engine grew louder, Clay looked back again. What he saw made him almost lose control of his bike. The truck was less than fifty yards away and closing fast, on a clear collision course with his bicycle.

Clay's eyes widened, his heart rate skyrocketing. *Oh, shit!* He thought. *He's gonna hit me!*

His mind whirling, he froze for a second. Then, looking to his right, he realized he was in the one area of Ponte Vedra Boulevard he hated riding because of short, pointed wooden posts a homeowner had buried in a line only a foot from the pavement, a line that stretched at least one hundred yards. Many times, Clay had visualized a blowout that caused him to fall and impale himself on one of the posts. Recognizing instantly that his overactive imagination might have been a premonition, Clay knew what he had to do.

He aimed his front wheel directly at the next post. Inches from impact, and with the truck only feet away from striking and possibly killing him, he jammed on his front brake. The combination of hitting the post at almost thirty miles per hour, coupled with locking up his front wheel, caused the bike to cartwheel. At the same moment, Clay twisted both feet out of his pedals and lunged up and to his right, grabbing for a fortuitously positioned tree branch about eight feet off the ground.

Unfortunately, he miscalculated both the speed and angle of his unplanned flight. Instead of grabbing the branch with his hands and swinging over, the left side of his chest took the brunt of it, knocking the breath out of him and breaking two ribs. Clay fell, slamming his head into the ground with such force that, in spite of his bike helmet, a concussion was added to his injuries.

At that moment, the wheels and body of a one-ton Dodge Ram truck struck his bicycle, shredding the carbon fiber frame and wheels into thousands of string-like pieces. The truck's right front wheel passed by Clay's head with less than a foot to spare. Still moving forward, the big vehicle destroyed at least twenty of the wooden posts before swerving onto the road, where it slid to a stop.

In severe pain from the broken ribs, and mentally confused from the concussion, Clay tried to get to his feet. He made it to his hands and knees, where the pain threatened to render him unconscious. Every breath felt like a knife poking around in his chest cavity. The truck's backup lights suddenly popped on. In his confused state, Clay thought the driver must have lost something and was coming back to check.

He saw the remains of his bike ten feet away, but the bag containing his badge and gun was nowhere in sight. Clay felt he should have them with him. He wasn't sure why it was important. It just was. He felt naked, like when he would dream as a kid that he went to school but forgot to wear pants. The badge and gun were two pieces of equipment that, on the one hand, identified him as a cop and, on the other, provided him with protection from harm. He wanted them. Now!

Clay's eyes scanned the ground frantically for the bike bag. Suddenly, as the truck came to a stop on the roadway only twenty feet away, he saw it in one of the deep ruts gouged by the truck's passage, little more than an arm's length away. Clay kept one eye on the truck while he began to crawl the short distance to the bag. The driver's door opened just as his hands closed around the bag.

Carefully, Clay slid his hand inside, gripping the small semi-automatic pistol as he turned to look at the driver. He could tell from the silhouette that it was a man, but his face was in shadow. It seemed like he should say something, but nothing came to mind. Meanwhile, the man didn't speak, instead watching Clay while he remained outside the illumination of the truck's headlights.

"I need help. I think I've got a broken rib," Clay gasped between pain-clenched teeth.

The unknown man continued to stand without moving, watching Clay's pain and discomfort, saying nothing.

"For God's sake, help me! I'm a police officer. Call 9-1-1!"

The man suddenly laughed, a sound that instantly made Clay's blood run colder than ice. His brain was whirling, still shaking off the immediate effects of the concussion. He knew the voice was familiar; he just couldn't quite place it.

Is that Ty? What's he doing out here. He doesn't ride, he asked himself. Then he thought it might be Mike Wilson, the new chief. *Sounds too young for Mike.*

Suddenly his thoughts grew lucid, and it hit him like a freight train.

"Stovall!" Clay spat out the name with such force that a fresh bolt of pain rushed through his chest and head.

"Is that you, Stovall?" he wheezed.

Emory Elliot Stovall stepped into the glare of the headlights. "Well, what do we have here? A cop begging *me* for help? And not just any cop. Oh, no. A *special* cop. An arrogant bastard who thinks he's a hotshot detective."

As he talked, he began moving toward Clay. Stopping a few steps away, he allowed Clay to see what he held in his right hand.

"See what I have for you?" Stovall asked.

His clarity of thought rapidly returning, Clay responded, "It's the knife you had on you when you attacked Corri Jennings, isn't it?"

"No, not that one. You bastards wouldn't give it back to me, but this one is just like it."

"Are you ready to confess you're the serial killer, Stovall?" Clay asked, tightening his grip on the little pistol.

Stovall laughed loudly, sounding almost inhuman. "I'll confess nothing to a piece of shit like you! But what I *will* do is cut your fucking throat and watch you bleed out right here. And when I'm finished with you, that short fucker, Honchen, has an appointment with death. And I'm death.

"Then when I finish him off, I'll spend some time with your wife. I'll do things to her that will make her beg me to kill her just to put her out of her misery. Does that sound like a good plan to you, Detective Sergeant Clayton Allen Randall?" he asked as he started toward Clay, turning the knife around to a stabbing position.

The pain in his ribs and his head was gone, suppressed by a massive rush of adrenalin. Clay pulled out the gun and, knowing Stovall was well within the zone for a killing blow with a knife, fired twice. Both rounds struck Stovall in the chest, only inches apart. He stopped in his tracks, looking down at Clay with a surprised expression on his face as his last few seconds of life ticked off.

Stovall fell dead, landing on top of Clay. He could barely breathe from the combined weight of Stovall and the pain in his chest that now returned with a vengeance.

As Clay struggled to remain conscious, he heard someone approaching.

"Hey, what's going on? What happened here? Was that a gunshot?" the property owner asked as he stood a short distance away, ready to dash back into the safety of his house if he felt threatened.

"Help me," Clay moaned. "I'm . . . a police officer. Man . . . just tried to . . . kill me. Had . . . to shoo-, shoot him. Call 9-1-," he mumbled, his head slumping over to rest on Emory Elliot Stovall's shoulder as everything went dark.

Chapter 45

The next few hours were a blur for Clay. He recalled hearing sirens and then people talking. At some point, a body was lifted off him, but he couldn't remember who the person was or why this person chose to take a nap on top of him. Clay vaguely recalled riding in a rescue unit. He figured that's what he was in because he was strapped down on a gurney, and the noise of the siren added to his already massive headache.

As rescue personnel rolled him into Baptist Medical Center, Beaches, he recognized some of his team members escorting the gurney into the ER; Ty Honchen, Cassie Broderick, and Shank Wygle. Later, he swore George Strait, his favorite country music artist, helped lift him onto the hospital gurney. Forgetting he was wearing bike shorts that had no pockets, he tried to pull a piece of paper and a pen out to get George's autograph, confused as to why he would be wearing pants with no pockets. Dana later told him he was hallucinating; George Strait hadn't been in Jacksonville in at least two years.

After being x-rayed, CT scanned, and having his fractured ribs not-so-gently poked and prodded, Clay was pronounced in good condition. As he rested in one of the ER treatment rooms waiting to be released, he heard the door open. Opening his eyes, the most beautiful sight he could behold, his Dana, came into view.

"Clay. Oh, Clay. Are you okay?" she cried, tears rolling down her cheeks as she rushed to his side.

"Hey, babe. I'm fine, I think. How did you get here?"

"Ann Honchen and Cassie Broderick came to the house. I was so scared when I saw who was at the door. I thought you had just crashed and got some road rash or maybe even broken a collar bone or something. But when they told me what happened . . ."

Dana's fear of losing her husband, coupled with the intense relief she felt at seeing him alive and not badly injured, finally overpowered the rigid control she had maintained over her emotions.

"I, I feel dizzy," she said, her legs buckling.

Ty Honchen had been standing right behind her, and he grabbed her before she could hit the floor. Clay started to jump from the bed.

Ty exclaimed, "Stay there, Clay! I've got her." He maneuvered Dana to a chair and sat her down gently.

"Cassie, get a nurse in here," he snapped.

Clay watched from the bed, realizing his broken ribs rendered him useless to his wife. That realization, coupled with his quick movement to get out of bed, sent a fresh wave of pain cascading through his skull. He laid his head back carefully on the pillow to avoid making the pain worse.

Cassie had run out of the room at Ty's direction, coming back moments later with two nurses and the ER doctor who had examined Clay initially. The impromptu medical team quickly took control of the situation, checking Dana's vital signs.

"Dana's pregnant, Doc," Clay said.

"How far along?" she asked Dana.

"I'm five months tomorrow," she responded. "I'm fine, Doctor. I just got a little dizzy."

Looking at Clay and Ty, she asked, "Did Dana ever lose consciousness?"

"I can answer that," Dana interrupted. "I didn't faint, if that's what you mean. I was just feeling a little dizzy. I'm worried about my husband."

The doctor said, "Your vitals are fine even being pregnant. But you need to take it easy for the rest of the day. And contact your OB/GYN if you start feeling bad, okay?"

"I will, and thanks, Doctor," Dana said with a smile.

As the doctor and nurses left, Dana came back to the side of Clay's bed. Ty put a chair behind her, saying, "Sit, Dana." She immediately sat down.

"Wow," Clay said with a grin. "Why don't you obey any of my orders that well?"

"I guess it's all in the delivery," she said with a smile as she took his hand in both of hers. "I love you, you big goof."

"Love you, too," Clay mumbled under his breath, afraid his macho image might crumble if he were to get all mushy in front of his cop buddies.

Ty stepped up to Clay's bed. "How are you feeling, bud?"

"Like I got run over by a truck."

"Well, hell, man, you almost did!"

"Hey, Clay, we're all glad you're okay," Shank Wygle said. "Listen, we've been talking, and we figured Dana would never let you get on a bike again, so we sorta flipped for your gear. I got your helmet, Three claimed your bike computer, and we're giving your torn bike shorts to Bobby Hawkins. And your bike? Man, we decided you should keep it. All four thousand pieces of it!"

"You assholes!" he gasped, laughing out loud, which felt like a million needles all sticking him in the side at once.

The hospital chaplain had come into the room while Shank was talking, and he was shocked at Clay's ability to laugh.

He thought, *The man was almost killed, got two broken ribs, and then shot the man who did it. How can he laugh at a time like this?*

Ty saw the look on the chaplain's face and read his mind. "Chaplain, if we can't laugh about the pain and suffering we see and endure, we'd go crazy. Trust me, Clay's gonna be alright as long as he can keep laughing,"

After ensuring himself that Clay had everything he needed, the chaplain left, still shaking his head over how crazy cops have to be to survive.

When he was gone, Clay looked at Ty, "I'm ready to talk about it."

"Hey, man, you don't have to do this right now if you don't want to," Ty cautioned.

"No, it's cool. I'm okay with it," Clay said as he recalled the sensation of pulling the trigger at another human being for the first time in his life. From the ages of ten to thirteen, he had gone deer hunting in South Georgia every fall with his dad until he died unexpectedly of a heart attack. Until this morning, he had never again shot a gun except during regular firearms training.

"Chief Wilson is en route. You want to wait until he gets here so you don't have to tell it twice?" Ty asked.

"Sure, I guess."

At that moment, Mike Wilson walked in the door. "Clay, how are you feeling?" Mike asked, concerned about his best detective and friend.

"I'm good, Chief. I'll be sore for a while, but the doc said it's nothing serious."

"That's great, just great," the chief said, the relief evident in his voice.

"Chief," Ty said. "Clay said he's ready to tell us what happened. I asked him to wait until you got here so he wouldn't have to tell it twice. I've also got my digital recorder in case you want it on tape."

Mike Wilson was hesitant to require Clay to give a recorded statement since he was still flat on his back in the ER. He didn't want Clay to think he doubted his word about what happened.

Clay, sensing his hesitation said, "Chief, I think it's a good idea to tape it. That way I can refer to it when I write my report later so I don't leave any details out."

"Alright, if you're sure," Mike said.

As Ty placed the recorder on the bed near Clay, Dana asked, "Mike, can I stay? I want to hear what happened, too."

"Are you sure you want to hear all the details, Dana? It'll be pretty graphic."

"I'm sure. He's my husband, and we share everything, the pain as well as the happiness," she said as a tear rolled down her cheek.

"Then you're welcome to stay, honey."

Over the next half hour, Clay went through the whole incident, starting from the time he rolled out of his driveway at home and ending when he lost consciousness under Stovall's body.

When he finished, Clay asked, "Was Stovall alive when the rescue guys got there?"

Ty spoke up, "No chance, Clay. Both rounds hit him dead center, no pun intended. We won't know for sure until the autopsy, but it looks like at least one and maybe both bullets hit his heart. He was toast before he landed on top of you. And after what he told you about Dana and me, I just wish I could bring him back to life long enough to kill him again!"

"Who is the truck registered to?" Clay asked.

Cassie said, "It's his. We're not sure where he kept it. The neighbors tell us they don't recall ever seeing it at his house."

"I don't understand how he knew it was me. It was still pretty dark, and it's hard to tell who someone is when they're wearing a helmet. And how could he have known I'd be riding there at that particular time? It doesn't make sense!"

"It doesn't to us, either," Mike Wilson said. "But we may get some answers when we search his house. Rivers and Jennings are in St. Augustine right now requesting a search warrant. Obviously, I would have preferred to get the warrant from one of our judges, but with his residence in St. Johns County, we had no choice."

Clay swung his legs over the side of the bed, sitting up slowly.

Dana stood up, alarmed. "What do you think you're doing?" she demanded.

"I'm going on the search warrant, babe," he said in a determined voice. "I have to. I've got a history with this guy. You do, too, Dana. Remember what he did to you at your show? And the most important thing, aside from the fact I killed him, is that we still haven't found the serial killer. This is *my* case!"

Chief Wilson stepped in front of Clay so that he couldn't stand up. "You're not getting within two miles of his house, Clay."

"What?! Why the hell not, Mike?!" Clay cried, frustration clear in his voice.

"Several reasons, son. Number one, you've had a concussion, and you probably still have some lingering effects. Two, you killed him, so your direct involvement in this investigation is prohibited by policy. Three, at the risk of repeating myself, you killed him, so, even if it wasn't a policy violation, you're way too close to it to be completely objective."

As Clay opened his mouth to object, Mike raised his hand, "Quiet. I'm not through. It doesn't matter whether *you* think you can be objective. If we find evidence that ties him to the murders, I mean very clear evidence, there will be an impression in some people's minds that you planted it there to try to claim credit for taking down the serial killer. The department's integrity, and yours, are too important to take a chance on that happening. Long story short, the answer is still no."

Clay's shoulders slumped. Nodding his head, he asked, "But can I at least be kept in the loop on anything they find?"

Mike thought about the possible ramifications and then nodded, "Sure, I don't see a problem with that. Cassie and Ty will be the lead detectives on the warrant. Rivers, Jennings, Sheasley, and Jones will assist with the search, and Childress will handle the ET work if they find anything."

Turning to Dana, he asked, "Do you have your car here to get your guy home?"

"No," Dana said. "Cassie and Ann Honchen brought me."

"We'll get them home," Cassie assured the chief.

Mike shook Clay's hand before leaving. "The media are raising hell wanting to interview you about Stovall. I guess the homeowner who found you and called 9-1-1 also contacted a buddy of his who works for a TV station. And the rest, as they say, is history. Don't worry about having to talk to them, though. I'll handle all the media requests. You just concentrate on getting well. We need you back."

Chapter 46

At five o'clock that afternoon, the search warrant was issued by the Honorable Judge John Parsons, and Jacksonville Beach police and St. Johns County deputies descended on Stovall's oceanfront home. As they approached the door, they saw Stovall's BMW still parked in the same spot it had been when Clay rode past on his fateful bike ride. Behind it sat a red Cadillac STS. Ty looked inside and spotted rental papers on the front floorboard. The doors were locked, and he couldn't quite read the name on the contract.

Cassie rang the doorbell while Ty and the rest of the officers stood by. Just as she hit the button again, the door was opened by Gerald Strahan, Stovall's attorney at his bond hearing. Strahan stood in the doorway, his large frame blocking it as he stared at the collection of officers.

"Yeah, what do you want?" he asked, his 'aw shucks' courtroom demeanor noticeably absent.

Displaying her badge and ID to Strahan, Cassie said, "I'm Detective Broderick, Jacksonville Beach Police Department. Who are you?"

"I don't have to tell you shit, lady," he growled. "Now, if you'll excuse me, I've got better things to do than to stand here and jaw jack with a bunch of cops." Stepping back, he started to close the door.

Ty moved forward quickly and put his hand on the door. Strahan tried to push it closed against Ty, but he might as well have been pushing against a block of concrete.

"You seem to misunderstand," Ty said, shoving the door hard enough to cause the bigger man to stagger back. "We're here to execute a valid search warrant for this residence. If you obstruct us in our lawful duty, it will give me great pleasure to arrest you. Now stand aside!"

Although a large man, Strahan recognized in Ty Honchen someone he could not intimidate. So he tried to bluster.

"I'm Attorney Gerald Strahan, Esquire. I've been hired to represent Mr. Stovall. You can't threaten an officer of the court, mister. I'll have you brought up on contempt charges!"

Knowing he was bluffing, Ty smiled, "Don't pull that 'officer of the court' crap with me, *Mr.* Strahan! You're not in court here, and we have the law on *our* side, not yours. Besides, you no longer represent Stovall."

"What are you talking about!" he yelled. "Of course I do! Why do you think I'm here in his house if I'm not his attorney?!"

"Former attorney," Ty responded.

"What did you say?"

"I thought I was perfectly clear. I said 'former attorney,' Mr. Strahan. Tell me, do you know where your client is right now?"

"No, I don't," he admitted, a puzzled look on his face. "I flew in from Miami this afternoon and drove straight here. Why? What's going on? Where is Emory?" he asked, starting to become alarmed.

"At the M.E.'s office," Ty answered.

Strahan was even more confused at Ty's response. "The M.E.'s office! What the hell is he doing there?"

Ty glanced at his watch. "Well, right about now, I'd say the medical examiner is probably stuffing his guts and various other organs back inside his body. He may be stitched back up by now, come to think of it," Ty smiled, obviously enjoying himself.

"Are, are you telling me Emory is, is dead?" Strahan stammered as his face grew suddenly pale and he slumped against the entryway wall.

"Yeah, that's what I'm saying, Mr. Strahan. Emory Elliot Stovall is dead, deceased, no longer among the living, kicked the old bucket, died and gone to hell. At least I hope so," Ty said with quiet intensity.

"But, but, how . . .?" Strahan stuttered. He turned and staggered to a couch in the living room where he collapsed, putting his head in his hands.

Strahan's emotional reaction caused Cassie to feel a little sympathy for the man. Sitting beside him, she patted Strahan on the arm.

"Emory Elliot Stovall tried to kill Detective Sergeant Clay Randall this morning. He first tried to run him over on his bicycle just a mile or so down the road from here. When that failed, he got out of his truck and came at Sergeant Randall with a knife. Stovall told Sergeant Randall he was going to kill him, followed by

Detective Honchen here, and then Sergeant Randall's pregnant wife. That's when Clay shot and killed him."

As Cassie related the circumstances, Strahan stared at her with a horrified look on his face.

"Oh my God! That's terrible!"

"Not as terrible as it would have been if he had succeeded in killing a couple of police officers and a cop's wife," Ty snapped.

"No, no, Detective. You misunderstand me. I didn't mean my client . . . well, I guess my former client now. I meant all of you. I know I probably came on a little strong, and I apologize for that. I sympathize with what police officers go through. You see, my son is a cop in Miami."

Shaking his head ruefully, Strahan continued. "He can't understand why I'm a criminal defense attorney, but even criminals have the right to a defense. Anyway, that's a philosophical discussion for another time."

He stood up, turning to Cassie. "Detective Broderick, I still have a legal duty to represent my client's interests until a court makes a decision concerning his estate. I will not interfere in any way with the execution of your search warrant. I will need a copy of it, however."

"Here it is, Mr. Strahan. And thank you for your cooperation," Cassie said, handing the warrant to the attorney.

Ty said to the assembled officers, "You've all been briefed on the parameters of the warrant. You know what we're looking for. Split up, and go to it."

Over the next four hours, Stovall's huge house was searched carefully and thoroughly. In an upstairs study, Corri Jennings found a stack of newspapers on his desk. Looking through them, she saw multiple news articles about the homicides in Jacksonville Beach.

One reporter wrote an opinion piece summarizing ten of the homicides across the state and speculating that all were the work of the serial killer. Stovall had highlighted and underlined every mention of Clay Randall throughout the articles.

As Corri picked up the papers, she discovered a small cardboard box underneath. Opening it, she found at least a half dozen items, none of which appeared particularly valuable. Corri put the lid back on the box, thinking she would mention it to Ty or Cassie when she finished.

She packed the papers, marked the evidence bag with her initials and the date, and set it down by the door to take to Jim Childress. She went back to the desk and retrieved the box, deciding she would take it to Childress along with the papers.

As she reached the door, Corri had second thoughts. *I don't want to look like a dumbass bringing Childress a bunch of junk. He'll never let me live it down*, she thought.

She hesitated at the door a moment, thinking, *Leave it, take it, leave it . . . aw crap! I'm leaving it. I'll tell Cassie about it. She won't screw with me if it turns out to be nothing.* Placing the box on the bookcase beside the door, Corri moved on to the next room, eventually forgetting to tell Cassie about the box.

As the evening wore on, the searchers grew frustrated at their inability to find concrete evidence of Stovall's suspected career as a serial killer. Finally, Cassie and Ty made one more pass together to ensure that every room had been thoroughly searched. When they checked Stovall's study, Cassie noticed the light flashing on an answering machine on the credenza behind the desk.

"The light's still flashing, so nobody's checked for messages. What do you think?" she asked Ty with a raised eyebrow.

"Sure, why not," he said, discouraged by their lack of success and willing to try just about anything.

Cassie hit the Play button on the digital answering machine. There were three messages. The first two were routine, dealing with reminder appointments Stovall had made. As the third message began, Ty was examining the books in Stovall's floor-to-ceiling bookcase. His head snapped around as he heard the person talking. Cassie gasped, looking at Ty with shock in her eyes.

When the message ended, Ty grabbed the machine and disconnected the phone and power cables. Wrapping the cords around the machine, he said to Cassie, "Let's go. We've got to get this to Mike Wilson right away. This message is unbelievable!"

"Does this fit the warrant parameters, Ty?" she asked.

"I'm not positive, but there's no damn way I'm leaving it here!" he exclaimed.

Gripping the machine in both hands, Ty headed for the door with Cassie right behind. He stopped suddenly, spotting the box left on the shelf by Corri Jennings. It was sitting at an angle as if it had been tossed there carelessly.

"What is it, Ty?" Cassie asked as he picked up the box and shook it gently.

"I don't know," he shrugged. "Let's find out."

Walking back to Stovall's desk, he set the box down and lifted the lid.

"Looks like a bunch of cheap junk to me," Ty said.

Cassie started to pick up a pair of sunglasses when Ty suddenly noticed a dark spot on the left lens.

"Stop!" he cried. "Don't touch anything, Cassie. See the spot on the sunglasses? I'm not positive, but I think it may be dried blood."

"Oh, crap!" she breathed. "You're right!"

Taking out a pen, Ty shifted the items around as he identified each one. "Lighter, small earring—"

"Not an earring, Ty, a nose ring," Cassie corrected.

"How do you know that?"

"I wore one for a while when I was in high school," she said, embarrassed. "They're made a little different than earrings. Trust me on this. It's a nose ring."

"Okay, moving on. Pink rubber bracelet, something about breast cancer on it . . . matching silver earrings. Are these earrings, Ms. Expert?"

"Yeah," she grinned. "They're earrings."

"Let's see, peppermint breath mints . . . breath mints? House key. Stud earring in the shape of a ladybug. Cheap metal cross . . . Wait a second!" he exclaimed.

Ty stared at the items for several seconds, the wheels turning. Then it hit him, hard.

"Do you realize what these things are?" he asked, his pulse racing.

"Uh, still a bunch of cheap junk?" she asked sarcastically.

"Cassie my girl, sarcasm is so unbecoming for a lady such as yourself," he said laughing. "No, this is not a bunch of junk. These are trophies. Serial killer trophies! I just remembered that the Atlantic Beach hooker, Donna Martin, wore a small cross. I'm willing to bet this is her cross. And the pink bracelet? Nita Caruso always wore one. And the girl in Panama City Beach had a ladybug earring in her left ear and nothing in her right. She also had a tattoo of a ladybug on her boob. And the blood on these sunglasses I bet will match one of the victims. Hell, the crime lab may be able to get DNA off the nose ring or the earrings! Emory Elliot Stovall is our serial killer!"

Closing the lid on the box, Ty headed for the door at a fast walk.

"Come on! We've got even bigger news for the chief!"

Ty quickly scribbled a notation on the search warrant receipt and then headed downstairs. Cassie told Gerald Strahan the search was complete, left him a copy of the items seized, and went out the door.

"Did you put the box on the seizure list?" Cassie asked.

"Yeah. I just put, 'box with miscellaneous items' to describe it. That's why I hustled out of there. I didn't want him seeing the box and asking questions about it before we get it processed. His son's a cop, but that doesn't mean he'll roll over if he thinks it doesn't fit the seizure parameters."

They thanked the St. Johns County deputies for their help and quickly headed back to the city. En route, Ty called Chief Wilson at home and told him there was a phone message he really needed to hear. Wilson agreed to meet them in fifteen minutes in his office. Ty next called Clay and briefed him on what they had. Clay immediately got dressed despite Dana's protests that he should be in bed and was waiting at the end of his driveway when Ty pulled up.

True to his word, Mike Wilson walked into the administration offices exactly fifteen minutes later.

"Okay, Honchen, let's hear what you got," he said, unlocking the door and leading the way into his office.

Ty placed the box and the answering machine on the chief's desk as Wilson settled into the high-backed chair left by his predecessor. Clay sat gingerly on the edge of his seat, trying to find a position that would relieve the pain from his broken ribs.

"The box first, Chief," Ty said, opening it to reveal the contents. For the next few minutes, he explained his theory concerning the items.

When he finished, Mike Wilson sat staring at each of the items in turn. "What do you think, Clay?" he asked.

"The little picture from the James Barton killing isn't in here, but that doesn't mean the rest of these aren't trophies from the other victims. I agree with Ty. I believe Stovall was our serial killer," Clay said, relief evident in his voice.

"I tend to agree with you. If any of these items can be matched to the victims, we've got our serial killer pretty well identified. Get your people moving on trying to identify the items. Meanwhile, what else do you have?"

Ty unraveled the cord and plugged it into a power strip. As the red light came on, he glanced at Cassie, about to explode with the information they had found on the machine.

"I'm skipping the first two messages. One's about a dental appointment, and the other is from some accountant he apparently used. The last message was left three days ago at 4:47 p.m."

The third message started, "Stovall, are you there? Pick up. I gotta talk to you."

There was a brief pause as the caller waited to see if Stovall was going to answer. In that pause, every person in the room looked at each other, immediately recognizing the deep voice of Roy Connor.

"Guess you're not there. Listen, that information you wanted on Randall, his social security number, address, the layout of his house, and the description and license number of his wife's car, I've got it all for you."

At the mention of his name followed by the reference to Dana, Clay's eyes narrowed.

The recording continued, "Man, I'm really sticking my neck out here, you know? If Wilson finds out I've passed personal information about a cop and his family to anyone, especially you, considering the stunt you pulled trying to rape another cop . . . I mean, c'mon! That has *got* to be about the dumbest stunt ever attempted! Anyway, if they find out, my ass is gone, you know what I'm saying? And not just fired, either. I'll be wearing handcuffs and an orange jumpsuit. You're familiar with those items, aren't you? So, if you burn me on this, I'll make you sorry you were ever born, you hear? Now my fee. I want five thousand in cash. Meet me in the morning at four o'clock on Ponte Vedra Boulevard at the county line.

"And in case you're wondering why I'm doing this, it's simple. I *hate* the son of a bitch! He thinks he's God's gift to law enforcement, all self-righteous and lookin' down his nose at me. So, whatever you do with this information, I wash my hands of it. I don't wanta know, you hear what I'm saying? Just don't implicate me in any way, or so help me, I'll do ten times worse to you than whatever you do to them!"

When the message ended, no one said anything, so stunned were they all by the absolute betrayal of a cop by a fellow officer. Clay stood up and started slowly for the door.

"Where are you going?" Mike Wilson asked.

He didn't respond at first. As he reached the door, Clay said, "Chief, I'm going home to protect my wife. With Stovall dead, I don't know what that bastard Connor might do. I intend to be there in case he decides to pick up where Stovall left off."

Clay's face grew hard, and his voice dropped almost to a whisper. "And if he shows his face at my house, then I'll just have to live with two killings."

"Clay," Wilson said softly. "You and Dana don't have to worry about Connor."

Turning to Ty, Wilson said, "Take as many cops with you as you need. Find Connor and arrest him for releasing Clay's personal information. Bring him to me. I'll be here waiting."

Thinking out loud, Wilson said, "The violation itself is a first degree misdemeanor, so that won't hold him long."

"Broderick, call the on-call state attorney. Find out if we can charge him with homicide, too," he directed.

"Homicide?" she asked in confusion.

"That's what I said. Connor gave Stovall personal information that Stovall obviously used to find out where Clay lives. He must have been watching the house and saw him leave on his bike this morning. Connor's actions directly assisted Stovall in his attempt to kill Clay, which in turn resulted in his own death. I think the state law will allow Connor to be charged with Stovall's death based upon the chain of events started by Connor. I'm not positive on this, so check it out."

Turning back to Clay, he continued, "In addition to the criminal charges, state law also calls for his removal, so it will give me great pleasure to fire his ass. He's skirted the ethical line way too long, protected by Cooper. Well, *no more!*" he said vehemently. "We'll handle Roy Connor, Clay. You go on home and take care of your wife and yourself."

Clay stood there a moment, thinking about what Wilson had said. "Okay, I'll go home. But I meant what I said. If the son of a bitch ever shows his face around my house . . .," the implication was left hanging in the air.

"Take him home, Ty, and then bring that bastard Connor to me!"

Chapter 47

On his days off, Roy Connor was a fixture in the bars of Jacksonville Beach. The unofficial policy for off-duty police officers was to stay out of bars in the city where they policed, the better to avoid running into someone they had previously arrested in the same establishment. Connor didn't feel the need to comply with what he believed were bullshit unofficial policies, so he took pleasure in hitting his hometown bars as often as possible.

Sitting at the bar, Connor had just downed his second beer in the Beachside Pub and his sixth of the night overall when he felt a tap on his shoulder. Turning, his eyes widened at the sight of five cops standing behind him. Ty Honchen was flanked by Shank Wygle, Cassie Broderick, Corri Jennings, and Three Rivers, all people he disliked to one degree or another.

"Whata you want, slick?" he asked, slurring his words.

"You're under arrest," Ty said.

"Don't play bullshit games with me, Honchen. I'm not in the mood. Get the fuck away from me," he said turning back around on his barstool.

Ty stepped to his side, shielding the TASER from other bar patrons as he showed him the weapon.

"I'm placing you under arrest for providing Clay Randall's personal information to Emory Stovall. Now you can come quietly with us and not make a scene, or I'll tase your ass. I think you may recall the effects from your last trip!" he hissed.

Connor looked down at the TASER and then into Ty's face. It was obvious the alcohol had slowed his thinking and that he had not processed Ty's message fully yet. It was also obvious from the look on his face that he was calculating his chances of punching Ty before he could use the TASER.

"Go ahead!" Ty exclaimed. "Try me. I'll take great pleasure in causing you pain, you fucking traitor!"

It slowly sunk in to his beer-soaked brain that he could not win a fight with five cops and a TASER. Connor slumped on his barstool, shaking his head. Then Ty's other message sorted itself out in his head.

"Arrest me? For what? What personal information are you talkin' about, Honchen?"

"We'll let the chief discuss that with you, Connor. Get off that stool right now and step outside with us. When we get to my car, I'm gonna cuff you. Just like you predicted to your asshole friend. And don't fight us. You won't win."

Ten minutes later, Connor walked into Chief Wilson's office, handcuffed and surrounded by the five officers. The chief was behind his desk as they entered, reading a document. Ty directed Connor to a chair directly in front of the desk and made him sit.

"Hey, man, take the cuffs off!" Connor protested. "I can't sit back with my hands cuffed behind my back."

Wilson looked up at Connor, studying him with a cold eye as if he were a new species of snake. Glancing at Ty, he nodded. Ty removed the cuffs and stepped back. All five officers continued to hover immediately behind Connor in case he decided to get violent.

Connor sat in the chair rubbing his wrists.

"Chief," he complained. "Honchen put the cuffs on me so tight it cut off circulation to my hands. Look at the marks," he whined, holding up both hands.

Chief Wilson continued to study Connor's face, saying nothing.

After a minute of total silence that seemed to go on much longer, Connor couldn't stand it.

"What? Why are you just starin' at me and not sayin' anything?"

Wilson finally spoke. "I've been studying you, Roy, trying to spot something in your face, anything that would help me understand how you, a police officer sworn to uphold the law, could betray your badge, your commission."

"I don't know what you're talkin' about, Chief. I was just mindin' my own business havin' a drink when these *cowboys*," he said, gesturing over his shoulder, "decided to roust me like I was a suspect. Claimed I did something with some personal information on somebody. I don't know what they're talkin' about."

"We know, Roy," Wilson said.

"Know what? I'm confused!"

"We have the recording you left on Emory Elliot Stovall's answering machine. Would you like to hear yourself, Roy?"

The light finally came on. Connor slumped down in his chair, dropping his head to his chest. After a few moments, he looked up at Wilson.

"No, I don't need to hear it. So what happens now?"

"You'll be booked on criminal charges, and you're suspended without pay pending an internal investigation. I can tell you right now, Roy, that the investigation will result in your termination as a police officer. You've violated your sacred trust to our citizens and to your fellow officers. To betray a citizen is bad enough, but to betray one of your brothers, as well as his wife, is unforgiveable."

"Take him downtown for booking," Wilson said in disgust. "And get his badge, ID, guns, and uniforms, too."

Chapter 48

Over the following six weeks, near-record heat and thunderstorms in August and September ushered in the annual threat of tropical storms and hurricanes. During that time, the police department tried to return to some semblance of normalcy.

Interestingly, the autopsy on Emory Elliot Stovall revealed a malignant brain tumor located on the hemisphere responsible, in part, for personality and behavior. The doctors suggested the tumor could very well have caused severe paranoia as well as violent behavior. While the revelation didn't make Clay's ribs feel any better, he now had a better understanding of what probably caused Stovall to engage in such bizarre acts.

Roy Connor had spent two nights in the county jail before bonding out. The criminal charges were under consideration by the special prosecutor's section of the state attorney, the unit responsible for prosecuting public officials who engaged in criminal acts. His termination from the department had taken less than a week. Connor was given the opportunity to plead his case before Chief Wilson, but he didn't bother to show at the hearing.

No new homicides matching the serial killer's M.O. were reported anywhere in the state. After several weeks passed, Clay was contacted by Daytona Beach detectives with the information that the dried blood on the sunglasses matched their victim, Mary Stein. Atlantic Beach detectives got similar good news when DNA on the nose ring was matched to their victim, Donna Martin. And while the metal cross had no identifying marks or trace evidence on it, a family member tentatively identified it as belonging to Marilyn Gibbs, the first prostitute killed in Jacksonville Beach.

Local, national, and even international media had a field day. The story had everything: murder, sex, attempted rape of a cop, attempted murder of a cop, a serial killer slain by a cop. On and on it went for almost two weeks until kickoff of the NFL season. The story then lost legs and quickly faded, a development appreciated by every member of the police department and their families.

Eventually, as the avenues of investigation dwindled, Clay and his team accepted the premise that Stovall had either destroyed any evidence of the other crimes or had stashed it so well they were unlikely ever to find it.

One of the last clues was almost forgotten in the crush of events, forgotten, that is, by everyone except the evidence technician, Jim Childress. He dropped by Clay's office one day.

"Hey Sarge, got a minute?" he asked. Without waiting for an answer, he dropped into a chair and sat grinning at Clay. "How's the ribs?"

"Hey, Jim. They're better, thanks. Still a little sore, but I'm back on the bike. So what's up?"

Jim held up a copy of the note left on James Barton's chest.

"Remember this? The watermark letters, **ESE**?"

Clay sat there a moment looking at the paper, then at Childress. Suddenly he understood.

"Emory Elliot Stovall. People sometimes do that, putting the initial of the last name in the middle with the first and middle initials flanking it."

Jim grinned at Clay, "My thoughts exactly. And remember the font the letters were in? Braggadocio?"

"Jim, you're a genius!" Clay exclaimed. "That SOB Stovall was so arrogant. He put the clue in his note assuming we would be too stupid to figure it out. Well, come to think of it, I guess everybody but you *was* too stupid," he said with a rueful grin.

"I'm nominating you for a departmental award for this, Jim, Great work! If you weren't a civilian employee, I'd make you a detective today!"

"Thanks, Clay. I love what I do, but I appreciate the thought anyway. By the way, how's Dana?"

"She's good. Still gets morning sickness, even at almost seven months, so that sucks. And she's getting bigger every day. Since she had to cut back on her running, she's put on about ten pounds, and she's really bitching about it."

"Tell her I said hello, and thanks again for the compliment," Jim said as he headed back to his office.

Chapter 49

Most years, September marks the height of the Atlantic storm season for Floridians. Everyone watches the weather forecasts nervously for information on possible storms that might strike their state. Fortunately, none of the seven storms formed since the season began in June had threatened Florida.

On September 21, that began to change when a tropical depression in the Caribbean developed into Tropical Storm Holli. Within forty-eight hours, it had strengthened to a Category One hurricane and became Hurricane Holli.

With favorable steering currents, Holli began a northward turn, paralleling the coast of Florida. When that occurred, the National Weather Service issued a hurricane watch for all Florida coastal cities. By September 24, the storm, now a Category Two, was just over one hundred miles east of Miami, packing winds of ninety-nine miles per hour and moving north at a steady ten knots.

Jacksonville Beach had not received a direct hit since 1964 when Hurricane Dora caused extensive damage as it came ashore at St. Augustine some thirty miles south. So many storm seasons had passed without a repeat of Dora that most residents assumed Holli would be no different.

The police could not make that assumption. Chief Wilson convened a meeting of the department's supervisors to assess the situation. They discussed what preparations should be completed in the event the call came for an evacuation of the city, a call that was likely if the storm track shifted toward the coast.

On September 27, Holli was due east of Jacksonville Beach, by this time about one hundred and fifty miles offshore and causing heavy surf conditions and wind gusts to 50 MPH. These were conditions seen every winter during a typical Nor'easter, so residents shrugged and went about their business as usual, once more convinced the storm would pass them by.

In the middle of the night, conditions changed as Hurricane Holli made a sudden, dramatic turn to the west. The Duval County Emergency Operations Center immediately notified all affected agencies that the National Weather Service had upgraded the watch to a hurricane warning for the immediate Florida and Georgia coastlines. The call to evacuate the beach communities came from the EOC that morning at 6:00 a.m. Employees were notified to get their family members out of town and report to work with extra food, water, and gear.

Clay headed home quickly to check on Dana, by now almost eight months into her pregnancy. She had gained seventeen pounds, an amount her doctor considered a little low for someone her size, but satisfactory for her considering the steady running and exercise regimen she had continued throughout the pregnancy.

As Clay walked in the door, Dana was just hanging up the phone.

"Hi, I just talked to Daddy," she said. "We're not heading up to Stone Mountain now. Daddy said the newest report has the storm track going in somewhere between here and South Georgia. So, we're going down to Sanibel instead."

Taking her in his arms, Clay hugged her gently.

"God, I'm gonna miss you, babe," he said, drawing in the clean smell of her, the unique essence that was his Dana.

Hugging him back fiercely, she said, "I hate leaving you here. Why do you have to have a job that forces us to be apart at a time when we have the greatest need to be together?"

Before he could respond, she said, "I know, it's your job. I've come to understand that police work is an honorable profession like you've said. I'm proud of you and what you do. But sometimes, I think it asks too much of you. Your time, your attention, your energy.

"Oh, Clay, I'm sorry. This isn't the time or place for this conversation," she said starting to cry. "Now look at me, bawling like a child! Since I've been pregnant, I've lost all ability to control my emotions!" she said, angrily shaking her head.

Clay smiled as he gently wiped the tears away.

"I understand. These past months have been hard on us all. Just as we get all the paperwork completed on the murder cases, and we think we'll have a little breathing room, Holli has to come along and screw it all up. But we'll get past this, too. As long as she makes landfall north of us, we won't get that much of it. I'll probably be sitting around playing cards or reading a book to pass the time," he said, trying to calm her fears.

"I'm the one who should be worried. You'll be out on the road with a bunch of crazy drivers all trying to get nowhere in a hurry!"

"Don't worry. We're leaving early enough that it shouldn't be a problem."

"Well, let's finish getting your car packed up so you can get on the road. I assume y'all are still taking two cars?"

"Yes, we are," Dana said, loving the feel of Clay's strong arms around her.

"Daddy's taking the Expedition, and he's got it loaded down. There's barely enough room for Mama in there. But better that she's stuffed into the SUV with Daddy than riding with me! I don't think I could take a five or six hour drive with my mother two feet away giving me non-stop marital, sex, pregnancy, and general life *advice*, as she calls it."

Clay grinned at her. "The way you describe it makes it sound like a punch to my tender ribs from Mike Tyson would be way better!"

Dana giggled at Clay, standing on her toes to give him a passionate kiss. They held each other close for a few moments, and then Dana reluctantly broke the embrace.

"I better get going. They've already left. I'm supposed to meet them at the exit to World Golf Village off I-95. Daddy has to go by a buddy's house in World Golf Village and drop off his golf clubs. He left them at their house last week after they played golf, and he's worried the storm will blow away the house with his precious clubs inside. Honestly, boys and their toys!"

As they walked out to the driveway, Clay studied the sky. It reminded him of a Nor'easter with its dirty, grey clouds that appeared to be flying along a few feet above the roof of their condo. The wind was continuing to pick up, too.

One gust hit Dana hard enough to cause her to stagger. He grabbed her arm to steady her, opening the door to her Lexus and urging her inside out of the increasing wind. One more quick kiss, and Clay stepped back. Dana backed out of the driveway and headed south. As she turned at the corner, he waved and blew her a kiss.

Man, this sucks! he thought. *I hate her being on the road, especially in her condition. At least she's in a bigger car so she won't get bounced around by the wind. And she can always call her dad on the cell . . .*

"Oh, crap!" he exclaimed. "Did she remember to bring her cell?"

Clay grabbed his phone and punched the speed dial number for Dana. After two rings, she answered, "I've only gone three blocks. Do you miss me already?"

"Always and forever, like the song goes," he said. "I was just checking to make sure you had your cell. Is it charged?"

"Yes, dear," she said in mock disgust. "It's charged, and I have my car adapter in case the battery gets low. I'm a very organized woman, didn't you know that?"

"Just makin' sure, darlin'," he said. "As this storm gets worse, we may lose cell service, so don't be worried if you call and get a busy signal. Just keep trying."

"I will . . . I love you, Clay. You take care of yourself, you hear?"

"You got it. Love you, too. Bye, babe," he said hanging up and heading to his car to go to work.

By the time Clay got to the station, the wind had increased to a steady forty with gusts to fifty-five. A rain squall cut loose as he stepped out of his car, and he had to make a run for the building to keep from getting soaked. Grabbing his raingear and rubber boots from his locker, he hit the street to check on the progress of the evacuation.

At the same time Clay was leaving the station, Dana was pulling off the freeway at the World Golf Village exit. She spotted the Expedition parked at a gas station, the monster SUV being fed its diet of high-priced fuel by her father.

As she stopped beside her parents' car, Dana reached up unconsciously to touch the gold cross Clay had given her at Easter, thinking of her husband and worrying again about his safety. But it was gone. She looked down, not believing her sense of touch. Sure enough, it wasn't there.

The cross was eighteen carat gold on an extremely fine, filigree chain. Although not terribly expensive, it was very important to her, both as an expression of her Christian faith and a token of love from her husband.

Dana had worried when Clay first gave it to her that the tiny links might break if pulled the wrong way. Apparently that had happened. She sat in her car staring out the window at the rain as she thought back to when she had seen it last.

Roberta was in the passenger seat of the SUV only a few feet away, staring at Dana and wondering what her daughter was doing.

"Dana," Roberta called.

Her window was up, so she couldn't have heard her mother even if she had been listening.

"Dana!" her mother yelled, this time getting out of the SUV and stepping over to Dana's car. "What are you doing?"

She snapped back from her reverie, looking up at her mother in surprise. She rolled down her window.

"I was trying to remember when I last saw my gold cross necklace. It's gone, and I can't leave without it."

"Now, Dana, darling, that's just foolish. It's just a tiny little thing. Your father and I will buy you a diamond cross when we get down to Sanibel if it means that much to you."

"I don't want a diamond cross, Mama. I want my cross that Clay gave me." At that moment, it hit her. "I know where it is! I took it off at Ethan Hunter's house yesterday and put it on the table by my easel. The cross kept catching on the chain, and I found one of the links partially broken. I didn't want to lose it, so I took it off and was going to put it in my purse when I had another bout of morning sickness. I went outside to get some fresh air and forgot about it when I left. I've got to go back to his house and get it," she said.

"What's going on?" Marty asked as he shoved the gas receipt in his pocket.

"Martin, please speak to your daughter," Roberta said, exasperated. "She claims she's going back to get a little necklace she left. The storm is getting closer all the time, and we need to leave. Tell her, Martin," she demanded in her most imperious tone.

Marty Cappella loved his daughter unconditionally, and he had always had trouble telling her no. But this time, he thought she was being foolish.

"Honey, have you been listening to the radio? The hurricane is heading almost due west. They're saying it may hit around Fernandina

Beach. That's only twenty or thirty miles from home. You can't go back there!"

"Daddy, we're wasting time here, time that I don't have. I'm going back for my necklace. I'll meet up with y'all in Gainesville in front of the Swamp," she said, indicating the stadium where the Florida Gators football team held court.

"I'll call when I'm getting close. Now, I have to go! I love you both."

Dana drove quickly away, leaving her mother and father to wonder when they would see their strong-willed daughter again.

She drove as fast as conditions would allow. The wind had continued to rise, even ten miles inland from the shore. By the time she reached Hunter's oceanfront home in South Jax Beach, the gusting winds and squalls were making her question the decision to return. She pulled into the long drive and stopped in the turnaround as close as possible to the front door. Figuring an umbrella would be useless in this wind, she decided to run for it.

As she opened the car door, the wind snatched it out of her grip, slamming it forward with such force that the hinges bent. Dana jumped out and was instantly soaked from the driving rain. She tried to slam the door, but the bent hinges prevented it from closing fully.

"Great! Now I'll be wet all the way to Sanibel!"

Silently cursing her bad luck, she ran to the garage door and punched in the code Hunter had given her when she started her project. As the door rose, she said a little prayer of thanks that the power was still on. Dana hit the button to close the door and went to the workbench where Hunter kept a supply of clean shop towels. She wiped her face, arms, and feet and tried to get her hair somewhat dry before going into the house.

With Ethan's car missing from the garage, Dana assumed he had already evacuated.

He's probably at some five-star hotel in Orlando getting a massage and a manicure right now, she thought. *Or at least someplace where Hurricane Holli isn't planning to visit.*

Going directly to the living room overlooking the large terrace, she stopped to stare, entranced by the power of Mother Nature outside the floor to ceiling windows, which had been covered with hurricane screens that allowed some daylight inside.

Seven-foot waves crashed into each other from odd angles, a condition she knew created impossible conditions for surfing. Gusts whipped the Sago palms at the edge of the terrace first one way, then another. Debris from the many trees and bushes around Hunter's lawn littered the flagstone terrace, making it difficult to see the pavers themselves.

Dana finally broke her gaze away from the dramatic weather taking place on the other side of the double-paned glass. Walking quickly to the table by her easel, she saw her necklace partially hidden under an art magazine she had brought with her to read when she took a break from the painting.

Now I remember, she thought. *I went out to get some fresh air to keep from vomiting. When I came back in, I sat in the chair and read for a while. I must have put the magazine on top of the necklace and then didn't see it when I got up. What an idiot!*

Dana picked up the necklace and put it in her pocket. Turning to go, her stomach flipped over. The familiar queasiness was back.

"Please, no! Not now," she begged her rolling stomach.

As the seconds passed, the nausea became stronger, and she realized another round with the porcelain throne was imminent. She headed at a fast walk for the bathroom off the den.

Opening the door, she groaned, "Crap! I forgot the toilet wasn't working right."

Apparently, Hunter had called a plumber after she left yesterday. The toilet had been completely removed, and plastic had been taped over the hole where it had recently resided.

Feeling the urge building, Dana took off, holding her swollen belly with her left hand while she raced up the stairs to the second floor. At the top, she paused, frantically trying to remember the direction of the guest suite. At the point of desperation, she dashed to the left, opening the door and running through what was obviously Hunter's private bedroom suite instead of one of the three guest suites.

Reaching the large marble bathtub, she felt everything in her stomach coming up fast. Dana knew she couldn't drop to her knees quickly enough with her protruding belly, so she simply leaned over, putting her hands on the side of the tub and doing her best to avoid splashing that morning's granola all over herself.

"Oh," she moaned, when the latest bout was over. "I'm so sick of puking! Why are you doing this to me?" she asked of the daughter she felt sure she was carrying.

She rinsed out the tub and splashed water on her face. Feeling only slightly better, she left the bathroom slowly, once again noticing the heavy rains and wind slamming against the hurricane screens covering the bedroom windows.

I've got to get out of here before this gets any worse and I can't leave, she cautioned herself. *Clay will be pissed beyond words if he finds out I'm still here.*

Halfway to the door, Dana paused to admire Hunter's taste in décor. She had never been in the master suite, and what she saw impressed her. The bedroom was huge, almost six hundred square feet, she estimated.

Occupying the wall to the left of the door was a massive bookcase filled with an eclectic mix of titles representing varied disciplines and interests. Marketing, general business, and leadership books were juxtaposed with authors as wide-ranging as Stephen King and Sean Hannity.

As she started through the door, she saw something out of the corner of her eye that seemed out of place. A picture of a little girl in a small, red plastic frame. Dana paused to stare at the picture a moment before picking it up. She read out loud the inscription scrawled across the bottom, "To Daddy from Meghan. I love you."

I had no idea Ethan had a daughter, Dana thought, temporarily forgetting her need to leave. *She's so cute. I wonder what happened to his wife?*

Something about the picture nagged at her. She stared at the little girl a moment longer before replacing the frame on the shelf.

She shrugged, *Maybe she reminds me of some kid actress I've seen on TV or something. I don't know. I just know I don't have time to stand here admiring Ethan's daughter while the house may be ready to come down around my ears.*

Dana left the room, closing the door behind her and going downstairs. The disgusting taste in her mouth from the latest attack of morning sickness caused another delay as she detoured to the kitchen. She opened the refrigerator and got a bottled water that Ethan kept stocked. Twisting off the cap, Dana took a swallow, swished it around and spit into the sink. Then she leaned against the counter, taking a long drink of the ice-cold water as she watched the wind continue its attack on anything capable of bending or moving.

The sweet face of Hunter's daughter popped into her head again.

She looks very familiar. Where have I seen her face before? Dana asked herself. *That young actress from the movie, Little Miss Sunshine? Abigail something?* She shook her head in disgust at her inability to remember. *Maybe pregnancy causes memory loss*, she laughed to herself, finishing the water and tossing the empty bottle into the recycle bin.

"Time to go," she said aloud to the empty house as she headed for the garage.

Dana had noticed a slicker suit hanging in the garage and thought she might need it if her sprung door frame let in too much rain during her escape from the storm. As she touched the garage door knob, she stopped. The subconscious part of her brain, that part that never sleeps or takes a vacation, had continued to noodle the problem of the little girl in the picture. It finally completed its job, pushing the memory toward the front of her brain.

Suddenly, her eyes open wide, she gasped, "Oh, my God!"

Running back up the stairs as fast as her pregnant belly would allow, she yanked open the door and ran into Hunter's bedroom. Grabbing the picture again, she stared at the words written there by a little girl so many years before, "To Daddy from Meghan. I love you."

The memory came flooding back at the speed of light. They were at Harry's the night she told Clay she was pregnant. They talked about Jimmy Barton's murder and a picture of his daughter, Meghan, that he supposedly carried.

"A picture in a red plastic frame!" she exclaimed. "And the inscription said . . . it said *this*! Clay said the picture wasn't in the backpack, and he thought the killer might have taken it. What did he call it . . . a trophy!"

Additional bits of information came crashing into her brain as hard and as fast as the Atlantic Ocean battering the shoreline outside. Ethan Hunter fit the description of the serial killer that was all over the news. He recently sold his blue BMW, saying he wanted a smaller car. A light blue BMW was the getaway car in Panama City Beach when the girl was killed there, and the physical description there fit . . . *him*!

Standing in Hunter's bedroom still holding the picture of little Meghan, Dana's mind was whirling. "I've got to get out of here! I've got to call Clay and tell him! I have to take the picture to Clay . . . oh crap! I have to pee!" she wailed.

Slipping the picture into her pocket, she hurried into the bathroom to relieve the relentless pressure caused by the baby pressing on her bladder. Finished, and fighting rising panic, she headed for the stairs, thinking she needed to get away before calling Clay in case Hunter came back unexpectedly.

As she reached the bottom of the stairs, Dana heard a sound that made her breathing stop and her blood turn icy. The garage door was opening, and through the living room windows, lashed by the driving rain, she had a clear view of her worst nightmare come true . . . Ethan Hunter had come back home!

Chapter 50

Dana stood frozen to the spot, her mind reeling. *Oh my God! When he finds me in here, he'll know! He'll see it in my face! He's going to kill me!*

That thought broke her paralysis. In full panic now, she took off running, a rush of adrenaline giving her wings as she flew up the stairs. Dashing into Hunter's bedroom again, Dana pulled the picture out of her pocket and dropped it quickly back on the shelf as close as she could recall to its original spot. She ran out and down the hall into the guest suite, easing the door shut and dashing to the bathroom. Inside, she closed the door, ran to the small linen closet, and concealed herself inside.

Her hands shaking badly, breathing heavily from the exertion as well as the panic attack struggling to overwhelm her, Dana pulled out her cell phone and, in the darkness of the closet, hit Clay's speed dial by feel. She waited impatiently as she listened for his voice with one ear while trying to hear Hunter with the other.

"Come on! Ring, dammit!" she hissed.

As the 'circuits busy' ring warbled in her ear, she stabbed at the disconnect button, silently cursing the storm that interrupted phone service when she needed it the most. It took all her willpower to remain calm.

She told herself, *Don't panic. Your baby needs you. Clay needs you.* She took two deep breaths, letting each one out slowly. Feeling herself starting to calm down, Dana hit Clay's number again, mouthing a prayer that it would go through this time.

It began to ring. Her hand so tight on the phone it was starting to cramp, she counted the rings. At the fourth ring, Clay answered, recognizing her ringtone.

"Hey, sugar. Where are you?" he asked, thinking she was well on her way to Sanibel Island.

"Clay!" Dana whispered fiercely. "Eth-- ---ter is - --rial ----er!" she said, not realizing the storm was breaking up the reception.

"What? Say again, Dana. You're breaking up something awful."

"Ethan Hun--- is the serial ----er!" she cried.

"Honey, I think I heard Ethan Hunter, and then you broke up again. What about him?"

So frustrated she could scream, Dana tried again. "Hunter! Serial killer! Serial killer!"

The panic in Dana's voice, coupled with what he finally heard her say, caused him to slam on the brakes and pull over, the rain sluicing down the side windows so heavy he could barely see the pier from where he stopped. While he was pretty sure he understood what she said, it didn't make sense.

"Did you say Ethan Hunter and serial killer?"

The reception suddenly became clear, if a little scratchy. "Yes! Yes, he's your serial killer! Not Stovall! And he's here!"

"What? Here where? Where are you?" Clay asked, more confused than ever.

"I'm hiding in the bathroom closet in his house! Clay, I think I hear him in the house now! My car's out front, so he knows I'm here. He's going to find me and kill me like all those others. Help me, Clay! I'm so afraid!" she cried, starting to shake uncontrollably.

"I'll be there in a second! Just hang on!" Clay said, throwing the phone on the seat and peeling out of the parking lot heading south on First Street. He was a little over two miles from Hunter's house at the extreme south end of Jacksonville Beach, and he stopped at no lights or stop signs in his headlong race to save his wife.

Dana knew in spite of her terror that she couldn't stay in the closet. Hunter would find her, and he would immediately recognize from her terrified actions that she had discovered his secret. She thought her chances for survival would improve if she could somehow convince Hunter she was upset over the weather and needed to get on the road to meet her parents.

Easing the closet door open, she stepped into the bathroom. By this time, she could hear Hunter calling her. From the sound of his voice, he was apparently ascending the stairs. She turned on the faucet and splashed water in her face. Taking a towel off the rack, she walked to the door, wiping her face as she opened it.

Hunter was standing at the door of the guest suite as she walked out. Pretending to be unaware of his presence, Dana looked up and exclaimed, "Oh, Ethan, you startled me!"

"Dana, what are you doing here? I thought you had already left town," he said, a puzzled look on his face.

"Well, I, I was already gone, and I, I," she stuttered, cursing herself for sounding flustered. "I remembered I had left my cross necklace here yesterday, and I had to come back for it. Clay gave it to me last Easter, and I wear it all the . . . oh, listen to me! I'm babbling. This storm has really rattled me. And I just finished a bout of morning sickness again. I'm a mess," she said, unable to look Hunter in the eyes.

"Hey, it's okay. You look beautiful even with morning sickness," he said, smiling. "Anyway, I heard the storm's turning more northward and will probably hit around Savannah. This is probably as bad as it's going to get. I decided I might as well come on back home and ride it out."

"Well, uh, I guess I better get going. My parents are waiting for me at World Golf Village. I guess we'll decide when I meet them if we're going to head on down to Sanibel or just come home," she said starting toward the door where Hunter was standing.

"Are you sure you don't want to wait it out here? This house is built like a fortress, so I don't expect there to be any problems, especially with the storm turning north like it is."

"No, no thanks. I'd better get going. Clay will be upset with me if he knows I stayed," she said, walking past him heading for the stairs.

Hunter followed along several steps behind, trying to decipher why she seemed so nervous. He suddenly noticed the door to his master suite standing ajar a couple of inches. Glancing at her retreating backside, he opened the door and looked inside.

Shit! he thought, seeing the picture of Meghan Barton on the floor where it had fallen.

Why is the picture on the floor unless she was in here, he asked himself. *Does she know? Can I afford to let her go?*

"Dana, wait," he called. "I need to talk to you for a second."

She had reached the bottom step when he called. She thought seriously about making a break for it but quickly realized that, in her condition, Hunter could catch her before she got out the door. She turned and looked up at the man she now knew had killed at least ten people.

"Y-Yes?" she stuttered.

Coming down the stairs as he spoke, Hunter said, "I was just thinking about the project you've been doing for me. You're almost finished, so I would like to commission a second painting. Same commission as before. I have some ideas that I—"

"No, I'm sorry, Mr. Hunter, but I've got a bunch of other commissions that are going to keep me busy for at least six months, so . . ."

"Mr. Hunter? What happened to Ethan?" he asked, eyes narrowing.

Dana panicked. She raced for the door, but Hunter caught her before she could get it open. He grabbed her arm and jerked with such force that her feet flew up in the air. She landed on her back, knocking the breath out of her. Lying on the floor, wheezing as she tried to draw a breath, she looked up to see Hunter standing over her, a look of contempt on his face.

"Please . . . don't," she gasped.

"Don't what, Dana?" he asked in a curious tone.

"Kill . . . me! Please don't . . . kill me!" she panted.

"Dana, I never planned to add you to my collection. I thought you were strong like me. But I was wrong, and it pains me to say that. Instead, you're just as weak as the rest of the losers in this world!"

"Get up," he ordered pulling her to her feet effortlessly.

When she stood, Dana suddenly felt dizzy as a wave of nausea hit. Her lower back and abdomen were hurting. She worried her baby had been injured in the fall. She had to do something, anything to save her baby.

In spite of the fear and pain, she found her voice. "I called Clay, and he's coming. And when he gets here, he'll kill you, you bastard!"

Hunter shook her like a rag doll, a look of pure hate on his face. "You bitch! You'll be sorry you called him. He's a dead man, and I'm going to make you watch while I do it! Then I'll make you pay for thinking you could beat me!" he raged, an insane look on his face that frightened Dana even more.

He dragged her across the room and started up the staircase. Dana, fearing he would hide and ambush Clay if he made it upstairs, suddenly fell to her knees, causing Hunter to fall on top of her. He landed at an angle, his neck across her face. The only weapon immediately available was her teeth, and she didn't hesitate to use them. She bit down hard, instantly drawing blood. Hunter screamed and jerked back, causing the soft skin of his neck to tear, increasing the flow of blood.

Hunter pummeled her body with his fists trying to get Dana to let go, but she held on, tucking her arms in tight to her body and putting her hands on her stomach to protect her baby. Dana's position on her back allowed Hunter's blood to flow into her mouth and down her throat as she continued to bite deeply into his neck.

As she began choking on his blood, she released her bite. Hunter sprang up and grabbed his neck, trying to staunch the flow of blood. Before she could react, he delivered a vicious punch to her left temple, knocking her unconscious.

He stood up unsteadily, still only halfway up the staircase. He knew he was losing blood rapidly and had to get it stopped or risk passing out. He staggered the rest of the way up, leaving Dana crumpled on the stairs. Making it to his bathroom, he grabbed a towel and held it to the wound.

Hunter assumed he didn't have much time if the bitch had been telling the truth about Randall coming. Holding the towel in place, he went to the vanity and tried to open it.

"Shit! It's locked!" he yelled.

Fumbling his keys out of his pocket, Hunter opened the vanity and removed the knife that had taken the lives of ten people.

Suddenly, he heard pounding at the front door. He rushed out the door and back to where Dana still lay unconscious. Sitting on the stairs with his back to the wall, he dragged her limp body in front of him as a shield. Hunter held the towel in place with his left hand, his right gripping the deadly sharp knife as he waited for Randall to join the party.

Chapter 51

Clay drove like a madman toward Ethan Hunter's mansion. Dana had given him a tour of the place a couple of months before when Hunter was out of town, so he knew exactly where to go. As he steered with one hand around small limbs and debris from the storm, Clay picked up his portable radio and called in a loud voice, "710, dispatch!"

Getting no response, he tried again, "710, I have emergency traffic!" Once more, he tried, "710 to anyone, respond!"

Still getting nothing but silence, he threw down the radio, unaware that lightning had struck the primary tower, thus knocking out all radio communications.

Clay wheeled into the long driveway that led to Hunter's house. He immediately saw Dana's Lexus blocked in by a red Mercedes. He leaped from the car, drawing his pistol as he ran for the front door. Finding the door locked, he pounded on it, yelling Dana's name repeatedly.

After a few seconds, Clay could wait no longer. He delivered a powerful kick to the door at the lockset. It bent slightly but held firm. Gathering his strength, he attacked the door a second time. This time, it flew open, the interior handset striking the wall and punching a fist-sized hole in the sheetrock. Clay went in low and to his left, his Glock held two-handed in tight to his torso.

He scanned the living room for movement. Seeing nothing, he continued moving to his left toward the door that led into the garage. As he neared it, Clay turned to look toward the second floor landing, worried Hunter might be above him. As he moved to his left to get a better view, he stopped cold.

Dana, the love of his life, was in the grip of Ethan Hunter on the staircase. Transfixed, his mind refused to accept what his eyes were seeing. Dana's beautiful face, so white, the blood covering her mouth and chin giving her an unreal, nightmarish appearance. More blood on the front of her shirt that partially obscured the "Baby Under Construction" logo.

Then he saw the knife held to her throat by Hunter. Dana's eyes were filled with such fear that Clay's reason almost deserted him.

All this he absorbed in a space of a second. Eyes narrowing in rage, he started for the staircase, his gun coming up to point at Hunter as he moved.

"Stop!" Hunter yelled, shifting the knife so the razor-sharp blade now rested fully on the side of her neck. "If you take one more step, I'll cut her throat! Tell him, Dana!" he commanded.

"Clay, he's crazy! He's going to kill us both!"

Clay stopped as if he had hit a brick wall, his gun still pointed up at Hunter.

"Let her go, Hunter!" he demanded. "She hasn't done anything to you!"

Ethan Hunter kept Dana's body in front of him to provide the smallest possible target, just in case Randall was a crack shot. He grimaced as he moved his head, the ache in his neck from Dana's bite a nagging reminder never to let his guard down with anyone.

Smiling through the pain, he drawled, "Well, now, Detective Randall, I believe the jury would disagree with you that Dana hasn't done anything to me. In fact, I believe I have a case for assault against Ms. Cappella were it not for more pressing matters. By the way, I bet you didn't know your wife was a cannibal, did you?"

The look of confusion on Clay's face caused Hunter to laugh, an angry, bitter sound.

"I was just trying to convince your wife to do another painting for me, and look at what she did to me," he said, gesturing at the blood-filled towel he still pressed to the side of his neck. "I would remove the towel and show you the actual bites, but, as I said, more pressing matters."

Clay moved slightly to his left to get a better shooting angle if the opportunity presented itself.

"Don't move!" Hunter screamed, moving the knife half an inch across Dana's neck, slicing through her skin.

Dana screamed as she felt the blood start to flow from the shallow cut.

"Stop! Don't hurt her, you bastard!" Clay shouted as he stopped moving.

"*Now,* do we have an understanding, Detective Randall? You are not in charge here. I am. And you will do exactly what I say or she will die, along with your kid," he said contemptuously.

"You know," he said as he began to rise, dragging Dana up with him, "I might have been tempted to taste your wife's delights had she not been carrying a kid. Pregnancy is just so disgusting, don't you think?" he asked, curling his lip in disgust.

Clay clenched his weapon so tight his knuckles turned white as he thought of his wife and unborn child at the mercy of this madman.

"You bastard! I'm going to—"

"You're going to do nothing, asshole! If I choose to cut her throat, I will. And you can't stop me! Now, here's the drill. You drop the gun. I don't like guns, you see. Too noisy. I prefer, as I'm sure you know, the quiet power and intensity of a sharp instrument.

"Then, after you separate yourself from your gun, I will leave with Dana in my car. At a point I deem appropriate, I will release her unharmed."

"Don't listen to him, Clay! Don't give up your gun!" Dana cried.

"Shut up, bitch!" Hunter snarled, yanking her back against him.

Clay calculated the odds in a split second and made his decision. Hitting the release, he dropped the magazine full of .45 caliber rounds into his left hand. Sliding it into his pocket, he ejected the round in the chamber, thus emptying the gun of its bullets. Then he tossed it on the floor at the foot of the stairs.

"There's my gun, Hunter. I'm not about to give you a loaded weapon that you can use to kill us both," he said.

Hunter smiled. "An interesting strategy, Detective Randall. Disarm yourself, but prevent me from arming myself with your weapon. Somewhat unexpected, but it still leaves me in the driver's seat, so to speak."

His voice once again turning hard, he demanded, "Now back up! Get over by the terrace doors! And remember that a slight flick of the wrist is all that's required to send your wife to wherever artists go when they leave this world. Now, move!"

Clay stepped back as he was told, never taking his eyes off Hunter and Dana. She was obviously in pain, and the fear in her eyes was almost more than he could bear.

As they reached the bottom of the stairs, Hunter quickly scooped up Clay's gun and put it in his waistband. He began moving backward toward the door, constantly keeping Dana between himself and Clay. When they got to the front door, still standing open from Clay's violent entrance, Hunter took a quick look over his shoulder at the driveway.

He turned back to glare at Clay.

"Your car is blocking mine. Since I can't let you get into your car to move it, I'll have to take it instead of mine. Come over here slowly and carefully, and toss me your keys. Don't try any shit, or you know what will happen to her," he threatened.

"Hey, I'm cool," he said, more an attempt to convince Hunter than himself since he was anything but cool.

Clay took the keys out of his pocket and started walking slowly toward the door. As he approached, Hunter backed outside, keeping Dana between them.

No longer protected by the portico, the wind and rain buffeted them both. As Clay came out the door, Hunter yelled to be heard over the storm, "Stop! Don't come any further! Toss me the keys!"

Clay's mind worked furiously. He could try tossing the keys high into the air so Hunter would take his eyes off him. That might give him enough time to get to the backup pistol strapped to his left ankle. Getting his pants leg pulled up, releasing the holster snap, pulling the gun, and shooting Hunter, all before he could cut Dana's throat, sounded impossible and probably was.

Rejecting that idea, he glanced at his keys, knowing he had to do something quickly before the man followed through on his threat. He just knew he couldn't let Hunter drive away with Dana. If he did, he would never see her alive again. Suddenly, in a flash of insight, he knew what to do.

Please God, make Dana remember, he pleaded.

"Dana, remember D. T.!" he yelled, staring into his wife's frightened eyes.

Suspicious, Hunter pulled Dana even closer. "What does that mean? What is a Dee Tee?"

Knowing the next few seconds were critical, Clay responded.

"It's a little inside joke we play on each other. It means 'don't talk.' We use it when the other is talking too much. I don't want her to say anything to piss you off," Clay said, hoping Hunter would buy the explanation and Dana would catch on to its real meaning.

"Smart move on your part, Randall," he exclaimed. "That goes for you, too. No more talking! Throw me the keys! Now!"

Clay braced himself. Would his crazy plan succeed, or would he condemn Dana and his unborn child to death? His heart pounding, he gave one last look at his wife and then pressed the panic alarm on his door opener. Hunter was standing directly in front of the police car when the horn began honking loudly, accompanied by flashing headlights.

Startled, Hunter spun around, the knife shifting away from Dana's neck as he did. She had gotten the message Clay had so desperately tried to send to her. Dana instantly shifted her hips to the left and drove her fist directly into Hunter's groin as hard as she could.

The killer screamed in pain, releasing her as his knees buckled. Dana ran for her life as Clay dropped to his knee to dig his pistol out of the ankle holster. In his haste to get the weapon out, it caught on his pant leg and spun out of his hand. Bouncing once on the concrete, the gun slid under a bush bordering the portico.

Though the pain in his testicles was agonizing, Hunter knew he had to move. There was no time to catch Dana and kill the bitch for having the audacity to hit him. Hobbling painfully, he staggered around the corner of the house, heading for the beach.

Clay dived under the bush and grabbed the weapon, shaking the dirt off as he rushed forward to his wife. Momentarily forgetting the serial killer, he held Dana tight.

"Are you hurt?" he asked, close to panic himself.

"Nothing that won't heal. Find him, Clay. If he gets away, we'll be looking over our shoulder the rest of our lives!"

Handing her the keys, he said, "Get in my car and lock the doors. The radio was down earlier, but you might get through now! Call for help! I love you, Dana!" he exclaimed, heading after Hunter.

Chapter 52

The storm was still pounding the beach with winds hitting almost sixty miles per hour, and rain came down so hard that visibility was limited to less than twenty feet. Clay ran around the left side of the house, sweeping in every direction with his gun.

As he rounded the back of the house, the driving wind, rain, and flying sand hit full force, almost blinding him. Holding his left hand in front of his face to protect his eyes, Clay moved deliberately across the expansive patio, failing to see Hunter crouched behind a large Sago palm.

As he eased past Hunter's hiding place, the killer leaped, stabbing at his back. Sensing the movement, Clay turned in time to avoid a direct hit. Instead, the knife cut his shirt and sliced through several layers of his ballistic vest, stopping just short of entering his back.

The force of Hunter's attack caused Clay to fall to the terrace, dropping his gun for the second time. The pistol came to rest several feet away under the adjacent Sago palm.

Hunter loomed over him, the black blade in his hand. Unarmed, Clay resorted to his ground fighting training. Rolling onto his back, he drew his knees up slightly, ready to lash out with his feet if Hunter came close enough. The killer tried to circle around to get behind Clay, but he moved with him, always keeping Hunter at his feet.

"You fucking loser!" Hunter raged. "Scuttling around like a fucking crab! Stand and fight me, if you've got the guts!"

"Drop the knife, and I will!" Clay retorted.

Laughing wildly, Hunter said, "I don't think so!" at the same time lunging at Clay, intending to stab him in the leg.

Anticipating the move, Clay kicked out with all his strength, aiming for Hunter's knee. But the angle was bad, instead striking Hunter's upper thigh. The killer went to the ground, screaming in pain as the knife flew out of his hand and bounced off the terrace into the sand.

Clay pounced on Hunter, punching him in the head, face, chest, wherever he could connect with the coldblooded killer who had planned to add his wife and child to his list of victims. But Ethan

Hunter was not ready to surrender. Screaming maniacally, he fought back, burying his face in Clay's chest as he tried to gouge out his eyes with one hand while he slammed his fist into Clay's body again and again, right at the spot where the ribs had been broken only weeks before.

Grabbing Hunter's ears, Clay yanked as hard as he could, trying to rip them off. Hunter screamed, pulling at Clay's hands to try to break his hold. As Clay held on doggedly, the killer managed to get a knee up and drive it into his groin, sending bolts of pain through his testicles and causing him to release Hunter's ears.

The killer then drew back his knee and drove it into Clay's ribs, once, twice, three times. The sound of the abused ribs breaking again was audible. Clay screamed, in such pain between the newly-broken ribs and his abused testicles that he almost passed out.

Hunter scrambled to the edge of the terrace and retrieved his knife, crawling quickly back to the man he wanted to kill more than any of his previous victims. Clay was still writhing on the terrace, the pain worse than anything he had ever felt.

Through the tears of agony in his eyes, he saw Hunter was back with his knife. He stared at the man who had killed so many people. The unknown killer he had pursued all those months. Now, he knew the truth, and there was nothing he could do about it. The anger and disgust he felt at himself for failing to defeat the killer was a bitter pill to swallow.

"Feel like dying, asshole?" the rain and wind continuing to pound so hard that Hunter had to yell.

As he raised the knife to deliver the killing blow, Clay's mind flashed on Dana and the unborn child he would never see.

Suddenly, Hunter staggered. He straightened up a moment and then staggered again, this time falling to his knees, still holding the knife. Clay scrambled painfully away as Hunter pitched forward onto the sand-filled terrace.

"Clay!" Dana yelled.

He turned to see his wife standing on the terrace, her little gun in her hand.

"Clay, is he . . . is he dead?"

He was in shock, as much from the vicious struggle as from the injuries.

"I, I don't know. Stay back, but keep your gun on him."

Clay stumbled back to where Hunter lay without moving. Keeping his arm tightly against his side for support, he tried to breathe as shallow as possible to minimize the pain from the broken ribs. Easing to his knees, he pried the knife from Hunter's hand.

Clay was beyond the point of pain and exhaustion. If Hunter managed to rise up from the ground, he knew he could not fight him again. He limped slowly over to the base of the palm tree where he leaned over to pick up his gun. A wave of nausea and dizziness hit him, and he bit his lip hard to keep from blacking out. After a few moments, it passed, and he was able to stand up.

He looked toward Dana, and a fresh wave of panic hit him. She had slumped to the terrace unconscious. Clay staggered toward her, still watching Hunter as he went, half expecting him to leap up, hidden knife in hand, ready to continue the death battle.

He kneeled beside Dana, frightened at how bad she looked. The rain was pelting her in the face, yet she gave no indication she felt it. He dropped to the ground beside his wife, shielding her from the elements as best he could.

As the minutes passed, the squall finally moved on, and the rain slowed to a drizzle, although the winds continued to howl. Clay held her tenderly, the pain from his ribs ignored in his desperate concern for his Dana. She looked like death, so pale, so fragile.

Her eyelids fluttered open. Seeing her man safe, she broke into sobs. Clay held on, letting the emotions rage through her.

Every few seconds, he looked over his shoulder to make sure Ethan Hunter had not somehow resurrected himself. Each time, he was reassured by the stillness of the killer's lifeless body.

Epilogue

In the days following, Jacksonville Beach became news central for the media. Chief Wilson became the de facto public information officer for the department, considering the notoriety of the case. He spent hours in press conferences explaining the deadly confrontation at Hunter's house and trying his best to squelch rumors that inevitably accompanied such a newsworthy event.

One reporter asked if it was true that Dana had gone into labor and delivered the baby lying right beside Hunter's dead body. Mike Wilson had almost reprised the Gordy Cooper meltdown at the stupidity of the question but ultimately shared the true facts with the media throng.

The truth was that Dana had started into labor on Hunter's terrace, brought on as a result of the extreme physical and emotional trauma she had endured. Somehow, in spite of his two broken ribs and battered body, Clay had managed to get Dana from the terrace to his car, stopping twice as she endured intense labor pains. They made it to Beaches Baptist Hospital five minutes before their healthy baby girl made her appearance, four weeks premature.

Every reporter clamored to interview the heroes, as they were calling Clay and Dana, but Wilson refused them all, knowing they both needed time to recuperate and decompress. Clay spent one night in the hospital for observation of his broken ribs and other injuries. Dana was released the day after Clay, kept there by her doctor to ensure the bruises and general trauma to her body did not cause other complications to her health. Officers stood guard outside their rooms to guarantee their rest and privacy.

While one group of reporters schemed to get around Chief Wilson's blockade to Clay and Dana, others attacked the Ethan Hunter angle, demanding to know how the police department could have erred so badly in claiming Emory Elliot Stovall was the serial killer.

Wilson knew he had to defend the integrity of his department, so he told them of the computer diary Hunter had kept detailing each of his ten murders. In it, Hunter chronicled how he broke into Stovall's house while the man was in custody for the attack on Corri Jennings.

Figuring the house would be searched, he planted mementoes from his previous kills to throw suspicion onto Stovall as the serial killer. Reporters demanded the release of the diary under Florida's public information law, but the chief refused, explaining the investigation was still ongoing.

Privately to his staff, all of whom were as curious as everyone else, he revealed many details, including Hunter's previous life as Edward Earl Shanklin. Hunter had created the watermark as an obscure clue to see if the cops were smart enough to figure out that the letters stood for his former name. Jim Childress groaned when he heard the news, embarrassed that he had been so certain the initials were those of Emory Elliot Stovall.

Two weeks later, the media having moved on, Clay and Dana were thrilled to bring Caterina LeeAnn Randall home from the hospital.

"She's so beautiful," Clay said, sitting on their bed beside Dana as he stared in awe at the tiny bundle in his arms. "I know this sounds crazy, but I counted her fingers and toes as soon as she was born. You know, just to make sure."

"I did, too," Dana said with a giggle. "She *is* gorgeous, isn't she?"

"Well, she couldn't help being a knockout. Look at her mama," he said, grinning at Dana.

"Yeah, right. I don't exactly feel like a knockout. More like I've been knocked out!"

They both laughed, something they had done very little of since the final confrontation with Ethan Hunter. Dana grew serious as the ordeal popped into her head for the hundredth or maybe the thousandth time.

"Clay, how did I miss seeing Ethan Hunter for what he really was?" she asked, still puzzled. "He seemed so normal, always so nice and friendly to me."

"Honey, he had the classic serial killer personality. Very smooth on the outside, but filled with demons on the inside. That's how he was able to fool his victims and everyone else who thought they knew him."

Dana said nothing. Staring at the ceiling, she shook her head as she reflected on that earth-shattering day. It was a strange dichotomy, terror and pain juxtaposed with indescribable joy.

On the one side, Hunter would have killed Clay if she had not made the decision to leave the safety of the car. He would have killed her, also . . . and their precious baby. Killing an animal like Ethan Hunter had been necessary, though not easy. The taking of a human life was a traumatic, life-altering experience, regardless of the circumstances.

Conversely, the joy she felt at bringing a new life into the world, tiny "Cat" Randall, was unsurpassed. And the happiness and relief at not losing Clay were impossible to express in words.

"Are you okay, I mean, really okay with what happened?" Clay asked, still worried about her emotional state.

Dana knew she would need to talk with Clay about the competing emotions she was feeling. But, for now, she wasn't quite ready. At this moment, she wanted only to snuggle up next to him as she gently stroked the face of their daughter.

"I'm not completely okay . . . not yet. But I will be. I will be."

THE END